THE WAR OF MARIAN

JG McCord

authorHOUSE®

AuthorHouse™
1663 Liberty Drive
Bloomington, IN 47403
www.authorhouse.com
Phone: 833-262-8899

Published by AuthorHouse 10/20/2020

ISBN: 978-1-7283-6496-4 (sc)
ISBN: 978-1-7283-6494-0 (hc)
ISBN: 978-1-7283-6495-7 (e)

Library of Congress Control Number: 2020911354

Contents

Prologue

The world had settled into an era of advancement and expansion. The gained ability of space travel opened new opportunities for Earth. Expeditions were sent to other planets to scope out land and resources suitable for life to prosper and further start new settlements. After two decades of searching, multiple planets were found to meet the needs of humanity. This would be Earth's greatest achievement and their greatest time of prosperity.

Soon, groups of people had settled into colonies on other planets such as Mars and Venus, along with planets on the outer belt such as Saturn and the moons of Jupiter. Engineers built domes to allow for human survival and stability until the foreign planets could be made habitable. With the quickly advancing technology, soon even that was easily accomplished. Humanity over three hundred years had made their mark on the universe by making well known that this galaxy was theirs.

Nations formed and grew on a multitude of planets, expanding the reach of the human race. Since the red planet, Mars, along with Venus, nicknamed the silver planet, were the easiest to inhabit, growth was rapid and fast-paced. Mars and Venus quickly became similar to Earth's atmospheric conditions with the ability to sustain life, this with the basic necessities for growing and harvesting food along with livestock.

The two planets developed their own government, laws, and military. Fields grew food and kept livestock as towns and cities were erected to sustain a growing population and the need for Earth's guidance and protection was no longer needed, and more importantly, was no longer wanted. With threats of war, Mars broke away from the rule of Earth while Venus became neutral ground. Mars and Venus easily obtained their independence from Earth. The vast distance between the planets made it difficult for Earth to control them for this reason, Earth relinquished their rights. The sister planets were able to make their own laws and govern their own people. Six centuries of peace passed. Life prospered and the three planets held neutrally beneficial alliances with one another.

Then the world appointed capital of Earth started to fall apart, divided through various reasons and separate agendas, the fighting escalated, and war broke out. Amongst the chaos of civil war many other countries took advantage of the weaknesses and attacked, trying to gain a foothold and win the rights to lead Earth. Soon a world war had broken out and no one was safe. War was fought on all fronts and the land became tainted and stained with the blood of the innocent lives lost.

The world was tearing itself apart and the neighboring planets watched as Earth would soon destroy itself. The Venus government sent forces to help, but with the threat of destruction reaching their planet, they removed their forces and left Earth to its own. Many people tried to escape to the other planets while they could, but it was too late. Mars and Venus refused to open the ports and accept any refugees, leaving Earth to its own demise. After twelve years of war, Earth reached an agreement of peace for the sake of the remainder of humanity.

A peace treaty was signed almost two hundred years ago. The Earth still bears scars of the past great war that almost destroyed humanity. Where the fires once burned, out of the ashes, humanity survived and started to rebuild itself determined to be a greater civilization then before. A century passed and it seemed humanity was on the rise once more, that was until unexpectedly a plague swept through Earth. The people of Venus and Mars were unaffected. Because of that, humanity would have a fighting chance.

Many accused the red planet of causing the disease as an attempt to take control of the planet. Mars's population had continued to grow and taking control of the Earth would present opportunities for expansion and relief from overcrowding.

Over the centuries that had passed, the citizens of Mars appeared to display differences in their genetic makeup to that of earthlings and this difference made them immune to the disease that had spread over Earth, it also gave the Mars citizens different outward appearances. The disease caused blood to pour from the eyes, ears, and nose of the infected. It was this reason the disease was given the name the red death. This accusation caused tensions between that of Earth and Mars. Soon all treaties and alliances with Mars were dissolved and it seemed Earth would once again see the destruction of war.

However, the Earth's military was in no position to fight Mars. The red death ravaged Earth and once again, humanity was on the brink of extinction. With the almost complete annihilation of humanity came the destruction of everything along with it. Cities burned while buildings fell, homes and towns were once again taken over by the land. Earth was returning to a time before it was touched by humans. In its wake left the ruins of a civilization lost to the test of time.

It has been just over a hundred years since the red death was neutralized. Humanity survived but just barely. The survivors gathered to form pockets of civilizations and societies around a now changed earth. The first nation constructed held the second largest number of people at a couple of hundred thousand following behind the nation of Tiffiledien. The nation of Helenia is protected by a wall that surrounds the eastern side along with part of the northern and southern sides. The southern borders are met with a vast amount of water with the nation of Tiffiledien sighted in the distant horizon. While the northern borders tapered off into the east and west were home to immense and treacherous mountains that generate strong, freezing winds and snowstorms making travel almost impossible. Beyond the western boarders, lay a desert stretching for miles.

The government of this civilization quickly rebuilt a functioning society led by military forces. Within their borders, the people lived by a four-tier system with towns and cities contained in each tier. The outermost tier, Consus, is home to those that live on the outermost of the borders. The people live in small towns in grassy plains near an over towering wall that protects the boundaries of the grasslands and the city. The people live simply but hold jobs that provide for the many by tending to the farmlands and the livestock.

The second outer tier, Lincoln, is split into industrial and manual labor. The people work tirelessly with the military to make weapons and machinery to strengthen the stronghold of the military defenses. The industrial tier, along with the military, makes up the mass of the workforce, providing textiles, weapons, and goods.

The third tier, Charles, holds that of the military forces. Not only is the military responsible for protecting the border and act as law enforcement for the nation, but also work on breakthroughs and advancements to help rebuild humanity and strengthen its forces from threats of otherworldly proportion.

The innermost tier, Otho, belongs to the aristocrats and leaders of the nation, the ones that pull the strings for the remainder of humanity. They live in wealth and security away from any possible attacks.

Then there are those that fall outside the tiers, outside the construction of a government, those that fall outside the wall and the borders. It is rumored that the people who live outside the wall can't even be considered human. There is something different about them. Their genes are different. Some of them even carry the red death gene but show no signs of illness. For that reason, the government fears another outbreak of the disease that would potentially wipe out humanity in its entirety.

The outer tiers think this might be the next step in the evolutionary chain, while others think that those on the outside of the wall are citizens from Mars lying in wait to attack and overtake the Earth. In reality, they are outsiders because they resist the rule of the structured government, disagreeing with the laws and social structure. Their goal is to overthrow the current government and rebuild a government acceptable for all, even those with a unique genetic makeup.

Though there is tension with those on the outside of the wall, a declaration of war has not been established, but there is fear and fear always make for rash decisions. Tensions are on the rise and it's only a matter of time before units are sent out in an action to destroy those that are different.

Chapter 1

DRILLS IN THE MORNING

"Hey Dans, did you read the paper today"

Liam jumped over the bench sliding into a seat next to his best friend, Dani. Even sitting down, he loomed over her, a task that was not at all hard given how tall he was. He grabbed the paper out of his back pocket and laid it on the table where it unfurled itself. Now anyone who wanted to read it could, allowing themselves to be exposed to all the exciting news being feed to the mindless masses by those in higher positions or influences.

"Yes, because between waking you up, the mandatory morning run, getting dressed, and waking you up again, I just have so much time to read the paper. Honestly, I'm not even sure where you found the time to read the paper and by the way you missed the run."

"Awe, don't be too hard on him Dani, we all know Liam is only good at one thing..."

"being devilishly good looking and hardworking" Liam interrupted.

Aiden spat out his breakfast of eggs in a fit of laughter. A girl with long blond hair that was kept up in a neat, tight bun with bangs falling loosely in her face, walked up to the table to join the group of cadets eating their breakfast.

"What's so funny, Aiden?" Sarah, the blond hair girl, asked.

The idea that Liam was anything but irresponsible not to mention a procrastinator was humorous. Liam had a talent for always showing up to formation, training, or anything that didn't involve food or sleep, late. He somehow managed to always slip under the commander's radar. His outgoing personality attracted a profusion of attention whether it was positive or negative. It was his mouth that unfortunately got him into trouble.

"Liam thinks he's hard-working.

"Hard-working, you? Now that is funny." Sarah sat her food down and joined the rest of her fellow cadets at the table, scooting in next to Aiden.

"What I was going to say is being a complete screw up" Aiden finally finished his sentence to the group of friends.

"Someone's just angry they didn't get their beauty sleep this morning" Liam stated with a hint of glee to his voice, preening like a ray of sunshine, putting on a show of it. He knew his comment would get Aiden wired up. Liam enjoyed watching Aiden get mad over silly things and any opportunity that presented itself to help that along Liam took advantage of.

"Not all of us have the ability to sleep in and miss the morning requirements while staying clear of the consequences. How you manage to do it fathoms me." Dani commented while her dark green eyes continued glancing at the paper Liam had now shoved in her face.

She was in a daze, her mind far off thinking about something else. One of the articles had caught her attention and she was currently entranced by it. Dani was by no means shy but she was quiet. She often looked lost in thought but anyone who knew Dani Mitchell knew that was never the case. She was in fact calculating every situation and was always studying her surroundings.

Breakfast time was the few minutes the cadets had in the morning to enjoy some friendly conversation before heading out to formation and receiving the morning brief that would set the tone for the full and exhausting day of training they would have to endure. Everyone lives for these few moments. At each table, comrades were building lifelong bonds through laughter and storytelling.

One person was holding their side laughing at something someone else had said at the table across from where Dani and her group sat. At the table adjacent from them, two girls gossiped over a fellow male cadet that had caught the eye of one of the girls. The table behind them, someone was leaning over into the aisle, head in hands, nursing a headache from too much drinking from the night before while his friend stood in the aisle making judgmental comments.

The dining hall was filled with conversation that created a noise that almost soothed her. Dani appreciated the simplicity of it all. The knowledge that all of them were there for a reason that combined them in a bond stronger than blood.

"What interesting news does the almighty paper give us today?" Aiden joked.

It seemed the daily newspaper was more rubbish then insightful. It spun tails ranging from super soldier Marsians who had come to Earth spying on humanity to that of possible alliances between Mars and Venus. There are even bits on war campaigns from the leadership and how they would put an end to the conflict between Earth and Mars. In all reality, there was no real conflict between Earth and Mars and even if there were, Earth would never stand a chance against the Marsian forces. Earth was still too weak, and humanity was spread too thin compared to the population Mars had built over the past few centuries. While Earth was suffering from war and disease, Mars was on the rise, building an empire.

"It seems the prince of Mars is looking for a bride. And that's not all. He would prefer to take a bride from Earth." Dani went on to inform the others. "it seems by taking a wife from Earth it will mend the tension and bring peace to our two worlds."

"That seems a bit... well old and barbaric. A contract marriage isn't something humans have done for at least a thousand years!" Sarah chimed in. "Furthermore, why would someone who is in complete power that isn't being challenged by any other force feel the need to establish a peace treaty of any means, especially with Earth?"

"Unless Mars is being challenged, possibly by Venus." Aiden added, flicking his fork towards the paper.

"Even if they are, Earth is still rebuilding, we're in no position to stand grounds. We're not really the go to here." Liam air quoted. "Plus, we have stable alliances with Venus going back hundreds of years, since their independence, in fact. So, there's no way we would side with Mars."

Liam was right. Earth held no power. We were weak. At one-point Earth was the foundation, but with humanity having to start over so many times, Earth had become a dying planet and it had taken everything to hold on to the little bit of life they had left. The last hundred years showed promise, the population was on the rise, nations had been rebuilt and functioning governments were in power, but the idea that a prince from one of the most powerful planets wants to marry someone from Earth was ridiculous. Unless it was a power play to take over Earth. After all, humanity might not survive, but there were plenty of resources to still be used and with Mars growing, they needed all the resources they could get.

The bell rang alerting the cadets to the end of breakfast and the beginning of another challenging day of training. Dani trained harder than most. Her father was a general holding a job at the eastern command, therefore the expectations of Dani were higher. As much as the commanders and other trainers pushed her, no one pushed her harder than herself. She was bound and determined to be the best that she could be, not because she was trying to live up to her father's expectations but because there were people she wanted to protect.

There was a chill in the air and the leaves on the trees surrounding the academy compound were starting to change. Fall had arrived. This time of year, had always been Dani's favorite. To her, the world seemed more peaceful. Everyone seemed to be happier and was enjoying the cooler days after suffering through the long hot and sticky days of summer. The vigorous training was somewhat more bearable when the blazing sun wasn't scorching Dani and her fellow cadets.

It was honorable and a desire to be accepted into the military's academic program. The nation of Helenia was one of the first pockets of humanity to retain any type of structure and gain stabilized mobility paving the way to take hold of smaller, still developing nations and towns that surrounded Helenia. It wasn't long before Helenia had tripled in size making it one of the largest nations. The military played a vital role in the success of the large nation. It was the force that controlled the people and implemented the laws set down by the leaders. The nation of Helenia was a military run state with a panel of generals at the control. The only person higher than them was the leader, a totalitarian of a man that goes by the name of King Foley.

Everyone had lined up and was in a tight-knit formation ready to receive the brief. The air was crisp, and the sun was hiding behind the clouds making the morning feel hazy and gray. The sky and dark, low hanging clouds teased the trainees with the idea of rain. Even though it was a bit chilly standing out in the wide-open courtyard it certainly beat the hot summer days when the sun was brutally unkind.

The brief was by far the most daunting and taxing part of the day. It seemed as if the brief would go on indefinitely. It didn't help that the entire duration of the brief was spoken whilst everyone was at attention holding still in complete unison. The government held the military forces, especially those who attended the cadet academy, to the highest of standards. Those who graduate from the cadet school would go on to join the ranks of the elite task forces with higher ranks.

The commander spoke with such stamina and excitement, one would think the cadets were receiving a heartfelt speech about standing together and fighting till the last man stood right before charging the enemy.

"Today will be the day that each of you will take your next step to join the glorious ranks amongst the elite. The tasks that each of you will face are meant to be challenging, they are meant to push you, to break you, to tear you down and then when you feel you can no longer continue you will find the inner strength and that will rebuild you into the cadet, into the leader needed to succeed and lead."

Liam leaned over towards Aiden and whispered. "Who do you think he's trying to convince with all this hero bullshit?"

Aiden in returned snickered at the comment. "You'd think he was preaching."

"Should we give a hallelujah shout out?" Liam commented.

Liam and Aiden were quietly taunting the commander while in the background he continued his speech about honor and glory. Droning on and on about duty and the self-sacrifice needed to better the lives of the remanding survivors of Earth.

Dani gave both of them a look that was a good indication of what she would do to them if they didn't stop fooling around, followed by an immensely disapproving shush. Dani actually enjoyed the two guys shenanigans, especially during an hour long brief that she had heard every day since joining the academy four years ago, but she would never let them know that. They wouldn't let her live it down.

"We will be running drills this morning and into the afternoon. Each of you will be assigned a squad. Once you receive your squad number, join your fellow squad members in your assigned area. Each team will pick a leader. That leader will be given an envelope that will give each team further instructions. Treat this like a real mission because one day your life will depend on how serious you take this today. Your squad will not eat lunch until the mission is complete so finishing in a timely manner would behoove you, that being said, accuracy is also key. Too many mistakes and your squad will do the mission over. Failure will not be tolerated. After lunch, half of you will work with arms and the other half in combat for two hours and then we will switch and go again for another two hours. At that time, we will reconvene. Now, the officers will call names, listen up because it will only get repeated once. When you hear your name move to the designated area."

Five officers started to call names and in a stampede of excitement, cadets started moving left and right. They were moving fast and swiftly with a purpose, but that's just how it was in the military. Time was precious and moving slowly could be the difference between life and death.

Dani heard her name called along with a few other cadets she was familiar with. They all moved to the east side of the courtyard where the trainees met Warrant Officer Reed. He was short for a male, but he was built like a tank. His hair was always slicked back, not one strand was out of place. He had brown eyes that were almost black as night and carried a fierce look of determination.

Amongst the cadets to join Dani's group, Sarah was one of them. Dani was ecstatic that she would be in a group with her. Sarah was one of the few people let alone females that Dani was close with. She just got along with her so easily, but Sarah was a happy person and was easy to get along with in general. There was also another female with untamable curly red hair that bounced with each step she took and bright green eyes that shone like emeralds. Freckles covered her face and she spoke with an accent. Her name was Erin and she was a fierce competitor. There were also two males, John and Cain. John was similar to Liam when it came to morale; lazy but charming. Cain on the other hand was quiet and usually had his nose in a book.

Warrant Officer Reed selected Cain to take the lead point for the morning's activities. His shyness and attempts at disappearing amongst the others only painted a target on his back. Officer Reed gave a laugh and immediately singled him out with not another thought behind his choice. Cain was handed a small white envelope. Inside were the instructions waiting to be read and followed. Cain pulled them out and looked on with confusion turning the paper over and over.

"Good luck cadets." Officer Reed's serious demeanor let loose for a momentary devious smile as he walked away. The five members of squad two watched as the officer walked away to join the rest of the officers on the side of the courtyard.

"Well…" Sarah paused waiting for a response from Cain. The other members' eyes were immediately drawn back from their task, and on to Cain. He stared blankly at her as if he just realized she and the others were standing there.

"What does it say?" John said a little more harshly and louder than he meant too.

"It just says run" he responded. Cain flipped the paper over and over and looked inside the envelope, one eye shut as he did so.

"Run? That doesn't make any sense. Run to what, to where? What do they expect us to do with that?"

Erin was as confused and apparently as anxious as everyone else, after all, these morning drills were meant to challenge the cadets. Each drill represented a possible real-life scenario and each drill became increasingly more demanding and strenuous forcing the cadets to use all the skills previously learned. They had to be able to think fast and act faster adapting to any situation. Now it seemed even the orders were cause for alarm. They, too, were given regarding think and think fast.

At that moment a gun fired from the west somewhere in the nearby woods. Everyone stopped but only long enough to realize the drill had started. They had run out of time to think.

"Everybody move! Head to the nearest cover!" Dani had figured it out and was shouting at her squad. She took off running towards the woods directly behind her. She had yet to put all the pieces together and she wasn't sure of the objective yet but through her training, she knew one thing, keep moving or die.

If they could just get to the trees and find a spot to hide for a few minutes, then they could collaborate an idea and unveil the plan behind this drill. John and Sarah reached the edge of the woods first, there long legs giving them an advantage of speed. Dani was right behind them. Erin was close too; it was Cain who was lost. He was running but not towards the eastern woods where the rest of squad two came together. In the chaos, he got turned around and now wasn't even sure where he was supposed to be running at all.

Dani reaching the woods, singled for John, who was the fastest and strongest of the group to go back out and retrieve Cain. While he did that the three girls, making sure to keep an eye out for trouble, started to discuss their next play.

"What the hell is going on!" Erin was furious. Her shirt had been snagged on a branch and ripped as the thin, low hanging branch broke. She was pulling the stick out of her shirt, while Sarah pulled a few leaves that had collected in Erin's hair when she disrupted the tree.

Dani spoke first. "I think it's an ambush drill"

"An ambush drill? What do you mean Dani?" Sarah's face was in disgust, she didn't like the idea of being attacked by her own leaders even if it was a drill.

"Think about it, at any moment, especially during a scouting mission, we could be attacked by an enemy. We need to be on guard and ready to counterattack at any given time. What better way to prepare us for that than for us to be attacked by our own leaders without warning, this forces us to act on natural fight or flight instinct. As military personal, we should be acting on our skill and training. That being said, they wouldn't just attack us without some kind of catch. That leaves me to believe that we still have a mission to complete. So, we need to figure out what the second objective of this drill is."

John and Cain returned soaked in sweat from running and dodging the chaos of other cadets running around still confused and trying to get to the woods clearing the square.

"What have you guys figured out so far?" John asked as he wiped his brow with the edge of his shirt and then took a swig of water from a canteen hiding away in his pocket.

"It's an ambush drill." Cain responded through heavy breaths. He had leaned over allowing his hands to rest on his knees, his head was feeling overheated.

"But that's not all, we still have a mission, and I believe we'll find out what that mission is by heading towards where that gun was fired from." Dani stated sure of herself.

Dani was sure that any answers they needed would be guarded or protected. So, heading towards a known weapon, though it would possibly be dangerous, would prove that the leaders had hidden clues close by. The only thing now was to strategize whether to run blatantly through the square out in the open or trek through the woods that surrounded the courtyard. It would add time, but they could stay in the shadows and undercover with the tall trees and thicket ensuring their rate of success to increase.

"Cain!" Dani snapped at Cain drawing his attention. Cain raised from the sitting position he had fallen into to meet Dani's eyes.

"You've been placed as the leader for this drill, so what's your order." She asked him already knowing what they should be doing but showing him the respect, he had been handed.

"I'm….I'm not sure." He stated shakily.

"You know every war strategy, every maneuver, every tactic! You have to have some idea." John was annoyed at Cain's lack of responsiveness. It was that kind of weakness that would get members of a squad killed one day.

"This isn't a situation where strategy is used, if we were ambushed, we would be thinking about survival, not the mission." Cain responded with an attitude. He was starting to get annoyed with John. He and John had a history of disagreements and arguments.

"Bullshit! We're soldiers we should be able to handle it, not freak out and shut down!" John became louder.

"Okay guys let's just settle down a bit." Sarah moved in between John and Cain, waving her arms attempting to ease the tension. "Getting upset isn't going to solve anything, furthermore it's only going to divide us, and we need to stick together with clear heads." Sarah looked to Dani. "Dani why don't you take point until Cain calms down."

Sarah was good at getting people to see reason and diffuse a situation before it became too heated or out of hand. Dani knew she was right, already she knew where they needed to go and that there was still a mission drill to complete.

"We need to head towards where that gun was fired, so we need to go west, across the compound into the forest. But we should stay to the tree line. We can stay in the cover of the woods but close enough to where we can see any activity occurring in the square."

"You want to head towards the danger, where most likely someone will be waiting... with a gun... to possibly fire at us again. Any of that clicking with you."

Erin was aggressive towards Dani. It made sense; she was envious that Dani was the first choice to take point. She felt her skills as a cadet matched that of Dani's, there was no reason she shouldn't be able to lead the squad as easily and efficiently as her.

"Erin, chill out. Dani's right." Sarah chimed in. "The best place to find out clues about a mission we have no idea about is to look at where the mission initially started. I say we go for it, beats sitting around here all day anyways."

Sarah's optimism made Dani feel at ease and as if she was on the right path. It brought a smile to her face and she once again was happy that Sarah was on her team, giving her the support, she didn't know she needed.

The squad started on the move towards the west side of the compound. It was about a two-mile hike through the woods and the sun was starting to shine through the clouds, breaking up the chances of a rain shower.

The trees helped to alleviate some of the sun's brightness and provided great coverage not only from the sun but from being seen by others. The members of the squad heard other groups making their way towards the western woods as well. Seems others had figured it out, this only reassured them they were on the right path. After the two-mile hike the squad reached the edge of the western woods.

"Well, now what?" Erin looked around without actually looking. She was making a show in hopes of putting Dani down.

Cain finally stepped up, voicing his opinion. "We should look for a clearing, we need to find somewhere that someone would have been able to shoot and know what they were shooting at. I imagine the person responsible probably had a line of sight to the square from their location, that way they could see our reaction. To see if we responded the way they wanted us too. From the moment that gun was fired we were being judged."

"I agree with Cain. This drill is meant to test our ability to maintain composure under pressure." Dani added.

"Well if that's the case Dans, we failed" Sarah nudged Dani, lovingly.

Dani gave a slight smile to Sarah. She was right. Very few people knew what to do when that gun went off. Most everyone started running around in a heap of confusion. Even if everyone finishes the drill and finishes it before lunch, she had a feeling the commander and officers weren't going to let the trainees off so easily.

"Let's stick to the tree line keeping the square in view. That should give us the best vantage point to see a clearing in the woods." Cain decided.

"It's about time you make a decision." John was still furious about having to run back to the square. He not only had to drag Cain to the woods, but he ends up running straight into someone else causing a huge lump on his forehead and a massive headache throbbing in his skull. Earlier that morning he had spilled coffee on his undershirt as well as tripped during the morning run. It just hadn't been his day. Now he was stuck in a group with people he really didn't care for such as Erin and Cain.

Squad two ran along the tree line. John took point in the front a little way ahead along with Erin to scoop out any more traps that might be lying in wait for them. Cain ran in the middle while Dani and Sarah stayed on the left and right sides of him towards the rear, ready to act if needed and intervene if they were attacked.

"There, on the left!" Sarah called out. The group slowed to a stop.

John and Erin rejoined the group at the sound of Cain's signal.

"Why are we stopping?" Erin commented once they returned to the group, heavily breathing from running.

"There's a clearing that looks promising, we should scope it out." Sarah announced.

"I think we should split up Cain, we can cover more ground that way." Dani discussed with Cain.

"Yes, I agree, Dani, you and I will take the left side, Sarah and Erin, take the right. John take up the middle." Cain commanded.

"Hold up, you don't think that's a little risky, that area is sure to be a trap, you're pretty much sending me into the lion's den!" John raised his voice.

"I know, but it needs to be checked out and you're the fastest runner here as well as the strongest. You will stand a better chance of holding someone off until we can get there to help you." Cain didn't like making the decisions. If something went wrong, it would be completely his fault. If they failed in the drill, it will be because he made the wrong calls.

"Fine, what should we be looking for?" John asked, accepting his role.

"Anything out of the norm, broken sticks, trampled plants, footprints. Something that shouldn't be there that might give us an indication of where we should go next. Look for a path. This isn't going to be our final stop. They wouldn't make it that easy." Cain's knowledge of strategy was starting to come in handy, shining through as he became more comfortable.

The group started to rake through the forest. John slowly made his way towards the center, wary of his surroundings, listening for movement, eyeing the trees as he moved. Sarah and Dani had the same idea, they both climbed a tree so that they could get a better vantage point. They would be able to see a path better, as well as see anyone trying to sneak upon them.

Erin, who had stayed close to Cain now whistled to the squad and motioned for them to head over her way at his command. Cain was onto something and was ready to piece the puzzle together with his fellow squad members. Dani climbed down from the trees while Sarah stayed on patrol, watching for any signs of trouble, but close enough to hear her squad.

As he approached, John asked them what they had found. Dani was standing with her arms crossed watching Cain examine the area. Cain was leaned over a patch of plants that had been trampled. He was testing the dirt, feeling for how soft and hard it was. It had rained recently, and the ground easily moved where it had not been trampled by footsteps.

"You see, right here. These twigs have been broken. And there, those plants have been stamped down also there and there too. Also, right here, there are seeds. Someone was eating sunflower seeds and spitting them out." Cain was moving about quickly now, pointing out the different signs of accumulation and disturbance. It was like tracking an animal, he was hot on the trail now.

"I found footprints in the clearing; it looks like at least four sets." John added to Cain's thoughts.

"So, four sets in the clearing, the three trampled spots here, and then there's this print here," Cain was mumbling to himself and making wild hand gestures, pointing this way and that. He was clearly strategizing the events that had passed, visualizing the events in his head. He walked a few steps one way and then a few steps another as if to look at something, he then nodded to himself confirming what he had concluded. "So, if we go that way..." he pointed down a path, still thinking.

"Hey guys, I don't mean to interrupt, but it looks like a squad is coming up the rear, at eight o'clock." Sarah called down from her place in the trees.

"Cain, which way?" Dani knew they needed to pick up the pace. The sun was now high in the sky and noon would be fast approaching.

"Assuming no other squads have come this way yet, it looks like there was a team of at least six people and probably more. They headed North. I'm going to guess at some point they headed out of the woods. What structures are north of us?"

"Uh, the barracks are north, aren't they?" Erin wasn't the best at directions, but she had a good general idea of where everything was located.

"Hey, Sarah come on down, we're heading out." Dani called up to her best friend hanging off a tree branch like a primate.

"Okay Dans!" Sarah climbed a few feet down then somersaulted out of the tree landing on her feet and hands just like they were taught in combatives. She had fallen with grace, and the perfect landing encouraged a smile and wink at Dani who in returned giggled, understanding the intent in her friends' facial expressions.

The squad took up the same position from when they had started and headed out, running towards the north, towards the barracks, still staying close to the tree line. It didn't take long for them to see the living quarters ahead. When they got closer and were about to exit the woods, Cain signaled for them to stop and regroup to discuss their next plan of action. The group huddled together in the brush to scan the buildings and the surrounding area. Nothing seemed to be out of place, and it didn't look like anyone was around, but the squad knew that wasn't the case.

Erin was the first to speak up breaking the silence. "I don't see anything."

"It looks like we're the first squad here." Dani wondered how Liam and Aiden were holding up in their squads. She didn't know if they were in a team together or had been separated. In the chaos, she hadn't even had an opportunity to catch their eyes after her name was called.

"We should stick to the shadows of the buildings, running in between the buildings. Two of us should take to the tops of the buildings though. We still need a vantage point, those two will be our eyes and can call down to us if there's any trouble ahead. That being said, those two will be exposed." Cain had finally started to act like a leader, displaying more confidence in his orders without second guessing himself. His abilities were sound.

"I think Dani and I should take to the roofs, like you said before I'm fast and strong, but so is Dani, I know her combat skills are almost unmatched. That should prove useful if we run into trouble."

"Agreed," Cain stated. "Then Erin, Sarah and I will head towards the innermost building." He pointed towards the center of the cluster of buildings.

"Why the inner building?" Sarah asked a tad confused.

"Because it's the hardest place to get too, we have to cross obstacles and overcome challenges that would ensure anyone weak or unwilled would never get close enough to finish the mission." Dani explained as she studied her surroundings calculating the best way to enter the center square of the barracks. "We should split up." She addressed John. "One of us takes the left side of the buildings the other takes the right, that way we can watch over the western and eastern borders as well."

"I'll take the left rooftops, sound good?" John asked.

"Yeah, I'm good with that." She replied.

"Okay, we'll give you guys two minutes to get to the tops, signal us when you're there. From that moment we'll give you another three mins to get a head start and start scoping, whistle to us if you see anything." Cain looked at his watch, noting the time.

"Right." Dani and John said in unison and then turned and ran out of the tree lines and to the nearest buildings keeping on their toes and listening for anything while the other three stayed behind watching for movement.

Dani got to the closest building to the right of her and entered through the back door of the barracks. She proceeded to climb the five flights of stairs that lead to the roof of the building. One min down a min to go and she was only halfway up the stairs. Forty-five more seconds down and she could see the door that opened out to the roof. She burst through the door and surveyed the roof along with the surrounding roofs. She could see John to the left of her. She signaled that she was ready. In return, John signaled to Cain back in the woods to let them know that so far everything looked clear and they would be moving on ahead.

Dani and John turned and started to run leaping across the roof's tops, scanning the area as they went. John was in fact faster than Dani. He was at least a full rooftop in front of her when he suddenly stopped. He motioned for Dani to do the same. Dani crawled to the edge of the roof and peered over while staying in the shadows. She could see a group of soldiers, carrying an air of authority, standing around and talking.

That confirmed it, they were on the right track for completing this drill. What happened next took Dani by surprise. She felt a cold piece of metal against the back of her neck. She stood up slowly as to not set the person on the other end of the gun on edge, her arms were up in a position of defeat and surrender.

"That's it, stand up nice and slow. No sudden movements. Now turn around slowly. Where are the other members of your squad?" The deep voice spoke easily to her.

Dani lifted to one knee but before she fully extended to a standing position, she jabbed her elbow into the side of the assailant's knee making him fall. She quickly jumped up and spun around to where she was now behind the person and kicked him from behind causing him to fall to his stomach. She pinned him there with his arm held tightly behind his back.

"What's the objective here? Are we after something or is this just a test to see how far we get?"

Dani figured while she had the "enemy" trapped she might as well pump him for answers or at least try too.

The stranger belted out a hardy laugh. "You've got spunk kid, I guess I should expect that though from Major General Mitchells's daughter." He struggled to get his other hand free. Dani gave him a little slack knowing that if he tried anything, she could easily overcome him again. He pulled off his mask to reveal his face. Dani retreated off the person taken aback by the persons' appearance. The black hair was stirred to a whistling mess with the quick removal of the face mask. The wrinkles told stories of hardship, stress, but as well as devotion and happy times.

*****

John looked over to see that Dani was not alone on the roof anymore. Instead, she was kneeling on the ground with what looked like a gun pointed at the back of her head. Before John could warn her, she was up and then in one smooth and flowing motion she had the assailant pinned on the ground. John wasted no time in rushing over to help Dani. He flew down the flight of stairs and rushed over to the other building but before he could reach the door, he was ambushed himself.

A male assailant came at him from the side while a smaller figure, most likely a female, was falling on top of him from the sky. He managed to dodge the attack from the female but in turn, ended up having to block a fist that almost collided with his sternum. He was having to avoid attacks from two different sides of his body now. He tried to kick out the knee of one person while simultaneously blocking a punch from his ribs.

If he wasn't careful this fight would turn very fast in his opponent's favor. Before the fight could get out of hand, Sarah was running towards them ready to engage. She came back to back with John, her fist already raised.

"Keeping all the fun to yourself, Johnny? That's not being a team player."

"You are more than welcome to take over." John was looking at the person in front of him, sizing up his opponent. "Dani has someone trapped on top of the building as well."

"Damn, what is it today, ambush day? I just want to be done with this shit so we can eat lunch" Sarah joked.

"Thinking about food again, are we?" John rolled his eyes as he readied himself for his attacker to make a move.

"Always."

'Sarah, always so playful', John thought to himself with a slight smile on his face. He was glad she was there. He enjoyed her company and although she was constantly joking, she was a powerful ally. Her skill in combat was almost as good as Dani's. That came as no surprise. The two usually sparred together in their off hours.

"I'll go left, you go right" Sarah strategized.

"Sounds good to me"

The two moved on instinct and charged their opponents each blocking attacks easily enough. But Sarah and John did not go easy on the masked covered people. Even though it was just a drill they took it ever so seriously, knowing that those two masked figures would be dealing with a few aches, pains, and bruises the following morning.

The two were able to incapacitate their attackers within minutes. They started for the building to help Dani before any more opponents could show up. The other members of their squad were already halfway up the building. They had snuck by when John and Sarah were engaged in combat. John and Sarah reached the top walking out to see Cain and Erin gawking at the scene before them. Dani had let her attacker up, he had removed his face cover, and the squad was left speechless at the sight of their visitor.

Chapter 2

FAILURE IN THE EVENING

The gentleman continued to laugh. In his position, fun was a luxury he often did not have time for. Visiting the academy brought back memories of when he was a cadet in training at the academy a lifetime ago and life was easily not taken so seriously. In his high office in Eastern Command, he saw more paperwork than action, and his eyes and mind had become weary and strained with the endless typed words that sat black on a white background. Even this little bit of action proved harshly on his body, his muscles growing weak from lack of movement, but he enjoyed the rush of adrenaline it had awakened within his aging soul.

"Brigadier general Alpine, sir," Dani said in shock. "Please forgive me?" She pleaded.

The general continued to laugh, letting it taper off to an end. "There's nothing to apologize for cadet. You acted as you should. Your combat skills are quite impressive, but I suppose I should expect nothing less from the daughter of General Mitchells. I'm sure your father is very proud."

"Thank you, sir." It came as no surprise that she was recognized as General Mitchells's daughter. She grew up around the higher-ups, attending balls and gatherings along with the occasional trip to her father's office. She and her father had become very close after her mother and her three sibling's passing when she was a very young girl and since it became just the two of them, she became her father's pride and joy.

"What do we owe the pleasure, sir?" Dani asked.

"Oh, Well I like to see that my cadets are on the right path every once in a while, and it just so happened this is one of my favorite drills. It really shows what each of you is capable of under pressure. So, I decided to take point today. Before we continue, why don't we head to the center square. We don't want other squads to see us up here, now do we?" He said rhetorically.

General Alpine turned to leave the roof with the trainees towing behind him. He was a tall man with impeccable posture. He had a beard and a head full of hair that was as black as night. Surprising for a man of his age. He was older than her father but, it was clear he still had fire within his soul. Dani's father used to tell her stories about General Alpine. How he was loyal to his men never leaving anyone behind.

"Hey," Dani whispered getting the attention of the other squad members. "Keep your guard up, this could be another trap"

"What?" Erin whispered back a bit harsher than intended. "What do you mean? Why would this be a trap?"

Keeping their distance from the general as to not let him over here their discussion, the trainees continued to whisper. The general understood their intentions and quickened his pace letting the young cadets strategize. He laughed inwardly still remembering his time here, walking these same stairways. The memories came flooding back as he allowed his hand to rest lightly on the walls; letting them slide against the rugged edges as he walked. One memory stood out in particular of a cadet that was a year behind him. Cadet Bartovics and himself managed to sneak away from the morning drill and hid away in the stairwell only to be discovered an hour into it by a commanding officer. He had been such a rascal in his younger days, and if his shenanigans from today proved anything, he still had that troublesome streak deep within him. Nowadays he sat cozily in an office as a general while Bartovics defended the wall as the stronghold of the western command. He smiled at the memory.

"Do you really think the general is leading us into a trap? I mean, he made it seem as if we completed the task. He even explained what he's doing here. That doesn't seem like a trap." Sarah said slightly disappointed but also with a hint of hopefulness.

She was an optimistic person. She would rather see the brighter side of things than the negative. The only problem with that was in war, optimism wasn't a luxury one could afford to have. A person needed to stay on guard and suspect anything and everything because once you have trust you could be looking down the barrel and it might be the last thing you see.

"Yes, I do, he never said this was over and if it were then why ambush us? Why not just let us carry on" Dani asked, raising the questions in her fellow cadets' minds, forcing them to think things through.

"Maybe it was a finale test, to see that after all that energy spent to get here that we could still fight and defend. These drills are, after all, meant to challenge us in every aspect. Using our combat skills would just be another tool we are supposed to utilize." Cain went on to explain.

The statement made sense, but still, Dani couldn't shake this feeling. Years being trained and taught by her father had forced her to be paranoid about such things. 'Question everything, to live on into the next day", her father used to tell her.

"You could be right, but it also wouldn't surprise me if he were here to make us feel at ease, letting our guard down and then lead us into a trap. After all, if this were a real mission, we wouldn't be getting off this easy, and like you said these drills are meant to challenge us. This...just seems too easy is all." Dani explained.

The general stopped and looked behind him at the students. "Is everything alright back there? You cadets are walking rather slow, your starting to fall behind. An old man like me is putting you to shame out walking you." The general gave a light-hearted laugh with glee in his soft eyes.

"We apologize sir, we were just discussing the mission and started to lag behind." Sarah replayed with a lightness to her voice as to not raise suspension. The general seemed to buy it because he continued walking.

The squad looked around at the barrack buildings as they headed to the square that was in the center of the living quarters. They paid close attention to the tops of the buildings and the shadows waiting for another ambush. Expecting more to this drill.

They paused when they reached the center of the square. A fountain loomed over them, flowing with cool crisp water reflecting the sunlight causing little droplets of rainbows. It was quiet and empty. The general was now talking to someone that had approached him. Upon a closer look, Dani realized it was the commander. What was he doing here? Maybe the others were right, maybe this was the end of the drill. Brigadier General Alpine and Commander Leon walked over to Dani and her squad. The sun catching their silhouette.

"Congratulations cadets, you not only completed the ambush drill, but you were the first squad to complete it. You may rest up and have free time until this afternoon's events. You are dismissed." Commander Leon addressed the group. His congratulation and release speech were surprisingly short. Usually, the man was a talker.

"Thank you, sir," the squad responded.

General Alpine address Dani before him and the commander took there leave. He was impressed by Dani and her assigned squad. He knew Dani's progression well having taken the time to study her file and constant drill success, in hopes that he would be able to have her transferred to his unit as his second lieutenant when she graduated the academy the following year.

"You and your squad were able to not only react quickly and efficiently while keeping your composer to the gunshot, but you made quick work in devising a plan that would set in motion a complete and, might I add, successful mission. Regardless of the unexpected, your squad managed to stay in control and assess each situation rationally, bringing you to this point. And to top it off you made quick work of the ambush we set for you here. Good work cadet Mitchells. I'm expecting great things from you, and I hope to see you among my ranks in the near future."

The general saluted Dani. It was a small gesture that held a great impact. He was showing respect and admiration to her by saluting to her, someone of lower rank, first.

"Thank you, sir," Dani said as she saluted back.

General Alpine turned to take his leave and Dani did the same rejoining her squad. She knew if her father were here, he would have been proud of her. Sarah watched her and smiled, and Dani felt Sarah was saying the same.

"Well." Sarah started to say as she stretched her long arms above her body cracking her neck while she also stretched her long legs in front of her. She then slumped back down on the fountain; legs crossed in front of her. The sunlight caught her blond hair turning it a golden color. "I don't know about you guys, but I'm starving. I say we head to the dining hall and grab some food." She smiled, soaking in the rays of the sun.

"Sarah, you're always starving." John was teasing her as he gave her an awkward light nudge on her arm. "I'm not quite sure where you put all that food."

"I'm not quite sure if that was a compliment." Erin said giving John a hard time.

Cain chimed in, "I think getting some food is a superb idea, plus if we leave now, we can ensure we make it there before the rest of the squads so we will have first pick."

"Then it's settled." Sarah jumped up. Everyone else followed and stood up from sitting around the fountain and started to take their leave. All but Dani that is. "Dans are you coming?" Sarah asked her friend.

"You go ahead, I'm going to hang back for a few, I'll catch up." She said with a reassuring smile, but Sarah could see through it in a heartbeat.

"Don't worry, they'll make it here in time. Aiden is smart and you know Liam will talk his way out of any situation." Sarah reassured her.

"Yeah, your right." Dani smiled at the hope that Sarah instilled in her.

"Well since I'm right then, come on, join us. We can celebrate our victory of being the first ones done by stuffing our faces." Sarah was hanging an arm around Dani's neck, gesturing to the sky as if the food was suddenly going to float down on a cloud surrounded by halos.

Dani laughed and smiled as she let Sarah pull her away from the fountain following the others. John looked back and motioned for them to hurry up.

"Come on! I thought you were starving" teased John, acting as if he were going to faint from hunger with the back of his hand hanging on his forehead to tease Sarah further. She just rolled her eyes and shouted back at him.

"I'm giving you a head start; you don't want me to get there first!" She and Dani laughed as they quicken their pace to catch up.

*****

"Hey Dani, did you read the paper?" Liam scooted in next to Dani at the dining table where she and the rest of her squad were enjoying their lunch.

She threw up her arms, fork still in hand and rolled her eyes. She starred at Liam dumbfounded. "Are you kidding me! When the hell did you have time to continue reading the paper? We were running drills all morning!"

"Yeah, I know." He rolled his eyes back. "I read it on my way here." As if that explained everything. "Anyways, apparently your father's going to be heading a conference with the leaders of Mars and Venus...on Mars. Did you know?" he asked her.

She took the paper to read the article mentioning this news. "No, he didn't tell me," Dani was a bit surprised and taken aback by the news. Why wouldn't her father tell her he was traveling to Mars. Surely, he didn't think this was information he should have kept from her. "I'm sure it's just routine diplomatic issues." She waved off the issue as if she wasn't bothered by it. "Anyways how did your squad do in today's events; I see you have a black eye. And is that blood? Did you gash your face too? What, did you run into someone's fist through your own stupidity?" Dani had her hand on Liam's chin moving his head about examining his face.

"That hurts that you think so little of me, give a guy some credit." Liam stated with pity in his voice, hoping it would gain Dani's affections.

"Oh, excuse me. Please, I beg your pardon. So, then what did you do?" She asked with sarcasm in her voice expecting a ridiculous answer.

She and Liam had grown up together, somehow, he always was injured in the most absurd ways. One time, when they were seven, he broke his arm tripping when he stepped into a bucket and somehow managing to fall into a wooden barrel while helping his mother pick carrots from there garden. She couldn't stop laughing at how ludicrous he looked when he attempted to crawl out of the barrel soaking wet slipping as he tried to balance using only one arm. Even then he laughed at himself. He must have been in pain from the broken arm, but he laughed right through it. He always said it wasn't where you ended up or the end result but how you got there, the adventure was what mattered. And that fall created a story he loved to tell over and over. Dani never saw a kid prouder of his broken arm.

"That's better," he patted Dani on the back. "Well, there I was, ready to lead the squad to success in the mission. We had just reached the edge of the woods, when I heard a noise, I immediately went into a defensive stance ready for whatever was about to come my way when...."

"when the dumbass tripped because he got his foot stuck in a hole and fell hitting a rock." Aiden had walked over to join his friends. As he passed Liam, he lovingly pushed Liam's head ruffling his hair just as an older brother would. He sat down next to Sarah, across from Dani where he started to enjoy his lunch.

"You are such a klutz." Sarah was laughing at Liam for his ability to be so wholehearted at such a low moment. She admired him for that. Whenever she was feeling down or needed a push, he seemed to always be around to lighten her mood.

"So, I'm guessing you two were in a squad together then." Dani assumed, watching the two carry on back and forth.

"Yeah, which in all reality, I'm happy about because the other people," Liam was explaining between bites of bread, "were hard to work with."

"Liam's' right, we had a high classed second year, and two third years." Aiden commented.

In the academy, there were the first years who started at the age of thirteen going all the way up to fifth years, graduating at the age of eighteen. Within each year there were different skill levels obtained and techniques taught. With each year the tasks and drills grew harder and became more in depth. How hard a person worked and studied would determine how fast they could progress or events and drills they could participate in. Someone who was a second year could easily work with third, fourth, or even a fifth year if they put in enough hours and extracurricular work.

Dani and Liam were fourth years while Aiden and Sarah were fifth years. They were preparing to take their final exam and go on a month-long exit drill where they will use all their skills learned and assets acquired to survive with an assigned squad in the wilderness. They will be required to complete different tasks and work in different areas of the military. This will later help to determine the branch where they would be assigned.

"How did your squad fair? I saw that you and Sarah were in a squad together Dans." Aiden was sitting in such a way that allowed him to naturally face Sarah. He was straddling the bench with his legs facing her, admiring her. His elbow was hitched on the table so that he could use it to support himself. Even though he was keeping conversation with the rest of his friends, everyone could see his attention was truly on Sarah.

Dani notice John was a bit jealous. He wished Sarah was giving him the attention that she gave Aiden, but it came as no surprise. Aiden was very handsome. His dark brown hair made his hazel eyes burst with lightness giving his face a luring appeal. He seemed to always have a five o'clock shadow, even after he had just shaved, giving his high cheekbones and square jaw a rugged look that made him seem relaxed and easy going. That was Sarah's kind of person, someone who made her feel at ease and could make her laugh.

So he would not be bothered by the flirting between the two, John tried to keep conversation with Cain and Erin who were more interested in their own selves then conversing. Cain had a book and was too busy reading to pay attention and Erin was paying attention more to another girl from the table behind her, turned around carrying on a conversation. Dani felt bad for John, after all, he was a nice guy and was helpful during the drill. She had never worked with him before, but he was a fourth year like herself. She had heard he could be a bit rough around the edges, taking his training a little too serious, but he mirrored herself.

"Oh, well we were the first squad to complete the drill, so that was in our favor and we did that with all fourth years except for Sarah, of course."

"Dans went one on one hand to hand combat with General Alpine." Sarah mentioned with pride in her voice.

"No shit! That's impressive, not many can say they've done that. I'm sure that will bump you up a few levels for sure! Not that you need extra help doing that, your head of your class. Liam on the other hand...." Aiden had started to say.

Liam was stuffing his face with pudding and cookies. He stopped only briefly with this eerie feeling that everyone was looking at him only to look up and see that they were doing just that. "What! They never have chocolate pudding."

Everyone started to laugh. Liam was left confused but joined in on the laughter as well. It was often that he was the joke of the group, but if it made his friends laugh, momentarily forgetting their worries and problems, then he was more than happy to be laughed at.

The bell rang to indicate the end of lunch. Everyone broke up into their squads and met back with their original officers who had given them their envelope for the morning drill. They would be informing the cadets if they would be participating in combats or arms first.

"Squad two, congratulations on being the first to complete the drill." Warrant Officer Reed wasn't the friendliest of people and when he congratulated them it was the furthest from sincere. He had not even bothered to look up from his clipboard. "All of you will be working in combats for the next two hours and then after you will switch to arms, that is all." He turned and walked away to rejoin the other officers.

"What a friendly person." John said sarcastically.

The squad turned away and headed to the training field. Once a long time ago, it was a field for sports but today it makes a great faculty to run training exercises without causing an excessive amount of damage to the body since the field was laid with artificial grass. Plus, the buildings held great storage space for all the extra equipment for various training exercises.

*****

Waiting at the field was a captain expecting nine squads to appear at the entrance of the field. There had been eighteen squads total and half of the squads were assigned to combats first while the other half were assigned to work within the arms building.

"Do you think Aiden and Liam are here?" Sarah looked at Dani, hopeful.

Dani had been looking for them as soon as they had proceeded to the field, but she had yet to catch sight of them. All squads had made their way to the field and were lined up in rows ready to receive further instruction from the captain.

"Each of you will first partner up with someone of an equal statue. When you hear the bell ring, switch and pair up with someone that will likely challenge you. There will not be a lesson today nor will I show you any new techniques. Today's goal is for each of you to teach one another a skill you have acquired and are good at. By teaching a person you not only help your comrade in arms but you also better your understanding of that technique or skill. Do not cheat yourself by picking someone who will not challenge you. This time of combats is meant for you to better yourself, strengthen your body, and for you to hone your skills. You are only as good as you want to be." He walked away from the crowd of cadets, an indication he had completed his instruction.

"Erin, would you like to spar?" This was Dani's attempt at smoothing tensions between her and the other cadet.

"Yeah sure, I guess." In reality, Erin liked the idea of fighting Dani. She could finally prove that she was better than her. Even if she couldn't, she would at least be able to do some damage.

The bell rang and the teams of two started to spar. Dani was reluctant to throw the first punch, so to speak. She always liked to measure her opponent before attacking and usually the first move gave the best insight and understanding to who she's fighting. She was petite and her size often caused the other trainees to underestimate her. She used that to her advantage. She usually could figure out how to defeat an opponent or determine their weaknesses. Did they favor their left side or right? Did they prefer to use their legs, fist, or maybe their arms?

Dani was on guard, ready, when in a blink of an eye Erin moved. She ran from the left side coming in low and fast with her fist at the ready. She was going to hit first, an unusual move, Dani had seen Erin fight several times over the years and knew she preferred to use her legs more. She was a fast runner and always did leg strengthening exercises at the gym. It made sense she would use her legs as her strong point in hand to hand combat. 'So why was she coming at me with her fist?' Dani thought.

Dani knew something was off, but before she could reason why, Erin had lowered her fist and lifted her leg, going in for an ax kick. She was aiming for Dani's shoulder in an attempt of a possible dislocation leaving Dani with a loss of one of her arms, not only that, but it was Dani's right arm that Erin was aiming for. At some point, Erin must have noticed Dani was right hand dominate or she was betting on it. Either way, if she lost the use of her right arm she could be in real trouble.

Dani turned at the last moment, dodging the kick. She, in turned, threw an arm up in hopes of knocking Erin off balance since she was unsteady from still being in mid kick. Erin was unable to recover fast enough from the kick and Dani managed to land the strike to her left shoulder blade. She knew the strike would weaken any attack Erin tried with that arm.

Erin attempted another kick, this time aiming for Dani's ribs. She landed the blow only to be welcomed with a fist in her thigh when Dani dipped down and maneuvered around Erin's left side. The blow left her thigh numb.

"Smart move going for my legs." Erin commented.

'One more blow like that and this fight might as well be over.' Erin thought. Erin twisted away from Dani but couldn't get far enough away. She was hit again, but this time on the opposite side. 'I knew it.' Erin thought. She was able to react just in time backing away so that she didn't get the full force of the blow. She countered by throwing a punch at Dani in the same spot as before, her ribs, and managed to land a hard hit.

'Shit.' Dani thought as she gasped for air.

She knew that the second punch to the ribs did some damage. Her breathing was laborious now. She needed to end this and end it fast in hopes of not receiving further damage. Erin came at her again and when she did Dani turned at the last moment so that her back was to her and jabbed with an elbow into Erin's stomach knocking the wind out of her. Erin was hunched over holding her stomach when she felt a jab in her back. Dani had delivered an elbow to the middle of Erin's back. When she hit the floor, Dani quickly pinned her. The match was over, and Erin was no longer able to safely continue fighting. She had been bested by her rival.

The bell rang and the cadets took a twenty-minute break to recover from the sparring matches. A team of medics was going around checking the status of the injured. They were hard at work cleaning up and bandaging cuts, relocating dislocated limbs, wrapping springs and twists, along with benching anyone that was far too injured to continue.

Sarah and Aiden wandered over to Dani. "Nice job," Sarah congratulated "I see you put miss. attitude in her place. It's about time someone did."

Dani took a swig of water. "Thanks, I have to admit, she was a tough opponent and she definitely didn't hold back. How did you two fair?"

"I fought another fifth year. He thought he had me, but one good kick and he was done."

Aiden was gleaming with sweat on his forehead and his face was red but overall, he looked unscathed, in fact, he looked unfazed standing there slumped to the side with his arms crossed, and pride in his heart. He seemed so much older and mature than most of the other cadets. Even so, his face gave his age away, especially with the strands of hair hanging in his eyes. It was a face untouched by war and chaos.

"Where's Liam?" Dani was still looking around for him, she was concerned that he had lost his fight.

He was strong willed and would give it his all during a fight, but he was irrational and acted with his heart more than thinking with his head. That got him into trouble and before he could think things through, he was getting a fist in the face and then spending the next few minutes on the ground unconscious.

"Oh, he's getting seen by a medic. He received a fist to the side of his skull. He has a nice size gash on his head, and they were fixing him up." Aiden explained to Dani.

"Will he be able to continue in the next round?" Dani was concerned but she had a feeling this would happen.

"I think he will, you know our Liam, he just can't sit still for too long." Aiden rolled his eyes at Liam's carelessness.

Dani must have had a look of concern on her face. When it came to Liam, Sarah, or Aiden, Dani's emotions and concern for safety was hard to conceal. This was the family she had built. The people she trusted with her life. She already lost one family to tragedy and she would do what it took to keep this family safe.

"Don't worry Dans. You know he's fine." Sarah was always good at comforting Dani and saying the right thing at the right time to make her feel better. Dani gave her a small smile, reassuring Sarah that her words eased the tension in her mind.

The next round was about to start. Dani decided she wanted to spar against John while she still had energy and was not too badly injured. John happily accepted, he knew Dani was an exceptional fighter and he probably could pick up a few new tricks. The bell rang indicating the beginning of the second round.

Just like the first round with Erin, Dani waited for her opponent to make the first move. From working with John, she already knew he was left hand dominate and he was all upper strength. Going for his legs wouldn't be the best strategy to begin with. She knew she would have to avoid getting hit by him at all cost. One good hit could easily leave her seriously injured, or worse unconscious. A full minute had passed, and no one had moved. 'What is he waiting for?' Dani thought.

"Well, am I just going to stand here looking pretty all day or what?" John remarked with his hands at his hips. He hoped his comment would rattle Dani into making the first move.

'I guess I'll have to make the first move.' Dani was still strategizing in her head.

Dani ran at John's left side fast, and brought her leg up readying herself to kick out his left shoulder. She jumped to land the blow when he turned away and caught her arm bringing her within his grasp. Her back was now up against his chest. He had her right arm pinned to her side and held her in a choke grip with his left arm. It took everything to hold his arm from crushing her throat, but the room she had was just enough to jab up with her head into his nose.

He instantly loosened his grip from the sudden impact and the sudden burst of stinging pain to his face, but he still had hold of her. She elbowed him in the stomach. He let go of her and immediately knelt over trying to catch his breath. She quickly turned towards him and went to knee him in the face while he was still leaned over, only to be thwarted. He blocked her with his arm and pushed her away. It gave him a moment and that moment was all he needed to steady his breathing and gain control once more.

This time he made the first move. He came in low and hit hard. He realized when he had captured her the first time that when he brushed against her ribs, she seemed more pained than usual. 'She must have got injured there during the first fight' he thought as he charged. Dani was able to detect what his end goal was and therefore able to avoid the incoming attack and counter with a good old fashion punch to the face. John's center of gravity became unsteady and he fell to the ground, he laid there for a moment as he waited for his vision to clear.

John started to laugh as he pulled himself into a sitting position. He was leaning back on one of his hands, one leg was laid out in front of him while he rested his arm lazily on his knee. Both were exhausted from the battle. The two were well matched. Dani was leaned over resting her hands on her knees dripping sweat, looking at him through strands of her dark hair.

"What's so funny" she spat between breaths.

"I haven't had my ass kicked like that in years." He looked dreamily up to the deep blue sky. The sun was high in the sky now, the constant, easy breeze was delightful as it streamed over the heated cadets, cooling them down. Dani was surprised by his answer.

Dani walked over to where he sat and joined him. She looked up to admire the sky with him. It wasn't something she did often. It seemed frivolous to do something so simple, to look up when there was so much to be looking down at, to be paying attention to what was on the ground in front of her. Dani had never been a dreamer, it seemed silly to be when there was no sense in the broken world, they lived in. She needed to keep her mind clear and her sight focused anyways. They sat in silence, an unspoken understanding of the memory that they were creating.

After a moment she got up and stretched. Halfway through her stretch she winced and grabbed her side, an indication of the toll the fights were taking on her. She turned to John and held out her hand waiting for him to grab it so she could help pull him up. "Let's call it a draw, shall we?" Dani was sincere. He grabbed her hand and hoisted himself up.

"Deal." He smiled down at her.

The bell rang indicating the end of the second fight. The two walked over to join the rest of their comrades. The two had worked together multiple times on drills throughout the years of training. John was an honorable man, falling in his family's footsteps by becoming a respected general working in central command under the king himself. John had made the comment 'A nation can only thrive when all its people are accepted' to Dani after a drill during their third year. She thought it was odd, but she agreed with the statement. Today, she was reflecting on that statement.

"What the hell happened to you, ugly?" Liam took a snap at John. Liam was leaning an arm over Aiden's shoulder. His hand was hanging on his pocket. He looked as if he didn't have a care in the world. Knowing Liam though he probably didn't. Aiden stood there with his arms crossed, gleaming with sweat from the matches.

'He must have won his fight' Dani thought.

"The same thing that's going to happen to you if you don't shut that trap of yours Liam!" John bellowed out, his fist shaking in the air.

Liam laughed. "Fine, you and me, next round. Should be fun."

"You're on, you're not going to be laughing long, I'm going to kick your ass!" John's tone suggested he was serious, but his demeanor said otherwise. He had a smile playing at the corners of his mouth.

"You think you can with your giant size. You must be so slow and clumsy; you're never going to be able to catch me." Liam taunted John. He really liked John and harassing him was just his way of caring.

"Save it till the bell rings, no one wants to listen to the two of you bicker. Honestly, Liam do you have to start shit everywhere you go" Sarah was walking, more limping than anything, over to join the small group that was growing bigger. She was clearly annoyed. Her last fight had not gone well leaving her ego bruised. She had a split lip that was swelling up and she was trying to keep ice on it. She had her boot swung over her shoulder and her left foot was wrapped in a bandage. She was supporting herself by walking with the injured foot on her tippy toes trying to avoid putting extra pressure on it.

Aiden jumped up and rushed over to her side to help her sit down beside them. He moved her leg over his thighs to help elevate it. He was stroking her leg while she laid back on her hands with her head slanted to the side. She was clearly exhausted. Aiden and Sarah were in their own world talking to one another while Liam and John were still arguing back and forth.

"You should set the next two rounds out, there's no point in injuring yourself further." Aiden was whispering.

"Will you sit out with me? I'll be bored watching everyone by myself."

"Sure, I'll stay." His face was shadowed, but a smile danced across his lips.

Dani loved watching Aiden and Sarah together. Their relationship was a special one, unique. Even though they weren't together, according to the two of them, there was no one else out there for either of them Dani thought they both just accepted that. Aiden was rough around the edges, some might say standoffish and a bit of an ass, but when it came to Sarah, he was soft and delicate. He was gentle with her, as if she was glass and she could break at any moment. Sarah was loud and abrasive, but with Aiden, she was quiet and calm.

Dani enjoyed seeing those different sides of her closest friends.

The bell rang and Dani fought another opponent. She dislocated a shoulder and had taken a blow to her head, right at her temple, when she failed to avoid a hit. The blow caused her vision to spot, the ending result was a dull pain pounding through her head. She had started to feel fatigued during the third spar, and she had exerted almost all her energy with the day's events. She wasn't sure how well she would perform in the last spar.

"Hey Dans," Liam came up behind her. She was sitting on the ground, resting, with her head down. Her arms laid over her upright knees, supporting her head where her forehead touched. She was holding a bottle of water but couldn't bring herself to drink from it. Liam sat beside her and put an arm around her, rubbing her shoulder up and down at an attempt to soothe her. Her body rocked with the motion.

"Hey Dans. Why don't we spar this next round? I know it's pointless to ask you to sit your stubborn ass out. The least you could do is take it a bit easy." He spoke softly. Something he never did, preserving that voice for her and only her.

She kept her head down and mumbled, too pathetic to be bothered to lift her head in a proper response.

"What?" Liam put his ear closer to her knees so that he could hear her.

She turned her head to talk to him. "I said, okay, Let's do it."

"Great!!!" Liam jumped up excitedly.

The bell rang for the finale spar. Liam stood up and stretched his arms to the sky. He reached out his hand down towards Dani to help her to her feet. She looked up at him. The sun caught his light brown hair causing it to look almost blond. Besides his hair, she could only see his silhouette against the sun and sky. She reached up, gladly accept his strong but gentle hand.

The two friends started to spar, each throwing punches and kicks just to turn around and block every move. They had spared like this with each other so many times growing up that they knew each other's mannerism and abilities, their weaknesses and strengths. They had become equally matched through the years of training together.

"You bothered by your father's proposition?" Liam suggested, breaking the silence.

"It's just work, he probably didn't think it was important to tell me. Besides we've been busy the last few weeks with all these drills and tests we've been running back to back. I'm sure he just didn't want to bother me."

"Bullshit, I know you Dans, I know you're just locking away all those little feelings of yours." He fluttered.

She accidentally threw a punch a little too hard and struck his cheek. Immediate the side of his face started to swell, and a red patch had appeared revealing three distinctive lines. An indication of her three inner fingers.

"See, told you." Liam rubbed his jaw, attempting to brush away the pain.

"Why didn't you block!" She had started to yell at him, furious by his intentions and deceit. She rubbed her hand feeling pain in her knuckles.

"How else was I going to get you to open-up and let out that frustration," there was a pause. "I mean we could...."

He trailed off. His chestnut hair was plastered to his face from the past three sparring matches making him look fierce and wild. His blue eyes bore into her. She paused looking stunned, blinking a few times. And as if nothing happened, she continued to spar with him.

"Don't be a perve." Another kick was thrusted towards Liam.

Liam just laughed and blocked the kick while throwing a punch only to be blocked in return.

"Is that how you get them? You comfort them to reel them in and then go for the kill, as it were. Do they actually fall for that bullshit?" Dani suggested.

He just laughed, as if that was enough of a response. His best friend would understand the answer behind the laugh, and she had.

The bell rang indicating the end of the match. He wrapped his sweaty arm around his best friend's neck bringing her in close, he gave her a peck on her bloody temple, only to wipe away the excess of blood softly with his hand. As they tiredly walked towards the benches to meet with Aiden and Sarah they continued to converse, Liam hoping the interaction would be enough to sustain the mood and ease Dani's mind of her father's mission.

Liam continued to joke about his ability to attract those of the opposite sex and even some of the same sex, even though, he affirmed, he didn't swing that way. Dani just rolled her eyes at him. Even though she didn't laugh or humor him, mostly out of exhaustion, she enjoyed his rants about his arrogance. If she was being honest with herself, she enjoyed listening to him talk because it felt like home which seemed to cheer her up.

Liam had been the one constant in her life. He was there when her mother, older brother, and younger twin siblings left the world behind in a fire and he had helped pick up the pieces every time she shattered. In those first few weeks after they buried her family, he was there every time she broke down and cried and he would hold her and let her cry until she fell asleep. He would then carry her to bed, tuck her in, and wait on the couch until her father got home. It was a side of Liam not many people saw as if it was reserved only for her.

Aiden and Sarah saw the two approaching and stood up to join them. Sarah was leaning on Aiden for support making sure to stay off her injured ankle.

"Ready to clean some weapons? Nothing like getting dirt and filth in open wounds" Aiden said as he rolled his eyes.

"weapon cleaning?" Liam asked.

"I overheard one of the officers speaking, they said the weapons needed to be cleaned and checked over for flaws and damages. Apparently, there's a substantial scouting mission in the works. One that will go beyond the usual route. One that scouts beyond the mountains." Sarah spoke as she reached down to adjust the ice on her ankle. The ice was wrapped within her bandage to keep it lodged there in hopes that the swelling would descend.

"A scouting mission?" First the meeting with Mars and now a new scouting mission, something was happening Dani thought. "That's odd. They haven't had a scouting mission that traveled past the mountains in at least a year. Why now I wonder and when winter's approaching too. They never go beyond the wall during the cold season. Too many accidents occur in those mountains."

Aiden supported Sarah while she was leaned over by holding on to her, helping to keep her steady. "The government is probably just being paranoid." He commented. "It's probably why we've been running so many drills lately. Every week there's more news about attacks. Whether they're true or false is another story."

The four friends walked disheartened from the training field and towards the square in the middle of the compound. They were silent, enervated from the last two hours of combat training. They had reached the square and then headed towards a building on the north side of the square, that was where the armory stood.

They arrived at the armory. The officer that commanded the armors building stood ready to instruct the grime-covered, sluggish cadets making their way into his territory. His scowl was hardened as if years of training had worn down his spirit. That, or he had seen the effects of too many wars.

The four stood slumped, drained of all energy from the busy day's events. They looked as if they were soulless, just existing in the world. 'These next two hours are going to be brutal.' Dani thought, feeling that her friends were thinking the same.

"The lot of you will be cleaning the remnants of this building. Floors three and four have already been graciously completed by your fellow trainees. I expect the rest of the building to be completed. Team up into groups of four to five and get to work." The officer stated and then walked away, feeling that the cadets understood their assignment and needed no further assistance.

The four friends looked at each other, shrugged, and then started to move in the same direction. It was an unspoken agreement to just stay with each other. They were in good company when together and it just made sense.

The four had always been like that, ever since Dani and Liam were first years and had been selected to be in a squad with Sarah and Aiden to run a drill during the second month of training. It was unusual for first years to run drills, but Dani had grown up within the military. She was expected to be exceptionally superior than that of other first years. The higher ups tested her and pushed her as soon as she entered the academy. For those reasons she had to work extra hard, putting in more hours and often exerting herself further then she should have just to stay miles ahead of her fellow trainees.

Liam on the other hand was selected because of his raw, formidable talent and high marks. Upon entering the academy every potential trainee goes through a series of tests to prove what their worth or possible worth is. Liam received one of the highest marks in marksmanship which had not come as a surprise since he used to go hunting with his father and brothers every weekend giving him plenty of practice. It was natural for a weapon to be held in his arms.

His combat skills were undeniable. He could thank his three older brothers for that. He was the youngest of four boys with a ten-year gap between him and his older brother and seven between him and the youngest of the three older brothers. So, he always had to hold his own against them when they decided to gang up on him. Therefore, fighting became instinctive to Liam. His scores on the computerized exam that tested overall knowledge were well above average as well, not as high as Dani's, but still impressive. His combined skills made him a desirable candidate to run drills during his first year.

The day of that drill came as a shock. Liam and Dani were called out of a techniques of war class and were requested to join the other trainees in the square. Upon doing so the commander approached them with two officers who held bags that were clearly packed full.

"Cadet Mitchells, Cadet Evens I'm assigning you to a squad for a drill."

Dani and Liam were wide eyed with surprise, dumbfounded, after all, they were only first years. They had only just started their training a couple of months prior and the commander already thought they were ready for a drill.

"Cadet Hunt, Cadet Pearce!" The commander called over the other two cadets; his hand high in the air waving them over.

Two cadets came running over. One was a female with blond hair cut above her shoulders. At fourteen, she had already come into her own and was well endowed. She wore khaki colored pants with knee high combat boots that complimented her long legs. She had a black long sleeve shirt on. Strapped to her hip was the military assigned knife. It wasn't until a person was in their fifth year that they were assigned their military issued handgun.

She was followed by a male. He was the true description of tall, dark, and handsome. He had light chestnut hair that shone golden in the bright sun. It complimented his hazel eyes that shifted colors with his surroundings and with the light. His hair was cut short and styled in a traditional military cut. He was broad and he wore the uniform with pride, the colors seemed to compliment him. The black camo pants with a black fitted shirt that showed underneath he was built as stone.

When they greeted the commander, they both saluted the traditional Helenia salute with their hands balled into a fist and placed firmly across their torso to their left shoulder and came to a halt with their backs straight and their heads held high. "Yes sir!" They said in unison, the proper response to a person of higher command.

"This is Cadet Mitchells and Cadet Evens. I am assigning them to your squad for this drill. They are the two brightest trainees of their class. I would like them to work with the two of you. I feel that the four of you will make an exceedingly excellent squad. This will be there first drill but with you two taking point I'm sure cadet Mitchells and Evens will catch on very quick."

"Yes sir!" Again, in unison while saluting once more.

The commander saluted back and then turned to walk away. The officers handed off the packs to Dani and Liam and followed suit. Cadet Hunt was named Sarah and Cadet Pearce was Aiden. Instantly Sarah opened up to the two of them and welcomed them to the squad, she treated them as old friends which really helped Dani to come out of her shell. She told Dani how excited she was to have another girl in the group with her. She droned on about how she and Aiden had been in the same squad together from the very beginning and she needed someone else to talk too, that his voice was starting to scratch at her ears. Aiden shook hands with Liam and they both instantly started to bond as if they were long lost brothers finally reunited. The four immediately connected on a level of inseparability as soon as the first words past between their lips.

The two second years explained that the drill was a week-long retreat into the woods. It was meant to test survival skills. They told Dani and Liam that they both had completed this drill twice before. They both thought it was fun especially in good company.

That week was indeed enjoyable, the four bonded immensely while out in the woods left to their own with no one around. Dani and Liam learned a lot as well, which gave them an edge to furthering and advancing their training. Since that day the four had been inseparable, always looking to each other for support, partnering, and even rooming.

Sarah was like the big sister Dani never had but always wanted. Liam and Aiden always gave each other a hard time but through their training, they pushed each other harder than anyone else. Dani didn't want to think about how there were only two more short months all four of them would be together like they were every day. After Sarah and Aiden graduate and move on to their new positions in the military, she and Liam will only have each other to share deep midnight conversations over a pint of ice-cream or beer depending on the talks, when they couldn't sleep. What were they going to do on the weekends? Or in their free time? Who were they going to sit with at mealtime? She didn't like to think about it.

The four walked into the building, up the stairs to the second floor and walked into a room that held rows of rifles placed neatly in individual slots. The lights from the ceiling were bright revealing the layer of dust on the wooded fixtures holding each rifle in their place.

"Well, I guess this room is as good as any" Liam sighed and looked around at all the cobwebs starting to gather in the corners. He slid his finger down the door frame and rubbed his fingers together inspecting the amount of filth gathered on his fingers.

"Let's clean the room first since that won't take but ten or fifteen minutes then we can get working on the weapons." Aiden took lead.

"I like that plan Aiden." Sarah smiled at Aiden from inside the room. Their warmth filling the air.

The group of friends started cleaning the room. Sarah stayed sitting on the counter that was placed in the middle of the room. It held drawers of cleaning supplies and oil for the weapons along with empty magazines. Aiden instructed Sarah to sit on the counter and start checking the weapons to determine which needed a good cleaning and which ones just need a spot cleaning or oiling. He wanted her to stay off her ankle as much as possible. There was not always time to let an injury heal properly during training at the academy, so any chance to stay off an injury or an attempt to not overexert oneself to prevent further injury should be taken advantage of. Once the layer of dust had been removed and the cobwebs swept away, the cadets began dismantling and checking the rows of weapons lining the wall.

The day continued on, time stretching. Without the reference of the sun's movements, it felt as if time was standing still, creeping by as slow as possible. The cadets were completely drained of energy, and for that reason, they sat in silence too tired to even mutter a word let alone carry on a conversation, their heads were down working on the weapons. Soon an announcement occurred over the buildings' intercoms system.

"Cadets, finish up what you're doing and head to the square for the end of day brief."

Everyone finished cleaning the weapon they were on, put it away and then disposed of the cleaning clothes they used. Leaving the room in better standing than when they entered, Dani turned off the light and shut the door behind her. The indications of the end of an extremely long day.

Others had already reached the square and were starting to form up getting ready to receive the end of day brief. After a few moments, the commander brought the trainees to a resting position where everyone had their arms locked behind their back and all eyes laid on the commander. His posture suggested what Dani and Sarah had feared, that he was not pleased with the assessment of today's events. He started to deliver his announcement.

"Today, was, to say the least, a disappointment. Yes, all squads were able to complete the drill in a timely matter. Everyone was able to work out the objectives of the mission, also every squad deduced that the end goal was to head towards the square in the middle of the barracks. This drill, however, was not meant to test your ability to perform, but was to test your ability to react. Which in that aspect most of you would be dead or captured? When a squad is ambushed, the quicker the reaction the better your chance of survival. Staying on guard at all times is key. Next time I expect to see a substantively better outcome because in the heat of battle there might not be a next time." He paused and looked at the cadets standing formally in front of him. "Dismissed." The commander walked off leaving the trainees behind.

The cadets snapped to attention bringing their heels together and saluting in their traditional form, with their arm to their shoulder. In unison, the cadets responded with a yes sir in correspondence to their commander out of respect. As soon as he was gone the cadets started their walks of shame.

"This was the longest day" Liam slapped his face with both hands and slide them down his face. He was slouched over frantically as if to make a show of how worn out he was. He walked as if he was part of the undead.

Sarah was still hobbling but was keeping pace with everyone thanks to Aiden's support.

"Well some good food should help with that dramatic display; I know food always cheers me up!" Sarah mentioned in hopes of lightening the darkness of gloom looming over her friends.

"I think we should all go take a hot shower, get out of uniform and into some comfy clothes. Then go grab some grub. Maybe a beer or two after that. Sound good?" Aiden smiled at everyone.

"I like that plan." Liam and Sarah both agreed, looking at each other as they did so.

"Okay, well then meet back in fifteen to twenty. Sound good?" Dani plotted, shaking her head.

"Sounds good" everyone nodded. Dani took over helping Sarah to their room, while Aiden and Liam went the opposite way towards the male barracks.

Dani and Sarah arrived at the dining hall before the guys did. 'Well, this doesn't surprise me.' Dani thought looking around thinking she might have overlooked Aiden and Liam, but of course she hadn't.

"Dani!" Sarah had already hobbled her way over into the food line and was now shouting in Dani's direction. "There serving beef stew with rolls and for dessert," Sarah looked like she was in heaven drooling over the glass while admiring the fresh food. "There's apple pie with ice cream!" She squealed with delight and clapped her hands together.

'Like a kid in a candy shop.' Dani thought shaking her head with a smile on her face.

"Here, let me grab you a plate." She spoke to Sarah, after arriving at her friend's side. "two beef stews please." Dani asked the server behind the counter.

The server filled up two large bowls with piping hot stew with buttered rolls on the side. She placed them on top of the glass in Dani's reach. Dani grabbed them and put them on a tray. She moved down the line with Sarah in tow. She reached a bar that held side items such as veggies, fruits, and items to make a salad. At the end of the bar was apple pie already cut into sections waiting to be eaten. Dani grabbed a small plate of salad for both of them and then of course placed two apple pies on the tray as well.

She and Sarah grabbed a seat at the nearest bench. Sarah started to eat while Dani went and filled up the cups with something to drink. By the time she had gotten back to the table Aiden and Liam had made an appearance and joined them at the bench. The friends enjoyed their hot meal with pleasant conversation. The day had been long, but the meal and her friends made everything worth it.

Chapter 3

SCOUTING MISSION

Sarah hobbled out of the barracks building where she and Dani lived. There was a layer of fog that had settled on the ground. The nearby woods were still clouded in darkness in the early morning. The air was cool, and a slight breeze was blowing, ruffling the leaves. It hinted at a winter that was fast approaching. But today it looked like it would be a cool autumn day with the promise that the sun's warm rays would make an appearance later in the afternoon. For now, the sun was hiding behind the clouds, refusing to wake up in the early hours, of course not many were up in the early hours.

Sarah saw a head full of dark hair sitting in a gazebo nearby already with a cup filled with something warm, immediately she knew it was Dani. The cold air made the steam from the hot liquid more visible, tantalizing Sarah, calling to her, so much so she could almost smell the hot liquid. She walked over to join Dani being careful not to put too much weight on her still throbbing ankle. She had continued to trade heat and cold compacts all the night before, but by the morning the swelling hadn't resided much and now Sarah was waiting for the medicine she took to kick in.

"Morning." Dani said without looking up from the newspaper she was focused on.

"Morning." Sarah grumbled, wincing as she sat down. Her hair was still a mess from the night's sleep.

Dani handed her a warm cup. Sarah held it up to her face and breathed in the strong smell of coffee. Her hands wrapped around the cup, hugging it. The drink was exactly what she needed to get her day started.

"You always know just what I need." Sarah commented as she attempted to lift her leg up and over Dani's lap. Dani rolled her eyes and momentarily placed her paper neatly down as she listened to Sarah grunt in her lame attempts. Feeling sorry for her friend, she helped and placed the leg over her lap, and then picked the paper back up.

"Speaking of things, you need." Dani handed Sarah a warm compress for her ankle. "If Aiden comes out here and sees you're not nursing that ankle, he'll throw a fit."

Sarah rolled her eyes but took the compress none the less and wrapped it around her ankle, hitting the paper jokingly as she did so. Sarah sighed with relief from the compress. Not only did it help her ankle, but it sent warmth throughout her body, chasing away the chill from the crisp morning air.

"Why are we up? The suns not even out." Sarah groaned, scooting closer to her best friend. She wrapped her arm into Dani's arm attempting to steal her friend's warmth by snuggling next to her.

Dani looked up from her paper and rolled her eyes. She then ruffled her paper and continued to read. "No one woke you and made you get up."

"True, but my best friend was out here all alone, someone needed to keep her company."

"Well in that case I appreciate your thoughtfulness." Dani laid her head lovingly on Sarah's head for a moment, patting her hair at her temple.

"That's more like it. Anyways, is there anything interesting in the news today?"

Dani put down the paper and folded it. It was clear she wasn't going to be able to continue to read it while Sarah was around. She was a talker after all. Dani didn't mind though. She enjoyed conversing with her friend more than reading the lies that filled the paper anyway.

"No, just a bunch of bullshit. Mars this, Mars that. Apparent relief efforts from the minor attacks on the outer wall." She tossed the paper on the bench to the side of her. Throwing it as if it was garbage just like the garbage that was written within the pages of the paper.

"Minor attacks? I thought we were the military," Sarah said sarcastically. "So why haven't we heard anything about any minor attacks?" She air quoted, "It's probably just a power play. The government showing the people they're still in control."

"Yeah, I agree. It's always been about fear and control." Dani added on to Sarah's statement.

As Dani and Sarah continued to converse, they watched as early morning cadets made their daily routines. One person, in particular, always caught Dani's attention when she sat out here in the mornings. A cadet named Hiromi Katsuki. Dani always saw her running with two beautiful dogs. One was white as snow while the other was black as night. Their face and build resembled that of a wolf. Dani never saw the dogs on leashes or restraints of any kind, but the dogs never left the girl's side, loyal to their master, always next to her ready to protect and serve.

"She's quiet, they say those dogs are her only friends. She keeps to herself." Sarah interrupted Dani's thoughts.

"Hmm, what?" Dani blinked lazily; her eyes dazed over from staring.

"That girl, Katsuki, you were staring." Sarah pointed with a finger; the rest of her hand still wrapped around her coffee mug as the steam warmed her chin.

"Oh, yes. She's intriguing to me." Dani said slowly. "I know she's one of the dog handlers, but I've heard rumors that she and her dogs have an unusually unbreakable bond making them the strongest k-nine unit of any other team. They're expecting great things from her when she graduates, so much so that she will automatically receive a rank of captain." Dani grabbed her own cup of dark, black coffee from the ledge of the gazebo into her hand and took a sip.

"I know she's about to graduate with Aiden and myself, but she's been doing actual fieldwork and missions in a real unit since her third year. She runs scouting missions on the other side of the wall. It is quite impressive." They both were staring at the girl now, watching her run drills with her hounds as she shouted out commands and the hounds, in turn, followed them.

"Do you know what she's going to do after graduation?" Dani asked, curious if she was headed down the same path as the dog handler.

"I think she's going to be joining a scouting unit." Sarah confirmed. "It makes sense, since she's already been scouting and I mean, as a dog handler the choices, I'm sure, are limited."

The two sat for a moment longer, still staring, watching the cadet continue running past with her dogs. The fog was starting to lift from the ground letting the grass seep through the gray air. The forest was starting to reveal the greenery that was still left, not yet zapped from the cold nights. Even the clouds were trying to break away, allowing the sun to shine through, in an attempt to warm the ground. The two friends could hear footsteps approaching from behind them and by the sounds of the heavy footsteps, they knew exactly who it was.

"Morning guys." Aiden walked past Dani and Sarah to enter through the opening in the gazebo. He handed both of them some fruit, along with a bagel that had bacon and an egg on it.

"What's this for?" Sarah asked holding the bagel up, a confused look on her face.

"Are you really questioning food? Who the hell are you!" Liam snuck up behind them.

"Anyways where's...". Before Liam could finish his sentence, Aiden tossed something wrapped in paper at him. It was warm and upon unwrapping it, a bagel was reviled. He smiled brightly, taking in the fresh baked smell of the bagel. "Awesome, thank you." He held it up after taking a giant bite from it, his mouth full.

"We're still going for a hike today, right?" Aiden asked the group of friends.

"Oh, shit, that was today wasn't it." Sarah smacked her head in realization. "Aiden, with my ankle, I don't think I can." She knew it would disappoint Aiden, he loved to hike.

Being able to go on hikes were the few times the friends could escape, leaving the world behind. Leaving behind all the other cadets, the military, the hardship they had to endure to become the next great leaders of their nation. It was an honor to serve, but every once in awhile, it was nice to get away and get to enjoy only each other's company.

"Well, we could always go into Falco. Walk around town, get some lunch, maybe go down to the water and watch the boats go by." Aiden was understanding of Sarah's physical condition. The last thing he would want is for her to injure her ankle further.

"That sounds like a relaxing day. Sarah, there is that new clothing store that we could check out." Dani knew that would put Sarah in a good mood. Dani was not much for shopping, but if it helped lift her friends spirt, she would of course shop.

"Well it's not hiking, but it still sounds fun. We can grab a few beers while we're out there too." Liam was always pretty easy going when it came to plans, as long as he was with his friends and a few beers were thrown into the mix, he went along with anything.

With only a few weeks left before graduation, the friends made a point to spend as much time together as possible. Once these few weeks were up Aiden and Sarah would be headed off to their permanent units and with that, seeing them, let alone spending time with them, would be rare and few and far between.

They made plans to meet back up in an hour, where they would catch a train to Falco, the town that sat on the boundaries between tier Charles where the academy and military training was conducted and tier Lincoln, the start to the industrial and mining towns.

The train ride down from the academy to the military town was uncomfortable. The seats were hard from years of being sat upon, the cushions dented from constant use. The downtown area of Falco was beautiful though and worth the uncomfortable train ride. The trees were bright with colors of orange, red, and yellow. Pumpkins sat outside store fronts and the streets were filled with the smells of freshly baked banana bread, warm apple cider, and cool crisp autumn. The sun was now peeking through the clouds, but the air was still cool. It was enough to warm their faces, but the air made them bundle in sweaters, scarfs, and hats.

Sarah leaned against Aiden, using him as her support, as they walked, attempting to relive the weight on her ankle. It was sweet how much Aiden was willing to do to help Sarah. They were all enjoying the sunshine as they walked in and out of stores. Liam acted as if he would rather be anywhere else but there. Everyone told him that he was more than welcome to go back to the academy on his own if he'd like but he stuck around anyways. The company of his friends was far more enjoyable than sitting in an empty room day drinking by himself.

The four friends had made their way towards the lake that was the heart of the small military town. They could see every small business in town from where they decided to sit and enjoy the scenery. The sun struck the surface of the water as if the lake was glass, reflecting the rays and brightening the surrounding area. There was a cool breeze wafting through the long grass where Dani and her friends sat as they watched the waves softly wash against the shore. There were a few birds that cooed overhead, occasionally diving down in an effort to catch fish. It was now the afternoon and Sarah had pointed out that food should be their next priority before catching the train back to the academy for the night. The restaurants in Falco had some of the best comfort food within a hundred miles. It made sense considering it was a military town, all sorts of colorful people made their way here as families were stationed at the academy as trainers and instructors.

Aiden led the other three to a small hole in the wall restaurant. It was dank inside with the low lighting and creaky wooded floors. They sat outside enjoying the perfect autumn weather eating their food and each enjoying a beer. Liam was quiet for one who was normally talkative. He was listening to the group of men sitting behind them speaking a little bit too loud for the peacefulness of the street, clearly becoming more intoxicated as the afternoon passed by.

"Did you hear? The eastern wall was attacked again. It's only a matter of time before those rebels get in and bring with them the red death." The first man started. The news of an attack on the wall had been in the paper only just that morning, but it was hard to believe the rebels were senselessly attacking the wall.

"Oh, that's hogwash, there aren't any rebels attacking the wall. Even if there was, there's no way they're getting through. This is just an attempt to tax us common folk more, so those rich assholes up in central can continue to sit on their high horse." A second man commented, clearly not giving in to the outlandish accusations the paper writes.

"My question is what the hell is the military doing? Even with these supposed attacks, I heard the military is pulling back cadets and sending them into the city." The final man chimed in, joining the conversation. "No doubt, they rather protect the rich than the poor. I tell you what. What happens when there's no poor to serve the rich, they're going to wish they hadn't pulled back all those soldiers then."

Liam was intrigued by the conversation. There were, of course, scouting missions being sent out but no attacks on the wall had been mentioned through the ranks and no attacks on the scouts either. Every scouting mission was a success with no causalities. If the rebels wanted to hurt the military, then why not attack the scouts? It was curious, what was the government spinning? Why was the paper writing such articles?

"Bunch of cowards if you ask me. Seems like the cadets are a bunch of good for nothing…"

Liam stood up in a flash, knocking over a glass of water and his beer. The rest immediately stop talking and looked at him surprised. He spun around to face the table behind them.

"That's enough. Shut your damn mouth." The three men stopped talking and turned to look up at the young man yelling at them. "You have no idea what the military is capable of, but I can guarantee it's more than what you're willing to do. So, if you're not going to do anything but bitch about shit you don't have a clue about then you're no better than those lies from the paper you feed into." Liam exploded on the three middle aged men. He had always been passionate about the military. All three of his brothers served, along with his father and his father before him. To Liam, it was an honor to follow in his father's, and brothers, footsteps and to continue the tradition.

"What did you say punk! I suggest you turn back around and sit down before you get yourself into a heap of trouble." One of the men spat at Liam.

"Liam, What the hell." Aiden sternly whispered as he stood up and grabbed Liam's shoulder and forcefully turned him partially towards him. Liam was still staring the man down, brows furrowed and ready to react. "You know how much trouble you'll get into if you start a fight! You might as well kiss your military career goodbye. The commander won't even give you time to pack your shit. Think!" Aiden held onto Liam's shoulder tightly.

Dani was now standing up, hands pressed against the table looking at Liam and Aiden. "He's right Liam. Come on, just let it go, he's not worth it and you know that, let's just go home." Dani was now pleading, hoping her voice would reach Liam's sense.

Sarah had stood up and gathered their things readying for an escape. "I think the train is getting ready to leave soon anyway, we should catch it and get back before it gets too late. We can grab a beer back at the academy." She thought the mention of beer would lure everyone away.

It must have worked because Liam finally turned away and started to walk towards the train, forgetting about the clueless men. His hands were still shaking with rage, but Dani was talking to him and helping to calm his nerves.

"That's what I thought, like I said the military is full of cowards." One of the men couldn't help himself. This young man had the nerve to challenge him and now he was itching for a fight.

Liam stopped and turned back around, but before he could take even two steps Dani had already jumped over the table placing her on the other side of it and had delivered a striking blow to the man's nose causing him to wince in pain. His nose was gushing blood everywhere.

"You're the coward, you should have just kept your damn mouth shut and left well enough alone when you had the chance." The other two men had grabbed hold of the man's arms to steady him. He spat on the ground next to Dani, blood flying, but Dani wasn't about to back down.

"You bitch, you just threw your military career away." The man took a step forward. Dani stood her ground, but the other two men pulled him away. It was one thing for a cadet to get into a fight, but for a man to attack a cadet, he would be facing major jail time.

When it was clear the three men were not going to make a move, Dani turned and walked away grabbing hold of Liam's arm and pushing him towards the train.

"Let's go, we're leaving." She proclaimed as if it was a matter of fact, now she was furious, herself.

Aiden and Sarah were right behind them. They were shocked by Dani's sudden outburst. It wasn't like her to take action in these types of situations, but then again, the man had threatened Liam. Dani had always protected her own no matter what the consequences would be.

"Well that's not fair, why'd you get to punch him?" Liam said looking over his shoulder at Dani as she continued to push him towards the train.

"Just keep walking." She told him looking around for signs of trouble. She hoped no officers had just seen them, if so then her military career really might be over.

The hour and a half train ride back to the academy was long and quiet. Sarah had fallen asleep on Aiden's shoulder while Aiden looked out the window. It was surprising she could sleep; the benches were hard as rocks, and the bumps did not make for a smooth ride. Liam was staring down at his hands avoiding eye contact with everyone. Dani felt that he was probably beating himself up enough for his stupidity and outburst and decided not to lecture him. His pride had gotten the better of him. She had acted no better, irrationally punching the guy, even if he had deserved it.

The train arrived at the port in San Pike, the town where the academy was located. The academy was hidden on the boundaries of the town and for that reason Dani and the others would have to catch a bus to get back, unless they wanted to walk the five miles. Which really wasn't that bad but with Sarah's ankle and the day they had, walking five miles didn't sound fun.

During the short bus ride back to the academy it started to rain. It was the beginning of a storm that was rapidly approaching down from the mountains. The bus dropped Dani, her friends, and a few others off at the front gates of the academy. There was a group of male cadets who hurriedly made their way towards the barracks to avoid getting rained on too much. Dani was in no hurry; the storm had not yet reached them, and the rain was a nice cool shower in the early night. They made their way through the gate. Just a little bit more distance and they could retire to their beds for the night.

"Cadets Mitchells, Hunt, Pearce, and Evens!" Dani looked up to see the commander standing under the cover of a nearby building with Brigadier General Alpine and....was that her father?

They stood for a minute confused and scared, wide eyed. Did news of their earlier confrontation somehow already reach them? Could this be the beginning of the end of their career? And to add insult to injury, Dani's father was here. How embarrassing.

"Well shit, now we're in trouble." Liam said not helping Dani's nerves. She thought someone must have seen them, or those cowards told on them. Her father here made her even more anxious.

"That's not helping Liam." Sarah said between gritted teeth as she attempted a smile.

The four rushed over to meet their leadership. In unison they came to attention, arm to shoulder over their heart, clanking the feet together in the usual salute.

"Sir!" The four countered.

"At ease" General Alpine proclaimed as he walked up to the cadets waving his hands in a relaxed indication. "It looks as if it might storm." He looked up at the sky. "so, I'll get straight to the point." The men's uniform hats were tucked under their arms as they stood under the cover of the building. "Yesterday's events were more than just a drill. It was a test to give us insight into the right cadets."

"The right cadets' sir?" Dani asked, slowly and confused. "The right cadets for what?" She felt this conversation was not going towards a speech that would end her career. She was starting to feel a wave of relief, but it was only replaced by a fear of where the conversation could head.

"I'm glad you asked Cadet Mitchells." General Alpine pointed towards her excitedly. "As I'm sure you have heard there have been attacks on the eastern wall. We've deployed troops to neutralize the threat, but we fear this could escalate from a simple riot to an all-out attack."

"How can we be of service sir? After all, we are still in training." Sarah asked.

"That you are Cadet Hunt. But we require the unique skills each of you possesses. Therefore, as of right now your training has been suspended. We are sending the four of you along with Cadet Katsuki and her hounds on a scouting mission. Her experience along with the sharp senses of her hounds should prove to be useful in helping the four of you adjust to a real mission." He was excited about the news and expected the cadets to be as well.

"To the outer side of the wall." Aiden asked confused.

"Precisely, Cadet Pearce, and I would like you to lead your squad. After all, your leadership skills have proven to be unmatched among your fellow cadets." General Alpine commented.

"Thank you, sir!" Aiden saluted. He was surprised by the compliment, but pride was building inside of him.

"Take tomorrow to pack your things. A list of items you need to procure, and pack is already waiting for you in your rooms. Each of you is expected to report to the eastern branch Monday by noon for further instructions."

"Sir!" The group said in unison all the while saluting.

The two generals turned and walked away leaving the cadets to the dim lights of the building and the rain as the storm approached, thunder and lightning growing closer. They were heading towards the gate where a car was waiting for them, the rain glistening in the headlights as steam could be seen in the cold air of the night. They were closing the distance between themselves and the running car when General Mitchells heard a voice.

"General Mitchells, sir!" Dani was running to catch up to the generals. The two stopped. When General Alpine realized who was calling, he looked at his comrade and nodded approvingly.

"I'll give you two a moment." He rested his hand on his comrades' shoulder and lightly squeezed reassuringly before removing it. He turned towards the vehicle and made his way out of the gate whistling as he walked away, the umbrella shielding him from the rain.

Dani reached the General and stopped short and in the proper stance saluted and came to attention. The gesture was formal, as she was unsure how to approach or react to the general.

"Hello, my daughter, you're looking well." General Mitchells addressed Dani.

"Thank you, sir." Dank was still standing at attention, her willingness to show her father, a commanding officer, the proper respect he deserved.

The General opened his arms to embrace his daughter in a warm hug, smiling to reassure her. She smiled back and then she gladly accepted, breathing in the scent of home and familiarity. She hadn't realized how much she had missed her father until now. He pulled away to look at her face.

"My, look how you've grown," He patted her hair, paying special attention to the darkness that was a replica of his late wife's. "Your mother would be so proud of who you're becoming."

She shielded her face feeling shy from her father's comment. The thought of her mother always saddened her. "Is it true father? Are you really going to Mars!"

"It's not set in stone, but I'm in a position where my expertise is desired and my presence at the summit would be beneficial for a stable and hopefully lasting union between our two planets."

"I understand, I guess..." Dani trailed off. She didn't want to voice her fears of losing another parent. She was afraid if she did somehow the universe would hear, and it would come true. Somehow her father understood. Somehow, he could sense her feelings of concern.

"Don't worry so much Dans. It's a routine meeting. I will be just fine. I might not even have to go." He lifted Dani's chin up as if she was five years old again. "Besides, you have other things that need your attention. You need to focus on this mission. You will be in a much more delicate position than I will be, and it is I who worries for your safety, as a parent should. I apologize for not telling you earlier about Mars."

"It's okay father. I understand." Dani hugged her father and the two said their goodbyes. Dani watched as her father got into the vehicle waiting for him and started to pull away. Soon she couldn't even see the red taillights as the vehicle drove further and further away. Dani, herself then turned and headed towards her barracks room, her clothes soaked through from the rain.

She wanted nothing more than to get out of her wet clothes, take a hot shower and snuggle into some warm dry clothes and into her warm dry bed. She had made her way into the shower when she heard a voice. She stopped in the middle of washing her hair, her eyes closed shut as the soap ran down her face. She was surprised by the break in silence.

"Am I not allowed to even take a shower in peace?" She wasn't sure why she was surprised by Sarah's intrusion. It had become a norm for her time in the shower to be interrupted by Sarah's presence.

"That was your father, wasn't it?" Sarah hopped onto the countertop and started to straighten the various items atop it, such as her lotions, and brushes.

"That doesn't answer my question." Dani continued to wash her hair and carry on with her shower as if Sarah wasn't there.

"When's the last time you saw him?" Sarah was now braiding her long hair, ignoring Dani's clear aggravation of the unwanted visitor.

Dani sighed, as she realized she had truly missed home. "I don't know, it's been at least two and a half years maybe three. Even though he's my father, they tend to frown upon interaction between us with him being a general and me being a subordinate." Dani shut off the shower and pushed her arm past the curtain reaching for a towel. Sarah jumped off the counter. She was sure to be careful to keep the pressure off her injured ankle but threw Dani the towel she required.

"See, if I wasn't in here, how would you get your towel? Admit it, you need me." Sarah said optimistically.

"If you weren't in here, I would have just gotten out and grabbed it myself." Dani countered.

"But then you'd be cold." Sarah said as she studied her nails. She was indeed a primed girl, always dressing up and making sure she was groomed when she left the room.

Dani had wrapped the towel around herself and was now opening the shower curtain to see Sarah standing there with a smug look on her face, arms crossed. Knowing there was no sense in arguing with Sarah, she gladly agreed with her. And though she would never admit it, she was pleased that Sarah was there to converse with her, even if she was interrupting her peaceful shower. It lifted her spirits and made her feel at ease, to feel at home.

It was late and Dani was tired from the beautiful day spent with friends. She decided to call it a night, crawling into her warm bed with thick covers and fluffy pillows. She knew tomorrow was the start of a very long day followed by longer weeks to come.

Dani woke in a cold sweat the next morning, frantic from a dream she had. She sat up in bed and shook it off not wanting to dwell on it, after all a dream of Liam dying by fire was just that, a dream. He was alive and well, that was a fact, still, it was unfortunately not rare for Dani to have dreams of fires. They haunted her ever since the death of her family, as survivor's remorse.

She exited her bed and donned the uniform pants and boots along with a black long sleeve t-shirt. She was headed towards the dining hall when she heard someone running up behind her calling her name. She turned to see Liam coming towards her. He skirted to a stop in front of her, smiling the usual boyish smile.

"Morning sunshine." He placed an arm around her neck and turned her back around, so they were both headed towards the dining hall.

"After your drinking last night, I'm surprise you're up so early." She wrapped an arm around her best friend's waist, hugging him as they walked.

"How did you know I was..." Liam trailed off, thinking. "Damnit! Sarah!" He smacked his forehead.

"Well you know Aiden is going to tell her and of course she couldn't wait to tell me of all the stupidity that you two were getting yourselves into." Dani was laughing at Liam as he nervously giggled while scratching the back of his head innocently.

"At least you guys had fun. You probably needed it after the week we've had and besides, it will probably be the last time you get to drink like that for a while." Dani mentioned, reminding him of the task they had been given.

"You could have come out and joined us last night." Liam told her.

"My bed was calling my name. Besides, you know I'm not much of a drinker anyways."

Dani and Liam had arrived at the dining hall and were about to go in when they spotted Aiden talking to another cadet and rather loudly at that.

The cadet was another fifth year that Dani had notice hanging around Aiden and Sarah from time to time.

"I recognize him, but I don't know his name. Do you know Liam?" she asked him curiously.

"Yeah, his name is...is Finn. He was out drinking with us last night. He said a couple of things about Sarah and Aiden got pretty pissed."

"Did he do anything?" Dani grew immediately concerned.

"No, we ended the night there, went back to our rooms after that." Liam settled her.

"Well it looks like he's handling it now, we should go over there and interfere if need be."

"Or we could just watch." Liam had a cheeky look on his face, amused by the idea of a fight.

Dani rolled her eyes as she started shoving Liam towards Aiden and Finn's direction. "Move it, your friend needs you." She demanded.

"Looks like he's fine on his own." He said jokingly, his hands waved about, as she continued her struggle in pushing him towards the other cadets. He dug his heels into the wet ground to slow her down and laughed, but only for a moment.

The two headed over in that direction when they heard a smack. Dani saw what happened, but she couldn't process it. Before her brain could catch up Liam had already started running towards Aiden and Finn. He reached the two and pushed Aiden away from Finn harshly and abruptly and started scolding him, hopefully trying to calm him down. Dani couldn't hear what he was saying but could only imagine.

She ran to the other cadet's aid and helped him up off the ground. Finn was holding his jaw, rubbing it. His lip had been split and there was a steady stream of blood running down his face where Aiden had punched him. Finn got to his feet and pushed away from Dani.

"Aiden! You bastard! You'll be lucky if I don't report you!" Finn spat blood into the grass and turned to walk away still holding his jaw.

Liam let go of Aiden and the two walked towards Dani, clearly more levelheaded than the few moments prior. Aiden had a black eye, but it didn't look fresh and he was still in the clothes that he wore the day before. He looked disheveled. His hair was wild, his clothes wrinkled, and even one of his shoelaces had come untied. But he looked unconcerned and unfazed by Finn's threat.

"Would you like to explain what just happened?" Dani stood with her hip swayed to the side, a manner she had seen from her mother many times when she and her older brother would get into trouble. Her arms were crossed in front of her, not because she was annoyed or angry but mostly because the air was a bit chilly after the rainstorm from the night before and a chill was starting to settle in her bones.

"Nothing, it was nothing, just some bullshit." Aiden attempted at straightening the wrinkles from his shirt.

"Some bullshit that enticed you to punch someone, not just anyone, but a fellow cadet, might I add, unprovoked?" She stated.

"Oh, no, there was definitely some provoking there." Liam snickered, only to get glared at by Aiden.

"Let's just drop it, okay. I'm starving anyway." His hair shielded his eyes, he seemed to be too embarrassed to even look up.

Dani paused starring at Aiden for a moment. Her thoughts calculating. "Yeah okay, let's go get some breakfast." Dani turned to walk away. She knew when not to try and push someone. Aiden would come around in his own way, on his own time. It was better to just let him sulk for a while.

"Hey, um, where's Sarah?" Aiden was looking around shyly.

"In bed still. She said last night that her ankle was really bothering her, and she was probably going to sleep in because of it. She hasn't been getting the best sleep since she injured it. I think it keeps her up. I was constantly bringing her pain medicine through the last few nights, so I just left the bottle with some water on her nightstand before I headed out this morning."

"Well, then why don't we get our food to go and bring her a plate. We can just eat at your table instead and that way she doesn't have to come all the way down here." Liam suggested.

"Sounds good to me" Dani agreed.

Dani, Liam, and Aiden grabbed four platters of food and headed upstairs to the second floor where Dani and Sarah's barracks room was located. Upon entering the barracks there was a small living area connected to a small kitchen and dining space. The academy was once a prestigious bordering school therefore the living quarters were overall roomy and quite nice. Each barracks was equipped with two bedrooms with a joining bathroom, and a shared common area and kitchen. They even had a washer and dryer. It reminded Dani of apartments, but then again that's probably what they were meant to resemble.

Dani knocked on Sarah's bedroom door. "Hey Sarah, you up? The guys and I brought you food."

Dani heard ruffling behind the closed door that was followed by a crash. She then heard Sarah moaning a string of curse words. A moment later Sarah opened the door, frazzled. Her hair was wild and untamed, her shirt was hanging off one of her shoulders and she hadn't even bothered to put on pants.

"Did I hear you correct? Did you say something about food?" Sarah looked wild.

"Yes," Dani said slowly. "We brought breakfast." Dani had swayed aside momentarily to where Sarah could see the rest of the living area. Liam and Aiden waved from the table. Aiden's eyes were wide at the sight of a half-naked woman while Liam was busy shoveling eggs into his mouth. He could care less. He always said Sarah wasn't his type anyway, with which she would always reply that she was everyone's type and that he just didn't have good taste.

"Maybe you should put some clothes on?" Dani whispered as she attempted to hide her friend by standing in front of her best, she could from a now gawking Aiden. Sarah was taller than Dani by a good few inches and her attempt at coverage was lost.

"That can wait, don't want this food to get cold." Sarah stated excitedly as she rubbed her open hands together.

Dani smacked her head with the palm of her hand and shook it knowing she shouldn't have been surprised by Sarah's priorities. She then stepped aside for Sarah to walk past her. Sarah and Dani join the men at the table to enjoy the breakfast. It would be the last breakfast they enjoyed at that table for a while. Scouting missions always took a few weeks to a few months to complete depending on what they were pulling reconnaissance on.

Chapter 4

NEW HORIZON

It was late in the afternoon before Dani was almost finished gathering all the items required for the mission. She just had to pick up a few more things. Most of the items on the list that had been left for her had to be bought at the military store located at the academy. She was expected to have camping gear that included everything from an all-weather tent and sleeping bag to cooking items. That wasn't all though, since she and Liam were still only fourth years, they had yet to be issued their handguns, unlike Sarah and Aiden.

She and Liam met at the armory after lunch with orders for their mission in hand. The officer in charge issued each of them a forty-five pistol along with two extra magazines. The ammo they would have to buy themselves.

It was starting to get late and she left the armory along with Liam, saying her goodbyes until dinner and headed back to her barracks. In her room, she was going over the newly issued weapon making sure everything worked the way it should when Sarah came barging into her room, unexpectedly.

"Can you believe this shit!" She was loud and her face was turning blush from aggravation.

"What happened now?" Dani asked while she was overlooking the action, ensuring it was clean of gunpowder residue.

"Finn!" Sarah shouted.

Dani paused looking up at her best friend standing there with her hands on her hips. "Sarah, I have no idea what you're talking about. What about Finn? Are you talking about this morning with Aiden?"

"No, I just found out he's joining us on this mission. Wait, what happened this morning?"

Dani stopped cleaning her gun and quickly reassembled it. She placed it in its holster and laid it at the end of her bed with the rest of her things that needed to be packed. She had been laying everything out and thoroughly going through all her equipment to make sure everything was in good condition before she packed it away in her rucksack.

She looked up at Sarah. "Aiden punched him this morning."

"He what! Why the hell would he do something so reckless? That moron!" Sarah was pacing, angry and upset that Aiden would act so immature as to jeopardize his position within their class along with possibly getting thrown off the mission and on top of it get thrown off his military career path.

"Stop pacing, I'm tired of bringing you pain medicine all hours of the night. Anyways he apparently did it for you."

Sarah stopped dead in her tracks. "For me, what the hell do I have to do with it." There were innocents in her voice. As if she had never believed that Aiden's kind gestures towards her were anything but pure.

"I would think that would be pretty obvious." Dani sat with her legs crisscrossed on the side of her bed, her arms folded in her lap. She was by far the worst person to talk to when it came to the opposite sex. She was a dunce when she was pursued by others not understanding or recognizing the settle clues. But she could see and understand Aiden's affection for Sarah.

"Yes," Sarah paused.

Her hands were hugging her neck and staring upward to the ceiling. Dani thought Sarah looked as if she were dreaming. Possibly of Aiden. "Yes, I suppose you're right." Sarah walked over and sat next to Dani on her bed. She put her hand to her chin resting it there and sighed. "What do you think this mission is about?"

The question threw Dani for a loop. But it was just like Sarah to change the subject when the conversation was getting too close to her having to possibly reveal her true feelings or talk about her disposition with Aiden. It was a touchy subject that Dani never could get straight answers from either of them.

"Oh, I don't know. Probably activity on the outsiders, I would imagine. According to the government, they are our biggest threat." Dani rolled her eyes.

Sarah sighed and laid back on the bed. "Well, whatever it is at least it gets us out of training. I'm so tired of routine drills and back to back running. And training. Five years of this shit. I'm just ready to be done and in an actual unit doing an actual job."

"At least you only have a few months left. I still have a full year."

Dani got up from sitting and looked at all her supplies on her bed. She was convinced everything was as it should be, and she had everything she needed. She started to neatly pack her rucksack. Starting with her clothes on the bottom. Leaving what she would use the most for the top. Sarah heaved herself off the bed.

"Well, I guess I should start packing myself." She rolled her eyes and left Dani to her thoughts and went to pack as well.

*****

Liam sat at a bench in the dining hall, reading a paper as his food started to go cold. He was reading an article that detailed the upcoming plans to meet with the leader of Mars to discuss a union of permanent peace between the two planets. The idea was to try and convince the prince of Mars that a diplomatic solution would be more appropriate and longer lasting than that of a matrimonial one.

It seemed leaders from Venus would also be joining the meeting to act as an intermediary since Venus has held an alliance with both Mars and Earth for a large expanse of time. Liam was so entranced by the paper that he hadn't even realized Dani was sitting by him enjoying a streaming roll with butter and honey.

He laid down his paper still scanning over it when he finally noticed Dani sitting next to him. He almost jumped off the bench with surprise. "When did you sit down?"

"About five minutes ago, that paper must have some interesting news." She looked over it. "Oh yes, like right here." She pointed to a snip in the paper. "Boy with red eyes and silver hair to be named as a new hybrid between Mars and the people from Venus. Is this a sign of a secret union between Mars and Venus? Hmm, very interesting."

"Ha-ha very funny, Dans." Liam shuffled the paper back together and rolled it away putting it in his back pocket. "Did you finish packing everything?"

She nodded yes as she finished her roll and started to eat the rest of her dinner. She was more than ready for this mission, excited even. All those hours spent training, now she could finally put her skills to use. She always knew that when she graduated from the program, she wanted to be a part of the scout's regiment. She would rather be on the front lines then sitting behind a desk watching the action from afar. She only wished Sarah and Aiden would be joining her. But Sarah was going to be working with intelligence, analyzing gathered information to assist the military while Aiden was planning on flying space crafts. He wasn't sure what, he just knew he wanted to fly.

"I guess tomorrow's the big day. We ship out..." Dani started.

"And we might not have to return to this place!" Liam finished.

*****

Dani woke the next morning feeling as if she hadn't slept at all. Her night was spent tossing and turning from unpleasant dreams. She had experienced another nightmare about Liam burning in an inferno of fire again and woke in a cold sweat because of it. The flames licked at the back of her skull, burning the scene into her eyes. It was still early, too early, the dining hall wasn't even open, and she knew her friends would still be fast asleep cuddled in their warm beds. She decided to go for a morning run until they woke, in hopes the nightmares would start to fade with every step she ran.

The run was pleasant. The air was cool and while on her run she was able to experience the sky begin to lighten from the sun promising a new day. The running route skirted the forest line causing the road to disappear under the falling leaves. They crunched underfoot as she stepped on them making it the only sound she could hear. When she returned to her room, the lights were still off, and Sarah's door was still closed.

The run, unfortunately, had not helped her shake the nightmare of Liam's death and Dani hoped a hot shower would do the trick. The heat from the water rolled over her sore body and seeped into her bones chasing away the chill and negative thoughts.

"It doesn't look like Aiden is going to get in trouble for his scuffle with Finn."

Dani jumped, startled by the unexpected presence. "Sarah! Why! Why must you always come use the bathroom when I'm in here?" Dani somehow, after four years was still surprised by Sarah's intrusion.

"This is the best time to talk to you, you have no choice but to listen. After all," Sarah pulled back the curtain just enough to see inside the shower. "You're naked!" Sarah laughed as Dani splashed her with water.

"Come on Sarah! A bit of privacy." Dani pulled back the curtain so that she was at least shielded. Sarah continued to laugh at Dani's embarrassment.

"How do you expect to shower or get somewhat clean when we're out in the field if you are too shy to be naked in front of anyone?" Sarah asked her as she started her morning routine.

"Well we're not in the field right now, we're in our bathroom, where you refuse to let me even have five minutes." Dani turned off the shower and stuck out her hand. "the least you could do is hand me my towel." Dani clapped her fingers together as she grabbed air, waiting for the towel. Sarah pushed the towel into Dani's open hand and told Dani she had coffee waiting for her and walked out shutting the bathroom door behind her. Dani quickly dried off and got dressed in the jeans and long sleeve shirt waiting for her.

She opened the door and walked out of the bathroom; her hair was still wrapped in the towel. She was handed a steaming cup of black coffee, just the way she liked it. The two friends sat in silence, enjoying the peace of the morning when they heard a knock at the door. They both looked up at the door only to look back at each other.

"You're closer." Sarah lifted her cup, pointing it up at Dani and the door. Dani rolled her eyes and sat her coffee down only to push off from the counter she had been leaning against. When she opened the door, she was surprised to see Finn standing there.

"The vehicles are here to take us to Eastern command. Do you guys need help with anything? Bags perhaps?" Finn looked at Sarah as he mentioned the bags. He knew her ankle had been injured during combat training a few days prior.

"We can manage, thank you." Sarah shouted from her spot at the table, rather rudely.

"I'll leave you to it then." His face conveyed an understanding of his unwanted presence." "They want to start loading in thirty." Dani thanked him, her eyes inadvertently passing a message of apologies and condolences, then shut the door behind him. She looked at Sarah with a scolding look.

"Don't look at me like that." Sarah continued to sip her coffee and then got up to wash the cups along with the remaining dishes in the sink.

"We're going to be on a mission with him, we all need to get along. Our lives could, no, will depend on it." Dani scolded. Sarah only rolled her eyes.

Dani walked into Sarah's room and gathered her roommate's gear. The friends loaded their packs on their back and locked the door to their room behind them. They knew when they returned there would be a layer of dust waiting for them. The room would smell musty and stale from lack of use and fresh air, the beds untouched from no one sleeping in them. The room would be different, but perhaps they would be too.

When they reached the front of the barracks building, they saw three cars along with Aiden, Finn, and Hiromi waiting in front of them, ready to head out. Finn and Hiromi were talking amongst themselves at the front car, while Aiden made sure to stay clear of them, or more importantly, Finn.

Dani looked around, looking for the last person of their party, but failed to spot his golden hair. "Of course, Liam is late." Dani said as she and Sarah walked over to the cars setting their packs in the open trucks of one of the vehicles. "Where's Liam?" Dani asked Aiden.

"He's coming. He wanted to grab a paper for the long drive out to Eastern Command." As Aiden explained, Dani saw Liam running up behind him.

"Good, everyone's here." Dani turned to see the commander walking up. Everyone saluted and then went to stand at attention when the commander motioned for them to relax. "I just wanted to come out here and wish everyone luck before send off."

"Thank you, sir." The cadets announced. The commander left them to their business, patting the roof of one of the vehicles before he left.

Dani followed Liam into one of the cars where Sarah and Aiden were already waiting. The door was shut behind her and the vehicle started to drive off through the gates of the academy. Dani looked back as the school she had spent the last four years had started to fade into the distance.

Chapter 5

THE CITY OF ICARDIA

Major General Robert Mitchells stood at the base of the large space shuttle gazing at the city before him. He was in the heart of Helenia at central command. It was the only place in the nation that space shuttles could fly out of and land. The conference on Mars was supposed to only last a week but he knew that by the time the earth party would return his beautiful daughter would already be on the other side of the towering wall on a scouting mission.

'Her first mission' he thought. 'A father could not be prouder, yet I wish it wasn't so.' The thoughts of his daughter doing anything that could bring harm or even death weighed heavily on his mind. He had become so protective over Dani after his beautiful, late wife had succumbed to death. The fear of losing his family grew more and more every day. And now with his departure to Mars, he would not be here to protect Dani.

The day she came home from school and told her father she wanted to train at the academy was the day he started to turn grey in his hair and a few wrinkles that did not lay on his face prior started to surface. He knew there was no point in arguing with her. He could see the fire in her eyes, growing as she spoke with determination. The passion to fight and follow in her mother's and his footsteps. He was indeed proud, and he knew his wife would have been too.

"Sir, they're ready to take off." A Lieutenant stood behind the General. She wore the traditional white and black dress uniform and held a cap in hand at her side. The General turned at the sound of the lieutenant's voice and acknowledged his needed presence.

He took another long look at the city that laid before him. The tall buildings glistened in the light of the sun. The glass looked like an ocean reflecting a sunset. Even though he was in the city he could see spots of colorful trees. The leaves were changing colors with bursts of reds, yellows, and oranges painting a scenery.

He turned away, leaving the city of his home and nation behind and walked up the ramp attached to the side of the ship, knowing well he was not looking forward to flying anywhere let alone Mars. In his older age, he had started to hate to fly. It was just something that didn't agree with him anymore. He'd much rather keep his feet firmly on the ground. Even though he hated to fly, there were worse ways to fly than the high-powered solar ship. The grand ship towered over Robert standing at three stories, the sheen on the sleek ship held a hint of blue that curved with the rounded propulsion rockets. It was such a large ship for such a small party.

He walked into the first floor of the ship where rows of seats waited for passengers to sit back and relax while leaving the atmosphere of the planet behind. He buckled into his seat and the doors shut sealing him in along with the other Earth passengers. There was another general along with two colonels and three majors. The two colonels were conversing with the majors, but General Mitchells kept to himself not wanting to be drawn into a boring conversation of politics or games.

He heard the rockets building in energy in anticipation for lift. The ship creaked as it started to leave the ground behind. The momentum gathered as the rockets worked to thrust the ship upwards from the ground. Soon the ship was gaining speed in an attempt to gain air. Going up wasn't terrible. It was the coming down that wreaked havoc on the body.

The ship was now soaring through the air gaining height and within the hour the ship would leave the atmosphere behind giving way to the openness of space. It would take the ship three days to reach Mars. It was just a matter of patience now. General Mitchells decided to retire to his room for the night even though it was still early in the evening. There was no point in keeping up appearances while they were aboard the ship.

Dinner would be brought to his room in the next few hours and he decided a quick nap would be a better use of his time.

He laid his head on the pillow wrapped in satin. The bed was soft and absorbed his movements. He felt he could melt into it if he laid there too long. His quarters were spacious. It could easily house a single family. There was a huge bathroom with a double sink along with a full-size kitchen, living area, and the bed was a queen size. The ship itself was the same as his room, spacious. There were ten quarters spread out over two floors along with accommodations for a full piloting crew and staff.

The ship was indeed huge, but Robert had seen ships that more than tripled the size of this one. The larger ships were not currently in commission. There was no need for such large vessels to carry whole families or large numbers of souls anywhere. Earth, after all, was still rebuilding from the countless decades of hardship and many of the other planets had closed their borders wanting to avoid further conflict with one another.

Time passed by quickly. Before Robert knew it, he was waking up to the sound of a sweet-sounding bell. An indication that dinner was ready and soon would be served. Moments passed and he heard a quiet knock at his door. He stood from where he was sitting on the couch and made his way to the door. It whooshed open and there stood a man with a silver tray covered as to help keep the food inside warm. He graciously took it and thanked the man.

'Alone again.' He thought. He had been alone since Dani left for the academy. He spent most of his nights in a dimly lit house with no one but himself to keep company. He kept a picture of his wife and three kids in every room just so he didn't feel so lonely.

The next three days dragged on slowly. The General kept to himself when he walked the halls of the ship, stopping only to make small talk when he was addressed or asked a question. For the most part, he stayed in his quarters, locked away from everyone else. As he understood it, so did the other general. Even though they were whirling through space on a mission he still had paperwork that came with his title. He passed his time slaving over the busy work.

Day three had arrived. The ship reached Mars's orbit. They would be touching down within the hour. Robert strolled down to the viewing bay where the rest of the leadership would be. Soon the red city, Icardia, was within view. There was a red haze of clouds surrounding the city, but as they cleared when the ship pushed through them, the round tops of the crystal buildings started to show. The city was clean and rich with the people all donning the highest and most desirable fashion of silks inlaid with red dyes and red jewels. However, the outer cities and towns were not in as good of condition and wealth as Icardia where the royal family lived.

The ship slowed down in anticipation of touch down. As soon as the ramp lowered the leaders of Earth were met by an entourage of Marsians servants. The females were wearing long flowing, red tinted dresses, and white makeup that brought out the red rings in their eyes, the trait that made them recognizable as Marsians. Their hair was pulled back into neat but unique hairstyles while the men wore deep red suits and had their hair slicked back. The servants were following a lengthy man in a white suit tinted red at the collars of the wrist and ankles. His top hat was white with red flowers native to Mars imitated on the side of the white satin band. His shoes where imported leather, stained red to match the red in his suit.

"Welcome, welcome, welcome." He exclaimed with his arms outreached over his head as if he were attempting to fly. "I am so happy to welcome you to my beautiful planet. I'm sure after your days of travel you are.... weary. Please come." The man was dramatic in his hand gestures, motioning everyone to follow. "Come this way into the dining hall. I have had a delicious lunch prepared for you in anticipation of your arrival."

The group of leaders from Earth followed the extravagant man into a large room made of glass that shone like crystal, matching the rest of the city. The floors were pristinely white and glistened with the many chandeliers that hung from the vaulted ceiling. The room overlooked the city. It was as bright as the room they stood in. The sun was starting to set, and the sky was different hues of reds and pinks causing the city to look even more brilliant, turning shades of pinks and reds with the setting sun.

"Please, please" the man gestured to the high back chairs and long marbled table. "Sit." He sat down at the head of the table and clapped his hands twice in a speedy rhythm to alert his waiters that he wanted them to serve him and his guest. The generals took the seats closest to the prince. The others in the Earth entourage followed suit. Robert looked around and noticed the generals along with the other military leaders from Venus had yet to arrive.

Prince Remilia Tachibana seemed to be as elaborate as the news said he was. Among his white suit, he wore giant red jewels and gold on each hand along with his neck. His hair was styled and there was a bit of red eye makeup to match his outfit as well. The sight was off putting for the general. He certainly was not used to such a flashy person holding such a high position.

Major General Robert Mitchells spoke first. "Your majesty, we thank you for your gracious hospitality in welcoming us to your beautiful planet and home."

"Yes, this city is quite...massive." The other general added trying to appease the prince. General Alice Hawkins was a woman not to be trifled with. She was a fierce person and an even fiercer leader. She commanded her brigade with an iron fist to the point where no other force would challenge them. It's why she was in charge of the outer wall that protected the people, that was until King Foley, Helenia's leader felt her leadership skills would be best optimized closer to the city.

The dinner was brought out and set in front of each guest. "I am pleased to welcome you. It is long overdue that our planet's alliance becomes more than just a piece of paper. A true alliance. But please enough about politics." The prince waved his hand in front of him as if waving the issue away. "Tonight, we shall feast and rest. Tomorrow can be a day of discussion."

They did indeed enjoy the night. There was a quartet playing in the distance while everyone was enjoying beverages endowed with alcohol, everyone that is except Robert. He was sitting on a lounge sofa listening to the music. The violin was soft and beautiful making him miss home all the more. The music brought back memories of his late wife sitting in the garden playing her violin for the flowers. When he asked her what she was doing she would respond simply with one word. Gardening, with a smile of innocence on her beautiful sun kissed face. She had believed that playing music for the flowers and plants it would help them to grow. The smell of roses surrounded their home as she tended to them daily. That's how his wife was, a little out of the box but behind every thought there was hope and a means to be helpful.

"Despicable, isn't it?" Alice came up behind Robert startling him. Her eyebrow raised as she noticed the movement. "You should stay on your toes when in the presence of a foreign and possible enemy. We may be at a time of peace at this moment, but we were not always so, and no one knows what tomorrow will bring. And yet these fools are drinking their sense away as if a celebration is in order." She spat the words harshly.

"Perhaps it's helping to shake off the nerves. It's not every day they meet a prince after all." He commented trying to keep the conversation casual.

"If they can't keep their wit about them, then it's surprising they made it into a leadership position at all. They won't last long if a real war occurs." General Hawkins stated. She wasn't wrong.

"I suppose you are right General, but let's hope it does not come to that. After all, humanity might not survive. I fear we only get so many chances to get it right and we've used up all our chances." Robert said sulkily. "But you are correct. Seeing them in this.... state has made me grow weary of the long day. I think I'll call it a night. Good evening General."

He stood and walked over to where the prince was sitting. He showed respect to their host by bowing before he spoke. He courteously asked their host if he could retire to his room for the evening. He wasn't one for entertaining others in such a manner as this. The prince reassured the general that he understood and had no ill feelings towards the general for wanting to retire. After all the flight had been long. He summoned his butler and had him show Robert to his room. Robert bowed once more before departing.

Robert was escorted out of the dining room and down a long open hallway lined with closed doors. The butler stopped in front of a door and motioned for him to head inside.

"Your luggage has already been brought in, sir." The butler spoke in a deep monotone voice, not even bothering to look at Robert. "Have a good night. Please do not hesitate to ring if you need anything." The butler turned and walked away leaving Robert to his own.

Robert opened the door and walked into the room. It was spacious with tall vaulted ceilings. The windows were adorned with flowing red satin curtains that reached from the ceiling to the floor. On the bed laid red silk sheets embroidered with gold. The bed was intensely inviting, and Robert listened to the call allowing it to pull on him. He climbed right into bed. He almost did not even bother to take his shoes off. Hopefully, sleep would pull away the weariness from the travel out to Mars and tomorrow he would wake refreshed and clear of mind.

Chapter 6

BEYOND THE WALL

Dani and the others stood in the office of General Alpine. His hands clasped together while his chin rested on them. He stared at the six cadets standing in front of him anxiously awaiting orders. The sun was starting to set over the eastern command. The light shone through the office windows blinding the cadets and showering them with the golden rays. Liam coughed and when he did everyone immediately held his attention. It was quiet in the office and time seemed to stretch.

"Hmmm." the General said rubbing his graying beard.

Behind them, a knock came at the door and then it opened. In walked a face Dani had seen many times. Colonel Harper strode in with his head raised high, his shoulders back, and a fierce look of determination on his face. Kyle Harper graduated from the academy fifteen years ago and immediately entered the scouts where he quickly moved up in ranks easily passing the others. This gained the attention of General Mitchells and he insisted Kyle join his leadership team. Being among her fathers trusted, Dani saw colonel Harper in her many visits to the office.

The colonel came to attention, saluted, and then acknowledged his summoned presence. Major General Mitchells came to him an hour before he left for central to board a space shuttle to Mars. General Mitchells informed him of the scouting mission that his daughter had been assigned too and his concerns of protection that came along with that. Colonel Harper volunteered his assistance, not realizing that entailed his time in actually going on the scouting mission. He had plenty of work to do while his leader was away entertaining the Prince of Mars.

"Oh good, now everyone is here. We can begin." General Alpine addressed the group as his hands raised when Colonel Harper ended his salute. He stood up from his chair and walked around his old, wooden desk, so he was standing directly in front of the group. He leaned up against his desk, his back against it, and begun to speak once more.

"Colonel Harper will lead the six of you cadets on a scouting mission over the wall into the eastern mountains. Our gathered intelligence has led us to believe that there is a compound run by the rebel forces. I'm sure you've heard of the attacks against the eastern wall. We think the rebels are trying to learn of our weaknesses so they can storm the wall and I don't need to tell you the trouble that would bring on our fragile society." General Alpine finished.

"With such a small group of cadets, I imagine it's not an attack you want us to accomplish sir." Colonel Harper deduced.

"Correct, the senior staff wants you to lead the cadets on a reconnaissance mission. We need intel on the layout of their compound, where they're located, numbers, weapons, means of supplies, etc. If, and I strongly mean if, we need to defend ourselves against them, if they truly are our enemy, we need to know how to defeat them." Dani felt his words had underline meaning but wasn't sure what they could possibly be.

"Not to be so forward, but you're not even giving me rookies, these cadets are still in training, are they not?" The colonel gestured to the six cadets standing there, trying not to take offense to the lack of experience they posed. "Don't you think a squad a little more...rehearsed would be better suited for such a seemingly important undertaking?" The colonel did not seem all too pleased at having to lead a bunch of kids over the wall into unknown dangers.

"I understand your concern, but these cadets are beyond your typical trainee cadet. Each of them possesses a talent and skill that will uniquely help you in completing this mission. I guarantee they will serve you well and not only meet your expectations but surpass them. I don't think we could have assembled a more suitable group of cadets to complete this mission" he emphasized on the word 'this'. Again, hidden meaning, Dani thought. "and you, as their leader, I have faith that you will be pleased. If you wish it, I will allow two additional people to accompany you. I will leave it up to you on who you choose colonel. Now I leave these cadets in your care."

With that, he dismissed the cadets and colonel from his office. They turned to walk out the door, the colonel shutting the door behind him. When out in the hallway he looked at each cadet to address them, his eyes stayed on Dani when he finally spoke. His face gestured his unpleasant feelings toward the situation. His nose and eyebrows were pinched in aggregation. "Cadet Mitchells, do you remember where the dining hall is?"

"Yes sir." She responded looking up at him. He looked as if his years of service were starting to catch up to him, he had more wrinkles then she remembered, and his dark brown hair held a few grey hairs. Surprising for someone still in his prime. He also looked as if he hadn't slept in days. He seemed to have let his standards of formality slip because his clothes were not as pristine and wrinkle free as she remembered.

"Good, lead the others there and eat lunch. Tell whoever is down there that I sent you and to send the bill to me." He took his insignia broach off his collar and handed it to her. Each broach was made special for the person wearing it. It identified who they were and marked their status. "I will reconvene with you there in an hour. I can tell you this," he spoke to everyone. "We won't be leaving until tomorrow morning. So, take the day to rest." He turned and walked away down the hall.

Dani led the others in the opposite direction of the hall to a set of stairs. They walked down to the bottom and turned down another hallway where the dining hall waited at the end. Liam pulled open one of the large, heavy wooded French doors and held it open allowing the others to wander into the open room. The room was round and beyond the windows was a courtyard where tables, chairs, and umbrellas were arranged so people could enjoy sitting outside to eat on their lunch break.

The ceiling was painted holding a mural of clouds and angels on it. It was quite a sight for a dining hall, especially when the cadets where use to low hanging wooded beamed ceilings in their dining hall. Dani remembered her father telling her once that Eastern Command wasn't always a fort. It used to be a castle before the new government was established, explaining why the building in no way resembled a fort or command center of any sort.

It was still early, and the dining hall was still fairly empty. Sarah was the first to get into line and gather food items to place on her tray, the others followed suit. At the end of the bar was a person waiting to ring the food in. Dani showed her the insignia broach and explained Colonel Harper would pay. She waved them on, and Sarah, Dani, and Aiden started heading towards the door leading to the outside. Liam followed while Finn and Hiromi were hesitant to follow. They reluctantly did, with thoughts that it would be better to stay together.

They were enjoying their lunch and the warm day from the sun when Aiden saw the colonel walking towards them followed by a woman. She looked well put together with her hair in a perfect bun. Not a strand of hair was out of place. She stood with poise and structure like a true soldier would.

"Cadets, this is my lieutenant. Elizabeth Reeves. She will be joining us on this little outing of ours. She will also be showing you to your quarters for the evening. We will be leaving at dawn tomorrow. Be fresh and ready to go in the morning and meet me in front of the building. We will have vehicles waiting to take us to the eastern wall. Any questions?"

He paused looking at everyone, daring anyone to speak up. After a moment he continued. "Good." He looked at his lieutenant and nodded. "Lieutenant." And then he turned and left not speaking another word, faith that his right-hand man, or in this case lady, could handle the rest of the necessary tasks.

First Lieutenant Reeves watched him leave and then turned to look at the cadets. "If you are done please follow me." Her voice lacking any real emotion. The cadets immediately got up and collected their dirty dishes.

It seemed universal that it wasn't a good idea to sit there continuing to eat while making a lieutenant wait on them. They followed her back inside the building. She waited patiently but quietly while they stacked their dishes in the disposal section of the dining hall and then they lined up, ready to follow her.

She led them down a hall and explained that she would have dinner along with breakfast in the morning brought up to the rooms and it would be best if they didn't go wandering around. The rest of the day they should be packing and resting anyways. Tomorrow would be a rough day and it would come very early. She showed them their quarters. Males in one quarter while the females were in the quarters across from them, she gestured. She told them goodnight and walked away leaving them behind.

The rooms were small. There was a living space large enough for a small couch attached to an even smaller kitchen. This was clearly not a room meant to be constantly lived in. In an adjacent room, there were three sets of bunk beds. Able to sleep six. The room had a layer of dust as if it hadn't been slept in in a while.

"So, I guess we can all call top if we wanted too." Sarah looked at Dani and Hiromi and let out a light laugh. They just looked at her blankly. The day had been long, the travel from the academy to Eastern Command was rough, and tomorrow would prove no different. "No? Well, I thought it was funny." Sarah moved into the room and flipped the switch for the light.

"May I take the bed by the window?" Hiromi asked shyly. Both Sarah and Dani looked at each other from across the room, confused, and then nodded reassurance at Hiromi. They were so used to just each other, adding a third female member into their group would definitely change things.

"Hey Hiromi," Sarah started. She was leaning against a bedpost, her arm resting on the mattress of the top bed. "If you don't mind me asking, why were you selected for this mission. I mean I know you've been running missions since the middle of your third year but that's because you're like a dog whisperer. But uh there's no dogs..."

"Oh, there will be." Hiromi gleamed. She then went and sat on the couch and pulled out a book. She began to read, already lost to her surroundings.

"Well," Sarah looked to Dani who was still leaning against the door frame to the bedroom. "I guess that's that. What do you want to do now?" Dani looked around. She really just wanted to sleep. The last few nights produced little sleep. The constant nightmares along with worrying about her father on Mars had disrupted her sleep.

"Maybe just a few games of cards?" It was something she didn't have to think about to do and Sarah enjoyed a good game of poker.

"Perhaps just a few, what should we wager?" Sarah held a devilish smile on her face forcing her eyebrows up and down.

"Bunk furthest away from the bathroom?" Dani wouldn't care either way but if she happened to win then she wouldn't have to listen to people constantly getting up to use it. Sarah shrugged. "Sure, why not."

The night was long. Someone had brought dinner to them an hour ago. Aiden and Liam had stopped by before that to play a couple of rounds of poker with them but when dinner came around, they disappeared to their room and had yet to return. Dani had grown weary and decided to call it an early night.

*****

The next morning approached. The sun threatening to rise. The cadets were already up and ready for what the day promised. It would hopefully bring about the beginning of a possible scouting career for Dani.

The morning dew had settled on the ground and in the green grass where the cadets stood. The cadets waited for the colonel and lieutenant to show up. The sun had already started to rise, and the vehicles were there waiting to take them to the eastern wall, the quiet hum of the engines buzzed in the silence of the early morning. Liam nudged Dani and nodded towards the right. Along came the colonel leisurely strolling towards them with his hands in his pockets. His hair was unkempt as if he hadn't brushed it that morning. He stopped in front of them and yawned, scratching the back of his head. The lieutenant was right behind him still emotionless and stern faced as if she expected this, as if this was a typical day and the colonel was like this on a regular basis.

"Oh. Hey guys," the colonel said lazily. "What are you doing out here so early?" He yawned and scratched the back of his head casually once more.

The cadet's jaws about hit the ground. They immediately relaxed from there strict stance they had held when they first saw the colonel and lieutenant approaching.

"Sir," Hiromi spoke up first, her voice small, "you told us to be out here before sunrise." She said it as if she were confused herself.

"Did I? Hmm". He pulled his other hand out of his pocket and put it to his chin, looking up as if he were truly thinking. "Lieutenant!" He excitedly said loudly pointing at her, arm outstretched.

She slightly jumped from the sudden outburst, her eyes grew wide, but only for a moment. She regained her composure just as quickly as she had let it slip. "Sir". She said it without a hint of emotion. As if she didn't truly even mean it.

"Did I tell them to be out here before sunrise?" He acted confused and sheepish.

"You did, sir." Again, with no emotion. She wouldn't play into his games. She knew them well.

"Oh, well, my mistake. I meant after sunrise." He bellowed out a laugh. The cadets about fell to the floor. Sarah shook her head while Aiden and Finn gave an audible groan of irritation. Dani stifled a laugh. He may have looked serious the day before and she knew him to be serious when it came to the job, but in reality, the colonel had always posed a humorous side.

"Well since you're all here and ready, we should go ahead and go." He started to turn away but stopped mid-turn. "Hold on. We seem to be forgetting someone... or someones." He turned and looked at Hiromi.

"Cadet Katsuki!" He shouted.

"Sir?" Hiromi straightened up, startled by his sudden attention on her.

"Where're your partners? Shouldn't they be here?" The colonel looked around. His hand hovering over his eyebrows. He was quite comical and dramatic. That side of him used to always entertain Dani when she was younger, even today it humored her. She had to stifle a giggle at his acting. Hiromi just shrugged looking around herself. But before she could respond, a man with two large hounds came running up. Hiromi left the group and met her hounds to take ownership of them.

"Sorry sir, we were just getting them fitted with new gear." The man said as he noticed the look of annoyance on the colonel's face. His foot was tapping on the hard ground and his arms were crossed. The man quickly took his leave before upsetting the supposed irritated colonel further. Hiromi rejoined the group now with her partners on each side of her person. They sat, alert and waiting for their next command, focused on their surroundings. The dogs were even more lethal and beautiful to Dani now that she could see them up close.

The colonel went on to speak. "Now that we're all here, load up! No point in burning any more daylight."

The squad loaded into the running vehicles. The colonel and lieutenant took the very center car while Dani, Liam, Sarah, and Aiden took the rear one. Hiromi, her hounds, and Finn were left with the first car and headed in that direction. The cars pulled away, one by one, from the old castle that stood as the Eastern Command Center and started towards the Eastern Wall located in the city of Socaster, a small military town that shared a border with Marian. It would take at least an hour to drive there, so Dani decided to close her eyes and try to rest in hopes she would sleep on the way there.

Dani awoke to a sudden jerk. The car had stopped and when she looked out the window a wall towered over her. "Dans," Liam motioned to her face. "You have drool on your face." She wiped her mouth with the back of her hand not even caring that she was a mess. She needed a nap. The endless nights of poor sleep had caused her to have headaches and she was starting to feel fatigued. She felt she was becoming sleep deprived. The hour-long nap took the edge off, now she needed to shake off the grogginess that had followed.

She stretched her limbs before grabbing the handle to the door. As she pulled the door open to get out of the car, she realized weakness had settled in her legs from the nap and she had yet to shake the weariness away. When she climbed out, she was overwhelmed by the looming size of the wall. She had only ever been to the wall one other time. She was young and her father had some business with one of the generals serving at the wall. General Hawkins, if she remembered correctly. They were only there for a short while and after the business of paper signing was complete, her father took her to enjoy the festivities of the yearly autumn festival in the town of Lomenersin.

Lomenersin was the town in which Eastern Command was located. Her father had been stationed at Eastern command several times. So much so that it was where he met Dani's mother, married her, and where Dani along with her three siblings had been born. It was home for her. The yearly festival had become a tradition for her family, and that year she was distraught that they were going to miss it. Her father had briefly been stationed in Central, and if it hadn't been for the untimed business at the wall, they would have missed the festival.

Liam walked up behind her, startling her when he let out a long whistle. She playfully backhanded him in his chest. He only met her with a laugh.

"Don't sneak up on me like that." She spoke to him as he started walking away.

She continued to admire the wall that towered over her at a hundred and fifty- two feet tall. She studied the architecture structure of it, the flowing stone and carvings at the entrance and at every window. The wall met the mountains, part of it even being built into the mountains. The grey and white stone stood out amongst the green and brown of the woods, that is, until the winter, when the snow fell. Then the wall almost became one with its surroundings as it blended in with the snow, disappearing almost all together. There were open ports and gates within the wall allowing entrance into the fort.

The wall had been built to also serve as a fort. Within its walls were tunnels and rooms serving different purposes such as living quarters, arms rooms where weapons and ammunition were stored, along with dining halls and work facilities or various other military affiliated occupations. Anyone stationed at the wall also lived within its walls. They even had medical facilities, labs, and space for mechanical inventing within the wall. Everything a soldier needed to carry on the day to day. On the outside of the inner wall, there were rows of windows and balconies. She wasn't sure what the outside of the outer wall looked like, but she imagined there were not many windows and certainly no balconies. Either way, she would find out very soon.

The town that they were currently in was a military town. The military provided homes for the soldier who had spouses and families. The downtown area had shopping and bars and the surrounding fields and grasslands grew the food needed to survive along with livestock. It would have been a quaint setting if there had not been a giant wall casting a shadow over the town.

"Are you going to gawk at it all day or what Mitchells?" Finn pushed past her unamused.

Sarah came to stand next to Dani. "Hey! Don't be a jerk, Carson." She had a fist on her hip and was using her other hand to enhance her shouting after Finn. "He's just being pissy because Aiden's in lead behind the colonel and lieutenant. Screw him, just ignore it Dans."

Dani looked at Sarah. Her blond hair catching the sun. "Oh, he doesn't bother me, honestly, I wasn't even paying any attention. Do you need help with your bag?"

"Oh no, thanks though. Aiden already offered. Well, he offered but as he offered, he was already getting my bag out of the trunk, so, ya know. Oh, and Liam got yours by the way."

"He what! Why? I could have gotten it." Dani stated slightly annoyed.

Liam tapped Dani on the shoulder. As she turned to face him, he sat her bag down in front of her. "It's called being nice. I am well aware you could have gotten your own belongings, but I was already there. Besides they wanted to move the cars. So, I believe the phrase you're looking for is thank you, Liam."

Dani just rolled her eyes but smiled up at him. "Thank you, Liam."

"You're welcome. Now see, was that so hard?" He smiled back at her.

Dani huffed her pack on to her back and the three walked over to the rest of the squad. Once everyone was together the colonel and lieutenant led them through an open bay door into a room where tanks and various other military vehicles were held. They walked in between two rows to the far end of the room where there was an elevator waiting to take them up to a different floor. They all piled in and headed up to the fifth floor.

When the elevator doors opened, they were met with bright sunlight from the many windows reflecting along the deep blue carpet lining the stone floor. The walls were a cream color and in various spots along the walls in between wooded doors, there were small wall tables with vases of flowers on them. They followed the colonel down the hall admiring the various pieces of artwork that hung on the walls. For a stone fort wall, they certainly made sure the inside was cozy and welcoming, but that was mostly for show.

"This wing is where the generals, officers, and other higher ups conduct business. Meetings, mission planning, so on and so on." The colonel waved his arm above him gesturing a motion indicated a long time, while casually walking with his hand in his pocket as if he didn't have a care in the world. He hadn't even bothered to look back at the cadets as he talked.

Dani understood the décor as the colonel explained. Leaders from other parts of the nation along with leaders from other parts of the world would come here, it made sense they would want to keep the halls presentable.

He stopped short at a door and knocked three times. They heard a muffled voice indicating a welcome to open the door. The colonel looked back at them. "Stay here, I will summon you to come in momentarily, maybe." He winked, smiled, then walked in with the lieutenant in tow.

He entered the room and announced his presence and business. After a few minutes of back and forth discussion, the colonel came out and motioned for them to enter the room and take a seat. Dani looked around as she entered the room. She had occupied plenty of meeting rooms as a girl because of her father but this one was different, it seemed more serious and surreal. This was a war room, the front lines, it was where the decisions were made that kept the rebels and other unwanted visitors out.

The walls were lined with maps of the nation and surrounding areas beyond the borders. Towards the west, Dani noticed the large desert, Alorea, that separated Helenia from the nation, Athelen. Towards the south, the large body of water separated Dani's nation from the extremely large and overpowering nation of Tiffiledien. They had a military force that could easily overpower their own along with any other nation that dared challenge them. But the two nations had a long-standing agreement of peace and often traded goods.

Another map showed a detailed area of the wall. On the inner side of the wall, Dani could see the cities lining the inside of the wall. There was Socaster, the current military town they were in, and when Dani followed the road leading out of Socaster towards Eastern Command in Lomenersin, she passed through Marian, a town that once thrived with life, that now sat in almost ruins. Dani was unclear why; in school, she was told the town came into hardship when many of the occupants fell prey to a poison found in their food. The poison was caused by a chemical the town was experimenting with to help with the agriculture growth. When people started dying from the poison the government had stepped in and quarantined the town to prevent further spread. The government's involvement quickly stopped the spread, but not before taking thousands of lives in Marian, leaving the town to quickly meet its demise with financial and economic instability.

On the other side of the Eastern Wall towards the southern side is the nation of Cade. A small nation that lacks an impressive military force but thrived in the technological development and agriculture field. They have a smaller population, but vast amounts of land with rich soil, making the growth of plant life abundant. With all the excess land they had at their disposal, testing new machinery and technologies without disrupting the farming land, was optimal to better life and the growth of life on Earth.

The west was protected by the large desert and the south side was protected by the water, even the south-east of the wall wasn't the problem with the lack of military Cade had, it was the north and the north-east side of the wall that posed threats. The wall was built into the eastern mountains and tapered off towards the west where the mountains doubled in size. Because of their enormous size, not many dared to try and attack from the west, nor could they, the travel would be dangerous to move a fleet along with almost impossible to move heavy equipment and artillery. The North-East Wall, however, was under constant threat from rebel forces. They used the mountains as coverage as they attempted to move into Helenia's borders.

Sitting at the head of the table was a general that Dani had not seen or met previously. He showed age through his graying beard that was streaked with black, and he was built husky, like a tank. The General scared Dani. He didn't look fierce or determined as most soldiers did, he looked haunted as if he was well acquainted with the effects of war, or death, his eyes were slightly sunk in and his cheekbones were prominent as if they were protruding.

He brought back a memory of a card she had received one Christmas from Liam. On the front of the card was a Skelton with a red Christmas hat on his skull. The Skelton was large as if to represent that at one point it resided in a larger person. On the inside of the card was a joke about Santa Claus and waiting on something. It had been so long ago that he gave her the card she couldn't remember, but the image of Santa's Skelton stuck with her.

Each cadet took a seat, all having the same idea to sit on the opposite side of the table from the General. The colonel and lieutenant also took seats managing to fill in the gaps between the young, unsure cadets, and the experienced leader of the wall.

"I am General Alaric Bartovics. I am head of the Eastern Gate Post. As I am to understand you have been given a scouting mission beyond the wall. As we speak my soldiers are saddling horses to take you to the first checkpoint. When you get there, you will take a night to resupply and rest up. The mountains this time of year can be hard to push through even for experienced soldiers. When you reach the second checkpoint, you will leave the horses with the soldiers there and travel on foot for the remainder of the mission. Any questions?"

The colonel spoke up on behalf of his squad. "Sir, how long is this mission expected to take?"

General Bartovics stood up and started to walk towards the window. "We expect a reconnaissance mission such as this should take no more than two weeks, three if you run into weather or any problems." He stopped at the window staring out at the mountains beyond the wall. He stroked his graying beard. "After all we will need a report back of any information you receive, and you will need to restock supplies, your packs can only carry so much." He looked back at Colonel Harper as he said that last part.

"I assume we will be able to relay any information through a radio at one of the checkpoints sir?" The lieutenant asked firmly.

Before General Bartovics could answer someone burst through the door, panting. The General looked at him enraged by the uninvited and unwanted disturbance. "Captain Caden! What is the meaning of this!"

"Sir I apologize for the disruption, but there's been an attack." The major had a large gun, a rifle, slung over his shoulder in preparation for a fight, sweat already starting to bead on his forehead.

"The six of you stay put. Colonel! Lieutenant! Come with me." The General spoke in a demanding and authoritative voice as he hurriedly strode with heavy steps to the door to leave. Immediately he took action and instead of the somewhat relaxed state he had been in moments prior, now a fire had been lit and he was sparked with energy and stamina. Colonel Harper felt the adrenaline rush as he was called to duty.

The general, captain, colonel, and lieutenant all left the room in a hurry, leaving the cadets behind. Colonel Harper had completed many scouting missions beyond the wall and because of that had spent a great deal inside the wall between rotations, helping where needed while he waited for clearance back to eastern command or anticipating the next scouting mission. To him, this just felt like his younger days as a fresh cadet out of the academy. He was only a corporal then but quickly moved up the ranks with his superior skills and stronger leadership abilities.

On one trip to the wall in preparation for a mission, a snowstorm had pushed down from the mountains delaying his squad's ability to leave the fort. The scouting mission was pushed back by a full three weeks. During a night shift guarding, Harper, who at the time had moved up the ranks to a captain, met Sergeant Reeves. The two continued to serve on the night shift for the remaining time he was there, their trust in one another growing stronger each night.

The snowstorm, at one point, had caused the mountains to completely disappear, concealing anything that might have been hiding in the storm.

What was hiding was a faction of rebels. They had followed behind the storm anticipating the opportunity to move against the military. The rebels staged an attack at night when the storm had subsided, but the darkness would still hide them, the clouds blocking out any light the moon or stars would have offered. It had been a smart play. The first shot rang through the quiet, still night. The sound of the alarms followed only seconds later.

Harper and Reeves took to action shooting whatever threat came charging towards them. Harper heard a shot and before he could react, he saw blood dripping into the white snow underfoot. It was his blood. He felt the pain, but he wasn't sure from where. Before he realized he had been shot in his shoulder, a man was charging towards him wielding a knife above his head.

At the last moment, Reeves slid in front of Harper swinging her rifle over their heads, blocking the knife that was coming down from overhead. She thrust her weapon and body forward pushing the man back. He slipped on ice and fell to the ground. Reeves took the opportunity and shot. Red liquid pooled around the now still body.

The moment of victory was short lived, behind the now lifeless body more people were emerging behind the tree line. She spun around to Harper and helped him back up to his feet, they ran towards the wall, back to where protection and backup were waiting to fire at the enemy. It was because of Reeves that Harper was alive today. She selflessly put her life on the line and defended him.

Since that moment he knew she was someone who would always have his back. The following week when he left for his scouting mission, he took her with him. The two had been inseparable as commanding officer and subordinate since then.

Now it seemed the two were right back where they first started, running into danger headfirst, weapons at the ready. The lieutenant at his side ready to defend his life, watching his back, like she always had and always would.

"Lieutenant, are you with me?" He asked her as he ran behind the General.

"Do you even need to ask sir? I'd follow you wherever you needed me too." Lieutenant Reeves's look was stern, as she was on the colonel's heels ready to follow him into hell if that's what was required of her.

The hallway opened up and the group was met with the blinding light of the sun. Their eyes quickly adjusted to the sight of soldiers running around carrying weapons and ammunition to stations readying for a counterattack on the rebels. General Bartovics was shouting out orders pointing to groups here and there. They acted as a well-oiled machine, not acting on survival or instinct but on the vigorous months and years of training.

Harper and Reeves had rifles and ammunition thrust into their hands and they took up a post taking aim at the tree line. They were ready for a fight. Long, silent moments passed. It almost seemed as if time were standing still. Harper caught out of the corner of his eye a shift in the trees. He could hear the branches ruffle and through his scope, he watched as a few leaves floated towards the frost-bitten ground.

"Lieutenant, the trees at my three o'clock."

"Yes sir, I see." The lieutenant aimed her weapon at the trees and waited, while the colonel continued to scan the trees.

Before he could locate any more rebels hiding out, he heard two gunshots to his left. When he looked up from his gun he watched as a fellow soldier fell forward over the wall grasping his chest. He was dead before he hit the hard, cold ground. Beyond where the solider landed a group of rebels had started to charge out of the trees towards the group of soldiers waiting at the bottom of the wall. They clashed with the squads. Harper could hear the sound of metal hitting and scraping against more metal. The soldiers above took aim and fired at rebels that had momentarily separated from the person they were fighting against. It was a small group of rebels that had charged from the trees, it didn't take long to either kill or capture the enemy.

"Lieutenant"

"Sir?"

"Do you notice any movement from the trees?"

"Yes sir." She was still as serious as she had always been. There wasn't a single hint of emotion in her voice.

"What are they waiting for? Why not fire. Why send people out just to be slaughtered?"

"Sir, the movements have ceased." The attack was over as fast as it had begun. Those who were in the trees hiding out had now started to retreat. The soldiers on top of the wall had either cleared out or gone back to their post as if nothing had happened. They made quick work of the enemy just as they had been trained. Those that had been captured were being escorted inside into the cells to be questioned later.

General Bartovics called after Harper and Reeves to return to his side. They handed their weapons off to a corporal and followed after the general. Harper continued to think about the situation, about the attack. Something didn't feel right.

'They must have been studying us. Looking for a weakness, studying our movements perhaps. Why else would they send people out knowing they would die. That's just wasteful. Unless they expected them to be captured and they wanted them to be captured. But why. What was their motive.' Harper was lost in thought trying to make sense of what he just witnessed.

"Sir," Reeves put a hand on Harper's shoulder. He startled as if just realizing she was there. "Are you okay, sir?"

"Oh, yes lieutenant. Sorry." He shook his head shaking his thoughts loose. He needed to be focused on his own mission. He needed to focus on keeping the young cadets alive, not worrying about those who were already dead.

The three returned to the room where the cadets had been anxiously waiting. Dani and Sarah were standing on either side of the window's edge. Hiromi's hounds were on edge, both at alert staring at the door, waiting. As soon as the leadership walked through the door everyone immediately went back to their seats ready to continue with their brief, fully expecting their mission to be postponed or even canceled.

The General sat down at the head of the table, taking his place once more. He crossed his hands, resting them under his chin. He looked as if he was contemplating a decision, most likely one about the mission. "Colonel Harper!"

"Yes sir." The colonel immediately responding. He had been expecting to be called upon, he waited for it in anticipation.

"I'm not canceling this mission; however, I no longer feel it is safe to leave from this port. I think it would be better suited for you and your squad to leave from the northeast port. It will add time to your mission but at least we can be sure that you won't run into any rebels straight out the gate."

The colonel stood up abruptly. "But sir, if we head towards the north it means we run into the higher altitude mountains, there have already been reports of snow. My cadets are not equipped for that. We're not...." the General put a hand up immediately hushing the colonel. The colonel's arms dropped to his side. His mouth still gaping from his mid-sentence.

The general slowly put his hand back down resting it on the table. "I am well aware of what you are equipped with, I am also aware of what your cadets are capable of. I am also aware of how crucial it is that this mission continues on schedule." Again, Dani picked up the difference in the general's voice, the underlying, but hidden meaning in his words was not lost on her. "One call is all it will take to get the equipment you need, not only that, but they will be there before you even arrive at the Northeastern Gate." The General was not going to back down. This judgment was final. They were going to have to trudge through the mountains to get to their checkpoints and finally to their destination.

"I will also have extra soldiers assigned to the squad until you reach the first checkpoint. Just to ensure the success of this mission." With those being his final words, he dismissed the squad.

By the time they had reached the front gates of the wall, there were already three new vehicles waiting for them, ready to take them to the next post. The vehicles were off-road capable and were painted to match the wall and snow, the only visible sign was the Helenia insignia painted a deep blue on the side. The symbol was a lion's head and body attached to the lower end of a mythical sea creature with a fin and tail instead of hind legs. The drive would take an additional three hours even though they were driving along the wall almost the entire time, doing well to avoid the towns and cities. It was already late in the afternoon and the sun will have started to set by the time they reached their new destination.

Dani leaned her head against the window watching as a rain shower started to wash over the vehicles. The raindrops danced across the glass, sometimes joining to create larger droplets before sliding off, falling to the ground below as the vehicle sped on.

Liam moved one of his legs onto his other leg, resting his ankle on his knee, the boredom was starting to take control of him along with everyone else. He started to tap out a rhythm keeping himself amused. Liam had never been one to sit still for very long.

"Well, this is an exciting turn of events." He huffed, speaking out, but not addressing anyone in particular, and not truly expecting anyone to answer. It was worthless rambling to fill the void of sound that had encased the vehicle. Only the hum of the engine turning over was a constant.

He watched as Dani started to draw in the condensation gathering in the window being caused by the cold water. "Dans! Why don't we play a card game?" He pulled down the centerpiece and unfolded a table that had been hidden away. He pulled out a deck of cards from his pocket and shook them trying to get Dani's attention.

She slowly took her eyes off the window and looked around the vehicle. Sarah was stretched out in the bench seat across from where Dani and Liam sat. Her head was laying in Aiden's lap and his uniform jacket was sprawled out over her shoulders. She was softly snoring against his leg. Aiden had his leg propped up on his seat, resting his elbow on his knee and his chin against his fist. He was deep in thought, lost to the world, staring out the window. Dani wondered what was racing through his mind.

Liam shook the deck of cards once more, this time a tad closer to Dani's ear. She looked at him and gave him a shy smile. "Sure, I'll play a couple of hands." They played until the sun had started to set and the cards became difficult to see without turning on the light. As Dani packed away the cards Liam brought her attention to the window.

"Look Dans, we're finally here." Liam kicked out at Aiden who had fallen asleep. When he slept his face became relaxed and set in a peaceful expression, a softer more innocent look than his usual stern, concentrated look. It was as if when he fell asleep all his worries melted away. Liam told Dani he only looked like this when he was close to Sarah. As if Sarah was his home. As if her grace could soften his serious outlook. Back at the barracks, he was still on edge but just as quiet, even when he fell asleep.

Aiden stirred awake at Liam's kick. He looked around groggily and then shook his head trying to shake off the hold sleep still had on him.

"We're about there." Liam said to him.

Aiden stretched and yawned, then looked at Sarah. She was still sleeping on his lap. Her blond hair had started falling out of her bun and strands were stuck to the side of her face. He gently pushed the hair away from her soft cheek. She tightened her shut eyes from registering the movement. He nudged her on the shoulder to try and rouse her awake, failing the first couple nudges.

"Sarah. Sarah. Come on it's time to wake up. We're here." Aiden spoke softly to her, his head close to hers. Her eyes fluttered open and she looked up at Aiden.

She stretched and smiled up at him. She raised up into a sitting position, his uniform jacket sliding off her shoulders. Even waking from a deep sleep with her hair a mess, Dani thought Sarah still held an air of grace and poise about her. "Good morning everyone!" Sarah said delightfully with a higher pitched voice. "Mmmm, that was a great nap. How did everyone else fair?" She looked around at her friends.

"You two were the only ones that slept." Liam pointed to Aiden and Sarah.

The vehicles stopped at the black iron gates. They towered at least fifteen feet high and twenty feet wide making it possible for larger military vehicles such as tanks to ride smoothly through or for a full platoon to ride through on horseback.

As Dani stepped out of the vehicle, she heard the colonel shouting at someone from above. A man was perched at a balcony on what was presumably the second floor. He was leaning over the balcony with his rifle slung on his back. "Harper! You son of a bitch! What are you doing here?" He teased the colonel. A smile danced across his face and there was laughter in his voice.

"That's Colonel Harper to you, Major Carter!" The colonel shouted up to the man, one of his hands around his mouth to push the sounds further out. "Now how about opening up the gate. Unless you would rather join me in the rain?" He said sarcastically. The man only laughed more but signaled to someone down below that the squad couldn't see.

One of the iron gates crept open slowly. "Okay, everyone move in." He looked to the side as if he were uninterested with the cadets. "I'm tired of standing in this unforgiving rain." He said the last part more to himself than to the cadets.

Once inside the wall, the cadets were met by a second lieutenant. He was dark skinned and had his head shaved. He was wearing sunglasses even though they were inside and there wasn't a need for them. "This way please." His voice was deep and rich. He turned and started to walk down the hallway.

The colonel came up behind the cadets, his hands in his pockets leisurely strolling by as Dani was growing accustomed to him doing. Lieutenant Reeves followed closely behind him back straight and firm as always. As he passed them, his hand left his pocket and motioned for them to follow. "Well, what are you waiting for, you've already been given an invitation. The man said to follow." He had not even bothered to look back as he passed them.

The male lieutenant led them to a large room on the third floor with couches. "This is where you will be sleeping tonight. Dinner will be brought up to you in an hour. Behind those doors," he pointed "are rooms with beds. Colonel, lieutenant, your rooms will be on the fourth floor. If you will please follow me." The man looked as if he wanted to be doing anything other than this. It was starting to get late and surely; he didn't want to still be working.

"Well go on, head on in. The lieutenant and I will be back in the morning to pick you up. Seven a.m. sharp. Be ready to go." Lieutenant Reeves cleared her voice and then leaned over to whisper something to Colonel Harper. He nodded realizing his mistake. "Oh yes. Cadet Katsuki, I will send someone down to take you to wherever you need to go to relieve the hounds, I'm sure there is an area for them to run around." Colonel Harper turned and followed the man down the hall where an elevator waited to take them to the next floor.

The cadets walked in the large room with Dani being the last to enter. She stopped and leaned against the doorpost; her foot propped up against the wall with her arms crossed over her chest. She watched as the colonel strode away. Her thoughts digging deep on all the interactions she had witnessed over the last few days. Something was going on, something their leadership wasn't telling them, and she wanted to know what. Liam poked his head out to see what she was looking at. "Ya know, I'm getting really tired of this sitting and waiting around bullshit. We can't even go outside." He playfully grabbed Dani's arms and slightly shook her back and forth. "I need fresh air! I need vitamin D!"

Dani rolled her eyes and giggled at his dramatic tantrum. "Don't be so ridiculous, it's only been two days, and besides," she said patting him on the shoulder. "You will have plenty of fresh air and... vitamin D when we're out camping and hiking through the woods for the next two weeks."

The colonel glanced back to see Dani watching them walk away. He had known Dani since she was seven. 'Has it really been ten years. She's gone from just a little girl sitting on the floor playing with dolls under her father's desk to a beautiful young woman. A fierce woman. What if something happens to her, what if I can't protect her? How will I face her father again?' Harper thought to himself.

Dani gave a slight nod in the colonels' direction as if understanding his concern. As if understanding the risk both of them faced. She pushed off the wall and started to jokingly shove Liam into the room, herding him and herself back into the room, and then shutting the door behind them.

"Something wrong sir? Lieutenant Reeves asked with concern.

"No, not at all Lieutenant." He turned his head back towards the elevator giving her an exaggerated, false smile trying to cover up his worries. Elizabeth eyed him, squinting at him even, knowing he was covering up his agitation but decided it was best not to push him and dropped the subject, besides, she had a feeling she knew what worries and concerns he was hiding.

Waiting at the elevator was the man Colonel Harper had shouted to when they first arrived. "Ethan Carter!" The colonel hollered with wide arms thrown in the air as they approached the elevator. Harper grasped the forearm of the major in a brotherly handshake when they reached the elevator. "Who'd you piss off to get stuck at this post?"

"Oh, you know, everyone." Carter laughed a hardy laugh. It wasn't like Carter to take anything seriously. It tended to make his superiors short with him, but when it came down to it, a person could not find a more loyal or hard-working soldier. It was his commitment to his fellow soldier that moved him up the ranks. His refusal to abandon his post or the mission.

Colonel Harper and Major Carter continued to converse as they made their way up to speak to the general of the Northern East Post. The elevator found its destination on the fifth floor. The three soldiers met with the brigade general, General Bridge, who instructed them on plans to leave the next morning and who would be joining them to aid in delivering them to the first checkpoint. It seemed Major Carter would be accompanying them as well, which is why he was in attendance at the debrief. He would be leading the troops that would further assist in the mission.

The brigade general also communicated to Harper that he was having the extra supplies requested delivered to the cadets as well as his and the lieutenant's quarters as they spoke. Colonel Harper acknowledged and thanked the general ending the brief with a salute, then he turned to take his leave along with First Lieutenant Reeves following behind him.

"Harper!" Major Carter bellowed from down the hall, frantically waving his arm above his head to gain the colonel's attention as Harper and Reeves put distance between the office of the general and themselves. Harper stopped in his tracks and waited for his long-ago friend to draw near.

"I fear I'm not going to be able to get rid of you while I'm here." The colonel bantered. He was starting to grow tired from traveling and wanted to relax before the next morning brought its hardship. "What is it, Ethan?"

"What say you and I go grab a beer. We can talk about things that need to be talked about. You're only here for the one night after all." He clasped his old friend on the shoulder with a smile that lit up his ageless face. His shaggy blond hair fell messily in his face and a hint of a five-o clock shadow started to raise on his young-looking face.

"After the day we've had, a beer actually sounds refreshing." The two strode away leaving Lieutenant Reeves to find her own way back to her room.

*****

Dani heard a soft knock at the door and looked up from her task. She was sitting on the couch cleaning her weapons, looking them over to make sure everything was ready and up to par for the mission that would finally commence the following day. With her, she had two handguns, the one issued and the one that her father endowed to her when she entered the academy, a knife that served multiple purposes, a few throwing knives, and her specialty, a dual short sword set. She loved having firearms, but her father introduced her to the art of knife and sword combatants from the moment she could pick up a knife and throw. A blade was natural in her hands and she preferred them to that of a firearm.

Finn was standing by the window, watching the rainfall, hoping that this wasn't an indication of what the weather would be like while they faced the already harsh terrain of the mountains. As soon as he heard the knock, he looked around at everyone's response to the unknown guest. "Don't everyone move at once." He pushed off the wall and took long strides over to the door to answer it.

Upon opening it he saw a cadet standing there with a cart behind her. The cart was filled with the additional gear General Bartovics had promised. He moved aside so that she could wheel the cart into the room. "Hey guys, the extra gear is here." He shouted.

The gear was sorted, dinner was delivered, and the night was starting to grow late. Dani decided it was time to lay her head down on a pillow in a soft bed. She wasn't sure when would be the next time she would get to lay in a bed after all, so she may as well enjoy it while she can. The rest of her comrades followed soon after, tired from the events that caused the day to drag on.

Chapter 7

THE MISSION

Dani stood atop the wall overlooking the forest and the mountains beyond. The sun was starting to peek over the horizon of the eastern mountains. There was a glow in the forest from the light reflecting off the droplets of water left behind from the rain. It almost looked as if the forest was on fire. In just an hour Dani and her squad would be departing into those woods on their first mission. This was what she trained for, what all of them had trained for. What she had spent years, even before the academy, preparing for. She was ready and the excitement of it all made her giddy, but anxious. Her bag was packed, her weapons ready, now she just waited for her horse to be saddled. She looked back at the home she had known, the nation she lived to serve and protect. It was an odd feeling to be leaving her world behind.

The wind tasseled the loose strands of her hair waving it in front of her face. She attempted to catch the wild hairs and push them behind her ear failing to keep them back. The wind hinted at the idea of a cold front rolling down the mountains. They might see a bit of snow on their mission. That may delay this mission even more.

Unknown to Dani, Harper was silently sitting up against a storage box that had been left out on top of the wall. He had quietly snuck up to the top of the wall without her noticing. She was evidently deep in thought. That kind of thinking could be dangerous on a scouting mission where a sense of alertness was needed at all time. He watched Dani for a moment, wondering what she was thinking about. If she was thinking about the mission or worrying about her father.

Finally, he spoke. "Are you worried?"

Dani jumped, startled by the intruder. She turned to see the colonel sitting on the floor leaning up against a crate. He was sitting casually with his legs stretched in front of him, crossed at the ankles. His hands were leisurely folded in his lap as he looked past her and towards the rising sun. She could remember when he would take her to the dining hall to get her food when her father was piled up with work. He would also sit and play with her in her father's office keeping her occupied until her father could return. He was like a big brother to her.

"No, why? Should I be? I've been training for this for four years." She walked over to where Harper was sitting and sat down next to him. She had not been this close to him in years. She felt at ease and safe as if she were ten years old again.

"That's not what I'm talking about and you know it." He looked sideways at her and then proceeded to look at the mountains beyond the wall.

She inhaled a large breath and let it out slowly. She did indeed know what he was referring to but she didn't much care to talk about it. "He's fine. It's just a diplomatic meeting. No need to worry." She paused feeling unsure of her response, feeling less confident in her answer. A frown crossed her face.

He stared at her for a moment, taking in the look of concern on her face. Realizing the touchy subject, he would have done better not to bring up. He needed her focus to be here, to be on this mission not on her father's well-being. "He'll be fine. I don't know anyone stronger or possessing more willpower than your father. Besides General Hawkins went as well, and you know how much of a hardass she is." He laughed to try and ease the tension he had created.

"I would hate to see the aftermath of someone trying to tangle with her." She laughed along with him, still feeling a little uneasy.

She only met the female general once, but the stories she heard of her, not only from her father but from her mother as well, were endless. She was a strong, unmovable force. They called her the Iron Fist because that's how she ran her soldiers or post, with an iron fist. Dani got up and brushed off her pants. She needed to shake off this feeling and get her head back in the game. Her focus was needed elsewhere, not only for her sake, but for those she loved.

"Do you remember the first time we met?" He asked her randomly, hoping it would help her to relax slightly.

"If memory serves me right, it was here at the wall. You were stationed here?" Her eyebrows frowned at the unsureness of her answer.

"Temporarily stuck." He rolled his eyes. "You were so tiny, this sweet little innocent girl who carried around a wooden toy horse. Your father was there to discuss my transfer to his unit."

"Wooden horse." She let out a small chuckle.

Her father had carved the little wooden horse out of a piece of oak tree her mother had found while the three of them were on a camping trip. Her siblings had all become sick and were stuck at home and her parents thought it best to get Dani out of the house and away from her siblings before, she too, became ill. Little did Dani know; it would be their last trip. Her mother and three siblings died shortly after that. The horse held a small compartment under its belly where Dani stored a picture of her mother along with her mother's wedding band.

"Well I may not carry it anymore, but the horse remains in my possession. It sits on my nightstand back at the barracks. Speaking of horses, do you think the horses are ready to go?" She turned to look down at him. He was still sitting against the crate.

He pushed off the floor and climbed to his feet. He walked to the edge of the wall and looked over it, spitting in the process. "I knew there was another reason I came up here." He turned back towards her and snapped his fingers as if just remembering something. He walked back over to Dani and leaned down until he was at eye level with her.

"The horses are ready, time to move out cadet." He smiled and then tasseled her hair. He turned to head back towards the door that led inside. "Are you coming?" He didn't even bother to look back.

She was in shock by his casual attitude. Dumbfounded and wide eyed she followed him inside to meet with the rest of the squad. She was ready.

Down on the ground level, the bags were packed, the supplies loaded, and the horses pranced in place ready to go. The cadets lined up waiting to receive the final brief before they headed out onto the other side of the wall. The colonel donned his jacket and hat as he walked to the front of the row of cadets. The lieutenant was at his side ready to snap to any command given to her.

The colonel stared at each one of them, serious, not even a hint of joy crossed his face. When he spoke, he said only two words. "Saddle up." He jumped onto his horse and the cadets followed suit. Taking formation with the colonel in front, the lieutenant to his right while Aiden was to his left, the rest of the cadets found their place. Hiromi with her hounds were in the middle behind the lieutenant and Aiden, while Sarah and Dani were behind either side of her. Liam and Finn covered the back of the first squad.

Behind them, there was a second squad of soldiers that would accompany them until the first checkpoint as a safeguard. The second squad numbered a count of eight cadets with a second lieutenant leading from the middle and Major Carter at the front. The four cadets heading the front were spotters. Their job was to run ahead of everyone else and look for signs of trouble alerting the squad of the danger. The four cadets in the back were a combination of fighters and medics. They would serve as back up as needed. The medics would be there to help any wounded but wouldn't get caught in the crossfire so they were less likely to get injured and could tend to the others.

The gates to the outside world opened. The colonel looked back to his squad. "Your mission has officially begun; you know what to do."

He kicked off and his horse started galloping out the gate into the mountains. The rest followed his lead. The pounding of hooves on the wet ground echoed in the cadet's head. The power of the stampede of horses vibrating into each of the soldier's bodies. As soon as they started riding, before they disappeared into the woods, the four spotters hauled fast on their horses to gain distance away from the crowd and get ahead of the squads. The four in the back dispersed giving distance to cover more ground. If there was going to be trouble, they would know about it before it ever reached Dani and her squad.

Hours into the mission they continued to trudge slowly through the wet mountains. Dani noticed the temperature starting to drop. The air was chilled for an autumn day. They would have to climb up the mountains and over to reach the valley below. The valley is where the rebel's camp was supposed to be located, but as they climbed higher it became colder. Dani could see her horse's breath along with her own. Colonel Harper held a fist up indicating that he wanted them to stop. He turned around on his horse to speak to the others.

"Dismount. Go ahead and put on cold weather gear if you haven't already and that goes for the horses too. They're not going to move fast if they're frozen."

Dani dismounted and took out her hat and gloves along with her wet weather jacket. It wasn't raining yet, but it looked like it would, as the clouds moved in. She then took out a jacket for her horse and attached it. The horse shook his mane and let out a snort along with a few other disapproving noises. Dani walked in front of the horse and gently brushed the horse's face with her hand.

"Easy boy," She attempted to soothe and calm him by enticing him with oats. It seemed to work and soon the squad was ready to start riding once more.

The day was starting to stretch on, and the clouds overhead were darkening. The colonel and the two lieutenants along with Major Carter were conversing ahead, they were too quiet for Dani to hear. When they parted and Major Carter and the second lieutenant rode away back to their squad. Colonel Harper slowed his horse forcing everyone else to do so as well. He held up a hand indicating he wanted everyone to stop once more. He dismounted his horse and indicated for everyone else to do the same.

"We're going to stop here for the night. It's starting to get dark and the temperatures will be dropping fast. We need to get a fire started and the horses fed, they need a break anyways." The colonel pointed to a thin row of trees revealing what Dani thought was a stream.

"Through those trees is a small stream. Take the horses to get water, go in groups of two, don't need you guys crowding each other after all. And if you're smart you'll go ahead and fill up your canteens while your there." He took the reins of his horse in his hand and nodded to the lieutenant. They would head to the stream first while the rest stayed behind to start setting up camp.

Thunder boomed in the distance threatening an oncoming storm. The squads hoped they could get the camp set up before getting washed out by the rain. They had found a thick canopy of trees on somewhat level ground. They cleared an area to set up tents and build a fire. The horses were relieved of all their gear except for their jackets to keep them warm through the cold, wet night.

The cadets of Dani's squad set up their tents in a circle around a fire pit facing inwards. The second squad had set up their own circle of tents with their own fire in the middle separated from the first squad. Sarah and Liam were on either side of Dani, while Aiden was on the other side of Sarah. Dani now sat in the opening of her tent looking at the burning wood in the fire. Her thoughts went to her father. He should be arriving on Mars. She wondered what he was doing, if he was alright?

"Dans, Dans..." Sarah had been standing above Dani for several moments trying to get her attention. She put a hand on Dani's shoulder. Dani stirred, startled by Sarah's touch. She looked up at her best friend and rubbed her eyes.

"Sorry Sarah. What's up?" Dani scooted to the side exposing space that would allow her friend to sit in her tent with her.

Sarah took a seat crossing her legs and arms in front of her. "You okay? You've been especially quiet all day." She had a concerned look on her face.

Dani never took her eyes off the raging fire. "Yeah, I'm okay." Liam walked over and sat down joining the two.

"She's lying." Liam called Dani out.

"Well, I figured that." Sarah rolled her eyes picking on Liam. They always picked on each other as if they were siblings.

"She's worried about her father." Liam commented not paying attention to Sarah.

"Thanks again captain obvious." Sarah strike back.

The sun finally set, and the night had settled in. It was beautiful out in the woods where no light touched the sky. The storm that had been threatening to wash them away all day never came. The wind had been strong, and it blew the storm clouds over them away. Dani could see every star in the sky along with a little red one. She stared at it knowing that that red dot was Mars, where her father was. She knew she needed to be focused on the mission and keeping a clear head, but she had a gut feeling that something was wrong.

"Cadet Mitchells, you'll be taking the first watch." The colonel walked over and leaned over in front of her.

She looked up at him from where he was standing above her. "Yes sir." She laced up her boots and grabbed her weapons, readying herself for the shift.

Everyone was asleep in their tents and the fire was starting to die down. Dani threw another log onto the fire dispersing ambers and throwing up ashes. In the distance, she could hear the sounds of the forest along with the other squad's watcher. An owl hooted in a nearby tree above while a wolf howled in the far-off distance. She looked around and caught the other squad member's eyes, he gave her an acknowledging wave.

She sat against a tree away from the camp and tents listening for anything that shouldn't be there. Soon her watch shift was over. She headed back over to the fire and sat on a log. She was chilled to the bone. She heard the tent next to her starting to unzip where Liam emerged from his tent stretching and yawning. His boots were still unlaced, and his shirt was wrapped around his neck, his torso exposed to the frigid air. Dani thought he looked boyish with his hair a mess and the sleepy look he displayed on his face. He gave her a sideways smile with his blue eyes still half shut from sleep. She wasn't sure if she felt warm because of the fire or because Liam made her unexpectedly blush, either way, she was glad it was dark.

"Alright, I'll be back. I'm gonna go take a piss." He walked away into the woods, so he was concealed.

Though he had not moved far enough away from the camp because Dani could still hear the ruffle of leaves. When Liam returned his white t-shirt was now around his body. The shirt was designed with a special material that prevented heat from escaping helping to keep a person warm, therefore the clothing fit snug and in Liam's case, this was no exception. The shirt hugged Liam's body, revealing a cut torso; the lines and curves of every muscle showing through.

He walked over to Dani, then grabbed her arms and pulled her to her feet. He wrapped her in a comforting hug and kissed her forehead. "Don't worry so much, you know he'll survive anything thrown at him. He's a tough old bat." He pulled away from her but only enough to see her face. "Remember all the shit we used to try. If he survived you, me, my three older brothers, along with your siblings, he can definitely survive some high fashion princess."

"Liam, he's a prince..." she stared blankly at him missing the humor.

"Yeah, I know. That's what I said. High maintenance girly prince. Same thing."

She gave a small smile and giggled as she returned his hug. "Okay, I'm going to bed." He let go of her and she crawled into her tent, zipping it up behind her. Even though she was on the ground, laying down felt relieving after riding horseback all day.

*****

The light shown through the tents melting away the frost that settled on the tops. Each squad member packed up their own gear starting with their tents. Poles were disassembled and fabric fluttered down to the ground only to be picked up and vigorously shook in hopes of relieving the tents of the melting frost. The fabric sprayed water in every direction, little droplets of water catching the light before they hit the ground, splattering.

A breakfast of fried eggs and meat was prepared. The cadets ate in silence still trying to wake from the trance of deep sleep the forest had cast on them. Even Hiromi's hounds, Luka and Willow, were cuddled together with their tails hiding their noses while they were fast asleep. Hiromi leaned down and gave each of them a pat rousing them from sleep, then gave them a bowl of dog food with a treat of dried meat. The dog's tails wagged happily as they devoured their food.

Colonel Harper finished his plate of food and set the plate down on the log next to him. He stood up and clapped his hands together a few times to get the attention of his squad. "Alright guys, clean up, I want it to look like we were never here. Do it quickly. We head out in twenty."

The second day of travel would prove to be much rougher than the previous day. The cadets were already sore from riding the day before and the horses didn't seem all that thrilled about treading up and down the mountain range as well. They were sluggish and slow to start moving.

The day stretched on, there was no rain, but the wind picked up making the trails treacherous. Colonel Harper instructed the cadets to dismount and walk beside the horses. They may not have gotten rain where they had camped the night before but the area in which they were hiking through did and the mountainside had become slick with wet, thick mud. It had become too dangerous to continue traveling on horseback until they had reached the other side of the pass.

Hours had passed since dismounting. The soft mud was starting to harden turning back into rock and stiff clay. The four spotters were returning to the second squad one at a time. Upon returning, they each spoke immediately with the second lieutenant and Major Carter who in turn spoke to the colonel. Soon the first squad had reached the other side of the pass. Not far behind them the rest of the second squad had regrouped and joined the first squad at the pass.

The colonel had taken out a pair of binoculars and was using them to scan the horizon. Lieutenant Reeves was looking at a map of the area while Major Carter was pointing to an area down the mountain. The colonel removed the binoculars from around his neck and wrapped them back up stuffing them in one of his sacks on the back of his horse while he nodded in agreement.

"Must be looking for the post." Finn said from behind the group. He had been chewing on something and now spat it out onto the ground.

"Looks like they found it." Liam commented back with a slight snip to his voice. Finn just snickered but let it go.

Everyone was on edge from the wet, cold weather and the two days of riding on a horse. Getting to the post meant a cot to sleep in along with a warm shower and a dry environment and the possible promise of warm food instead of the dry food the squads had been eating.

The colonel looked back to the squads. "The ground here is drier. We should be able to ride on horseback the rest of the way down. The post is halfway down the mountain. We'll have to take it slow, but we should reach it within the hour." He jumped back on his horse and turned her, so she was facing the open face of the mountains.

The twist and turns heading down the mountain proved to be more difficult than originally perceived. The cadets had to gather in a single file line as the pathway became narrow. But as dusk was starting to settle in, the two squads finally made it safely down the mountain and to the first post.

Dani dismounted her horse and unloaded her gear as she was instructed. They were met by scouting cadets who approached them and took the reins of the horses guiding them to a nearby barn where the horses would be fed, watered and relieved of all the saddling equipment. From here on out, Dani and her squad would walk the remainder of the mission, while the other squad would head back to the wall the next morning.

Colonel Harper had walked into the post building but had shortly returned with another woman beside him. He clapped to gain the attention of the cadets and then waved everyone over. "Okay, listen up. This is Major Sophia Morris, she is the commanding officer for this post, what she says is law so listen well."

"Thank you, sir." She nodded in Colonel Harper's direction. "Now," She shouted loud enough for both squads to hear. "this is not a hotel, we do not have maids or attendants, so you will clean up after yourself. We do have a cook on staff so dinner will be served at...." Major Morris looked down at her watch then back up at the small crowd. "Eighteen hundred in the dining hall on the main floor. That's in forty-five minutes. Plenty of time for each of you to head up to your rooms and get the filth off from the last two days. You may have had to sleep outside last night, but you are not animals and I do not particularly want my post smelling like a barn. The living quarters are on the second floor. Females with females. Males with males. That is all"

The colonel, who had been leaning against a column stretching the length of the floor to the underside of the overhang to the large five story building, now pushed off to address everyone once more.

"My squad! Tomorrow we will be headed out by eight am, no, make it nine. I think I would like to catch an extra hour of sleep after that ride. Breakfast will be served between seven and eight am. I suggest you go to bed early, get a good night's rest, and eat a filling breakfast. Tomorrow will prove to be a tiring day as well." When he finished speaking, he, Lieutenant Reeves, and Major Morris disappeared inside the building out of the cold wind of the coming winter.

Dani heard a laugh come from the colonel and... the lieutenant. 'That was a first.' Dani thought to herself. The three leaders must have been old friends. In the military, at one point or another, a soldier seems to meet just about everyone. There is no greater bonding experience than facing death together in the heat of battle and war.

Dani saw Sarah walking with Aiden and Liam and rushed to catch up. She called out for them bringing attention to herself in hopes that they would slow their pace and wait for her. Naturally, they waited on the person that completed their tetrad.

"Share a room?" Dani asked Sarah when she had caught up with her friends. She would have been surprised if the answer was anything but yes. Sarah happily agreed all the while making jokes about having had shared a room with her for the last four years, what was one more night.

Liam and Aiden shared a room as well. While waiting for dinner they unpacked clothes to wear after they take showers before heading down for a hot, filling meal. Aiden suddenly looked up at the door hearing a soft knock. He looked at Liam with a look of curiously and confusion. Liam just shrugged.

"Maybe Dani and Sarah?" Liam suggested. Aiden laid the shirt he had dug out of his pack on his pillow and answered the door. He was surprised to see Colonel Harper, Major Carter, and Hiromi standing at the door.

"Sir." Aiden spoke softly.

Before he could ask his leadership about his presence at their room the colonel pushed past him and motioned for Carter and Hiromi to do the same. He took a seat at a small round table in the corner of the room. Carter guarded the door by leaning against it after Hiromi quietly shut the door but not before checking to ensure there were no peering eyes.

"Best to speak behind closed doors." Harper said in almost a whisper. "Please" he kicked out a seat. "Take a seat." He smiled up at them.

Liam and Aiden looked at each other but did as they were told. Aiden took the seat that Harper had kicked out while Liam pulled out a second chair to sit in. Hiromi stood behind the colonel, watching the scene play out.

"Well, this is... weird. Are we in trouble?" Liam asked scratching the back of his head. He was feeling nervous and a bit on edge. This was exactly how his mother would pull him and his three brothers into the living room to be scolded for fighting or some other ridiculous thing they would do to get themselves into trouble.

Harper let out a small chuckle. "No, Evens, nothing like that. I however need to discuss some important matters with the two of you."

"What does this have to do with sir?" Aiden asked baffled.

"I'm glad you asked Pearce." The colonel adjusted, leaning forward in his chair. He placed his arms on the table, resting his elbows on the top, his chin laid on his closed hands. "This mission is about more than recon on some rebels. We are also meeting with an informant in the rebel camp."

"And why exactly would we do that sir?" Liam contributed to the conversation.

"Simple, he has information that we want or more importantly need." Harper leaned back in his chair once more.

Aiden adjusted in his seat. The look on his face indicating he was starting to feel uncomfortable. "Sir, why are we not discussing this with the rest of the squad?"

"I'm not ready for everyone else to know quite yet. Especially Mitchells. Her focus is already spread thin with her father on Mars, I need her attention here."

Liam now questioned the colonel. He did not like to keep secrets from his childhood best friend. "What does this have to do with Dani, why would this bother her?"

"Because the person we're meeting with is Dani's older brother." Hiromi spoke up, clearly aggravated at Liam and Aiden's lack of ability to accept the colonel's request and follow orders. In their position, their duty was to follow orders, not question commands.

Aiden was stunned by this new information. He knew Dani had an older brother but thought he had died in the fire with their mother and her other two siblings. News that her brother was alive and well was the last thing he thought he would hear.

"Evens!" Liam snapped to attention; his blue eyes focused on the colonel. "You don't seem as stupefied and phased by this information as I thought you might be. Which means you already knew. Didn't you."

Liam looked down into his lap, thinking before he spoke. When he did speak, he was quiet.

"That night, it was cold like it is tonight. The wind was howling. I had said goodnight to Dani only an hour or so before when I started to smell the smoke. I looked outside my window and I saw the light from the fire." He paused looking up to the ceiling his eyes vacant. When he looked back down at everyone his baby blue eyes had turned to ice filling with sorrow. "By the time I had gotten there it was already too late. Her mother had died trying to save her children. Robert was holding one of the twins in his arms, his wife and Abigail, Dani's younger sister, were laying on the frozen ground beside him dead from the smoke in their lungs. Dani had already been rushed to the hospital."

Liam rubbed his eyes attempting to chase away the tears gathering in the corners. "Nobody knew if Dani was going to make it. Her condition was critical, but her younger brother, he had escaped almost unscathed. Her older brother though, he was nowhere to be found. At the time I was so worried about Dani I wasn't thinking. News of her brother alive doesn't surprise me."

"How old were you when it happened?" Harper asked him.

"Seven. Dani and I were seven, the twins were four, and Grayson, her older brother was fourteen." Liam exhaled. He hated thinking about that night. He was helpless and felt useless when he was unable to help his best friend.

"Do you know why Major General Mitchells claimed the twins along with his eldest son to be deceased while Dani survived?"

Liam shook his head no in response. "Because very few people saw his sons alive and since they were not injured in the fire and were not taken to the hospital it was the perfect opportunity to put them into hiding. Unfortunately, Dani was taken to the hospital. He had no choice but to keep her in the light of the government."

It was Aiden who spoke this time. "But why falsify their deaths in the first place, sir? It doesn't make sense. And what do you mean in the light of the government?"

"Because Robert suspected foul play within the government."

Both Aiden and Liam startled with realization at the colonel's words. Liam's hands shook from anger. Aiden did not want to accept the reality of the situation. "No, it can't be. This isn't what I trained for!" Aiden's voice starting to rise, he jumped to his feet. The chair falling to the ground behind him.

"Calm down cadet. It's not what you think. It wasn't the military that ordered the hit on the general's family, but it was someone within our government. Someone who knew that Robert had imperative information that could cripple leaders."

"Then why not use the information. If there's corruption in the government, why not bring it to light?" Aiden was asking, furious.

"Because of Dani." Liam said silently. "They would hurt her maybe even kill her. He would never risk that."

"Exactly." Harper confirmed.

Liam looked up at him. "So, then this mission, this is to get Dani to safety, isn't it? To get her to Grayson?"

The colonel hesitated for a moment, looking at Liam. His eyes were dark from having to remember the events of that night. "Yes. Once they sent down the order to send General Mitchells to Mars, we decided it would be best if Dani was away and safe from the government's hands."

"You think the Mars mission is a cover up. To get rid of Dani's father?" Aiden asked picking up the chair off the ground.

"It's possible. We're not sure, but we sure as hell didn't want to take a chance." Carter commented from the door where he still stood.

"With the General gone, it doesn't seem Dani would be much of a threat, you think they would just leave her alone, unless she had inform..." Aiden trailed off realizing how dire and complicated the situation was becoming. He smacked his forehead. "Damn. Damnit!" he slammed his fist down on the table, the legs shaking from the force.

"I doubt she even realizes she knows the information, that is if she even had it to begin with. In reality, she doesn't have much knowledge on anything that's been carrying on. Robert kept her in the dark as much as possible for that exact reason. He thought it would be best that way." The colonel explained.

"Her father. That's why you don't want her to know. She would piece it all together. Putting her in danger. It makes sense now. We were assigned this mission as soon as it was released her father would be going to Mars after all." Liam connected.

Harper snapped his fingers at Liam. "Exactly. Evens, if you knew that Mitchells's sons were alive, why not tell your best friend. Why keep it from her. Why not tell Dani her two brothers were alive?"

Aiden turned on Liam with anger in his voice. "I can't believe you've known for all these years and you didn't say anything to Dani. You, of all people, know how much her family's death has affected her."

"Robert told me not too." Liam shut Aiden down before he could continue. "He said if Dani knew it would put her life in danger. That's all the motivation I needed. I would do anything to protect her, and if that meant lying to her, then that was a burden I would carry."

"Makes sense." Harper agreed, his head slightly shaking in agreement. There was a pause between the three of them.

"So, question, not to be rude but, why is Hiromi here? I mean I've put together that Major Carter is in on it all, but..." Liam asked unexpectedly.

Harper looked up at Hiromi standing behind him. She just shrugged her shoulders. "I'm here because I was one of the closest people to the General. All those missions I ran were always led by him. He shared many secrets with me, so I know things that others do not. Therefore, I can be of assistance."

"Good enough for me." Liam affirmed, satisfied by her answer.

"The time will come when all will be revealed. But for now," The colonel moved in close to Liam and Aiden. "Keep your damn mouths shut or your military careers will be over faster than they began."

"But they haven't begun... sir..." Liam said matter of fact not picking up the colonels' meaning.

"Exactly cadet Evens." Harper replied. Aiden backhanded Liam in the chest.

"Oh, gotcha ya." Liam attempted to rub the pain from his chest.

"Well now," The colonel stood up and pushed in his chair. "I do believe it's almost dinner time. Hiromi," The colonel indicated she should take the lead in exiting the room. "after you." The three of them left the room with Aiden and Liam still sitting in the chairs trying to simplify the information they had just been loaded down with.

Down in the dining hall, Sarah and Dani were already eating dinner with Finn. Aiden could see them laughing from where he stood on the top of the grand stairway. They were enjoying the warm meal and the cozy comforts of the building away from the harsh winds of the frigid outside.

Liam hid a small smile that slipped onto his face. Without truly looking in Liam's direction Aiden took the opportunity to pick on Liam. "I saw that."

Liam looked at Aiden. "She looks so happy. It's the first time I've seen her truly smile in months. How do we keep something like this from her? From either of them."

Aiden clasped his friend on the shoulder. "We just have to buddy. You know it's for the best. We need to keep her safe. To keep both of them safe." Sarah looked up and noticed Aiden and Liam standing at the top of the stairs. She lifted her arm up and waved them over, mouthing something that was unrecognizable with the distance between them. "Come on, if we stay up here any longer, they'll know something's wrong." Aiden gave a slight nudge to Liam's back and then started down the stairs.

"What took you guys so long? We've been down here for like forever." Sarah grabbed on to Aiden pulling him down onto the bench beside her. She caused him to be off balanced and he almost spilled his tray of food all over himself and the table.

"Sorry, we just got talking about the mission and lost track of time." Liam sat next to Dani.

She was enjoying a stuffed chicken with steamed vegetables and rice. Liam looked up at Aiden and he just stared back. An unspoken understanding passed between them that neither one of them liked the situation their commanding officer had put them in.

*****

"Dani wake up!" Sarah was shaking her friend trying to rouse her awake. "Wake up Dans, it's just a nightmare." Dani was laying in her bed tossing and turning, her sheets soaked with sweat. Her eyes jolted open and she sprang up into a sitting position. Falling into her friend's arms. She buried her head in the nape of Sarah's neck.

"Shhhh, it's okay. It was just a bad dream. You're okay." Sarah was rocking her back and forth stroking her back up and down trying to calm her friend, just like her mother used to do to her when she was a child. After a few moments Dani started to relax and settle down. Sarah pushed Dani's hair aside so she could see her face. "You okay now."

"Yeah, I'm okay." Sarah slowly released Dani from her arms. "What time is it? I feel like I haven't slept at all."

Sarah tucked back a loose strand of hair behind Dani's ear. "I don't think you did sleep. What's going on? This isn't the first nightmare you've had. And they've been occurring more frequently."

Dani rubbed her eyes trying to brush away the clutch sleep had on her. "I don't know. I have these dreams of fire and Liam is there. But he's...he isn't...." she couldn't bring herself to say it.

"He's dead." Sarah finished for her. Dani just shook her head and looked down. "Dani you know he's alive and well. In fact, he's right across the hall probably still sleeping. Maybe you're just having dreams of fire because of your past and it's the only way your subconscious can cope with your father's mission. You're just stressing yourself out so much that it's manifesting into nightmares. Do you maybe want to talk about it? It might help." Sarah gave Dani a reassuring smile.

"Honestly, I wouldn't even know where to begin. Yes, I'm worried about my father. But I'm also upset about you and Aiden graduating in a few months. I have no idea where that puts Liam and myself. And now this whole mission. I'm worried about screwing it up."

"Well, as far as the mission goes, I don't know anyone more qualified to handle a scouting assignment than you. So, don't even worry about that." Sarah paused and looked out the window. She could see a flurry of white fluffy snow. "Hey!" She jumped off the bed and ran to the window, sitting on the bench laid out in front of it. "It's snowing."

Dani crawled out of bed and joined her. Without looking at Dani, Sarah continued to talk. "To be honest I don't know where graduating puts me either. I'm lost and hopeless without all three of you to hold me up. Especially you." The two sat for a moment more before getting dressed and gathering their gear to head downstairs.

"Good morning cadets" Colonel Harper stood at the end of the table looking down at his squad. He was dressed in a heavy parka and thick snow pants. He looked as if he was ready for a blizzard. "I hope everyone got some much-needed rest because today we make our way down the mountain and trekking through these woods will be treacherous with the snow."

Lieutenant Reeves glided up behind him holding a box. "Sir, Major Morris handed these to me this morning, she said they're great to help keep warm." He turned to her and opened the box revealing hand warmers.

"Oh good, now we shouldn't hear any moaning or groaning about the cold." He turned to his cadets and smiled a devilish smile. "Alright, cadets it's time to head out! Load up your gear. We move in ten. Come lieutenant."

"Yes sir." She followed him out of the dining hall. As they walked away the two conversed.

"Sir, are you sure about informing Evens and Pearce about Mitchells's situation?" She asked Colonel Harper.

"No, but its already done. I can only hope they can keep it to themselves until the time is right." He replied.

"Then why tell them at all sir. The information doesn't seem relevant for them to need to know at the current moment."

"I suppose your right Lieutenant." The two had made it to the front entrance of the building, away from the ears of the cadets. Colonel Harper looked to his most trusted subordinate. "but I needed to know how much they knew and if we will be able to trust them with the next phase of the plan plus it's great motivation for them.

"And?" She inquired.

"It might be an adjustment at first for them, but I do believe they will fit into the plans perfectly." The two turned and left the building behind, out into the white of the world beyond.

*****

The cadets loaded up their gear and lined up ready to venture down the mountain towards the rebel's compound. Hiromi's hounds, Willow and Luka, were prancing anxiously, ready to move. Their giant paws making indentions into the freshly laid snow.

Colonel Harper stood in the front of the formation as he spoke to Major Carter before he departed, leading the second squad in the opposite direction, back to Heleina. On his mark, Harper started out of the clearing, leading his troops back into the woods, away from the safety of the post.

The snow was starting to disperse as the sun rose higher, allowing the air around the squad to warm. The once frozen ground thawed making way for muddy slush. The ground caused everyone to have trouble staying balanced on their feet. Dani almost slipped a few times but was able to recover. The calming view of the mountain chain aided in lifting the soggy moods of the cadets. The caps were covered in a light dusting of snow while the trees underneath released an illusion of warmth with the deep colors of reds, oranges, and yellows from the ocean of leaves.

Sarah was having trouble staying on her feet. She had already slipped twice. Her ankle had never had proper time to heal and the effect of it was causing her problems now. Dani was walking a few steps behind Sarah watching her closely, afraid for her friend's safety when all of a sudden Sarah stepped on a loose rock, dislodging it. The rock loosened from the ground and started its descent down the side of the mountain, hitting and bouncing off the rock face.

Sarah's foot slipped off the side of the trail causing her to lose her balance. Dani watched in horror as her friend started to tumble over the side. In a flash, Finn was there just in time to grab Sarah by the wrist.

"Hang on!" Finn was shouting at a frightened Sarah. He looked back looking for assistants from the others. "Someone give me a hand!" He shouted.

He was holding onto her, but she had started to slip. The weight of her pack proving to be too much for Finn alone. Dani had already raced to his side attempting to help. Aiden was on the other side of Finn reaching out for Sarah's other arm, while Hiromi and Liam were behind the three supporting them, pulling them back as they pulled Sarah up.

Sarah's torso was bobbing above the ledge when she was able to kick one of her legs up and push herself back over to safer ground. Once she was safely on the ground Finn and Dani let go of her while Aiden held on even tighter.

"Are you okay?" Aiden asked lovingly and concerned.

Sarah shook her head to startled to talk. "Cadet Hunt!" Harper had raced over when the group was still pulling Sarah up. "Hunt, are you okay?" Sarah nodded a positive response to her commanding officer. "Giving us quite a scare there, aren't ya?"

"Sorry, sir." She was quiet, embarrassed that she had to be saved. Embarrassed that she had been so stupid as to not pay attention, letting herself get distracted by the scenery.

Harper clasped her shoulder and gave her a look of understanding and forgiveness before standing back up from the kneeling position he had been in to meet her eye. "Okay everyone, here is as good of a place as any to take a break. Thirty minutes to refresh and refuel and then we move on."

The sun was high in the sky reflecting off the puddles of water still left on the ground from the storms. One of the dogs was lapping the water while the other took point in guarding the group. Dani's nerves were still high on alert after she watched her best friend tumble over the edge of a cliff, almost to her death. She walked over and stood behind Finn. He was kneeling over his pack digging through it, trying to find something.

"Thank you." She exclaimed drawing his attention from his objective. He looked up at her and then shook his head.

"I was just doing my job. I would have done it for anyone. I don't see the point in thanking me for that." He had continued in his task in searching through his bag. He must have found what he was looking for because he held up a bag and exclaimed a feeling of delight and success.

"Even so, thank you." She walked away leaving him to his business.

She was sure he appreciated someone speaking out even if his attitude suggested otherwise. Finn paused at his task and watched as Dani walked away out of the corner of his eye. He didn't expect her to be the one to come over and thank him. She wasn't as quiet as Hiromi, but Dani was still the quiet one amongst her group of friends, always so focused. Finn never understood why someone who was clearly more studious then the others surrounded herself with them.

"Finn, Finn!" Finn was abruptly disturbed from his train of thought. He swung his head around to be greeted with a large black dog's hot breath in his face. Hiromi was standing above him, shadowed by the sun's rays. She was blocking the sun from his eyes, but it still did not help him to see her. He pushed Luka's snout out of his face but not before Luka licked him.

"Luka, get out of here." He pushed off the ground using his own knee as a support. "What is it Hiromi?" The two had often found each other's company, even before the mission. They grew up close to one another in the same town and went to the same school. They were each other's familiar face and because of those connections, it made it easy to converse with one another.

"The colonel and lieutenant want us to scout ahead. Make sure the path is clear of any dangers, environmental or anything else. Don't want another Hunt repeat." She nodded towards Sarah and the others.

"Shouldn't you know this path pretty well. After all, this isn't the first time you've been on it." Finn was hinting at a deeper meaning.

His eyes and brow frowned at her. They locked eyes, staring at each other in a showdown of wits and nerve. Finally, Hiromi backed down and looked away, her arms crossed. Finn didn't have all the pieces but knew this mission was about more than just recon on a town. He saw Harper and Hiromi leaving with the major from Liam and Aiden's room the night before. He knew a squad like this would never perform a scouting mission in the approaching winter. Something was amiss, and Hiromi knew what it was.

She motioned to her hounds. "Luka, Willow." She made a clicking noise and the hounds stood up and returned to her side imitating her every move. "Let's just go." She walked away and started heading towards the path expecting Finn to follow without further command. Finn shook his head but leaned down, closed his pack, and heaved it on his shoulders to follow her into the thicket of woods.

Hiromi and Finn were walking along a cut out in the woods. The path had been worn into the mountains through the years of small squads traveling to and fro from the first and second posts. At the rate they were going they would have to camp in the woods tonight and carry on to the second post in the morning. Hiromi gazed up towards the sky determining the weather they would have to face that night. Her hound's noses were up sniffing the air. She leaned down to pat Willow behind her ear. Her white, furry face turned up to her master, grateful for the sign of affection placed upon her.

"The clouds are moving fast. We might be looking at a cold, rainy night again." She looked to Finn who was now examining the sky himself.

"Yeah, I think you're right. What a terrible time for a mission. Constant rain and cold. Even with the hot shower last night I can't seem to shake the chill from my bones. I wonder why now, what's the urgency to go on a mission into the mountains this close to winter. It hasn't been done before after all. And with a bunch of trainees at that." He was fishing for information.

Finn continued to ramble on. Hiromi decided to let him instead of explaining. She didn't think there was any reason to reveal to him the whole story quite yet. "Well, it must be important if they sent us out here when they normally wouldn't." Hiromi pushed a branch out of her way and then ducked under another one.

"That's what I mean, if it's so important, then why send trainees. The colonels right, we're not even rookies." Hiromi looked back at him and gave him a look as a reminder as to whom he was speaking too. He quickly swung up his arms in front of him and shook his hands to warn off her flare. "Not you, of course, I mean you're not just a trainee. I mean..."

She continued on her way. She was focused on the trees looking for signs of stirring. "Yeah, I know what you mean Finn. If I remember correctly there's a clearing up ahead that opens up to an overlook. That would be a good place to examine the surroundings. If there's anyone around, if we stay low, we'll be able to see them, but they won't see us. Follow my lead."

"Roger." He needlessly saluted her.

They walked in silence a few yards more until the trees started to thin. Finn noticed the exposed rock of the mountain indicating the sight of the clearing. The hounds on cue got low and started to scoot on their bellies until Hiromi clicked implying her want for them to halt. The hounds did as commanded and laid down but stayed alert with their ears high. Hiromi and Finn paused at the edge of the clearing studying the surrounding, confirming they were alone, and it was safe to move into position onto the lookout. They moved in unison to the ground, low crawling to the edge of the clearing. They could see the valley below and with a pair of binoculars they could see the second post below as well.

They studied the mountain and forest around them. The sun was directly overhead when Finn looked for Hiromi's attention. She removed the binoculars and looked to him. "We should head back. It's starting to get late and the squad will be waiting on our report."

She agreed and they backed up from the cliff still staying low. When they reached the edge of the woods, Hiromi motioned for her hounds to stand and lead the way back to the squad. They jogged all the way back making quick work of the distance they had put between them and the other members.

The lieutenant was the first to notice the movement in the trees when she saw a white and then a black face poking through, they were followed by long slender bodies. "Sir, they've returned." As she spoke Hiromi and Finn burst through the trees.

"Report!" He didn't even give them time to catch their breaths.

"We're clear sir." Hiromi stated with a salute.

"Good." His next words were louder to address the whole of the squad. "Gather your gear, we're moving onwards." Dani was glad to be moving again. Sitting there, waiting, set her nerves on edge, and made her feel as if she should be doing something. She had wished she had been sent with the others to scout.

The squad progressed forward towards the second post. Hiromi informed Colonel Harper and Lieutenant Reeves personally that they would have to stop and set up camp before too much longer. There would be no way to reach the second post by nightfall with the treacherous slopes of the wet mountains.

As the day grew long so did the faces of each cadet. The constant fighting of the up and down terrain had caused their bodies to become weary and worn and a good night's rest was crucial to be able to continue their journey. The colonel stopped them when they found themselves in an open field down in one of the many valleys they would have to pass through.

Just like the first night, tents were set up in a circle centering around a localized fire. Dinner was made and the cadets ate in silence, exhausted from the day's travels. Colonel Harper and Lieutenant Reeves were quietly whispering with one another as they studied maps and other papers.

Harper pointed to something and Reeves nodded in agreement. "I've received intelligence, sir, that General Bartovics will cover our return. It was a smart play to inform him of the senior staff's betrayal ensuring a permanent alliance with the commander in control of the wall."

"I thought…" The colonel started.

"Smart, but reckless. What if he had been involved? What if he had been working with the leaders? Sir, you shouldn't be so open with your intentions and motives." Lieutenant Reeves scolded him.

"True, it was a calculated risk, but it was one that clearly paid off. Besides are plans our too far along. By the time the leaders catch wind of any ruse, the rebels will have moved their forces in and be ready for the final attack. The riots have already escalated, to a point where any ruling will raise suspicions on their part. First, we get Mitchells to safety." Harper explained.

"I understand your connection to the family, but wouldn't have been easier to hide her somewhere in Helenia, sir?" Reeves mentioned.

"She knows her father's secrets, if anyone can coax them to the surface, it will be her brother." He explained.

"Yes sir." She disapprovingly agreed.

Liam walked over and sat down on the ground next to where Dani was perched on a log. He scooted down, making himself comfortable and tilted his hat. "What do you think those two are whispering about?" He gestured over towards Harper and Reeves.

"Probably the mission dummy." Finn walked over slapping Liam on his uplifted knee with the brim of his hat as he passed by him. Liam swung up his leg in an attempt to kick the backside of Finn's legs, missing only by a hair when Finn's quick reflexes set in and he skipped to the side and out of the way.

Finn looked back at Liam and blew him a kiss while winking, joking at Liam's failure to successfully trip him. "Missed me." He looked at Dani. "May I sit?" He gestured at the empty space on the log next to her. She nodded a welcome for him to join them and he gladly accepted. "Thank you."

"So, Finn, see anything interesting while you were out scouting with Hiromi?" Liam inquired while chewing on a piece of dried meat. The fire crackled and squealed as Finn threw a twig onto it from where he was sitting.

"No, just a bunch of trees and rocks. We were able to see the second post. If we keep at the pace, we're going we should reach it by afternoon tomorrow, maybe sooner." Finn threw a few more twigs in the fire, it was something to do as the night carried on.

Liam reached up with a piece of meat in his hand and offered it to Finn. He leaned across Dani and humbly accepted it. "Thank you." He took a bite of the spicy but savory meat, the flavors melting in his mouth. His nose began to run from the sudden relief of sinus pressure caused by the strong spices. "Whoa! This is strong. Where did you get it from?"

Liam laughed a hardy laugh at Finn's inability to handle such strong spices.

"He made it." Dani clarified as she held out her hand for a piece herself.

"My brothers and I go hunting every year and some of the meat from the deer we kill goes to making jerky. I made this with the spiciest peppers I could find. Really clears up the sinuses, doesn't it?" Liam breathed in deep, his chest doubling in size and his head rising.

Finn wiped away a tear while stifling a cough. "It does have quite a kick, but it's addicting, to say the least. So, then it's deer jerky." He clarified.

"Sure is." Liam handed him another piece. Finn once again accepted, pleased that Liam and Dani were feeling so accepting of him. That they were willing to allow him into their circle of trust and friendship.

The three conversed while the other cadets had already turned in for the night. Colonel Harper said goodnight to Lieutenant Reeves. She clicked her heels together and saluted with her fist hovering over her heart and to her shoulder. And then turned, heading into her tent. He waited until she was gone and then walked over to the three remaining cadets.

As he approached them, Liam and Finn gave out a quiet howl indicating a romantic gesture between that of Lieutenant Reeves and Colonel Harper. When he got near, he raised his arms to motion he wanted their silence, but he still let out a humorous snicker followed by an eye roll. "Okay guys, that's enough. Nothing is going on between myself and the lieutenant. She and I are commanding officer and subordinate."

"Doesn't mean you don't want there to be....". Liam was poking fun at him.

"Shush Evens. We just have history, that's all." Harper had kneeled down so he would be eye level with his cadets.

"What kind of history?" Finn asked more as a curiosity than anything else. He like to know better who he was blindly following and taking commands from on this little outing. But he was also feeling sheepish alongside Liam. He was just curious.

"A sexual one." Liam spoke up before Harper could answer.

"Damnit Evens. Stop being so immature. It has always been professional between the two of us." Harper rubbed his brow and sighed.

"I'm seventeen. Turning any situation into a sexual one is my main talent right now. When the opportunity presents itself, I pounce. And you're just such an easy target Colonel." Liam shrugged as if his words were a matter of fact.

Harper inhaled a deep breath and let it out slowly. "Don't you think the three of you should be getting some sleep. It's getting late."

"Yes, let's call it a night boys." Dani stretched and then lifted up from the log she had been resting on. "Sir, would you like me to take the first watch again?"

"No Mitchells, I think that honor has been won by Mr. Evens here. You go on to bed and get some rest. Evens! First watch." He had stood up and was now pointing at Liam with serious intent.

"Yes sir!" Liam rocketed to a standing position and saluted. He spoke half joking but also serious. When it came down to his duty as a solider to protect, he took it very seriously. Finn said his goodnights, crossing the camp and then climbed into his tent. Dani waited a moment more holding her hands together and looking down not wanting to offend anyone.

"Oh well, I guess I'll be heading to bed myself. Goodnight Mitchells, Evens." The colonel gave Liam one last look indicating him to stay out of trouble.

"You'll be okay to take the first shift?" Dani was quiet, tired from the long day of walking.

"Oh yeah. I found a piece of wood earlier and it's perfect for carving. So, I'll just work on that." It was just like him to brush off any situation. Dani thought he would take the weight of the world on if it was for her.

"Okay, well then I'm going to go to bed. Goodnight Liam." She placed her hand on his shoulder and standing on her tiptoes reached up and placed a loving kiss on his cheek. She brushed past him and headed towards her tent.

She was at her tent when Liam responded with a goodnight himself. She turned back towards him and smiled before disappearing into her tent, relief washing over her as she laid down. The hardship of the day started sinking away as she slipped into a deep slumber.

Chapter 8

TOGETHER FOREVER

A bird chirped in the near distance, its beautiful melody welcoming the new day. Its lovely morning solo turned into a duet and soon Dani could hear a plethora of bird calls joining in, creating an orchestra of vibrant and colorful sounds. The forest had started to awake and come alive. Plants and leaves opened, spreading their petals to absorb the morning light and dew that had settled on the ground from the cool temperatures of the night. It seemed the troubles of the world could not reach this seclusion of nature.

Dani laid in her tent listening to the beautiful music of the forest, wishing she could lay there all day absorbing the peace from it. She knew she needed to get up, if she didn't someone was sure to attempt a rude awaking. In fact, she was a bit surprised no one had yet to come and see if she was even awake, but she was okay with that.

"Dans, you up?" Dani heard a voice. She had thought too soon. It was as if the universe dug into her mind and pulled her thoughts out to where karma could snatch hold of them and enact the very thing she didn't want to happen.

'Damn.' She thought to herself. "yeah I'm up Sarah, I'll be out in a minute." Dani rolled herself out of her laying position and rubbed the sleep from her eyes. 'Time to spend another day walking.' She rolled her eyes to herself. She wasn't sure why she was complaining, after all, isn't this what she wanted. Didn't she want to be a scout? This is what scouts do, this is what she would be doing.

She shoved her right foot into her boot and laced it up, then repeated the process with her left. She threw on her jacket and zipped it, then

141

clasped the ends of the sleeves. She breathed out reading herself for the day, then unzipped her tent, letting in the glow of light from the sun creasing the landscape.

When she emerged from the tent, she could see everyone was already up and breaking down camp, all except Hiromi and her hounds that is. Liam came over and handed her a plate off eggs and toast.

"Morning sunshine, didn't think you'd ever join us." His hands rested on his hips as he took in the morning air. The layer of dew was starting to be chased away as the morning was in full bloom.

"Why did you let me sleep so long?" Dani was engulfing the eggs trying to hurry so she could help with camp. She spoke in between bites of food.

"You needed it, the colonel said it sounded like you were having a rough time last night. Apparently, you were moving around a lot. Bad dreams again?" He looked towards her, a bit more seriously.

"No!" She said a bit harsher and louder than intended. She looked down at her half-eaten plate of food feeling bad about snapping at her friend. "Okay, maybe."

"Fires again?"

She slowly let go of a long breath. "Yes." She slumped to the ground where the log she had sat on the night before rested, wet from the morning dew. She handed the plate up to Liam expecting him to fulfill his duty as a human garbage disposal.

He took the plate as he leaned down in front of her, resting on the ball of his feet. He sat the plate down next to her. She looked over at it and then back to the ground. "How embarrassing that the colonel heard my sleep commotion." She leaned back.

"I don't think he cares, Dans. He's known you since you were a little kid. I think you're good. Now come on." He grabbed the plate of food and set it in her lap. "Eat up, you need your strength." He patted her knee and then lifted to a standing position but not before he placed a gentle kiss on his best friend's forehead. He walked away leaving Dani to her thoughts.

Dani finished her breakfast and cleaned up. She quickly disassembled her tent and packed it away, clicking it onto the bottom of her pack. While she finished packing her gear, she noticed Hiromi entering the campsite from the eastern woods, followed by her hounds. 'She must have been out scouting again.' She thought to herself. She watched as Hiromi conversed with Colonel Harper and Lieutenant Reeves. At one point she pointed towards the east, her hounds sitting patiently by her sides never wavering.

Dani sat on her knees leaning over her pack. She was tying it up tight as she continued to deduce the conversation taking place only a couple of yards away from her. Shaking her head, she gave up, unable to hear.

Suddenly a shadow was looming over Dani, blocking out the rays of the morning sun. "Hey, need any help?" Finn stood behind Dani; his pack already hoisted onto his back. She looked up at him shading her eyes in an attempt to block out the sun.

"Oh, no, thank you. I'm okay. Just finished up actually." As she started to stand, he steadied her by holding onto her elbow. He knew she wasn't weak, quite the opposite, but he felt he was growing a friendship with her and Liam and wanted to continue. Once she was standing firmly on her two feet he let go of her elbow. She gave him a small smile, unsure of how to perceive his kindness. "Thank you."

"Yeah, of course. Just want to help." He turned to walk away but stopped before doing so. "Hey, do you, um, get the feeling this mission is about something more?"

"What do you mean." She looked at him confused, her head tilted, and eyebrows frowned.

"Like we're doing more than just recon?" He scratched the back of his head and looked around to make sure no one was listening in. He didn't want to sound paranoid, but perhaps he was. "I don't know but when Hiromi and I were out scouting it seemed as if she was holding something back. Like she wanted to say something but couldn't bring herself to do so."

"Did you ask her?" Dani inquired. She didn't think there was really anything going on, but ever since they stopped for the night at the first post Liam had seemed off. He didn't joke around as much, and he seemed to smile a little less than usual. He also seemed to be a bit clingier and loving towards her as if he was shielding her from something. She knew this feeling, she felt it often from her father when he was keeping a secret from her, trying to spare her feelings or her heart from pain.

"What would I have said? Hey, Hiromi! Are you hiding something from me?" He spoke sarcastically.

"No, you're right. I don't think that would be the best way to approach a sensitive subject." She was remembering the tone of voices from General Alpine and then the undertone from the general at the wall. It was as if there was hidden meaning in their words when they gave a command.

"Approach what?" Liam stalked over to the two, cutting the conversation short. Finn looked down at his feet and kicked some leaves up, acting distracted. He opened the door to letting Dani explain to Liam what they were discussing if she would say anything at all.

"Oh, we were just talking about how we are going to approach the facilities when we get close to recon." Finn looked up sharply at Dani. 'She lied!' He thought. She lied for him to her best friend. 'Which only means she does think there is more to this as well and Liam might know more then he's letting on.' He concluded.

"Well, I'm going to go see if I'm needed elsewhere." Finn quickly walked away before Liam could stop him. He looked back to see them staring. Liam watched him as he walked away curious by his demeanor. When Finn was out of earshot Liam looked to Dani with a questioning look in his eye.

"Dani, what was that really about?" His arms were crossed looking down at Dani. It wasn't hard to do when she was a full foot shorter than him.

"It was really nothing. He was just telling me about scouting with Hiromi yesterday." Technically she wasn't lying, but she still felt weird about the conversation.

His eyes bored into her a bit longer. Her eyes were unmoving from his. She swallowed unsure of the silence that was turning awkward. "Okay, if you say so." He shrugged. He saw her pack still sitting on the ground. The colonel was calling for them to line up so they could start heading towards the second post. "Here let me help you with that." He grabbed her pack and helped her place it on her shoulders.

As soon as he let go of the handle, the bag slid down weighing heavily on Dani. Her shoulders immediately felt as if the ground was pulling her down by a few inches.

"Thank you." She adjusted the pack aligning it so that it was sitting properly on her shoulders and back. The two walked over to the rest of the squad and the group started to move out.

*****

It was early afternoon when the squad finally reached the second post. It was smaller than the first one and instead of being a grand five story white building with towering round columns, this one was a smaller two-story log cabin blending into the woods that surrounded it. The only indication it was there or even inhabited was the stream of smoke from the chimney and the smell of wood being burned.

"Oh good! A fire." Sarah bumped up behind Dani and Dani regarded her presence. Sarah rested her arm on Dani's shoulder and looked to her. "It's been a long few days. Are you sure this is still what you want to do every day?"

145

A breeze of cold wind blew past them blowing loose strands of dark hair into Dani's face. Using her hand, she delicately brushed them behind her ear. "Yeah, mom did it. I can do it too."

Sarah smiled and gave her friend a light squeeze. "Well, I can't have my best friend doing it alone. Guess I'll just have to keep you out of trouble by joining you."

Dani paused for a moment and looked at Sarah with shock on her face. She never, in her wildest dreams imagined Sarah would accompany her out in the woods. "Oh, Sarah! Really! But what about administrations? What happened to sitting in a padded chair behind a desk in a cozy office?"

Sarah waved her hand pushing aside the remarks. "Who needs a cozy office when this could be my office. Freedom to speak how I want, be who I want. No upper government constantly looking over my shoulder. Yeah, I could get used to it." They stared for a few moments longer. "Aiden said he would too. We're going to try and stay together, all of us. We're family after all."

Dani hugged her friend unable to speak. A single tear breaking free and running down her cold, soft face. Silently she said one thing, not even sure if Sarah heard. "Thank you." She sniffled.

Dani heard the footsteps of an unknown person coming up behind them. Suddenly there was the weight of an extra arm around her shoulder. Sarah, too, had an extra arm around her as well. A moment later Aiden was popping his head in between Dani and Sarah. "Wow! Look at that, someone already has a fire going!"

Sarah laughed while Dani gave a dramatic eye roll. Lieutenant Reeves hollered out for everyone's attention. "Cadets! We're moving out." The three friends looked in her direction and then moved on her command. The motivation of a warm fire waiting for them was enough to get them moving once more. They were wet from the constant mist and fog that loomed over the mountains, intertwining and weaving threads of white throughout the thicket of trees.

The weather was a good indication that a possible snowstorm was on its way. Dani was jubilant at the notion that the location they were going to be conducting recon was in a lower elevation and they would be out of the threat of possible snow. Usually, Dani loved the snow, but while they were out here, unable to escape the cold, it wasn't ideal.

The squad had made its way towards the cabin. Up close, Dani could see the log cabin had a wide-open window that stretched halfway across the house and reached to the roof that came to a point. She could see chairs and couches inside the window. 'Must be a sitting area.' She deduced. The cabin may not have had but two stories, but it was long giving it plenty of floor space. A deck wrapped around the entirety of the building on the ground level.

A man stood out front, a rifle was slung over his shoulder. He was wearing the military uniform with the hat pulled down covering his eyes or perhaps shielding them from the wind. As soon as the squad had lined up, the man called them to attention. The colonel and lieutenant joined him on the deck where they discussed matters before addressing the squad once more.

"I am Major Hayden Thatcher. I am the leading command at post two. As you may have realized we are a bit smaller compared to that of post one. This post serves as a telecommunications site. We relay messages and information back to central command. Therefore, there are not many troops here. We do not have the luxury of a cleaning staff or a kitchen staff. What we do have is a roof and a hot fire. You're welcome to those things. Rooms are upstairs, you're adults. Figure it out." He paused looking to Colonel Harper. Harper nodded to him and he and the lieutenant turned to go inside.

"Dismissed." The major spoke.

He took his leave out of the cold into the cabin. Hiromi was the first to move heading towards the deck. She paused and looked back when she realized nobody had followed.

"It's warmer inside. Unless all of you prefer to stay frozen icicles." She continued up the set of stairs, Willow and Luka following their master. This wasn't the first time she had been to this post and she knew Major Thatcher well from the last two years of running missions, even her hounds had become excited when they came closer to the cabin and picked up on the major's scent.

Sarah followed Hiromi towards the cabin attempting to shake the cold off. "Well, I'm not going to stay out here and freeze. Come on guys." She grabbed Dani's hand and pulled her along. After that, the rest immediately followed.

The night was quiet. The threatening snowstorm that had been following the squad finally caught up and broke loose a light flurry of white, fluffy snow. Dani sat by the towering window in the living space, her head and arms resting on the back of the leather chair. She watched as the ground started to disappear with a layer of ice covering it. Brief pauses in the clouds revealed the moon, it reflected off the snow casting the scene in a blue haze while beyond the clearing of the cabin the trees were dark, hiding away, hiding the secrets they may have held.

The fire crackled and popped as it blazed in the wide-open fireplace. Dani heard the burning wood fall onto one another as it charred and turned to ash unable to support its formal structure. Almost everyone had turned in for the night, all but Liam and Aiden who were enjoying a game of chess at a small table on the other side of the room. And of course, Dani herself was awake. She was tired and she knew if she laid her head down on a pillow, she would fall asleep, but the weight of another possible nightmare was on her mind.

She heard a clock chime from another room indicating it was half past nine. The light in the room was starting to fade from the dying fire. Dani's eyelids had grown heavy and she gave in to the sweet song of sleep. She stood up and stretched, and without a single word to anyone, she shuffled up the stairs and headed into a room where a sleeping Sarah laid. She didn't even flinch from the door creaking when Dani opened it. She crawled into the empty bed and fell asleep before her head even snuggled into the pillow.

*****

The sun was starting to creep in through the sheer curtains that laid over the bedroom window. Frost lined the outside of the window, illuminating the snow flurry that transpired the night before. Little droplets of water were starting to trickle down, the sun already starting to melt the unimpressive amount of snow that had fallen.

Dani lay awake in her bed refusing to move. The aches and pains had settled in her muscles and joints causing her body to become stiff and rigid. When she commanded her body to move it resisted, unwilling to make the effort needed to become flexible and malleable once more. After a few moments of struggling, Dani gave up the fight and continued to lay in the soft bed that had embraced her and wrapped her in a cocoon of warmth and comfort.

She turned away from the window trying to escape the light that was attempting to command her into getting up, but as soon as she turned over, she was smacked in the face with a pillow. The pillow landed with a soft thud on the ground revealing a giddy Sarah.

She was laughing. Unable to contain herself with the well-placed throw. She was propped up on her elbow, her head resting on her hand. Her hair was a tangled, mess of blond that cascaded around her, water falling to her mattress. The light wrapped her in a glow accenting her natural curves.

"And what, may I ask, was that for?" Dani leaned over the bedside, her hand grasping the side, steadying her and supporting her as she successfully attempted to grab the pillow. She pulled the pillow up in a hurry almost losing her balance and falling to the floor herself. She took the pillow hostage, using it to prop herself up.

149

Sarah continued to laugh, now void of any type of pillow. "You were snoring last night. It was so loud! I'm wondering if anyone else in the cabin got any sleep."

Dani was shocked by her comment. Her mouth dropped and she grabbed the pillow from underneath her and threw it back at Sarah. As it smacked into Sarah, she laughed harder.

"For someone who is usually so quiet, you were so loud!" Sarah continued to tease Dani lovingly, as an older sister would.

"I blame these damn pillows." Dani grabbed her other pillow and smushed it in between her hands. "They just do not have enough support." She threw that one at Sarah as well. Before she could look over to see if the pillow found its mark, she was over-casted by a shadow and then a large mass of weight was on top of her.

"Sarah! You're so heavy!" Dani yelled, jokingly as she joined in the laughter.

"Now that's not very nice!" Sarah was a bundle of joy, full of laughter and playfulness that morning. She snuggled beside Dani, joining her friend in looking at the ceiling. "Did you see? It snowed!" She spoke dreamily, "I love the snow."

"Is that why you're so happy this morning?" Dani acquired.

"No, I'm happy because... I get to wake up to your smiling face." She turned so she was facing her best friend.

They were within close proximity of each other, so close in fact, that they could smell each other's morning breath. The bed, after all, was only the size of a twin, making it big enough for one. Dani looked back at her. Her look was stern and serious, an indication that she never woke up smiling. Sarah fell under the spell of another fit of laughter. "Okay, okay, come on. Let's get up. I'm hungry and I'm sure the lieutenant will be pushing for us to get going. That is, if she can get the colonel going as well." They both burst into another fit of laughter.

Dani and Sarah pulled themselves out of the bed and proceeded to get dressed. With no kitchen staff, they would have to cook their own breakfast and then clean up after themselves before they started on the trail once more. Dani imagined they would not have a lot of time for a hearty breakfast.

By the time the two girls had made their way downstairs, everyone was already up and eating. Aiden was in the kitchen flipping pancakes and stirring eggs, while Liam sat at the table reading the paper. Finn was next to him enjoying a hot cup of coffee.

"Morning!" Sarah yelled out, grabbing everyone's attention. She walked up to Aiden in the open kitchen to assist him in cooking. He snuck a small peck onto her cheek. She giggled and grabbed a spatula to flip pancakes.

Dani joined Liam and Finn at the table, sitting across from them. Neither one of them seemed to notice the affections of Aiden towards Sarah. Dani looked around; besides the colonel and lieutenant, Hiromi was nowhere to be seen.

"Where's Hiromi and the hounds? Don't tell me she's already out scouting." Dani acquired.

"No, she's just out walking willow and Luka, dogs got to poop after all. Can't have them doing their business in the cabin." Liam stated without looking up from his paper. Dani thought he was a little too obsessed with the daily paper. He knew the news in it was nothing but rubbish. Most, if not all, of it could not be taken to heart.

Before a conversation could be started, the front door swung open. In entered two wet pawed dogs followed by a very cold Hiromi. The hounds shook off the extra water from their coats before heading towards the fire to lay down and soak up the heat. Hiromi joined her fellow cadets at the dining table. Aiden and Sarah served everyone breakfast, saving some for Colonel Harper and lieutenant Reeves.

The group of cadets enjoyed the hot food and the company of one another. Everyone smiled, joked, and laughed all together for the first time. It was in this moment a squad was finally formed not only by command but by spirit and heart.

"Well isn't this a nice sight." Colonel Harper wandered up to the heavy wooden table. "I'm happy to see everyone enjoying breakfast together."

"What can I say sir, it's hard not to be happy when pancakes are involved." Aiden joked, his arm resting on the back of Sarah's chair. Her leg sat bent up allowing it to rest in the seat of her chair, her knee resting against the table as she was slightly leaned towards Aiden's direction.

"Oh, do they now, well maybe I'll serve some to the lieutenant." He snickered, a grin stretching across his face.

"Serve me what, sir?" Lieutenant Reeves came up behind him as the cadets remained expressionless at her approach.

Colonel Harper stifled a scream, but instead, let out a squeal. His body convulsed from the sudden shock of Lieutenant Reeves standing next to him. "Lieutenant! What have I said about sneaking up on me like that, I swear I'm going to put a bell on you?"

"My apologies, sir." She adjusted her stance. "Oh, look sir, there are pancakes." She was a blank page as she compiled two plates of breakfast food together. She handed one to her commanding officer and then took a seat at the far end of the table saving the seat at the head of the table for the colonel.

He gladly took a seat and the two enjoyed their breakfast conversing with not only each other but also with the cadets, their cadets.

*****

By the time the squad had started their trek, making their way further east towards the known rebel compound. The snow from the night before had melted away causing the ground to turn to mud and slush. Come nightfall the ground will have hardened once more and the mud will freeze, until then the cadets were cursed with trudging over the wet ground, their boots occasionally getting stuck. Their legs tired faster with the constant fighting.

The day passed the same as the past couple of days had. Hiromi and Finn would run ahead with the hounds to sniff out any possible signs of trouble. When they felt the trail was safe, they would radio back indicating so and the squad would continue onward. When the afternoon had started to stretch, and the sky had started to turn golden with strips of bright pinks, oranges, and purples, the squad would stop and make camp.

The fire was kept small, enough to make food and keep the chill at bay. But the squad was getting close to the rebel's camp and didn't want to give away their presence. To the cadets, any false moves, loud noises, or bright lights could alert the enemy of their position and bring disaster upon themselves.

"Okay, listen up. Tomorrow we will be reaching the rebel's camp. Where we are now is considered enemy territory, so be suspicious of every sound and movement as you patrol tonight and as we continue onward tomorrow. I cannot express this enough, be careful of your sound levels. We need to be vigilant and cautious. I want two patrolling at a time tonight. Now try and get some sleep. The lieutenant and I will take the first watch."

Aiden and Liam looked at each other. A silent understanding of the false words the colonel had spoken passed between them. They were sure the rebels would not attack. After all, they were supposed to meet with a rebel leader. As of tomorrow, all the secrets and lies would be revealed. As of tomorrow, Dani might have her heartbroken at Liam's well-kept betrayal or might be overjoyed at having her family returned to her. Either way,

Liam had a feeling that Dani would not be returning to Helenia anytime soon.

*****

"Hey Mitchells." Lieutenant Reeves shook Dani awake. Two hours had passed since she fell asleep and it was now her turn to take a two-hour shift guarding the camp. She slipped on her boots and ducked out of her tent. She was joined by Hiromi and, naturally, her hounds.

Colonel Harper and Lieutenant Reeves said their goodnights and sleepily crawled into their own tents. It was late at night or early in the morning depending on the view, the moon was high in the sky illuminating the camp. Dani was happy for that since the use of a big fire was prohibited being so close to enemy territory.

"Good morning." Hiromi had walked over to Dani, her hounds following their masters' every move.

Dani took a sip of water from her canteen. "Morning. I'm not sure it's good though." She was making small talk. It was a start. The two had never shared a conversation together, just the two of them.

"That is true. I, personally, would much rather be asleep." She turned to face her hounds and clicked. "Willow, Luka. Scatter and circle." She commanded, her hand swinging up and pointing. The two dogs immediately went in separate directions and started to circle the camp. Hiromi looked back at Dani, seeing and understand her facial expression. Dani was confused but intrigued. "They're going to circle the camp, sniffing, listening, making sure there is no danger lurking nearby. After a few rounds, they'll come back."

Dani shook her head in understanding, intrigued by the bond the three had, but the dependency they had developed. She was extremely impressed. "Your relationship with them, the bond the three of you have developed, it's quite incredible. I would be lying if I said I wasn't envious

154

of it." Dani shared her thoughts, hoping it would open Hiromi's friendship to her. Hiromi smiled and thanked her.

Dani sat on a log near the fire. Hiromi joined her; she was too tired to have any motivation to continue standing. "The way you can relay your thoughts and emotions to them, and they understand or vise-versa." Dani commented.

"Well, thank you." Hiromi gave Dani a shy smile. "Having them, it's been, well enjoyable. They're more than just my partners, they're my family. I didn't, I mean I don't have parents anymore. The military has been all I've known."

"Oh, I didn't know. My mom died when I was young, along with my younger brother, sister, and older brother, but I still had my father." Dani kicked around some dirt with the toe of her boot. It hurt talking about her family, the wounds still feeling fresh and raw even though it was years ago.

"Yes, your father." Hiromi looked to the sky. The stars bright and collective forming waves of iridescent lights. "He's the reason I'm here. I mean not here," she looked down and pointed towards the ground. "But I mean here in the military. I guess he knew my parents and when they were killed, he sought me out and got me to where I needed to be. And then when I received Willow and Luka, it was your father who brought me along on the missions."

Dani was surprised by the information. "I didn't know that. I knew he was running a few scouting missions here and there, and of course; I knew you were running missions, but I guess I never thought to put the two together." Dani wondered what else her father had been hiding from her.

Hiromi paused for a moment, unsure of why she was telling Dani so much. She never spoke to anyone like this. Maybe because Dani was so much like her father that it was easy to open-up to her. "My father was a dog handler too. Willow and Luka are brother and sister from the same litter. From my father's hound. It seemed...poetic that they would become mine." She looked down, in thought.

155

"And your mother? What did she do?" Dani asked intrigued by Hiromi. So many times, she had watched this girl from afar never knowing a single thing about her, but always wanting too. Now she could learn about the girl that always runs with her dogs.

"Oh, my mother." Hiromi smiled. Dani could see a tear running down her face. "My mother was a florist. It seems silly, right. Something so frivolous and useless as flowers when we are under the constant threat of war, but I suppose in a life that can be so dark, we need a bit of beauty to cut through the darkness and brighten the world even if it's a little. She used to tell me that a flower could change something negative and turn it positive."

Dani sat, letting Hiromi talk. She was delighted to hear her speak. While she spoke, the dogs retired for the night and laid by the fire, cuddled on one another, enjoying each other's heat. Hiromi leaned down to pet them, scratching each of them behind an ear.

"She was right. A flower always brought a smile. I remember she would come home and smell of roses and sweetness. I don't think I'll ever forget that smell." Hiromi was smiling even though many tears now streamed down her face.

Dani was unsure how to respond to her, how to comfort her. Hiromi wiped her eyes. "I'm sorry, I must be making you feel awkward."

Dani straightened up. She moved her hands in front of her waving Hiromi's notion off. "No, not at all. Honestly, it's refreshing. To be honest I've seen you and wanted to know more about you." She paused and then smacked her forehead. "Now who's making who feel awkward."

Hiromi started to laugh and after a moment Dani joined her. The two continued to talk for the remainder of their shift, sharing stories of their past.

"Who's next?" Hiromi asked looking around at the tents.

"Well, Liam was next to me. And I think Finn was next to him."

"You wake Liam, I'll wake Finn?" Hiromi asked pointing to Finn's tent.

"Sounds good to me." Dani pushed off the log and headed towards Liam's tent to wake him. She unzipped the front and started to shake him. He swatted her away as if she were a fly that was bugging him. "Liam come on!" She gently slapped his cheek. He mumbled something and Dani leaned back frustrated. "Liam!" She grabbed his shoe and hit him in his arm. He jolted awake sitting up fast into a sitting position.

He looked at Dani, the flashlight was dim, but he could clearly see it was her. "What the hell Dans!"

"You are impossible to wake up!" She sat back on her knees. Her hands resting on her thighs.

"What are you taking about. I'm awake ain't I?" He rubbed his head; his hair was an unruly mess and then he yawned.

"But it took forever to do it along with violence, it took violence!" she repeated. "Now get dressed, put pants on! It's your turn to take guard." She lifted up out of his tent leaving him to dress. A few moments passed and he crawled out of his tent and stretched. He grabbed his best friend and pulled her into a hug.

"Okay, go to sleep grumpy butt." He was patting her head causing her hair to be misplaced and tangled. She pushed out from underneath his arm and attempted to straighten her hair back into place.

"Good night everyone." She looked around at Liam, Finn, and Hiromi. That was it for Dani, the pillow was calling out to her and she answered its sweet call.

Chapter 9

SHOTS FIRED

The leaves rattled as the squad hiked through the trees. It caused everyone to stay on guard and anxious expecting something or someone to jump out. The trail they had been following had thinned from lack of movement on it. It made travel slow as the cadets took their time, making sure to be careful not to trip on lose branches or debris.

Hiromi, Willow, and Luka had already gone ahead, scouting. Dani thought it was odd that no one was accompanying her like they had been doing, especially as they closed in on the enemy. Was Finn okay, Dani wondered, or was Finn right in assuming Hiromi and the leadership were hiding something.

"What's wrong?" Sarah studied Dani's face. She could see the look of concern displayed in her friend's eyes.

"Doesn't it seem odd that Hiromi went scouting by herself? I know she has Willow and Luka, but still, someone else should have gone with her. Especially now that we're in enemy terrain." Now Dani felt like she was the one being paranoid.

"Yeah, I suppose your right. It does go against what we've been taught, but maybe it would be easier for her to sneak around, ya know. One person can be a lot quieter than two, right." Sarah didn't seem that concerned with the arrangement and Dani thought she might have just been being over analyzing the situation, but she had a feeling that something was off.

"Yeah, maybe your right. Maybe I'm just overthinking it." The two walked in silence next to one another listening and keeping a watchful eye on their surroundings.

The mountains had started to level out, turning into rolling hills. The thick trees that had been hiding the rest of the world away had started to thin, letting more light peek through. The valley where the rebels were said to gather would be just beyond the hills towards the bottom, it wouldn't take long now for them to reach their destination. The colonel motioned for them to stop and take a break. Hiromi had reconvened with them and was privately discussing plans and movement options with Colonel Harper and the lieutenant before she was off once more.

Dani was leaning down sipping water from a canteen by her bag as she watched the scene play out in front of her. The feeling in her stomach was steadily growing stronger that something was amiss. Finn was right, this was about something more, Dani was sure of it.

"Dani! Earth to Dani!" Liam was snapping at Dani trying to get her attention. Realizing her name was being called, she shook her head clearing the daze from her eyes. She looked up to see Liam leaning down, his hands supporting him on his knees. "Aiden said we're about to head out. Are you about ready?"

"Oh yeah, I'm ready." She held her hand up for Liam to take and help pull her up to her feet. "Hey, do you know what Hiromi said to the colonel?"

Liam looked back at the colonel and Lieutenant Reeves speaking amongst themselves before looking back at his childhood best friend. "No clue. I was talking to Finn and Aiden." He pointed back to the two other males.

The two joined their squad, taking to their points ready to head out to their destination once more. The colonel motioned for the squad to move out, staying quiet as they moved. Less than a mile now till they reached the town that would mark the first point of entry to the rebel's forces.

It wasn't long before Dani heard something nearby. She immediately stopped and listened. Sarah, who had been walking towards her right, motioned up for the rest to stop and take point. Everyone listening to a sound that wasn't an animal or the natural sound of the thinned woods surrounding them. Dani looked around trying to pinpoint where the sound was coming from. She looked towards Sarah, her brows serious, and signaled that the mechanical sound of a gun being cocked was to her left high in the trees.

They readied their weapons expecting an ambush towards the front when Finn and Liam shouted out that the attack was coming from behind. Four rebels cloaked in masks came down from the trees knocking into Finn and Liam. Finn hit the ground causing him to be stunned momentarily. He quickly recovered and immediately jumped in to assist Liam.

Liam had been holding his own against the four assailants, but being four against one, he was starting to succumb to the poor odds. Dani and Sarah were the first to rush to his and Finn's side to assist, being the closest to them. But it seemed as they fought the four rebels off, more were appearing to fight. Their numbers had indeed doubled within seconds from four to now eight.

Sarah had spent much of her time in classes at the academy that involved medicine and first aid, for this reason, she acted as the squad's medic. She was leaned over Finn helping him into a sitting position as Dani and Liam fought. If she needed too, she could easily drag him away from the danger and then return to fighting herself.

"Looks like just a nasty bump, you'll be fine." She had quickly examined Finn's head making sure that the smack to his head that he had received from someone forcing him to the ground via body weight was not more serious or bleeding. She jumped to her feet, Finn followed suit and joined their squad members in hand to hand combat.

Within a few short moments that stretched on for what felt like hours, the entire squad was involved in defending off their attackers. As Dani fended off one attacker another would just replace them. She had her dual short blades out and was busy slashing over and over until she heard a gunshot go off. She jumped suddenly, startled by the loud sound. She was unsure where it came from or the destruction it had left in its wake. Her heart was sinking as she looked to each of her squad members, wondering where the bullet found its target.

Suddenly Dani felt a warmth emerge from her stomach and as fast as she felt the warmth it was gone, replaced by cold. She fell to her knees gripping her side, she wasn't sure why she felt pain there. Everything was moving so slow, as if time was coming to a stop. Running towards her, she could see Liam. He was calling her name not realizing the danger he was in. Someone was behind him, running at him holding a weapon above the attacker's head. Dani tried to warn him, but no sound would come out. Before he reached her, his arm already outstretched to grab her, he was knocked sideways in the head. He immediately collapsed from the attack. He had been knocked unconscious, but he was alive.

Finally, she was mute no more, but instead, let out a scream calling for Liam. She felt so weak; her energy zapped from her. With what little strength she had left, she shakily pulled out her gun and aimed. She fired a shot and hit the attacker in the shoulder before everything went dark and she collapsed to the frozen ground, but not before she heard someone shout her name.

*****

Harper heard the gunshot echoing through the mountains but couldn't worry about it at that moment. He was currently engaged with a rebel. Four of them had attacked from the rear and while everyone was distracted trying to help Liam and Finn, four more dropped down from the trees overhead and ambushed the rest of the squad. Hiromi and the hounds were probably still ahead of them most likely meeting with a young rebel leader named Zachary Ryder. The plan was to meet with Ryder and then move together to the compound where they would meet Dani's older brother, Grayson. Then the real intent of the mission would be revealed.

'What happened? Was there a betrayal amongst the ranks?' Harper thought. He took down his assailant and came back to back with someone. When he jumped back to put distance between him and the person to be able to fend himself against the person, he noticed it was his lieutenant staring back at him, her guns raised and pointed directly at him.

She started to lower her weapons but not before taking a shot at someone running towards her and her colonel. "Sir."

"Lieutenant. Have you seen cadet Katsuki?" He asked in a panic.

"No sir. What happened? We weren't supposed to be ambushed!" She was fiercely calm. This wasn't the first time she had seen the sight of battle and her experience gave her the ability to think things through and react properly when faced with a fight.

"I don't know. I don't think these are Grayson's men." He took a shot at a person running towards him catching the person in the leg. The assailant fell to the ground holding his knee.

"We need to end this quickly and get out of here." As he said it, he noticed two of his cadets laying on the ground. One was Liam laying face up, his breathing steady. Next to him laid someone with dark hair. He could see a red stain on her tunic, his heart immediately stopped from the sight.

"Mitchells!" He started to race over to her. Before he could reach her though one of the masked assailants swooped in, throwing Sarah off the girl laying still on the ground, and grabbed her, stealing her away. "Dani!" He yelled effortlessly understanding that his yelling would not get her back. When he looked around the rest of the assailants had disappeared. Finn, Aiden, and Lieutenant Reeves had fended the rest of them off. Proving to be a more difficult task than originally thought, they had retreated leaving the squad to their own.

Harper looked down to see Sarah slumped on the ground. Her hands were covered in Dani's blood, tears streaming down her face. Her breathing was sporadic, frantic from the sight of her best friend being shot. The colonel grabbed her shoulders and shook her, retrieving her attention.

"What happened?" He yelled at her.

Through inhales of breathes, she spoke. "I don't know. The gunshot. She was just, and then she." She couldn't finish, too worked up to continue talking. Aiden rushed over to Sarah's side, skidding on his knees to a stop in front of her and started to try and calm her down. He was grasping both her shoulders attempting to soothe her while trying to maintain his composure. He was furious, feeling betrayed, mostly by his commanding officer. He was angry that he had been useless in saving Dani, and he was distraught that he could not even begin to heal Sarah's broken heart.

Harper stood up and walked towards the lieutenant when Hiromi returned. She was being followed by a man with silver hair. They paused taking in the scene in front of them, confused by what they saw. Harper looked up and saw the two of them standing there, he waved them over.

"Harper." The man shook his hand. "What happened?"

"We were ambushed. Dani's been shot." He was surprisingly calm. His rage was building inside, but he knew he needed to stay composed for his squad's sake.

The man looked around a bit more on edge, understanding the trouble they were in. He didn't see a girl laying on the ground though, only a man. "Where is she?" He was afraid to ask.

"They took her. So, this wasn't you're doing?" The colonel asked.

"No, it wasn't. We would never betray your trust. We need to get her back, if Grayson..." Ryder started to explain.

"We will get her back. Katsuki! Get on Mitchells's scent. Ryder go back to the compound. Let Grayson know what happened. We will start following the trail, send reinforcements to meet with us."

"Will do. I will alert the patrol of the dire situation. If any new information is relayed to me from my men that are already out on patrol, I will be sure to reach out." The man with silver hair turned to leave with haste, pulling out his radio to call in the situation. Even though he had a good idea of what went wrong and who was behind them, he just hoped that Dani was alive and well.

Chapter 10

NEWCOMERS

Ryder slammed open the door and stormed into the room, he was furious ready to kill someone. He took two large strides over to the man he presumed shot the girl currently laying still in the bed. He grabbed the collar of his shirt to better hold him in place as he took a swing at him. His fist landed in the guy's face.

The man fell back a few steps before regaining his balance, his hand braced on the counter behind him. "What the hell was that for!" The man rubbed his jaw, wiping away blood in the process. A bruise was already starting to appear where Ryder's fist had made contact.

Ryder wanted to hit him again but knew it was for the best if he didn't. Instead, he started to yell. "What the hell happened out there! I told you we needed her alive! You almost killed her. You were completely out of line out there!" He pointed outwardly indicating the woods. "You got lucky! If she had died it would be your head."

Ryder had unintentionally moved closer to the man as he yelled. The guy pushed away from Ryder. "If I wanted to kill her, she would, in fact, be dead. She's not. So clearly, I did my job. Next time have your men do a better job capturing her and I won't have to step in and intervene." His voice was calm and easy. It was aggravating how composed he was.

"We weren't going to capture anyone! The plan was to meet with the squad and bring them back here! Not ambush them." Ryder was furious.

"Oh, well I guess I missed that memo or perhaps misunderstood in general, I thought when you said to bring them back here, I thought it wasn't on such…friendly terms." The man air quoted. "Oh well." He pushed past Ryder and walked out of the door. Ryder huffed, rubbing his head.

"Let him go. I will deal with him later." Someone said.

"I'm so sorry about this Grayson." Ryder looked at a man in his early twenties sitting at the bedside of the young woman. Grayson pushed up from the chair and leaned down to kiss the young women's forehead.

When he leaned back up it was to look at Zachary Ryder. "She's alive, that's all that matters." He inhaled a deep breath before speaking once more. "I wish I could stay, but unfortunately, I have to head back to Fort Ridge Crest to settle a few matters. Plus, the rest of the squad should be headed that way. I need to meet up with them before things get out of control. You understand."

"Yes sir." Zachary wasn't much younger than Grayson at twenty, but the four years Grayson had on him, he had spent growing in ranks among the rebel forces, gaining the title of major, while Ryder was still a captain.

"I'm entrusting you to take care of my sister. When she's ready bring her to the compound. I'll be waiting."

"Yes sir." Ryder said. He was exhausted from the last few days. He had been traveling back and forth between the main rebel's compound at Fort Ridge Crest and the rebel town, Amire, where defectors and other castaways had made a home and a living. It was all in preparation for Colonel Harper and his squad to arrive at a fixed point in the forest at the base of the mountains and then along with Ryder, travel to the town, where they would then transfer to the fort.

Grayson looked at his sister one more time and pushed the hair from her eyes. She looked exactly like their mother. He then looked at Zachary and nodded and turned, leaving the room completely. Zachary let out a sigh. This was a more difficult task then he was expecting.

Dani was out of danger, the nurse had expertly removed the stray bullet and stitched her up. She was now at the sink in the corner of the small room washing her hands. "She'll need rest and lots of it. When she does wake don't expect her to do much. She needs to take it easy and heal. If she does, then I expect her to make a full recovery, no problem. In a few days, she can be moved to a new room, if I see she's healing nicely."

"Thank you." Zachary spoke to the nurse. She finished drying her hands and threw away the paper towel. She nodded to the young officer and took her leave from the room leaving him and Dani alone.

"Dani Mitchells." Zachary walked over to her bedside and looked down at the girl laying before him.

She was quite beautiful. Her skin fair against her dark hair. Zachary even noticed small light-colored freckles dotting her cheeks and the bridge of her nose. Even though the color was washed from her face, she looked peaceful. "This isn't how I wanted to meet you. I only hope you don't hate me when you wake. Your injury is my fault. I should have had more control over my men, over him." He looked to the side, his eyes revealing his thoughts. "I'm so sorry. I hope that when this is all over you will be able to forgive me and understand."

Dani stirred, moaning in her sleep. Her closed eyes squinting as if she were in pain. After a short moment, her body and face relaxed and her breathing once again steadied. Zachary took one last long look at her before he left the room allowing her to rest and recover. They would move her to private quarters close to his in a few days when she was able to be moved.

He exited the room with his next plan of action filling his head. He needed to reach out to Colonel Harper and inform him of the situation. That Dani was safe and in the town resting. That he should head towards the compound instead of the town. Ryder would send for a vehicle that would get them to the compound faster instead of having to continue another week's worth of trekking. He knew Hiromi was who he needed to catch up with to relay his message.

Chapter 11

A NIGHT AT A BONFIRE

Dani woke in a strange, dark room. She sat up realizing she had been laying on a soft bed. Her head ached and when she placed her hand to her head, she could feel dry blood. She had been stripped down to her undershirt that had a huge bloodstain on the side along with her other undergarments. Was that her blood? She looked around and spotted her other clothes and belongings sitting on a chair with her boots on the floor.

There were also fresh white clothes sitting on the back of the chair. However, her holster for her weapons was missing along with her weapons themselves. She started to get out of bed when she heard a voice coming from the dark shadowed corner.

"I wouldn't move to fast if I were you, you might reopen your wound." He was watching her, studying her movements. "Don't bother looking for your weapons, they've been," he paused" well disposed of." The mysterious person was still masked in shadow. His voice though, was calming to Dani. As if a lullaby was being sung to her. For some reason, she recognized it as well.

Her head was foggy, the last thing she remembered was being with Liam and Sarah. She had been talking to Sarah, but what about? They were walking on the trail...and then what? Dani rubbed her eyes as if attempting to rub away the cloud looming in her mind. Suddenly the events came rushing back like a flood gate was opened. They were ambushed! Attacked from the trees and the bushes. And then she was wounded. After that everything was blank. Dani couldn't remember much else. "What...what happened to me, where am I?" She asked a little shaky, panic was starting to creep in.

"You took a bullet to the gut, you're lucky to be alive. As for where you are, well I'm simply not at liberty to discuss that with you at this point in time. For the time being, let's just say you're safe."

Dani was taken back by the venom that now laced the stranger's voice. She looked for a way to escape, calculating her odds since she had no idea where she was, nor did she have her weapons. She doubted that she and this stranger were truly alone.

"There's no point in escaping, especially in your condition. Even if you somehow made it outside and back into the woods, you wouldn't make it very far."

'Damnit, he's right.' Dani thought to herself. "How long was I out?" she inquired from the stranger still masked in the shadows.

"Five days. I'm sure there's a rescue party out looking for you, if that gives you any hope or peace of mind, but the likelihood that they will find you is slim to none." Ryder knew there would be no point in trying to convince Dani that she was safe amongst the rebels. He had no way of showing her the truth and making her believe it. He would have to wait until she could come to terms and start trusting him before he could truly explain everything. She was nowhere near ready to travel, her wounds had not even begun to heal, and until she could travel, they would have to stay in the town. Hopefully, in the time spent here, he would be able to ease her into understanding, but that time was not now, so for now he must play the bad guy.

"So much for that hope." Dani murmured under her breath, rolling her eyes. All things considered, she figured she might as well stay put and not cause any trouble. This would also be her best chance to not only recover more, but also increase her chance of survival. After all, she was rescued by whomever these people were, so they obviously were not going to go out of their way to kill her, at least not right now. She could use this time to try and obtain some information.

Dani could see the leg of the stranger move. He jumped to his feet and walked with heavy footsteps over to Dani. She could now see the outline of a man who was noticeably strong. He loomed over her from where she was sitting up in the bed. His arms were crossed. His face was still crowded in darkness but the little bit of light that shone through the closed blinds gleamed off his head exposing silver hair. Dani was surprised by his appearance, 'Silver hair, that's a trait from Venus.' Dani thought to herself.

"Your clothes have been washed along with a few new garments to replace the ruined ones you're wearing. There's a bathroom through the door" He pointed to a door to her left. "Get cleaned up and dressed. I'll return for you in twenty minutes. Think you can stand?"

Dani attempted to stand. She was a bit wobbly at first. She even fell back onto the bed for a moment. She held onto the bed frame for support. After a few moments, her legs had begun to gain strength. Moving slowly, she was able to proceed to the bathroom on her own.

"Good, I'll be back." The stranger turned and walked out of the room shutting the door behind him. She heard a distinctive click indicating that the door was locked. On the other side of the door, Zachary leaned up against it and let out a relieving breath. He had been so nervous when first confronting her and it was hard to put on an act, but until he could prove Dani was in a safe place, that the rebels were not the enemy, he would have to keep her at a distance.

Dani entered the bathroom and looked around. There were two windows but when she looked out, she saw that she was on the second floor of a building. Below her, there were armed guards standing at posts along with what looked like regular people walking around. From the windows, she could see a few other buildings that were just as tall along with a few smaller buildings. This wasn't an old, destroyed city though. It looked more like a small town. Beyond the town, she could see the edge of a forest and there was only one road that led out towards those woods.

At this point, there was no use in attempting an escape, Dani went ahead and took a hot shower. There were shampoo and body wash for her to use and a towel waiting for her on the sink when she got out, along with a brush and something to put her hair up. After drying off she headed back into the room where her clothes were neatly folded. She hurried up and got dressed and put her hair up in a small ponytail. She straightened her jacket and while doing so, noticed the hole where the bullet had passed through. She stuck her fingers through it and examined it momentarily. She returned to the bed to lace up her boots when the stranger knocked on the door but entered without waiting for her to respond.

"Follow me." He stated coldly.

"Where are we going?" She asked the stranger.

"I assume you're hungry, now let's go" he paused. "or you can stay in here and starve." Dani started to get up to follow him out. "Furthermore," he turned to her, his silver hair falling in his face. "it's in your best interests if you just do what you're told. You're a soldier, so that should be pretty easy."

"I would at least like to know your name." she asked innocently.

"What did I just say? You must be a shitty soldier. I said no..."

"It wasn't a question, more of a wish or a desire." Dani tried to make herself seem as least threatening as possible. The stranger just rolled his eyes at her as if he could see right through her act.

"Zachary," he paused and looked her in the eye. Dani saw the red ring that surrounded his silver colored irises. The mark of someone with Mars blood. The mark of a Marsian. She stifled a gasp. "Zachary Ryder. Now move."

She followed him in silence. She was unsure what to make of Zachary. He had silver hair which marked him as a Venus citizen, but he also had the mark of a Marsian. Should she trust him or not? She was being held captive, but she could have also been left for dead. There was something about him that was so familiar, and she wanted to trust him.

He took her downstairs and down a hall into an open space. There were tables lined up and people were sitting in small groups carrying on conversations. He guided her to a table and sat her down. Someone brought over a plate of food at his command. He sat the plate down in front of her and took a seat across the table.

"This place is a safe haven for runaways, outsiders, defectors, anyone needing a place to lay their head and start a new life." He looked around at the people eating, playing card games, laughing and smiling. Enjoying the freedom and safety of the town. "People come and go as they please but while they're here they contribute in some way."

"In other words, if you want to eat you work." Dani interrupted.

"It's only fair. A person cannot expect a free meal, or anything for free, for that matter." He commented.

Zachary stared at Dani for a moment. He was stern, a fierce look on his face as if he was always ready for something to happen, for something to go awry. He was looking around again, scanning the crowd, scanning the room.

"So then, what is it I'm expected to do?" Dani had barely touched her food. Zachary's eyes focused back on her.

"You should eat. You need to eat, or you'll grow weak and, in your condition," He trailed off, looking around again. Someone caught his eye and he nodded in response. He got up as a man walked over to him. They convened in private a few feet away from Dani, she was unable to hear their conversation. They glanced her way, but only for a moment. Zachary was clearly in charge. He had that air of authority surrounding him.

The two walked back over to where Dani was sitting. Zachary clasped the man on his shoulder squeezing it a bit too tight. The man flinched and let his shoulder fall at the hard touch.

"This is Gabe. He will be taking over watching you until I get back, making sure you don't go anywhere you're not supposed too. I won't be long. It probably wouldn't be a bad idea to go get some sun, some fresh air. Maybe take a walk." He indicated.

He looked at Gabe with a hard look and nodded. Ryder walked away reluctantly. Dani followed his movements trying to unravel what was happening or the position Zachary held. Who was Zachary Ryder?

She saw him meet with a group of people where he stood talking to them for a moment. Then they dispersed. Three exiting through one door, four exiting through another door and then Zachary exiting through the door they came through earlier, all by himself.

"You should be focused on finishing your lunch instead of what Ryder's doing." Gabe sat down next to Dani, sitting backwards on the bench. He was leaning with his back against the table not bothering to even look at her. "Besides you won't figure out plans just by staring. It only makes you look like a creeper." He laughed and looked at her. It was the first time since he had walked over to the table that he had done so.

She looked at him and saw that his eyes were completely red. She quickly looked away in hopes she was not caught staring. He only laughed at her clear intentions. "Oh yes, the red eyes of a true Marsian. Striking fear into humans for years, or is that pity I'm sensing?"

"I don't pity you and I'm certainly not scared, after all," she looked back at him with poise and composure, pulling out the strength her father had instilled in her to be afraid of no one. "Your human as well."

He laughed even harder at her. "Human! That's a new one. I assumed all earthlings just thought we were all monsters."

"Those from Mars only evolved to conform to the conditions. It's a new gene. Maybe not one found on earth but that doesn't make you any less human. You have red eyes while earthlings have blue or perhaps green.

We consider those from Venus human, and they have silver eyes and hair. It's just a difference in genes. Nothing more."

"And the special abilities we have, is that human?" Gabe questioned.

"Like I said. You evolved. It doesn't make you less human." Dani stood her ground.

"You've got some fire to you, don't you? No wonder you survived that bullet shot. Or maybe," He paused looking her up and down. "Maybe your different too. Maybe your genes aren't strictly earthling." He slid down the bench, stretching his legs. "What a relief that would be, and here I thought I was losing my touch." He looked at his hands examining his nails. They were painted black. "I'm usually such a good shot." He inhaled deeply and let out his breath with a slight sigh. "Oh well."

Dani's eyes went wide with realization. "What did you just say?" She said a bit quieter than expected. "You were the one that shot me!" She said it more than asked it.

"Don't take it personally love, I had a job, just like you, soldier girl. I just happen to succeed at my job whereas you failed. Now if your done eating, I would like to get out of here. I grow bored just sitting around." His casual attitude was already starting to annoy Dani.

Gabe had a sense of superiority of himself. He was proud of himself and enjoyed gloating over his accomplishments. He was a person who held nothing back and was not shy to express his thoughts. It was arrogant, Dani thought to herself. Shear arrogance. She disliked him from the moment he started to speak and now she had good a reason too as well.

"Yeah, I'm done." She spat.

"Good." He sprang up and held out his hand for her to grab raising his brow when she didn't immediately take it. It was a gentlemanly gesture with hidden meaning. However, she knew she was in no position to deny any acts of "kindness". After all, she was still in enemy territory and was still injured. She needed to seem as least threatening as possible, at least for the time being. She accepted his hand and allowed him to help her to her feet.

She winced as her side exploded with pain. She immediately grabbed her side and waved it off as if nothing happened. "Here, allow me to get your plate for you, my lady." She felt as if he was poking fun of her. Of course, he was, she thought, why would he not, but she stepped aside allowing him to grab the plate. She needed to be careful with her movements or she could reopen her wound. If Gabe was willing to extend a helping hand, she might as well accept the help.

"Thank you." She acted as if nothing bothered her. She would not let him get a rise out of her. She would keep her composure. She needed to stay strong until she figured out her next move.

Gabe put the plate away and started to walk towards the exit. Dani followed suit. He led her outside the building where Dani felt the warmth of the sun's rays hit her face, followed by an autumn breeze. A ruffling of leaves swirled by her, twirling as they passed. She looked around taking in the scene before her. They were in the middle of a town. It was a quaint little town. Overgrown oaks lined each side of the street paving the way for a broken and cracked road that had seen better days. Buildings lined the road, and beyond the buildings and towards the north and west, Dani could see many homes dotting the hillsides along with fields that stretched to the base of the mountains.

"Where are we?" She looked up and down the street. Beyond the buildings towards the northern mountains where her squad would have been heading, she could see nothing but a road and more forest.

"This is Amire." He pointed to the northeast leading out of town. "If you head that way, you'd find yourself at the compound, Fort Ridge Crest. But to answer your question, we are about twenty miles outside the wall. The compound is about a five-hour drive away, I believe. I've actually never been to the main compound, so I'm really not sure."

"Why tell me all this, why tell me your secrets?" She kicked a rock, then looked up at Gabe. She had her arms crossed in front of her, a chill from the wind starting to creep in. "Don't you think I'll divulge your whereabouts to my military. After all, I am your enemy. It's not like I'm here out of free will." Dani was confused by Gabe's willingness to talk so freely about information that she felt should be kept secret.

"Well, I don't think you'll be running back to your military anytime soon. Not in your condition at least." He pointed to her side and then kept walking. "Besides you think your military doesn't already know where this town is, you think us coming across your squad in the woods was just a happy accident?" He looked back at her; waving his arms in a theatrical manner. "Well happy for us, not so much for you."

"What do you mean? About the military, I mean." Dani was confused. Maybe Gabe was just talking, just rambling about nonsense. What would he know about her military anyway?

"Well Dani Mitchells, I'm sure everything will make sense, eventually that is, maybe we can bring you to the light." Before she asked him further questions two females walked up to him and started to whisper. Dani tried to listen, but it almost sounded like the three were speaking a different language. Dani looked around acting as if she wasn't listening, acting as if she didn't care. After a few minutes, the two girls left Dani and Gabe behind.

"What was that about?" Dani asked not expecting an answer.

Gabe just looked at Dani and then gently grabbed her arm pulling her towards a building. "You should see the library in this town. Surprisingly, it's books and scrolls that survive the test of time. Through war and disease, paper tends to be mightier than the bullet."

Dani pulled away from him and stopped. He looked back at her blinking. "Is there a problem?"

"How..." she looked up at him, her brows frowned, eyes serious. "How did you know my name, my full name?" He looked at her for a moment thinking, thinking up a story, perhaps debating something. He then turned away and started walking towards the building once more.

"Ryder told me. Now come along." He didn't miss a beat. Still biding her time, she reluctantly followed Gabe towards the library. But she had a feeling that was a lie. Gabe was different from Zachary. There was something more maniacal about him. Something deceitful and unnerving. When he smiled it wasn't genuine, but instead villainous?

Dani walked through the heavy wooded double doors. Upon entering, she was cast into a huge open room. The ceiling was tall and rounded with dusty glass panels dimming the natural light in the open space. The windows on the wall held stained glass giving the light in the room a rainbow effect dancing upon the walls. The sun that did shine through revealed a layer of dust that scattered through the air when there was movement. Dani looked around, spinning where she stood. She had never seen so many books in her life. Each aisle of shelves towered over her, and when she looked towards the top of them, she could see a second floor containing just as many shelves filled with more dusty books. She knew she could spend a lifetime in here and not even make a dent in reading the books.

"Pretty neat isn't it?" Gabe was leaning against a table in the middle of the room. "The first time I saw it I don't think I left this place for a week. I wanted to read everything and know even more."

Dani looked at him, almost forgetting that he had been there. "This is…it's," she trailed off unable to find the words to fill her dry mouth. "I can't believe all these books survived."

"This library was locked away, well, sealed away more or less, as I understand it. Everything stayed preserved." Gabe got up and held out his hand motioning for Dani to follow him. "Here, come this way. I want to show you something you might find interesting."

Dani looked at him curiously but followed him, nonetheless. He led her to a section down one of the middle aisles. He paused in front of a section filled with thick books and scrolls. They were in a case of glass that had, at one point, been locked away. She frowned her brows. Her eyes held a look of confusion after glancing at the books for a moment. "What is this?"

"This, soldier girl, is an archive of war."

"War?" She was more curious about Gabe and his intentions than the books. What could books of past wars tell her that would help her or help her military against the constant threat of Mars.

"Yes, war, a clash of two planets, between two worlds or more precise two cultures," he smiled revealing his teeth. "battling it out for dominance."

"Between whom." She stared at him, pausing. "Between Earth and Mars?" She asked confused.

"Give the soldier a golden star." He gave Dani a slow clap.

"Earth and Mars never went to war though." Dani returned.

"Are you sure about that? Books don't lie, and here is a whole section devoted to one war. Maybe you should take a read. Maybe you should learn some history. I'm sure you'll get some spare time; we can even get you a library card. You can check out up to five books at a time." He was making fun of her.

"Do you ever take anything seriously?" Dani asked as she took a closer look examining a few books that were not behind glass, touching a few of them that held titles that spoke to her. The dust rubbed off onto her fingers. She was indeed intrigued by the books and wanted to rummage through them. Her interest had been caught.

"Life is uncertain, I want to make sure that if I die, my leading moments are pleasant, why live in the shadows when the light is so inviting." He explained.

Before their conversation could continue, they could hear footsteps approaching. They both turned to see Zachary approaching. "Finally! I've been looking for the two of you everywhere." He stopped short of Dani and Gabe.

"Ryder, I was just showing...our guest" He looked to Dani. "our fantastic library, I feel most people do not read enough. Wouldn't you agree?"

Ryder just stared blankly at Gabe with his arms crossed. He then pointed at Dani. "Let's go." Dani was quick to follow him. The last thing she wanted to do was upset the person who was seemingly in charge.

He led her out of the library and down the stairs putting them back on the sidewalk under the cover of the overgrown oaks. The sun was already starting to set turning the sky a bright orange and pink hue. The forest beyond the town was shadowed in darkness. Dani could see a light at the edge of town. Zachary lead Dani towards that light. As they approached, she could hear laughter and music. The town opened up into a field where Dani could see a bonfire with people singing, dancing, and carrying on. Many seem to be enjoying drinks of alcohol and all were laughing, enjoying the moment, enjoying the night.

"They seem so at peace. Aren't they scared?" Dani took in the sight before her.

"I told you, this is a safe-haven. Don't mistake though, every one of those free-spirited people out there is ready to fight if needed." He walked a few steps forward and turned back to Dani, "I'm sure a soldier from the academy like yourself hasn't had an opportunity to be a free spirit herself. Come, see what you've been missing." He helped lead her down the rocky slope towards the bonfire.

They walked to a far point of the fire, away from everyone else. He took a seat against a log leaning into it. He stretched out and interlocked his hands behind his head. "Well sit down, standing there you just look... well odd."

She took a seat on the log a few feet away from him. "What's the point of me being out here?" She inquired.

He took a beer from out of his pocket, opened it and took a swig from it. He looked at her and then shook his head and proceeded to look at the fire all the while drinking more of his beer. "To change your mind." He said as a matter of fact.

"What do you mean change my mind, I don't und..." before she could finish, she was interrupted by someone walking up to Zachary clasping his hand in a strong handshake.

"Ryder! Man, I've been looking for you everywhere." The man said, pulling Zachary up onto his feet. He wrapped his arm around Zachary's shoulder and pulled him away, leading him to a group of people. In the group, Dani could see a mix of people. There were a couple of guys jumping around making fools of themselves undoubtedly intoxicated. There were also a few females, two of them laughing and outwardly flirting with Zachary.

She watched at the display of everyone laughing and dancing, as they drank and had fun leaving the world's worries behind. The scene laid out before her made her miss her friends, her family. She wondered what they were doing. How they were doing. Were they looking for her? Did they miss her, certainly they did? Sarah would have no one to talk to during showers and Liam would have no one to pick on. What about Aiden? He was the one person she could talk with seriously at any time. And undoubtfully she was the only one he could usually talk to seriously. Liam and Sarah were just to bubbly.

Sarah and Liam were all laughs. Would they laugh without her being there? Would they just carry on? The thoughts upset her, and she felt a tear run down her face. She quickly wiped it away making sure not to show any vulnerability. She scrunched up her legs bringing her knees up to her chest and wrapped her arms around her legs. She wished she was in the room instead of out here around the bonfire.

"Don't worry too much about him." Gabe walked up and took a seat next to her on the log. His drink sloshed out of his open cup, spilling liquid onto the ground. "Ryder's a pretty popular guy. One would expect that from the people's great hope." He said it sarcastically waving about his arm that held his drink.

"Are you drunk?" She asked him as she eyed him up and down.

"No lass can't be, I just started drinking an hour ago and have only had....". He looked at his hand trying to count his fingers. "Perhaps, maybe just a tad." He paused and looked down, thinking about something.

He looked back at her where he caught her staring. "What were we talking about?" he asked, confused.

She rolled her eyes and took a deep breath. "Nothing. We weren't talking about a damn thing."

They sat for a few minutes more and watched the crowd in silence. "Is it always like this? She asked Gabe.

"No, not always. But occasionally, people need to relax and let loose. Get a little drunk and let go of the worries, maybe make some trivial mistakes that they'll regret in the morning. In a world so unsettled and compromised, people need a chance to feel in control. To be in control. If they can't control the world then maybe, just maybe they can control their own world. If getting intoxicated and unruly is the only way to grasp a fleeting moment of power or control, then why take that away from them. I say let them be free to be, well reckless."

Dani listened as he droned on. She thought to herself that he really must like the sound of his own voice.

"Trivial mistakes, huh?" She continued to listen trying to stay focused, but she kept looking back towards Zachary. He was still with the group of people, but his attention was only on one person now. A pretty girl with long hair. She wore a skirt and a low-cut top. Dani was feeling envious of the attention the girl was receiving. She doubted it was because of Ryder, but more because she felt so alone.

"Yeah, everyone needs to make a few mistakes in their lifetime. So, uh, what about you soldier girl. Do you need to make a few mistakes?" Gabe scooted a bit closer to Dani. His breath was hot and was saturated with alcohol.

Dani was surprised by Gabe's forwardness. With people like this strong arming the rebel forces, how have they been able to elude her military forces for this long? How was she able to be captured so easily?

It infuriated her that she was so easily overcome by someone like Gabe. All her training and it was for nothing. She thought it best to move away from Gabe. She shook her head in disgust. Without another word to Gabe, she simply got up and walked away leaving him behind in his drunken stupor. She was confident he hadn't even noticed. When she glanced back, he was still laying there. 'He fell asleep or, hopefully, passed out. What a complete dumbass.' She thought to herself.

She found a spot away from everyone else and sat, waiting. She wasn't sure what she could or couldn't do and she assumed it would just be best to wait for someone to take her back to her room.

The night seemed to stretch. She was resting her head enjoying the warmth from the fire along with the silence. No one had bothered to come over and talk to her and she was perfectly fine with that. She had been left to her thoughts and she used that time to work on a plan of escape. The crowd had started to fade, and the fire had started to die down as the night grew late. The flames were not as intense as they were when she was first was brought to it, they didn't tower over her in an explosion of light, but instead was now just a spark losing its flame.

Since Zachary has been involved in conversing with other people the whole night, Dani hadn't noticed when he strolled over to where she sat and joined her. She could smell alcohol on him and assumed he too wasn't sound of mind, just like a drunk Gabe who was still passed out on the ground nearby.

Zachary had noticed Dani sitting by herself all night. He hated how he needed to keep his distance for the time. How his distance was allowing Gabe of all people to wiggle his way closer to her. He had some nerve, especially after he almost killed her. He had kept himself busy talking to people he was acquainted with, but he rather be anywhere else. He hated how the females acted so desperate for attention and refused to leave him alone. Finally, he had been able to escape and was able to join Dani.

He sat down next to her. He could smell the alcohol on his shirt from where one of the guys had accidentally spilled his beer on him. He was unsure of what to say to her. He knew she must be feeling alone, he was certain she must be missing her fellow squad members, and she was probably worried about them as well. How could he even begin to comfort her, as if she would even want him to anyways. To her he was an enemy keeping her trapped. To her, she was a prisoner. He opened his mouth to speak, to perhaps try to explain, but he wasn't sure how to even start. He thought better of it and stayed quiet. He thought to himself maybe he should have drunk a few beers, then he might have the courage to speak his mind, and, more importantly, the truth.

He stayed quiet as he sat there for a few moments. Dani didn't bother to talk to him either. It's not like she had much to say anyway. After a few minutes, he lifted from the ground and turned to walk away. "I'll take you back to your room now, I'm sure you're tired." He started to walk away, as he did, she heard him speak under his breath. "I know I am."

She moved to her feet and followed him back into town. The town looked deserted in the late hours. There were no lights on, and no one was out. The streets were entirely empty. Dani recognized the building she was staying in and walked towards it. Zachary escorted her inside and upstairs to her room. At the door, he unlocked it and opened it wide for Dani to walk through.

"I'll be back to pick you up at eight tomorrow. Be ready." He didn't even give Dani a chance to speak. He turned to leave, but before he walked away, as an afterthought, he quietly said goodnight. Dani was unsure if she heard him say it. He walked away leaving the smell of alcohol to loom in the hallway. He seemed confident that she wouldn't run, that she would be a good girl, that she would be smart, and walk into her room closing the door behind her. He was wrong. She didn't stop to think twice. She ran. What's the worse they could do to her. Put her back in lockup?

*****

"What the hell are we waiting for!" Sarah was pacing back and forth in the clearing of woods where she and the others had set up camp. She was yelling, furious at the fact that they were just sitting around doing nothing when they should be trying to rescue Dani. She knew Dani had been hit by that gunshot, the blood staining her hands. She was worried that her best friend was seriously injured or possibly even dead.

The colonel sat on a rock with his fingers laced, resting under his chin. His eyes were closed but anyone could tell he was deep in thought. As Sarah continued to yell, he moved his hands to his temples attempting to rub away the headache Sarah was causing. Other than Sarah's yelling the forest was still. Not even a bird chirped in the quiet woods, but how could they when she was scaring anything off with her tantrum. Until he heard word from Ryder, he knew the best position was for him and his squad to sit tight and unfortunately wait. At least they were close to the town.

"Cadet Hunt!" He finally snapped at her. "If you would please, shut up." Sarah was surprised by his outburst and immediately stopped in her tracks. She backed away a few steps feeling her pride was bruised. She was on the verge of crying, tiny tears starting to squeeze involuntarily from her eyes. She was completely outraged, feeling useless.

"Things are not so black and white as they may seem. We need to assess the situation and come up with the best strategy possible." He tried to explain to her.

"Screw that. They didn't just shoot her and leave. They took her! We need to go get her back!" Sarah snapped back at her commanding officer. The tears now streaming fully down her face.

Colonel Harper swiftly stood up. His height effectively causing Sarah to rethink her previous actions and outbursts. "You forget yourself, Hunt! I am your commanding officer! I suggest you learn your place cadet before you have to be reminded of it!" He spoke with such fierceness and demand everyone in the camp stopped. "Make no mistake, you're not the only one here who concerned for Mitchells's safety. I never said we weren't going to rescue her. I'm just not going to run in moronically making our attempts futile. Now sit down and think of something helpful instead of standing here yelling like a child."

He turned away from her. As he did so he noticed Lieutenant Reeves watching him. He understood her look. He knew she felt strongly about telling the cadets the truth, that it would help to ease the tension he was assisting to create. As he passed her, he acknowledged the look in her eye. He whispered as he passed her, speaking softly to her, but still fuming from Sarah's insubordination.

"Yeah, I know lieutenant." He grumbled.

"If you know sir, then maybe you should do something about it." Reeves was the steady hand Harper needed to keep him straight. He knew if he were to stray away from his path of determination to help shape the nation into something better, she would be there to lead him back onto his path.

Sarah did decide to sit down, hoping it would clear her head. She walked over and sat next to Aiden who was wrapping up a long strain of rope. When she sat down, he lovingly patted her leg relaying a message of concern and comfort. "We're going to get her back. Don't worry. Harper isn't going to let whomever took her to get away."

Liam jumped down from the tree he had been sitting in. "Sir." He spoke gathering the attention of the colonel and lieutenant.

"You better have good news Evens." The colonel had walked over to a small table where a map and other items were sitting. He hovered over the map that showed the area's topography hoping to gain knowledge of where a force that wanted to hurt both the military and the rebels by taking a prisoner might go to stash her.

"There's a town a few miles away. Maybe a mile and a half, two max. It's due east."

"Yes, I know about the town." He sighed, understanding and reminding himself that his cadet was only going off the knowledge he had been given, which was none.

He didn't know that the town was a rebel town, or that they had allies there, waiting for them to arrive. It was either he spilled his secrets and revealed the complicated truth or continue with this cover and risk completely losing his squad's trust. He looked up at Liam and gave him a reassuring smile.

"Um, good work Evens. Go eat, and then get some rest. You'll be taking the first night watch shift." Harper relayed to Liam.

Harper thought to himself. Ryder assured him his men were not responsible for the ambush and there was no way Grayson would allow such danger to befall his younger sister. Was it possible the group who took Dani was still hiding in the town somewhere without Ryder's knowledge though? Could it be a group with the rebel forces that had their own hidden agenda? Only time would tell, but for now, he knew they needed to get Dani back and he needed his team's conviction to follow him. Nonetheless, his lieutenant was right, he needed to be honest with his squad, but where to start.

The camp had been set up close to a stream. Liam grabbed a towel, soap, and fresh clothes and headed towards the stream. He hadn't cleaned up in a few days nor had he slept since Dani was captured the day before. The stream was cold but refreshing. He dunked his head under the water and waited, holding his breath. The possible life or death situation he was causing by staying underwater helped him to clear away the fog in his head that had been looming.

The moment that he heard that gunshot, his heart stopped. It was as if his heart and gut knew before his head did on what just happened and before he could react, before he could get to her, he had felt a burst of pain in the back of his skull. Everything went dark and he woke what seemed like hours later with a drumming in his head making it feel like it was going to explode.

He blamed himself more than anyone. He was supposed to be looking after her. He should have been by her side. Instead, he had been by Finn's side fighting along with him. Dani had come to their aid and yet when she needed them, they had failed her. If only he had been there, if only he had stayed by her side.

His vision was starting to go fuzzy and he lifted out of the water and inhaled a deep breath of air. He trudged to the bank of the stream and climbed out grabbing his towel to ruffle through his soaked hair in an attempt of sponging the excess water out. He donned his clean clothes and walked back to camp with his towel slung over his shoulder. Sarah had started to settle with Aiden next to her. He noticed Finn and Hiromi still weren't back from scouting. 'Hopefully, they're okay' he thought. With Dani gone and the colonel's lies, it felt as if his squad was starting to fall apart.

He climbed into his tent not bothering to make small talk with anyone and before he could lay down allowing his head to rest on his pillow, he was fast asleep exhausted from the week of turmoil.

Finn and Hiromi entered the camp followed by Hiromi's two hounds. The colonel looked up from the map that he and the lieutenant were going over pointing at various things. "any news?' He asked them, hopefulness in his voice.

"Not yet sir." Hiromi answered.

"Evens said the town was close, within a two-mile radius towards the east. You didn't happen to pick up her scent in that direction, did you?" Lieutenant Reeves asked them.

"Yes, ma'am we did." Finn responded.

"Damnit!" Colonel Harper announced realizing the trouble this could cause. "The lieutenant and I are still working on a strategic plan to extract cadet Mitchells, but we will head towards the town tomorrow and do some reconnaissance. We'll figure out if she's there or if the people that kidnapped her, are just passing through there."

"Sir, the town, but that's where..." Hiromi was cut short when the colonel raised his hand to quiet her.

"Yes, I know." His attention turned to Finn. "Carson go get cleaned up and eat. You're taking a shift after Evens." He dismissed the cadet before their conversation continued. Finn did as he was told but was immediately suspicious of the dismissal. What was Hiromi confirming? That's where what was, he wondered. Now he was sure of it. They were unquestionably hiding something. There was more to this mission than originally led to believe.

Colonel Harper pulled Hiromi off to the side to speak in private with her. "Katsuki, I need you to relay a message to Ryder, inform him of our plan. I won't move out until you get back, so make haste. If Mitchells is in that town, then there's been a betrayal and he needs to be made aware of the possible danger he faces, as well, he should send a search party for Mitchells."

"Will do sir." Then she and the hounds left once more with a quickened pace before the dusk of the setting sun and tall trees of the forest clouded them in darkness making travel treacherous and dangerous.

*****

Hours had passed since the colonel had sent Hiromi towards the town to relay his message to Ryder. He was pacing back and forth through the camp unable to sleep. Liam was up as well pulling his nightly guard shift, while everyone else had gone to sleep, unable to stay up any longer from the weary and emotional events that had played out over the course of the few days. The fire crackled and popped, hot embers spurting towards the edge of the fire pit.

"So, who really took her." Liam finally asked the colonel. The question stopped him dead in his tracks. He looked down at the young cadet. His chin was resting on his hand as he used his other hand to hold a stick he had found and was using to carelessly poke the fire. He looked drained of all emotion and the usual humor he carried. He was a void, keeping his thoughts at bay with the mindless task of doing something as simple as poking a fire.

"I don't know. Our contact said this wasn't his doing." He took a seat next to Liam. His head hanging low, his forehead hitting the palms of his fist. He too was drained, but it was because he felt like there was a war being fought inside him.

"Do you believe this guy? Ryder was his name? Do you know him well enough to trust him?" Liam stopped poking the fire and stab the stick into the ground repeatedly in front of him.

"Yeah, Ryder and I have a long history. Plus, he was handpicked by Grayson to oversee his sisters' transition into the rebel's control." The colonel raked his fingers through his hair pushing the loose strands back.

"Well, we see how well that worked. All I'm saying is maybe it's time to tell the rest of the squad what's really going on. This whole façade of spying on rebels but were actually with the rebels is only going to get more complex the longer you hold out."

Harper straightened up and looked at Liam sideways. "Well look at you, acting all grown up, telling commanding officers what they should and shouldn't do. Some might look at that as disrespectful and an act of defiance." He raised his eyebrows at Liam.

Liam took a piece of food out of his pocket and proceeded to take a huge bite of dried meat and spoke with his mouth full. "I call it as I see it, what can I say...sir." He added the sir in as a sarcastic gesture to the colonel's previous comment of respect. He knew Harper well enough to know when he needed to be professional and when he was able to make light of the situation.

Hiromi pushed through the trees into the clearing where her squads camp was located, interrupting Liam and Harper's conversation. She was out of breath from the constant running back and forth. The dogs slumped to the ground, their tongues hanging out of their mouths as they panted. She sat water down in front of them and gave each a loving pat reassuring their good work. They immediately started to lap up the water.

"You know if I were an enemy, the two of you would be dead." She strolled over to the two men sitting down. "Mitchells's there, in the town. She's safe. A nurse was able to retrieve the bullet and stitched her up. She's resting now, but she won't be able to be moved for a couple of days and won't be able to travel for at least two weeks if not more. Apparently, there was a...." she stopped and rolled her eyes. "misunderstanding amongst the ranks."

"A misunderstanding. A misunderstanding! You got to be fucking kidding me! They shot her and it's chalked up to a misunderstanding!" Liam was on his feet, his voice starting to rise. Hiromi was trying to shush him. Her hands motioning that he was being too loud.

"Evens. You're going to wake everyone. Please." She was pleading with him. Hoping she could gain enough of his attention to calm him. She knew how passionate he was when it came to Dani.

Liam sat back down realizing he was getting excitable. The last thing he wanted to do was wake everyone, especially Sarah. He didn't think she would be able to handle the news right now. He was quiet but was still steaming. Hiromi continued to speak.

"Ryder said we should go ahead and move towards the compound and skip the town. Grayson left earlier, about a day ago, in fact, and he will be there waiting for our arrival."

"And Mitchells?" The colonel inquired.

"Ryder will be moving her there once she's able to travel. She's out of danger but that bullet came close. She needs time to heal. Even though she has a lot of determination, I think even she will agree she needs to take at least a couple weeks before she should travel the distance to the fort."

"Okay, then in the morning. I will explain to the squad the situation and inform them of the underline intention of the mission. Hopefully I haven't lost their respect or trust and they will be willing to listen." Harper looked at Liam. "Our true intent."

Hiromi looked at him surprised. "Sir, are you..."

"Yes, I'm sure. It's time to come clean. This is getting too complicated and we need the trust of our squad. Anyways, we should get some sleep. Except for you Evens. You're still on guard." The colonel had paused and looked back at Liam, waiting for a sarcastic remark.

"Damn." He snapped his fingers sarcastically, while Harper and Hiromi went to their separate tents. While in a tent close by, Finn laid awake listening.

The next morning the colonel gathered his squad in anticipation of the information he was about to unload on to them. All eyes were on him ready to receive instructions on the day's plan.

"Mitchells is safe." He started and he was immediately ambushed with shouts of concern and questions from various members of the squad. He was already regretting this. "Settle down and shut it." He paused for a moment and then continued, starting over. "Mitchells is safe and yes, she is in that town, but!" He said louder stopping any sudden outburst of voices before they started again. "We are not going to go get her."

Sarah started to speak up, standing as she did. "Excuse me, we're..."

"Shut it Hunt and sit down." She slowly sat back down. "We are not going to get her, because she will be brought to us. She is with trusted allies."

"Sir, I think you're confusing them more. Perhaps you should start from the beginning." Lieutenant Reeves motioned.

"Oh geez." He scratched the back of his head and audibly sighed. "This mission is not to pull recon on a rebel compound, but instead we're meeting with a leader from the rebel compound."

"And why would we do that? Isn't that treason?" Finn asked slowly.

"Technically, yes, but there is more going on here then you cadets understand." He tried to explain. He didn't want to be the one tasked with explaining this to them. He sat down on a log and looked at everyone without truly looking at them. He was searching for his next words.

"We are meeting with the rebel leader to help establish peace. For now, that's all you need to know. Understand." He looked for confirmation.

"Yes sir." A few of the cadets responded, Finn not being one of them.

"Right now, we need to head to the main compound where Cadet Mitchells will be meeting us. Once she is clear to move and we talk to the leader we will head back home, without Mitchells.

"What do you mean without Mitchells? Finn inquired.

"She will be in danger if she goes back to Helenia. Her father knew information that put Cadet Mitchells's life at risk. If she had stayed in

Helenia, she would have been killed." Lieutenant Reeves shorthanded for the others. "Understand?"

"So, we are on a mission that will take at least two weeks if not more, just to talk to some guy? Why not just radio him, send him an email, a letter, a pigeon for crying out loud!" Finn started overloading the colonel with questions.

"No more questions. We're doing it this way and that's that. I'm not sure why you're really complaining. It got you out of training didn't it cadet? Now pack up, we're moving out in ten."

The colonel pushed off the log and started to pack his own tent up wondering if this was the right move. How could they know of the corruption spreading throughout their nation? That many of the higher ups and generals were acting out of hysteria rather than rationality. Because of their nervousness, they were building tension not only with the people in Helenia but with allying nations and on a larger scale, other planets such as Venus.

If things didn't change it could mean the end of humanity.

*****

It was quiet in the hallway. Dani had noticed the moon high in the starry night sky before she and Zachary had made their way inside the building. She deduced it was after midnight. She made her way towards the stairs. Stairs would be better to take since she could take them slow and without causing any noise. Once she was on the first floor, she slowly opened a door leading into a hallway attached to the lobby area. She was nervous and on edge. She had no weapons and no gear. She had no idea what she was truly going to do when she reached the outskirts of town. She was trusting that a rescue squad or better, her squad would be somewhere close by waiting.

She was at the end of the hallway where it opened. She looked around the corner and moved slowly so she would not be spotted in case someone was lurking. The room was dark. She knew she was taking a huge risk. The dark would conceal her, but it would also conceal anyone hiding.

With the help of the moonlight, she could see the door leading to the outside. It was a good fifty feet away. She started to move, staying low and close to the wall so she could feel her way towards the door without bumping into anything. She tried to remember what the lobby area layout was like when she was escorted through it just that afternoon.

Thirty feet down. She moved swiftly. Twenty feet. She could see the light from outside. She was so close. Ten, almost there. And then her hand touched the door handle. She closed her hand around it and started to turn it. 'Almost free.' She thought to herself. Before she could push the door open, she heard a click, but it didn't come from the door.

She stopped in her tracks raising her head up looking out the glass door. She could see her darken reflection in the window. The little bit of hope she had immediately drained from her body. She just wanted to go home. She wanted to not feel so helpless.

She rested her head on the glass and let out the breath she hadn't realized she was holding. The person behind her holding a gun walked closer. She could hear the heavy footsteps. She dropped her hand off the doorknob knowing it was futile, all that hope she had built just disappeared. She laid her forehead against the cool glass as she raised her arms above her head, her clear intent of surrender understandable.

She could attack. Knock the gun from the person's hands. It wouldn't be hard for her, but she was afraid the stitches might pull in her side. That was the last thing she needed. Even if she managed to get away, she would be bleeding, and her life would be in danger from her wound.

The stranger lowered the gun and holstered it on his hip. "Did you honestly think I would trust you enough to expect you to just go into your room?"

"If you knew I would run why even bother giving me the opportunity. Seems pretty ludicrous on your end. Perhaps you enjoy making life challenging for yourself Zachary." Dani finally turned around to face him. She was surprised by his stance, by his straight voice.

She thought it had been odd that when he walked down the hall only moments ago, he had walked with grace and there wasn't a slur to his voice. Maybe he hadn't really been drinking at all. Maybe that was all part of his rouse. To steer her thoughts towards an idea of comfort giving her the confidence to try and escape. In other words, he had played her, and she walked right into it. She felt like such a fool. 'But why.' She wondered.

"The best way to learn about someone is to watch their actions. What will they do when they think no one is watching?" Zachary crossed his arms. "Now if you don't mind, it's been a long day and an even longer night. I would like to go to sleep and you need sleep as well, your wounds won't heal if you don't rest, and we can't have that." He pointed towards the elevator indicating he wanted her to lead the way.

"Well, you didn't have to take me to the bonfire. I am a prisoner after all. Why show me any type of benevolence or hospitality. And furthermore, if it's been such a long day, then a bit of advice, don't go to a bonfire and stay out till all hours of the night." She held spite in her voice.

"Prisoner?" He said it as if he were surprised by the word. As if the idea of her being his prisoner never even crossed his mind. As if the idea was ludicrous, that he was surprised she even made that assumption.

"Who said you were a prisoner? At the bonfire, how long were you just sitting there left alone?" He grabbed her arm and stopped her, turning her around to face him. "You could have left at any time. You chose not to. I left you in the hallway because I honestly believed you wouldn't have walked out that door. I assumed you wouldn't actually go through with it. That you wouldn't be so stupid to throw away your life like that." Dani refused to look at him. He released her arm as she forcefully pulled it away from him.

"Maybe I was wrong but, damnit" He pointed towards the door forcefully. "You're smart, do you honestly believe you would survive out there with no supplies, no food, and in the condition you're in. Don't paint me to be the bad guy here Dani Mitchells. Your still here because you want to be. And furthermore," he copied her. "if I didn't have to go to the bonfires, I wouldn't."

Dani was glad the lights were off, and that Zachary couldn't see her face clearly. She was sure her face was turning red from embarrassment and anger. She could feel a few tears streaming down her face.

She turned and walked towards the elevator without saying another word to him. She pushed the arrow indicating up and the doors slid open with a shallow creek. She entered the elevator and turned to lean against the back wall crossing her arms in front of her as if to protect her ego from further damage.

She didn't even bother to look up and see that Zachary was watching her every move. The doors shut and took her to the floor where her room was waiting for her. The day had indeed been long, and she imagined tomorrow would be even longer.

Chapter 12

SECRETS AT THE LIBRARY

Dani woke to a knock at her door. In her wake, she wasn't sound of mind and thought she imagined the knock and didn't think much of it. Sleep was starting to claim her once more. With her eyes growing heavy she started to drift back into sleep when the knock came again, this time much louder. Her eyes flew open at the sound. She knew she didn't imagine it at that time. Before she could respond the door started to rattle from the loud banging.

She sprang out of her bed startled by the sudden turn of the knob. She had fallen asleep in her clothes that she had been wearing from the night before, so she knew she could at least seem like she had been up. Before the door could fully open, she had sat on the edge of the bed and started to put on her boots. Before she looked up at the intruder her uniform jacket was hitting her in the face. It slid down and landed on the floor with a thump.

She looked up to see Zachary Ryder leaning against the door frame, his arms crossed over his chest and his legs crossed at the ankle. "Who do you think your fooling? You were still sleeping, weren't you?"

She looked back down and continued to lace her boots with a sour look on her face. "Well, there's no fooling you, is there Zachary. I'm not sure why I even bothered to try." She finished lacing her boots and grabbed her jacket off the floor as she sat back up and tried to stand. She must have been sleeping pretty hard. Her body was as stiff as a board. It was as if she hadn't moved a single time through the night.

At least her wound didn't feel as sore as it had the day before. That was good news. She lifted her shirt slightly up to look and make sure the

197

bandages were still in place. She noticed they were not as ragged as the night before and it looked like there was fresh tape. The skin around the new dressing was fresh and had turned a soft pink. A sign she was healing or that tape had recently been ripped off.

"You were completely out of it. I was pretty surprised when you didn't even stir when the nurse ripped the tape off." Ryder walked over towards the bed and took a seat in the chair. He relaxed into it and stretched, letting out a yawn.

"When did you..." Dani started to ask.

"About an hour ago, when I knocked on your door the first time." Ryder interrupted her before she could finish.

"So, it's..."

"Nine, yes. Now let's go. Obviously, we're running behind." He exited the room shutting the door harshly behind him to let her finish getting dressed.

She laid back on the bed and sigh a breath of relief. She laid her arms over her head stressing about the day ahead of her. She missed home; she missed her friends. "No point in laying around, might as well get this day over with." She said to herself as motivation to get up and head out.

She made her way downstairs towards the dining hall where she saw Zackary waiting for her. He was sitting on the side of a table talking to a group of people, one of those people included Gabe. Zackary noticed her and nodded her acknowledgment. He finished what he was saying and clapped one of the guys on the shoulder, laughing as he did so. Dani thought it was strange to see him laugh because he was so rude and direct when he spoke to her. He walked over to her and when he was a few feet away he stopped and crossed his arms. 'Here we go' Dani thought to herself.

"Go ahead and get breakfast, after your done eating I'll take you to where you will be working while you're here, healing."

"Working?" Dani asked him confused.

"Like we discussed yesterday. If you want to eat, you have to work." He pointed to a table in the corner. "I'll join you at that table, I have a few people I need to go around and speak to first."

He left her to fend for herself. She headed towards the line that formed to gather food. People behind a bar were serving different food items upon request. After she got her food, she sat at the table she was instructed to by Zachary.

At least the food was good, she thought to herself. Her breakfast was suddenly interrupted by the scooting of the chair across from her. A girl with bright blue and green hair sat down. She was dressed head to toe in black attire. Dani was somewhat shocked by her appearance. In the military, Dani, nor anyone else, could dye their hair so it was unusual for her to see someone with unnatural hair color.

"Hey, so you're the new girl, right?" She was loud when she spoke, her voice booming in the early morning. Dani thought she recognized her from last night.

She looked around stunned. Dani thought the girl must be mistaken. She may be new to these people, but this wasn't permanent. She was leaving as soon as she completed her mission. She would gather information, find her weapons, and get the hell out.

"Um, I guess." Dani tried to make herself as least threatening as possible. Amongst the bursts of colors in her hair, there were black curls that strewn wildly everywhere. Her face was long and skinny with a chin that came to a point, and she sported a piercing along her nose. Dani never saw someone look so expressive.

"I saw you at the bonfire last night. Gabe can be so annoying, I know. Don't pay any attention to him. I know I don't, and I'm related to him." Dani was getting so used to seeing the red rings around the eyes of the people here that she didn't even pay attention to it when the girl sat down, although she was noticing it now.

"Oh, it's fine, I mean, yeah, he was a bit much last night, but I guess he was drinking." Dani tried to make light of the conversation. "I'm sorry, who are you?"

The girl wiped her had on her shirt and thrust it across the table to shake Dani's hand. "I'm sorry, I'm Nadia." She gleamed as if revealing her name was an indication of who she was, as if it explained everything. "I'm a cousin to Gabe. But that doesn't matter."

Dani shook her hand and introduced herself. "Dani Mitchells, I'm sure it's nice to meet you."

Dani looked around as Nadia continued to talk. She spotted Zachary walking around talking to different people before he made his way to her table. When he reached the table, he smacked Nadia on the side of the arm as an old friend might do.

"Nadia, what are you doing here? Shouldn't you already be helping in the greenhouse?" He took a seat next to Dani, which surprised her.

"Yeah, yeah, I was heading there now." She got up to walk away. "It was nice to meet you, Dani. Hope to see you again tonight." She teased Zachary as if she was going to hit him on the arm, she laughed and took a few steps away only to return and truly hit him before she ran off laughing and calling him vulgar names. He reacted by shaking his head and calling her names under his breath.

"Don't pay any attention to her, she's just as weird and out of her mind as her cousin."

"You mean Gabe." Dani took a bite of her pancakes.

"Oh, she told you, she's such a chatterbox. Can't keep her damn mouth shut to save her life. I'll warn you now, don't trust either of them with anything, along with Penelope."

"Who's Penelope?" Dani acquired.

Zachary looked around and then pointed to a table with a group of people sitting there enjoying their breakfast. "See the girl with black curly hair with the streaks of pink in it?" Dani nodded. "That's Penelope, she's Nadia's older sister. And she's trouble. So, watch yourself around her."

Dani finished her breakfast. She walked over to where she could dispense her food tray while Zachary waited by the door for her. When she had caught up to him, he led her out of the building towards where she would be working or really helping out at while she was there.

"You'll be putting in hours at the library. You can check out books if you so desire, I'm sure it will help to pass the time by while your healing." He stopped and turn to look at her. "I would highly suggest you take a look in the section that I found you at yesterday."

"The section on the supposed war between Earth and Mars?" She carried on the conversation with him. It was the first time he spoke to her without a tone that suggested he would rather be anywhere else or perhaps talking to anyone else, but he was unfortunately stuck talking to her.

"Yes, there is some... interesting information to say the least that I think you'll find, well, let's say intriguing, I even have a few books from the section checked out at the moment." He said it with a hint of mystery as if there was some hidden meaning behind his words that Dani was supposed to pick up on. She looked at him sideways unsure of the supposed hidden message she was sure wasn't even there. What she was focused on was that in his spare time he enjoyed reading just like her.

"Okay?" She asked it slowly.

She thought she was probably overthinking his intentions though. What could he possibly want her to know that he couldn't just say or that would change her views on the rebel forces, or betray her own military? There were many times when they were alone after all. However, he was keeping her there and taking care of her. He made it clear she wasn't a prisoner even though she still felt like it considering he escorted her everywhere. Dani was starting to develop mixed emotions.

They reached the library doors. It didn't take long since it was across the street from the building that she was temporarily living in. Zachary held the door open for her and waved her inside. Dani was hit with warm air. It instantly chased away the cold that had settled within her. He guided Dani over to a round desk near the front where a woman with dark skin sat. Her hair had tiny tight curls and was cut so short it was almost gone.

She stood up from her chair to welcome her guest. "Good morning Ryder."

"Morning Miss Mackenzie." Ryder set down a cup of coffee on the desk counter. "This is for you, as a thank you for letting Danielle help out here." Dani looked at him sideways at the mention of her full name. No one ever called her by her real first name, she didn't even think Sarah and Aiden knew it.

"It's going to take more than a crappy cup of coffee to butter me up, Zachary Ryder." She held a hand on her hip and carried a strong English accent.

"Oh wait!" Zachary started to dig in his pocket. "Here we go." He pulled a small box out of his pocket and handed it to Miss Mackenzie. She opened it up and lit up with glee.

"Oh, you're the devil! Where did you get these from?" She asked excitedly.

"Miss Katherine made them special for you. She knew they were your favorite." In the box were six chocolate coated coconut bonbons. Dani hadn't seen coconut in years. It was a rarity because it was hard to grow tropical foods such as coconuts in the high altitudes of the mountains.

The trading industries shipped the coconut in from other civilizations, but it was usually reserved for those in the higher tiers because they were the only ones who could pay for it. After the seven-year war that ravaged the Earth with warfare and other harmful bioweapons, much of the land had become tainted and unsuitable in sustaining crop life. Hundreds of years may have passed since the war, but the Earth was still healing. Much of the land had been reclaimed by nature with the lack of human technology cultivating it. Growth and expansion to overtake those lands back was not humanity's first priority.

The pockets of civilizations had advanced technology and medicine. The civilizations themselves were advanced. The ability to fly in space was as easy as turning on a vehicle, but many foods, especially exotic fruits, were mostly left to the wild, at least for the time. And what was available was in limited supply.

Zachary looked at Dani. "This is Miss Mackenzie. She will be watching over you and giving you direction as to what she needs of you while you're in the library. She will take good care of you." He turned back to the woman. "This is Danielle Mitchells. She's a hard worker, so I know she won't let you down, Miss Mackenzie." Dani again gave him a look, what did this guy know about her. First her name and now her work ethics. Who was he and how did he know so much about her?

"Oh, I'm sure she will do just fine. Now get out of here. We all know you're too busy to just be standing around." She was shooing him away with both hands.

"Okay, okay, I'll be back around three then?" He started to walk towards the door. The two watched as he walked away. Before he could get to the door, he turned around still walking. "Don't forget to eat lunch, you need to keep up your strength." He hollered back at Dani. Then he was gone, through the door.

"Okay, Miss Danielle." Miss Mackenzie started to speak when Dani politely interrupted.

"Please, just Dani. No one calls me Danielle anymore." The only person who called her Danielle was her mother and sometimes Liam when he was teasing her, but after her mother's death, he knew better than to call her by it now. When she heard her name, it brought back memories of her mother and it was hard for Dani to move forward, almost unbearably so.

Miss Mackenzie smiled at Dani, acknowledging her wishes. "Okay, Miss Dani. First, I would like you to take that cart of books," She pointed to a grey wheeled metal cart near the desk, "and put them all back where they belong. There's a three-letter code followed by three numbers. The letters are an indication of the aisle and section and the numbers are rows and placement. There's a map attached to the cart to help with location and there are brass plates at the end of every aisle as well. Sound easy?"

"Yes ma'am." Dani replied. She walked over to the cart and pulled the first book to start her task.

*****

The day in the library passed by quickly, between lunch and all the books Miss Mackenzie had for Dani to put away, it felt as if Zachary had left only an hour ago. She was sitting in front of a section of books in the very back of the library, where it was dark and dusty, when she heard footsteps turn down her aisle and start to approach. She looked up expecting to see Miss Mackenzie or Zackary, but to her surprise and dislike it was Gabe.

"Well good afternoon Dani Mitchells." There was something uncomfortable about Gabe. There was an air about him that rubbed Dani the wrong way and caused her to instantly become tense.

"Good afternoon." She said with a lack of emotion. She looked back down at her stack of books. She may not have liked him, but she wasn't afraid of him and knew she could hold her own if she had too. "What can I help you with today Gabe." There was a hint of annoyance in her voice. She genuinely was in no mood to deal with his approaches.

"Why so annoyed? Is it something I said?" He acted innocent, shocked by Dani's aggression towards him.

She stopped and looked up at him. "Honestly I haven't been around you enough for you to have said something that would 'annoy' me as you put it." She smiled not giving away her dislike for him. She tried to walk away but he put an arm in front of her on the shelves and blocked her from going.

She was forced to stop. She moved the short stack of books she had been working on from in front of her to a nearby shelf, allowing her arms to be free. She was ready to defend herself if needed. She gave out a slight sigh. "Excuse me." She said without looking up at him, staring straight forward.

"You need to loosen up a little, Dani. I can help with that." Gabe's smile turned wicked.

She pushed his arm out of the way and moved past him without responding. Before she could pull out of his reach, though, he lunged forward and grabbed her wrist holding her back. "Hey now, it's rude to just walk away from someone talking to you, you know."

"Gabe, I would suggest you..." Dani was speaking through gritted teeth, her blood starting to boil.

"Dani! There you are." Before she could finish Zachary rounded the corner and started to jog down the long aisle to meet her. Gabe had immediately dropped Dani's wrist when he was startled by Zachary's booming voice. Dani looked down at her now freed arm and then thrust it up to her chest rubbing her wrist. Cradling it from where Gabe had twisted it.

"Ryder, what a surprise. What are you doing here?" Gabe asked innocently as if nothing happened. His expression smoothed once more.

205

Dani caught the look that quickly faded over Zachary's face. He clearly understood what had happened.

"I could ask the same of you, Gabe. I heard you didn't go to work today, to busy sleeping in, huh? Guess not all of us can hold our alcohols." Zachary spoke as if he was kidding around with an old rival.

Gabe ignored the alcohol comment and moved forward with the conversation. "Oh well, I was just, uh, checking on our new guest, Dani." He clasped her on the shoulder. She moved her shoulder up as if trying to shake his hand off. She was noticeably uncomfortable. "I heard she had been left all alone at the bonfire last night and wanted to make sure she was okay." He smiled knowing the comment would get to Zachary and as soon as he said it he was right. A moment of anger flashed across Zachary's face. Just as fast as it was there it was gone.

He stared at Gabe for a moment longer and then turned to Dani. "Dani, are you ready to go?"

"Oh, um, yes. Let me just go put these books away. Meet you at the front?" Zachary nodded a confirmation. She moved past him making herself seem small. There was too much testosterone between the two of them at that moment that Dani wanted to be as far away from them as possible. She walked to the front of the aisle where the cart she had been using had settled. She stacked the books on the shelf and pushed the cart back to the front desk.

Ryder watched as Dani walked away and turned towards the front. He then quickly turned back towards Gabe. "I know what you're trying to do. Don't." He hissed at Gabe.

"I have no idea what you're talking about Ryder." Gabe pushed past Ryder in an attempt to leave, but before he could get too far, Ryder grabbed his arm.

"Stay away from her. If I catch you around her again…. alone. I won't haste to put you down." The look in his eyes was stern, serious. As if he was challenging Gabe to step out of line and give him a reason.

"What, Ryder? You don't like a little competition. You worried I might woo Miss Dani to my side?" Gabe taunted. Ryder stared at him for a moment more before he shoved past him. He refused to even acknowledge the comment with a response.

"I guess I'm done for the day, Miss Mackenzie. I'll be taking my leave now?" She asked, bringing the librarian's attention away from her work. Dani stood at the front desk where Miss Mackenzie remained at the computer. She looked up at Dani and smiled.

"Thank you so much. You did a great job today. I'll see you tomorrow. Have a good night." The woman looked frazzled from the strenuous work she had been engulfed with at her computer. Dani had the instinctive feeling it had something to do more with the rebels and less with everyday librarian tasks.

"Thank you. Good night." Dani replied.

Zackary had walked up beside her leaving Gabe in the aisle. The look on his face indicated he knew what Gabe had been attempting and Zachary was not happy about it. Dani could not deny there was a heat rising from the inside of her chest to her neck at the idea that Zachary was trying to be protective over her, but she was sure that was not necessarily his intention. She recognized the competitive nature between the two, and she had nothing to do with it.

"Night Miss Mackenzie." He guided Dani towards the door encouraging her to walk outside. He waved back to the woman at the desk, her nose already back into the computer and her fingers flying over the keys on the keyboard. He had wanted to react to Gabe's forwardness towards Dani. How dare he try to touch her after he had almost killed her. Gabe was chasing after Dani at an attempt to hurt Zachary, and it infuriated him further. He would not let Gabe use Dani against him.

"You be good now Zachary." Miss Mackenzie hollered back at him. She stated it as an afterthought, as if she finally realized that Dani was leaving, and Zachary had been with her.

The two walked back across the street towards the building where Dani was staying. They stayed silent while Zachary walked in front of her. When they had reached the elevator and stepped inside, he finally spoke to her. "Did he hurt you?"

She looked up at him taken back by the question. She wanted to believe it was out of concern for her safety, but she was feeling unsure. Still, maybe Dani was wrong. Even though his attitude towards her had been less favorable, his actions for her spoke of something different, something more protective and caring. She wondered if there was a reason or what the reason was that he felt the need to be more of a brute towards her. Why he kept her at a distance but protected her and escorted her everywhere.

"No, he didn't hurt me." She spoke softly.

"Okay, I'll pick you up in three hours for dinner. You should take that time to relax, maybe take a shower since you didn't have time this morning. I'll make sure no one bothers you." He didn't even bother to look at her. He was staring at the buttons on the side of the doors seemingly lost in thought. Dani assumed other pressing matters were on his mind.

If he was so busy why didn't he just assign her a guard since she obviously was not allowed to be unsupervised, she thought. The elevator doors opened, and he walked out and waited for her, expecting her to follow. When they arrived at her room, he opened the door to reveal her dark room with the still closed blinds from the morning, she walked in the room and felt for the light switch.

"Three hours, get some rest." And then he was shutting the door without so much as a goodbye.

She was alone once more. She let out a long breath of exhaustion and relief. She was thrilled to be alone, to not have to put on a front or talk to anyone especially someone who didn't want to talk to her. She sat on the bed and unlaced her boots, kicking them off one at a time. She stretched her toes not realizing how cramped her feet had felt. Her body ached all over and she concluded the warmth from a hot shower would help to ease the stiffness in her back and the ache in her bones.

The hot water poured over her. The steam collected in the closed bathroom hiding her away from the world. It was quiet, too quiet. She missed the intrusion of her best friend and roommate barging in to converse with her. She wondered when she would see them again. If they were okay, alive even. After all, Dani was shot, could the others have been mortally wounded? She started to panic and took a seat on the shower floor. As she sat there thinking she finally did something she hadn't allowed herself to do in a long time. She cried.

She opened the bathroom door wrapped in a towel and walked into the rest of the room she was living in. She expected to put on the same grunge clothes she had been wearing, since she didn't have any of her belongings, she had been carrying with her on the scouting mission. Along with her weapons, her bag was also gone, which meant all her clothes as well. She wasn't even sure when they took her and brought her back here if they grabbed her bag or if that was left, lost forever on the forest floor. The locket her father had given her was in that bag. It held a picture of her mother with her father, and a picture of her three lost siblings. More than anything she wished she at least had that back.

As she walked to the bed, she noticed a bag with an envelope laying on top. Sitting next to the bed was a stack of books. She drew closer to the bed and noticed her name displayed on the envelope. She picked it up and turned it over noticing a stamp on the back with the initial R on it in a deep blue wax seal. She opened the envelope and inside was a letter.

Dani Mitchells,

I imagine you're tired of wearing the same old military uniform. Maybe try something new. The books are a good read too. Take some time to read them.

-Ryder

She placed the note down on the bed beside the books and proceeded to open the large duffel bag. Inside were clothes and undergarments. She dumped the bag out onto the bed and sorted through the new clothes examining all of what was graciously given to her. Sprawled out on her bed were a couple pairs of pants along with some long sleeve shirts and a heavy jacket with gloves, a hat, and a scarf. There were also undershirts and other undergarments along with clothes to run in. 'Too bad I don't have running shoes' Dani thought to herself.

She grabbed hold of a pair of fresh, fluffy socks, and held them in her hands, squeezing them tightly. A tear ran down her face from the joy of having fresh clean clothes to put on instead of the mud-stained ones she had been wearing.

She gathered up underwear, an undershirt with a bra, and a pair of socks to put on. She moved the rest of the clothes into separate drawers of the dark wooden dresser. If she was going to be staying in this rebel town for a while she might as well get comfortable. Before packing away all the clothes she selected a shirt and a pair of dark washed jeans. She slipped into the undergarments and then the jeans with the shirt. The shirt was soft and the jeans stiff as if they had never been washed. After she got dressed, she walked back to the bed and moved the books to the top of the dresser.

The only thing left on the bed was the bag the clothes came in. She grabbed it up off the bed and kneeled down on the ground next to the bed to slide the bag underneath. But before she could do that, she noticed shoes. There was a pair of running shoes and a pair of warm winter boots lined with fur on the inside. It was truly unexpected. She grabbed the running shoes and look them over. They were light, perfect for running. A small smile escaped her face. She scooted the shoes over so there was room for the bag.

With two hours still left before Zachary would come for her, she laid down on the bed and took a much-needed nap, resting just as she was instructed.

Ryder shut the door leaving Dani in the room to herself. He quickly ran to his room and grabbed the duffle bag and books along with the letter he had written earlier that day. While she had been working hard in the library, Ryder was running around the town collecting the articles of clothing and shoes for her. He hoped this would help her to feel more comfortable and maybe start opening up to him. He slung the bag over his shoulder and carried the many books in his arms as he left his room and headed back down the hall to Dani's quarters. He knocked on the door but received no response. He was happy about that; he was unsure how to approach her and would rather leave the bag waiting for her. He cracked open the door and peeked inside, where he saw no Dani, but instead heard the water from the shower running. He quickly deposited the bag on her bed along with the books and tiptoed out of her room before the water shut off.

Chapter 13

WHEN ON MARS

"Psst, Mitchells. Wake up. Mitchells! Wake up." General Hawkins was shaking Robert to try and stir him awake. It was early in the morning and it was still dark in the room. The curtains were drawn hiding away the first hint at a sunrise starting to peek through. Robert started to move around waking up to his body being shaken.

"Come on Robert. Wake up!" She was quietly yelling at him almost frantic in the late night.

"General Hawkins? What are you... what's going on? What time is it?" He sat up in his bed trying to wake up. He had been in such a deep sleep and the grogginess from the slumber refused to let hold the grip its claws had in him.

He rubbed his eyes and yawned. "There's no time. Hurry up and get dressed. We need to get out of here." She was already across the room at his suitcase digging through it trying to find him clothes. She pulled out a shirt and threw it at him. It caught him in the face finally breaking him from the spell of sleep he had been entranced by.

"Hey! Hawkins! What the hell?" He jumped out of bed and in three large strides was at her side grabbing her wrist trying to gently stop her from her frantic search. "Calm down. What's going on? Why are you in my room?"

"Everyone's gone and we're next. We need to go." She continued her search again and Robert didn't stop her this time. He took a step back confused before he started to understand. His eyes in a daze, but only for a short moment before snapping too. He quickly threw on the shirt she had thrown at him along with the pants that she now handed him.

"What do you mean everyone's gone? I don't understand." Robert was lacing up his boots and then stowing his knife on the side.

Alice moved to the side of the window frame and peered out from the edge of the cascading satin curtains. The window overlooked the courtyard. She could see movement amongst the dark and hear the clanking of metal. No doubt soldiers wearing black carrying weapons. Surly getting ready to attack or apprehend any enemies trying to escape.

Robert grabbed a jacket enhanced with additional pockets for stowing extra magazines in the zip-up pockets along with a picture of his family that he placed in the inside breast pocket. He clipped a magazine in his gun and pulled back the lever. When he released it, the gun allowed a bullet to fall into place in the chamber.

"Where are we headed?" He hid the gun away in the small of his back.

"I think we need to search the palace, probably the lower levels first." Alice let lose the curtain on the window and walked back over to where Robert was standing.

"I went to bed maybe half an hour after you. The party was still roaring and carrying on. It seemed it would go on for at least a few more hours." She looked around clearly on edge. Robert continued to listen to her. He was starting to grow concerned. Robert felt uneasy, fearing where her story was headed.

"I couldn't sleep, so I headed back out to the dining hall maybe an hour after I had left. When I got there, everyone was gone. The room cleaned up. All evidence of any party or person completely erased."

"Maybe they all called it a night." Robert said, knowing it wasn't true. Something was wrong and he was worried Alice and himself were the only two left un-captured.

"No, I checked all the rooms. They're empty. When I started heading back to the hall to see if there were any clues, I overheard some voices. I hid and listened in. I couldn't hear much, but something about a knockout drug and moving something."

"You think they spiked the drinks and when everyone fell asleep, they moved them into a prison?" Robert was now listening for unusual noises that might be taking place outside his door.

"That's exactly what I was thinking. Can't hold a planet hostage if you don't have any hostages." Alice double checked her weapons.

"At least it was a knockout drug instead of a poison." Robert's face indicated he was thinking about the situation, trying to plan their next move. His thoughts were interrupted by a sudden commotion outside.

"Time to go." Alice looked at Robert and nodded towards the doors to the balcony.

They headed towards the doors. With their hands on the handles already starting to turn the cold brass of the door, they heard a click from the other side of the room followed by a thin sliver of light that was growing bigger as the seconds ticked on. Someone was opening the door, most likely to take Robert prisoner.

Robert and Alice pushed open the crystal glass doors and threw themselves onto the rounded balcony as the enemy threw open the door behind them. They looked back and locked eyes with one of the soldiers.

"They're escaping!" The male voiced frantically started to yell looking around for his backup. "Get them before they jump!" Five more soldiers rushed into the room attempting to capture the escaping Earthlings. Each sporting the Mar's uniform with the red insignia and weapons fully loaded, ready to take the enemy.

"I guess we're jumping." Robert looked at Alice and shrugged, holding out his hand for her to take. They were up on the balcony and hailing over the side before the soldiers were even halfway across the grand and luxurious guest room.

The two landed with a thump in the soft bushes planted under the balcony. They laid there only for a moment shocked by the event that just transpired.

"I'm really glad your room was only on the second floor. Mine was on the third." Alice looked towards Robert and started to pull herself up. Robert followed but stayed in the shadows of the palace.

They could hear the soldiers above shouting out orders. They stood there in the dark, listening hoping to gain information as to where they would be searched for first so they could avoid those areas. They heard nothing but quiet whispers. Failing to hear much more the two moved on in the hopes that they wouldn't run into much attention.

"Come on, we should look for the others. Obviously, they're still alive if they were trying to take us captive." Robert walked along the wall keeping himself shielded from overhead.

"Of course, they do. They think our lives are meaningful enough that the government is going to meet their demands for us to be handed over. Despicable." Alice hated the idea of herself being used as a pawn. She would be no one's prisoner, she would not be used as a bargaining chip to overtake the remainder of humanity.

The two made their way back into the palace and headed towards the lower levels trying to keep out of sight. The sun had started to rise making the task of staying hidden that much more difficult. The palace was dimmed. The sun still trying to rise on a new day casted the grand palace in a sensational glow. Every few feet there was a half oval sheer lighting fixture, allowing for a moment of brightness before the marbled hallway dimmed once more.

They overheard guards speaking, indicating that they were still looking for them. They had control over the Earth ship, keeping it under guard to prevent anyone from trying to sneak on and using it to escape. They had also added extra security around other docking ports just in case the Earthlings had ideas to commandeer a Mars ship.

"Sounds like they've been preparing for this for a while." Alice whispered to Robert. They had been peeking around a corner listening to the conversation, but now they were silently running down a hallway trying to put distance between them and the guards. It would be easier to stay low if they didn't have to fight. If it came to that, Robert was confident that between him and Alice, they would have no problem.

Soon, the hallway met a wall and they had to make a decision on which way to go. "Left?" Robert shrugged.

"Sounds as good as any plan to me. We need to find a map or a layout. Something to help us get around. There should be servant hallways hidden within the walls. That would make it much easier to get around and avoid detection and run ins with the guards." Alice predicted.

They looked down the new hallway making sure it was clear of the enemy before proceeding. The darkness was helping with ensuring their success. They started down but before they made it very far a door suddenly opened and there was nowhere for them to hide. They tried to look as if they were supposed to be there, hoping it was just a servant that would pay them no mind. But as they walked past the door two guards emerged.

"Hey! Stop!" One of the guards shouted at them immediately.

Before they could take off, the guards had hands on Alice and Robert. "You are under arrest by order of the pri...". The other guard started to tell them. Before he could finish both Alice and Robert where on the defense, attacking.

They looked at each other and gave a restraint nod to indicate each other's intentions. Without missing a beat, the two worked as a combined force using their shared military knowledge and training to overcome their opponents. Alice grabbed the guard's hand that had been resting on her shoulder. With the weight of her body to steady herself, she used her strength and flipped him on his back using his momentum to help thrust him over.

Once he was on his back, she acted, making quick work to restrain him. When he started to call out, she delivered a satisfying blow to his cheek, slamming her fist into his face. The force was enough to temporarily knock him unconscious. His body went limp on the cold marbled floor.

Robert had subdued his guard as well. He had managed to swing his body around abruptly, intimidating the guard causing him to remove his hand from Robert. Robert grabbed the front of the shirt of the guard pulling him in close. As the guard swung forward off balance, Robert smacked into him headfirst breaking the guard's nose. As the guard held his nose, blood gushing everywhere, he comically fell hitting his head hard on the slick floor.

Robert brushed his hands together. "Well, that was...exciting to say the least." He held a handout for Alice to grab. She accepted the gesture and grabbed his hand heaving herself off the unconscious guard. Robert kneeled and started to frisk their pockets for weapons or anything that might assist them in finding the others along with aiding in an escape. They needed to get back to Earth and warn the military of what happened. This was an act of War.

He stopped when he heard a click followed by muffled sounds. He investigated a pant leg pocket and there it was, a radio. "Perfect, now we can monitor their movements." He swung the radio in front of Alice to bring attention to it. She brightened at the new hope that was sparking to life.

As Alice fiddled with the radio, Robert searched the second guard. He didn't find a map like he would have preferred, but he did find a set of knives and a small electronic device that resembled a small tablet. 'That might come in handy; he thought to himself. He handed the tablet to Alice for her to examine.

"Oh, this is good." She started clicking on the tablet.

She explained how it could display a layout of not only the palace but military bases on Mars and in 3D at that. It also indicated the whereabouts of every ship and fleet. This would help them to escape. They could even remotely start a ship for a faster escape. Robert lifted back onto his feet. He leaned over and took the guards guns, handing one to Alice and stowing the other on his waistband.

"We should move. Staying in one place for too long is dangerous and I'm sure these guys will come to at any moment. Personally, I would like to get some distance before they do." Alice spoke to Robert as she stowed the tablet into her side pocket, but not before determining a path that leads to the lower levels. They started running down the hall once more. They turned down another hallway and then another. The palace was like a maze of white. The sun was now rising, brightening up the hallways from the many windows. They wouldn't be able to get around now without being spotted. The darkness that had been their saving grace was now eliminated.

"There should be a door coming up on your left. Take it. It's an entrance to the servant's hidden halls. We should be able to make our way downstairs using them." Alice notified Robert. He looked at her with a bumbled look.

"There was a map of it stowed in the tablet." She explained. They arrived at the door and made their way in heading down towards the heart of the palace.

After taking three flights of stairs down they came to a set of large double doors. It wasn't guarded which seemed suspicious, but Robert noticed something in the corner. He pulled Alice to the side and pointed. Whispering, he informed her of the camera watching the door and hallway.

Alice had the tablet in hand looking at the map. Keeping her voice low she spoke. "Maybe I can disable the camera with the tablet. This should be an entrance to where they keep prisoners. What do we do? We can't just barge in. But we need to get down there."

"I'm not sure what else we can do." Robert started to make his way towards the doors after Alice was able to hack into the camera and electronically turn it the opposite direction of their position. Alice followed behind him, holding her weapon at the ready. They reached the doors and pushed through expecting and hoping to see cells with their fellow comrades locked away inside.

What they were met with took them by surprise. It was a single person. A person sporting a tailored purple suit and dramatic, purple top hat. He held onto a cane steading it in front of him giving the appearance of poise and elegance.

"Surprise!" The prince shouted out, throwing up his arms only to go back to holding onto the unneeded cane.

"What! How did you..." Robert started to say exasperated. There was disappointment in his voice having come so far for nothing.

The prince spoke with glee. "Know? Oh, it is just one of my many... talents. You could say. After all, I do come from a very strong Marsian bloodline. My ancestors even founded the first colonies." He gloated. His voice then turning serious. "You think I wouldn't inherit the strongest abilities we Marsian's can have?"

He looked up outstretching his arms. "The power of precognition. I knew what your intentions would be as soon as you sat down at my table and we toasted. I knew before you even knew."

He nodded bringing his arm up and waved his guards in. Guards rushed around them. Two guards each grabbed Alice and Robert subduing them. They were met with a total of eight more guards surrounding them with guns all pointed at them. Alice tried to shake one of the guard's grips lose on her upper arm, knowing she would fail.

"Where is everyone else! What have you done with the other Earthlings? Were they ever even here!" Robert was struggling against the guards yelling at their so-called gracious host.

"Are they even still alive?" Alice said with hatred lacing her voice. Her teeth barely showing through her grinding jaw too angry to even properly function.

The prince laughed, grabbing his side as if the two were dressed as clowns and he had never seen such humorous performers. After a moment, he acted as if he was wiping a laugh tear from his eye and then became intensely and overly serious all over again.

"Oh, don't worry, they are very much alive. In fact, you'll be joining them right now." He stated slowly then commanded his guards. "Take them away!" He smiled a Cheshire smile as the guards hauled them away.

Chapter 14

THE FIRST CONFLICT

Only half an hour had passed since Dani had fallen asleep. Try as she may, she couldn't seem to get her eyes to stay shut. With time to spare she rummaged through the books that Zachary had left for her. The books seem to be about past wars, battles, and conflicts between that of Earth and other planets. One book was labeled 'Mars, Seeing Red'. Another one 'Finding Faith In Venus'. She wasn't sure why Zachary would want her to read these, then a book caught her attention. It was small and thin wrapped in a dark brown leather-bound cover.

When she opened it the pages seemed frail and thin. She easily flipped through the pages, thumbing a few of them. The ink in some places had seem to run before drying, an indication that the beautiful font was all accomplished by hand instead of typing and printing.

She studied the small book noticing words such as war and resistance. This was the book that caught her attention the most. Not the glossed ones with firm book bindings, but the dusty journal that looked as if at any moment it would disintegrate in her hands. It was a book well read. She put the rest of the books away and sat down on her bed to read from the dull looking book with beautiful penmanship. The first page was titled 'A Broken Earth'. As she read, she started to understand why Zachary would want her to read this book. Why he would leave it for her. The meaning behind it was deeper than she could have ever imagined, and her eyes were starting to be open to truths kept from not only her but from the hard working, and just people of her nation.

The book started to unravel and reveal a dark, but recent past. A conflict between a peaceful region within the borders of Helenia of

Marsian descendants and the government. They were attacked by the military and killed. Those who were lucky, escaped beyond the wall and searched for a new place to call home. She noticed the timeline was when her mother was in the military. When the conflict started, she would have just graduated from the academy as a fresh officer.

She remembered asking her mother once when she met her father. She had told her they had met at Eastern Command before shipping out to answer a call to assist in establishing peace. She hadn't realized that what her mother meant was she and her father answered a call to fight against other citizens living within the nation of Helenia, her nation.

As she read, she understood the conflict lasted seven years with five years of peace before another conflict occurred lasting another three years. Dani would have been two at the start of the second conflict. Her older brother would have been nine at the time and her parents hadn't even been pregnant with the twins yet. She had no idea that something like this had occurred on Earth let alone within the nation that she lived in.

Before long she heard a knock at the door followed by a click. She looked up in time to see Zachary walk through the open door.

"Oh, good you're up." He paused in the doorway looking at her, staring just a little longer than usual. He shook his head hoping she hadn't noticed him staring at her. It was the first time he had seen her with her hair down and without a military uniform. He wasn't looking at a soldier anymore. But a young woman entranced by a book. Someone who was starting to relax and open-up. His hand rested on the doorknob before she invited him in.

He noticed the dark leather bond book in her hand and a smile played at his lips. He was hoping she would read it. "It's an interesting read, isn't it?"

She closed the book and laid it down on the pillow. She stared at the book refusing to remove her hand. When she did, she was slow, letting her hand slip away. She was quiet when she spoke.

"I... I had no idea. I had heard there were conflicts at one point, but it was played off as something that was normal. Natural problems of a growing nation. Not an attempted genocide. We were always told that the conflicts weren't the problem, but a sickness that swept through the town. Why would they do this? How were they even able to cover it up?"

"Fear Dani Mitchells. Fear makes people do stupid things. The government fears anything that is different and those who have any amount of Marsian blood coursing through their veins is a cause for concern." His voice conveyed sadness, hinting at something more, something he was hiding, or maybe remembering.

"Were you there? I mean in the region of Marina when it was attacked. I know you have Marsian blood." She spoke slowly. She knew it was bold of her to ask and she didn't certainly expect him to answer.

He stayed silent, debating on if he would open-up to her or not. He thought if maybe he started to open-up, maybe it would make Dani feel more at ease and, in return, start to trust him. "Yes, on my father's side. He was half Marsian. It was more than enough to isolate him to a region away from the rest of the tiers. It was by my mother's Venus blood that I was able to pass as a normal citizen. For a time at least."

He took a seat in the chair at the small table near the window. "I was five during the second conflict. My mother was able to run away with me in the middle of the night. My father, unfortunately, had not been so lucky. We were able to escape to other family members within tier Lincoln."

Dani was shocked by his willingness to talk to her. "How did the military cover this up?" She asked him.

"They're the government, they can cover anything up." He stood up and pushed his chair back in. "Anyways are you hungry? Downstairs is serving a rotisserie style chicken smothered in gravy. It's probably the best thing you'll ever eat." His attitude changed from the depressing worries of his childhood to a lighter mood, in hopes of leaving the past where it should be, in the past. The moment of weakness he allowed Dani to see was the first step he took to allow her in, to breaking down the walls. Not only the ones he had but hopefully the ones she had up as well.

Dani was flummoxed by his excitement of dinner, or food in general. She resolved that she was in fact hungry and the idea of comfort food such as chicken and gravy made her mouth water. As she rose from where she was sitting on her bed, she commented back to him. "Well, that does sound really good."

"Then, follow me, Dani Mitchells." The two exited the room and walked down the stretch of dulled colored hallway towards the elevators. Silently gliding across the dark green patterned carpet. Zachary made no effort of conversation and she was content with the silence. He wasn't a very pleasant person to talk to, at least he wasn't towards her. What could she expect though, he assured her she wasn't a prisoner, but she was still a soldier of Helenia, but his wiliness to speak deeply to her was something new and Dani was deep in thought about what his intentions were?

They rode in silence down the elevator and not a single word was spoken until they reached the designated dining area. He pointed at a table and told her he would meet her at that table and to go ahead and sit. He then went to retrieve two plates of food. He placed the plate of food in front of her and she had to admit it did look amazing and smelled even better.

"After this, we'll head to outskirts of town again. There is another bonfire that I must make an appearance at. This time if you find yourself lacking in entertainment then feel free to leave." She nodded in understanding. The rest of the dinner was eaten in silence.

Dani missed her friends, the family she had chosen, and built through the years of training. The bonds she had developed with them. She missed Liam reading his paper at every meal, Aiden and Sarah's light flirting. Even the occasional appearance of Finn, John, or Erin adding a bit of drama to the meal.

This dining hall carried the noise of people conversing and living their lives, but it was somehow different than the ambiance of sound she had grown to crave. The chaos clash of voices that soothed her. She wondered when she would hear those sweet sounds again if at all.

When she finished her meal, Zachary stood and took her empty plate and dirty silverware towards a window where used dishes were disposed of to be cleaned and prepped for the next service. As he walked back towards her, she stood and pushed in her chair only to be passed by him. An expectation of her to follow him did not need to be stated but was felt.

She walked a few paces behind him dreading attending another bonfire. She had no desire to deal with drunken fools and obnoxious people hollering obscenities and callus phrases. If she couldn't be with her fellow comrades and friends, then she rather not be with anyone at all. She felt so alone and unwanted it made her want to cry.

The air was cool and refreshing when it washed over Dani's face as the doors swooshed open. Immediately, she could smell the burning of wood from the fire. The leaves rattled in the trees overhead, the night sky shimmering through the branches. The dim light from the moon ever so slightly reflecting off the edges of the remaining dry, crisp foliage. The wind howled as it passed over the old lamp posts throughout the town. In the distance, Dani could see the glow from the roaring fire. She understood why he took her to the fires, the tactic of sympathizing with the rebels, and thus letting her own guard down. She had to admit it was a well-played game. Even if her government was wrong for chasing out the Marsians, that was almost thirty years ago. She alone could not write that wrong.

Zachary once again led her towards the edge of the small town where the bonfire was already blazing. The fire was so massive Dani could see the fire before they even came over the hill. Dani stumbled over a few rocks and branches in the dark of the unlit path to the open field.

"Here." Zachary paused and turned back to look at Dani.

She was so focused on her feet she didn't pay attention to his sudden stop and almost ran into him. He held out his hand for her to take. Her hand was warm in his. She was surprised by his touch, but it was a fleeting touch. As soon as she was down the dark slope he let go of her hand and continued to walk a few paces in front of her. He seemed to be unfazed by her hand, by her in general, but still, it was the first act of kindness he had shown her.

Zachary noticed Dani's trouble with descending the hill and offered a hand. He was stunned when she almost fell into his arms. He could feel his cheeks starting to blush at the sudden embrace. She quickly backed away from him, but not out of repulsion, but out of embarrassment. He tried to collect himself best he could, hoping to not look foolish.

As soon as they were at the bonfire, Zachary was gone, already distracted by someone speaking out to him. Dani noticed he seemed to relax when they came out here. She wondered how much of it was an act, a show of popularity. How much he played up that he was happy to appease others. She sat on the logs that surrounded the fire pit. She let the flames lick at her, enjoying the warmth that chased away the chill that was starting to settle around her.

She covered her hands with the ends of the sleeves of the shirt, stretching the material slightly to do so. She brought her knees up to her chest and wrapped her arms around them to help keep them put. She rested her chin on the top of her knees and watched the fire and people enjoying the cool night. People danced and jumped, excited that the long workday was over, that they had their health, their loved ones, or perhaps their freedom. She, somewhat, envied them. Their resolve to live as open as possible knowing at any moment it could be ripped away.

As she watched the fire leap and bound in an inferno of heat and smoke, she felt the small hairs on the back of her neck start to rise. She heard footsteps and before long, two people sat on either side of her.

"This doesn't seem very exciting. What do you think Penny?"

"Oh, I agree Nadia. On a night like tonight, I feel no one should be sitting all by their lonesome selves. They should be out there," The girl indicated towards the fire where everyone was dancing and laughing, enjoying life. "getting into trouble, or...". She had a devious smile plastered on her face. "making trouble."

"So then, Dani, which would you like to do." Nadia leaned down, uncrossing her long legs for her elbows to come to a resting place along her knees. Her hand was supporting her chin and her large red ringed eyes bore into Dani's.

"Excuse me?" Dani tried to seem unthreatening and friendly.

"Would you like to make trouble or get into it?" Penelope prompted before her sister could respond.

"Oh, I, um, would rather watch?" Dani hoped they would leave her alone. Getting attached to the people here would make leaving complicated and difficult, besides that, Zachary told her to stay clear of the two girls now keeping her company. Their statements only proved his warning was well placed, their intentions were not of good favor.

"Nonsense. As I understand it you've been cooped up in some military prison being forced to train and fight for the twisted government." Penelope's feelings towards the government were one of informal taste. She was not shy about speaking her ill will towards them or her lack of affection.

"Nadia! Penelope! I have been looking for you guys everywhere. Come, cousins! There are some people I want you to meet." Gabe walked over towards them, grabbing their attention and intriguing them with a proposition of enjoyment and foolery. This was the one-time Dani appreciated Gabe's unwanted appearance.

Nadia and Penelope jumped up excitedly and skipped away towards a group of people that had been hovering nearby. They hadn't even stopped to look back at Dani, as if she was already a distant memory starting to fade in the back of their mind.

"Gabe!" Someone yelled. Gabe looked over but ignored the call.

"Well Dani Mitchell, shall we continue our conversation from earlier?" Gabe's wicked smile showed his row of bright teeth as it stretched his face. He placed his hand on her shoulder and she looked over at it. His finger lightly stroking her upper arm.

Dani slapped his hand away and stood up from where she had been sitting. Every other time she didn't want to seem threatening. She thought it would be best while she was in the rebel town. But with Gabe that was not the case. She wanted him to know she was fierce and was a force not to be messed with.

She looked him square in the eye and with a look of repugnance she spoke. "I suggest you go and join your friends. I guarantee there will be no type of enjoyment or pleasant conversation between us." She made clear of the venom in her voice.

Gabe held her eyes, unblinking. His smile had started to fade as her words sunk in.

"Gabe!" One of the dolled-up females called out, her voice laced with a spoiled attitude.

Dani crossed her arms and smiled. "Guess you're being summoned. Why don't you run along and play? Trust me, I won't be waiting when you get back."

"You're going..." Gabe started.

"Gabe! Let's go!" The girl shouted a bit more forceful, stomping her leg as she did so.

Gabe snarled but fulfilled the wish of the girl. He turned away and headed towards the group of people. Dani let out a sigh of relief. She knew it wasn't a good idea to infuriate Gabe, considering he was the one who shot her, proving that he did, indeed, have skill, not only that, but she was still healing from her wound. If Gabe tried to physically approach her again, she might have to fight. She wasn't sure how well she would be able to hold her own in her condition.

Once Gabe and his entourage had settled on the other side on the bonfire Dani decided there was no point in staying out in the cold. Zachary was off entertaining other rebels. She could see him clear across the field. He looked as if he had a drink in his hand and she could see he was laughing. He seemed so normal, so natural, surrounded by people he enjoyed being around.

It hurt her to see him so happy, enjoying the night. It caused her to miss her friends even more. She refused to sit out alone for another night. She'd much rather be in her room reading anyways. She starred at Zachary for a moment more before turning away and heading back into town.

*****

Zachary noticed Dani sitting alone. He wanted to sit with her, to converse with her. He wasn't sure why, but she made him nervous and because of that, he felt he needed to distance himself from her. She probably hated him anyway.

Before long Dani wasn't alone anymore. He could see two people talking to her. He was sure it was Nadia and Penelope as the light from the fire caught the neon blue and pink in their hair. He watched carefully. He knew the two were dangerous. The two of them along with their cousin, Gabe, had been trouble ever since they arrived in the town only a month ago. He thought it was suspicious how they appeared in the town without any warning. Usually, if there was a defector from Helenia then the scouts would either bring them or inform them before the defectors would arrive. And worse, their eyes were completely red. All three of them had remarkable skills in combatants and weapons. He had his suspicions about them. That they weren't from here, as in Earth, but couldn't prove it…yet.

Not those three. And the story they spun had holes and disconnections. Zachary was immediately suspicious of them. He noticed the two girls leaving after someone came and spoke to them, but the dark figure had stayed, looming over Dani. Zachary heard someone call out for Gabe and notice the dark figure standing close to Dani react to the name.

He was about to head over there when he watched as Dani slapped away the hand Gabe had placed on her. She stood straight up as if a storm was starting to brew. He couldn't hear what she was saying but soon she was crossing her arms and her powerful stance indicated she had the situation under control. In that moment Zachary witnessed the fierceness that was Dani Mitchells reveal itself.

Gabe stormed away. Clearly whatever Dani had said enraged him. A modest smile passed over Zachary's face. The smile didn't last long though. Dani was now alone once more. He wanted to go over there, to talk to her and explain everything.

"Hey, Ryder." One of his friends called out to him. The conversation, momentarily, drew Zachary back in. He was laughing and enjoying the company, but when he looked back over to where Dani had been standing only moments prior, she was gone. He frantically scanned the field for her. After a moment his eyes laid on her. She was walking back up the hill towards town. She looked cold with her arms bundled in front of her. He wanted to run up to her, to make her feel welcome, but he didn't think she was ready.

*****

Dani reached her room. Before she walked in, she rested her head against the cold wood of the door and closed her eyes. Her thoughts went to desperation. She couldn't believe this was happening to her. A simple recon mission and she had been captured. 'Maybe Zachary was right,' she thought, 'maybe I am a shitty soldier.' She found the door handle and fiddled with it. She turned the knob and headed inside. The darkness encased her. She was mentally drained, and she couldn't bring herself to read or do much of anything but shove her face into the pillow and let sleep take her, only after allowing herself to cry once more.

Chapter 15

A TRUTH REVEALED

Although it probably wasn't wise, Dani woke up in the early morning and went for a run. The crisp icy air and the pounding of her feet in line with her heart helped her to feel alive once more. A spark stirring inside her as if hope were starting to grow. The run reminded Dani of who she was and because of that, she gained back the strength and determination of the soldier she had been trained to be. The confidence she had nurtured over the years to act and be a force rose to the surface. She would survive this; she would escape and make it back to the wall whether a team came for her or not. This was her resolve.

She ran around the outer side of the town. Even though the town was small and condensed after half an hour of running she hadn't even made it halfway around. When she could see the building she was living in, she slowed her pace to a jog and soon a walk to cool down. In the early morning, there were not as many people on the streets, but still, she could hear voices and early morning work being completed. Vehicles were coming in and out of the town from the east. People sat in the back of a few trucks that were headed towards the fields to harvest the last of the vegetation for the season, while others headed towards different buildings to work various jobs to better the community.

As she approached her building, she even noticed the guards changing shifts. She looked down at her watch and noted that it was exactly half an hour past six. Dani thought it was odd to change in the middle of the hour so either someone was extremely late, extremely early, or it was a strategy to throw an enemy off. She decided she would keep mental note and be more mindful of the guard shifts, it might help aid her in an escape later.

When she walked through the doors, she was hit with the overpowering, but mouthwatering smell of bacon, eggs, and biscuits. There were already people in the dining area enjoying the fresh hot meal. She quickened her pace up the stairs to the floor that held her room. After her exhilarating run, she was famished, and she rushed to get back downstairs for the food that teased her senses. She laid out clothes for the day, while she waited for the water in the shower to heat up.

The hot water seared her aching wound. The run was a bit harsher on her then she realized, but the wound was healing fast. Where a dark purple bruise had been was now replaced with an ugly yellow. A soft pink ring surrounded the edge of where the bullet hole had been. It was tender to the touch but was clean and as the days progressed Dani felt she had more mobility. She wasn't favoring the opposite side of her body as much as she had been, too afraid that she would hit the wound and reopen it.

She finished her shower and hurried to get dressed, throwing on a pair of jeans and a thermal shirt graciously given to her. She laced up the warm fur-lined boots and grabbed the winter jacket and scarf before she ran out the door. She didn't even bother to wait for Zachary to come fetch her. Honestly, she felt perturbed by him, constantly taking her to those ridiculous bonfires so she could just sit around while he flirted and enjoyed the surrounding of people he knew.

She enjoyed her breakfast in silence, no Zachary, no Gabe nor his mischievous cousins. She, however, wondered what news the paper was bringing back home. Liam was always so good about informing her of the daily news, about Mars and their plans to enact peace with Earth. About all the stretched truths the government relayed. The thought of Mars brought images of her father. She hoped he was safe; he should be returning home from Mars soon.

Looking across the table, she could see her friends in her mind. She could see Sarah and Aiden sitting closer to one another than that of others, the innocent flirting by Sarah and the soft, light touches of Aiden pushing the strands of loose hair away from her face revealing her bright blue eyes.

Dani looked beside her to the empty chair. She could imagine Liam sliding into the bench next to her excited by the daily rubbish of the paper, as he stuffed his face full of food.

She even missed the other cadets such as Erin and Cain. Erin's attitude and competitive nature. Cain's ability to solve and work out any problem. 'He probably would have already strategized a plan in escaping this town if he were her.' Dani thought to herself. She continued to eat, hoping it would help her to choke down the tears she could feel starting to sting the inside of her eyelids.

Instead, her thoughts traveled back to her father. 'Just a peaceful diplomatic resolve', she thought, what could be more suspicious. The idea that something went wrong, that something happened to her father was snarling its way into her head. Before it could overtake her, she stood up and took her plate to the disposal window and headed to the library, hoping work would clear her mind of stray and worrisome thoughts.

*****

Zachary had been up early helping load the trucks with supplies to be taken to the main compound. Grayson had reached out to him not soon after he finished with the trucks. He had been inquiring about his sister's health status and when Zachary would be bringing her to the compound. He arranged with Grayson for a car to be prepped. He felt Dani would soon be ready to be moved, especially after seeing her run that morning. He had the car arranged to receive them within a weeks' time. Plenty of time for him to start explaining things as he eased her into the idea that they were not enemies.

Zachary was headed back to the main building that housed the living quarters. He planned to talk with Dani that morning about her brother and the compound. He wanted to tell her last night at the bonfire, but he had been pulled away and before he could return, she had already left and headed to her room for the night. He knew she might not be ready to listen to him, but his actions seemed to be pushing her further away. He felt she was closing off from him instead of opening-up. He needed to fix that. He needed to talk to her.

Before he could make it to the building though, he noticed Dani walking out the door and heading across the street towards the library. He started to head in her direction, but before he could take more than two steps, he heard his name called. Just like the night before he was pulled away once more. He stared after her as she disappeared into the library building. He sighed heavily as he looked towards the graying sky and then turned away, hoping he would get to talk to her later.

*****

Dani entered the library building, Miss Mackenzie was already sitting at the front desk, her coffee cup steaming from a fresh brew. She was so entranced by something on her computer screen that when Dani walked in, she hardly even flinched at the sound of the heavy door closing behind her.

"Good morning Miss Mackenzie." Dani announced as she unwrapped her dark green, navy blue, and cream plaid scarf from around her neck. She peeled off her forest green jacket and neatly folded it up. Holding onto the two items, she joined the librarian at her front desk, she peeked at the computer screen expecting to see military information, but she couldn't make heads or tails of what she was looking at. The only thing she recognized was the nation of Oakden. A nation even further northeast from Helenia that specialized in military weapons.

"Good morning Miss Dani. How are you doing today?" She moved on to shuffling a pile of books. It seemed no matter what, there was always a stack of books on her desk. They seemed to multiply even though Dani rarely saw anyone in the library.

"As good as can be expected. Is that pile for me?" She came around the desk and laid her jacket and scarf in a cubby designated for her use.

"Yes, ma'am it is." She stopped what she was doing and looked up at Dani, her arms still laid across the books. "These books need to be re-categorized. After you get done with that then your free to go."

"It's going to take me that long, huh?" Dani joked.

Miss Mackenzie laughed at Dani's forwardness. "No, I just don't have much that needs to be done and you should be resting anyways. I don't see any point in making you hang around."

Dani went straight to work appreciating the act of kindness. The idea that when she completed this task, she would be able to leave and perhaps get some rest pushed her to work steady but fast. Even though the easy work at the library distracted her, she would still rather be resting in her room with the books Zachary loaned to her. Her window, too, was in a prime location to complete some recon on the town, hopefully giving her valuable intel on the rebel forces to report back to her military.

She had found herself working with books about the conflict between the nation she had thought she had known so well and the Marsian territory. In the open floor of the library, tables and chairs sat for those to research or read in silence. They sat empty with a layer of dust piling on them.

Nobody was in the library except for a single person. An older man sitting on the far side at one of the tables. He had a stack of books with him and he seemed to be writing down notes. Dani walked over towards him, intrigued and curious. The darkness of the library almost concealed him, but the small, golden brass lamp with the emerald glass shield attached to the end of the table had shed just enough light to reveal a face impressed with sadness and self-loathing.

"Can I help you with anything, sir?" Dani asked quietly, unsure if it was the right thing to do.

The man stopped writing and looked up at her. His face immediately scrunched in concern and fear. "Amelia?" He was so quiet Dani almost missed the name.

"Excuse me?" Dani asked. Did her ears deceive her?

"No, it couldn't be." He said the last part so quiet; it was absorbed into the silence of the still library.

From the sight of Dani, he started to gather his papers and close the books in front of him. Dani caught words relating to the medical field along with pictures and diagrams of anatomy laced within the pages not being concealed. When she looked at the titles of the book, they all related to medicine, anatomy, or the medical field. The man started to rise from his chair looking for an escape but sat back down when he noticed the look on Dani's face.

"How do you know my mother's name?" Dani asked confused and hurt. The sound of her mother's name felt like a bullet to the heart. No one ever said her mother's name, not even her father. She thought it was more than a coincidence that this person knew her mother's name and because of it, she needed to know more.

"I apologize, I've confused you with someone else. My mistake." The man tried to play the confusion off as a misstep on his end, knowing well that the play would not cross over Dani's eyes as such.

Dani could see through his act. "No, you've mistaken me as my mother, you knew who she was, and you know who I am. Don't you?" She was desperate for information. The sound of her mother's name sending her head into a frenzy. Her voice started to rise. A mix of emotions unable to be contained. She was demanding of him.

The man looked back at his books. He was contemplating his next move. When he looked back up at Dani there was a single tear in his eye. "Yes, I do. I... knew your parents, fought alongside them in the conflict." He paused for a moment.

"Your mother was one of the bravest people I've known, but I'm afraid I've already said too much." He gave Dani a sad smile, but it seemed the smile was more for him then for Dani. "Please excuse me." He looked down at his watch and then stood up shuffling his pages and books together once more. "I have somewhere I need to be."

"No, wait." Dani had a hand on one of the books. He grabbed the book and pushed past her.

"I'm sorry." He exclaimed back as he rushed towards the front of the library not bothering to look back. Dani stood there befuddled by what just happened. She walked up towards the front where she rested at the desk. Leaning against it, she looked over at Miss Mackenzie. She had been looking at the scene playing out in front of her.

Dani spoke first. "Do you know who that was?"

She didn't hesitate to explain. "Jaxon Black is his name. He tends to keep to himself. As I understand it, he was in the military as a brigadier general." She paused and look towards the exit only to look back at Dani. "What was that commotion about?"

"I'm… I'm not sure." Dani said it slowly still trying to process what the gentleman had said to her. She wasn't sure of his connection, but she knew one thing, he knew her parents and she would get answers.

She said her goodbyes for the night and took her leave heading back to her room. As she strolled back, she noticed people bustling around carrying cases of flowers and other such objects resembling decorations. They all seem to be heading in the same direction. A large building with a round top that came to a point. 'Town hall.' Dani imagined. She assumed someone or many someones would be making an appearance, no doubt to discuss movement against the government. This might be a good opportunity to gather information.

She had made it back to her building when she realized she hadn't seen Zachary at all that day. Maybe she had been up early enough that they missed one another. Dani thought it for the best and made her way to her room.

She opened her door and was welcomed by the warmth from the light that poured into her room. She was sure when she left this morning, she had left the curtains closed. The sunlight shone brightly through the opened windows, highlighting an object on the chair. Laying there was a beautiful dark blue satin dress. It was cut short in the front and frilled longer towards the back. A layer of lace laid over the satin. The sleeves were long and made entirely of lace revealing flowers and leaves engraved into it. Underneath the chair stood a pair of strapped, golden heels. She touched the dress feeling the material, she had never seen a dress so beautiful before.

An envelope had been placed on the table next to the chair where the dress laid. Dani picked it up and turned it over and again she noticed the wax seal with an R stamped into it. She picked open the letter careful not to ruin the wax and pulled the note out.

Dani Mitchells,

Tonight, is our annual celebration of the coming winter season. I will pick you up at seven if you would like to join me.

-Ryder

She wasn't sure what to make of the gesture. Why invite her to a ball if he had made it clear he didn't enjoy her company. She had a few hours to contemplate whether or not she would join him. After the night before, at the bonfire, it wasn't something she could see herself going too. Perhaps, Zachary would just have to attend the celebration by himself.

Chapter 16

A SOLDIER FIT FOR A REBEL

Dani was about to dive into the books Zachary had left for her to read when she heard a soft knock at the door. Dani frowned; she was really hoping to enjoy the warm afternoon to herself. Upon answering the door, it was Nadia who surprisingly stood in the doorway. She was holding with her a small duffel bag that seemed to weigh heavily on her shoulder. Her hair was pulled up in a ponytail and her clothes looked ragged and smelled of soil. 'She must have just come from the greenhouse not bothering to clean up after work.' Dani thought.

"Hi. May I, um, come in?" Nadia asked nervously. Dani looked up and down the hallway expecting someone else to come around with the way Nadia asked. "It's just me." Nadia gave her a small smile.

Dani didn't want to be rude, so she stepped aside to let the girl in. Nadia seemed less abrasive and obnoxious than her older sister, Penelope, or cousin. Nadia saw the dress as she walked in while Dani shut the door.

"I'm guessing you're going to the ball?" Nadia turned to Dani; the bag swung on her hip.

"Oh, I'm not sure. I doubt I'm truly wanted there. I was captured and brought here. I'm a Helenian. Remember. I don't belong here, let alone fit in." Dani walked over to the bed and sat down crossing a leg underneath her. The same way she used to when she was home with Sarah. She felt there was no reason she should beat around the bush. She was still an enemy.

"Nonsense! This is such a mixed bunch of people. There's those from Mars, obviously." She flipped her hair indicating herself. "People from Venus, and of course from Helenia. There are even people from Saturn. I'm not actually sure why because it's not like their planet is doing bad. As I understand it, there one of the most successful planets out of the planets that have been cultivated. Probably something in the gaseous air. Apparently, they hit it big with a mineral and everyone wants it, so there like crazy rich." She said it carelessly, her intentions to make fun of the planet clear.

Venus was a neutral planet with no intergalactic issues with other planets. The last time they had a conflict it was at least a hundred years ago, and it was with one of the outer planets. The conflict only lasted six months, but there were still many immigrants from Venus that had settled on Earth because of it.

"Well, even so, I may have a dress," Dani indicated the chair by nodding at it. "But it's not like I have any way to..." she trailed off not wanting to admit she couldn't do her own hair or anything else girly that Sarah was always going on about.

"Get all dolled up?" Nadia said, her hand placed dramatically on her hip. "I figured not, and that's why I'm here." She dropped the bag on the floor. It clanked with a heavy thud. The items inside shifting.

She leaned down and opened it to reveal hairbrushes and styling utensils. She pulled the items out and laid them out on the floor. Next, she dug around and pulled out a black leather case. When she unraveled the case, it revealed a plethora of makeup brushes. Still in the bag were eyeshadows in every color, along with every makeup essential a girl could ever need.

Dani's eyes went wide, shocked by all the items that had been able to fit into the small bag. Sarah did Dani's make up a couple of times when she and the boys would go out into Falco, but even Sarah didn't have this much makeup. Nadia indicated that she wanted Dani to sit in the chair patting on the back of it. Dani grabbed the dress so it wouldn't get ruined, moving it to the bed. As she sat in the chair, Nadia moved the items to the table, organizing them as she would use them. Dani sat nervously in the chair. She was told by Zachary not to trust Nadia or be around her and now Nadia was there wanting to play dress up with her.

Dani decided to play along, it couldn't hurt and maybe she could get Nadia talking. She would play dress up if it meant she could possibly get crucial information. Nadia took a look at Dani; her hand was on her mouth and she was humming. Her red eyes focused. Dani looked side to side, feeling awkward as she was being studied.

"Maybe a little concealer for those dark eyes. Your skin is so fair they stand out." Nadia commented to Dani. Dani rubbed her own face feeling self-conscious about her dark eyes. She had never been one to sleep well, but she never paid attention to how it had affected her look. She felt she must look like death, or like Sarah before she had her first cup of caffeine.

Nadia grabbed a tube of light tan substance that resembled a lipstick. She dotted it under Dani's eyes. "You must not sleep well, nightmares?" Nadia asked her. She was so casual about the topic. Was Dani that easy to read?

"Yeah actually." Dani's thoughts went to Liam. It had been almost two weeks since she last saw him or saw any of her friends and fellow squad members. If they weren't looking for her then they should have made it back to the wall by now.

"I get them too, sometimes, about Mars." Nadia continued to talk. She wasn't really paying any mind to Dani as she spoke. Although, Dani had started to pay more attention to her. The mention of Mars was intriguing and entirely caught her attention.

"Mostly about the military training. It's a bit intense because if you have abilities then they want to harness that power. Then the use of your abilities becomes your job or determines your job, and they're not great jobs. Ya know." Nadia carried on, apparently enjoying the sound of her own voice, Dani concluded. 'Must be a family trait.' Dani thought.

However, Dani was surprised she was willing to talk about her military so openly. If Nadia was having nightmares about Mars and was indeed a soldier, then what was she doing here. As Dani understood not many people left Mars since the king passed away five years ago and the prince took the throne. Especially those who served in the military. Dani wondered if Nadia was possibly a spy of sorts, and if that was so, what did that make her sister, or better yet, her cousin, Gabe.

"So, you were in the military on Mars then?" Dani inquired, hoping to entice Nadia to continue talking.

"Oh yes! We defected from Mars to Earth because of the twisted demands of the prince. He's become paranoid and hungry with power." She exclaimed with pride in her voice. It was as if Nadia understood what Dani was thinking. The lie seemed believable enough, but Dani wasn't convinced.

"You mentioned the vigorous training, so then do you have any abilities?" Dani inquired curiously.

It had always been well known that some citizens of Mars have the ability to control energies. It was caused by a mineral native only to Mars. When colonies started to cultivate the red planet, the mineral reacted with the colonist's DNA triggering a line of new genes such as the red circles around the iris to emerge and develop. The new genetic make-up allowed some to gain the ability to harness the movement of energies. The military naturally used this to their advantage against threats, and at one point the Earth's military thought they could do the same with those who had the red planets mixed blood, but it seemed only true, full-blooded Marsians could possess the ability.

Nadia was silent for a moment too long. Dani immediately became suspicious. Whatever answer Nadia gave Dani, she was sure it was going to be a lie.

"No, not really. My parents did, so they thought I might. But no luck. Oh well, right! Anyways your makeup is done." It seemed believable enough, but Dani was sure there was more to the story than that.

She stepped back to admire her work. She held up a small mirror for Dani to look with. What she saw was a completely different person. She almost didn't recognize herself.

"I didn't need to do much, you have so much natural beauty. But I highlighted your eyes, so they look brighter and bigger and added a little color to your face. You're so fair. What do you think?" Nadia was gleaming with pride at her fine work.

"Thank you, Nadia, it's... it's absolutely perfect." Dani was a bit shy about it, but she did feel beautiful.

"Now for your hair!" She took out a few brushes and hairpins. Nadia was quiet as she did so. It was obvious she was no longer going to spill any more information about her home planet.

Dani tried a different tactic, one that she hoped would gain her more information about the rebel forces and their young leader. "Who is Zachary?" Dani probed. The question was completely out of the blue, she hadn't even realized she had been thinking about him, to begin with.

"What do you mean?" Nadia brushed Dani's hair pulling it into her hand as the comb caught strands of hair.

"He has the red circles in his eyes, but the silver hair, he's clearly in a leadership position here." Dani tried to seem casual about the topic.

"Red eyes and silver hair, hmmm." Nadia said slowly as she continued at her task. "I hadn't even noticed. But clearly you did Dani. Am I picking up on an attraction here?"

"No!" She said with haste and a bit louder than expected. "No." She spoke softer and calmer this time. "I mean, sure, he's attractive but he's rude, and irritating, and..." Dani started to fidget with the ends of her sleeves, picking at the soft fabric.

"And taking you to this ball." Nadia squeezed the statement into Dani's unfinished sentence.

Dani looked over at the silky dress that laid on her bed. At that moment she started to feel like a fool. What was she doing going to a ball or celebration of any kind? This might be the best opportunity to find her gear and escape. She wasn't worried about her wound reopening, and every day she felt stronger and stronger.

"There I'm done." Nadia patted Dani's hair one last time and moved around to where she was standing in front of Dani. "To answer your question. Zachary Ryder is a rebel leader who was hand-selected by one of the majors from the main compound. I believe the major's name is Major Mitchells. Yes, that's right, Major Grayson Mitchells. You never know, he might make an appearance at this celebration tonight."

Dani's eyes went wide with shock and realization. It couldn't be a coincidence that that was her brother's name, her brother who was supposed to have died in a fire when she was seven.

"Guess you have a reason to stick around and go with Ryder to the ball instead of making an escape, don't ya?" Dani looked up at Nadia. How did she know? It was as if Dani was an open book and Nadia was thumbing through the pages carelessly, reading all the little details and emotions.

Nadia gathered up her makeup and brushes and stuffed them back into her bag. She hoisted the bag onto her shoulder and turned to leave, but before she exited through the now opened door she turned and looked at Dani.

Her voice grew serious. "Marsians can control energies, that doesn't just apply to the elemental energies. People give off energies too. Imagine what we could do with that. Oh," Her voice was once again filled with energy and delight. "and this was fun we should do it again." Then she was gone, shutting the door behind her, and leaving Dani to her thoughts.

She wondered why Nadia would so willingly give up such tactical information. It was as if Nadia knew her and her two other family member's plans were unstoppable no matter what information they gave out, perhaps that's why they parade around as they do. Or maybe Nadia was in something she didn't want to be in, fearing for her life and Dani was a possible lifeline for her. Too bad she wasn't Marsian and couldn't read energies.

Dani had heard rumors circling the towns back home that Marsians could control minds, but she chalked it up to paranoia. She still didn't believe it, but maybe instead of minds, it was a person's energy they were reading. An energy could change depending on moods and could convey messages, or somewhat predict actions. It would be almost the same as reading a mind. Perhaps not details but enough to understand action, emotion, and plan.

Dani looked at herself in the mirror admiring her hair. Her thoughts going to the major's name. She decided she needed to go with Zachary to the celebration. She had to know, was this her brother.

*****

Zachary arrived at Dani's door and stood there waiting to knock. He was considering if he was ridiculous for asking Dani to go with him or not. He had not given her the best impression of himself, in fact, he had been standoffish and downright mean to her. He was telling himself it was to protect her, keeping her at a distance, but was it, or was it really to protect himself?

After his mother had escaped with him, they came across Robert, and for whatever reason whether it was pity, guilt, or something he hadn't understood at the time, he looked after him and his mother. Sheltering them from the government. When he was ten, He asked Robert if he could join the military. He wanted to change the way the government thought about people like him and the only way to do that was to work from the inside. Robert entered him into the academy before the legal age, forging paperwork to solidify his age and race.

At the age of eleven, two years before the average cadet, he had entered into the academy. He studied tirelessly and pushed himself harder than most. By his second year, he was running missions, mostly working under the command of Robert himself and his most trusted officer, Harper. During his fifth and final year, his Marsian blood was discovered. He had to flee in the middle of the night or risk imprisonment. Colonel Harper was waiting with supplies and a car to get him to the wall. From there he rode horseback to the rebel's camp where Grayson was waiting for him.

In his fifth year at the academy, Dani was in her first year. It was then that Robert had tasked him with watching over her before he had been discovered. Robert had been able to protect her when she was still at home but now, she was alone, and at the academy, she was an easier target for the government. After he defected from the academy, Grayson still had him tasked to watch over Dani. That's when Zachary approached Hiromi upon her older sister's recommendation. It was easier for her to watch over Dani since they were in the same year then for him to set up camp outside the academy and risk being discovered and thrown in prison, or worse, killed.

Now four years later Dani was here, right behind the closed door that Ryder stood at and he still couldn't bring himself to tell her the truth. He took a deep breath and knocked on the door softly, hoping not to disturb Dani if she didn't particularly want to come with him. He waited a minute without receiving any answer. He started to move his feet in an attempt to turn and walk away when he heard the doorknob rattle.

A moment later Dani emerged from behind the door. Her hair was up in a simple braided bun, but the look complimented her high cheekbones and dark eyes. The dress that he had left for her hugged her curves and accented her legs. The sleeves hung off her shoulders, exposing her bare, fair skin. He was stunned speechless, his mouth gaping at her beauty. His eyes became dry from staring. He attempted to blink away his daze hoping it was working.

Dani had been standing on the other side of the door, pacing back and forth, her nerves starting to tingle as the time counted down to when Zachary said he would be there to pick her up. She looked down at herself and started to feel ridiculous all dressed up. She looked up hastily when she heard a soft knock at the door. She hesitated, standing there, her hand on the doorknob, waiting. Finally, she worked up the courage and took a chance. She opened the door. In front of her stood Zachary dressed in a navy suit that complimented her dress. His usual wild hair combed to the side letting his face soften.

"Oh, you're going." Was all Zachary could verbalize, his mind lacking the necessary words to convey his message or have a proper conversation without sounding rude.

Dani looked down at herself curious as to what Zachary was staring at. "Well yes, you asked me.... oh, were you hoping I wouldn't go?" Dani had started to feel foolish and silly.

Zachary came to terms with what Dani was implying and responded hastily and loud. "Yes! I mean, no! Yes, I want you to come. No, I wasn't hoping you...." He stopped talking and scratched the back of his head feeling like an imbecile. "I'm sorry this isn't coming out correctly."

Dani had never seen Zachary so unraveled and on top of it, he apologized to her. He was usually so careful and composed. He looked almost boyish as he stammered over his words. So much so, she almost giggled at him. She was immediately curious about this side of Zachary, not only that, but she enjoyed it.

"I'm glad you're joining me. I would have felt foolish coming up here and you not...". Zachary trailed off. He realized the conversation wasn't going smooth and he felt there was no way of fixing his first impression. "Anyways," he held out his arm, pointing down towards the elevator allowing Dani space to exit her room. "Shall we go?"

Dani released a small smile and moved down the hall. Zachary shut her bedroom door and met her at her side. Her small physique stretched with the heels of the shoes. Still, she was comparably shorter to Zachary's height. He enjoyed standing next to her and she was enjoying it too.

"Thank you." Dani said quietly, avoiding Zachary's eyes.

"For what?" He asked confused.

"The dress." She said shyly.

He looked down at her, taking in her beauty. Her skin looking fair against the dark blue of the dress. Her shoulders delicately displayed where the lace from the sleeves hung off.

"Also, I never had a chance to thank you for the clothes. It was unexpected and I'm grateful for the act of kindness you showed me."

Zachary finally found his voice, clearing his throat. "Oh, of course. I'm glad they all fit. Oh! That reminds me. I have something else for you." He stopped her, pausing in the hallway.

"You're missing something." He said.

He pulled something out of his pants' pocket. The light caught it, but only for a second. Dani could see the glimmer of gold. He reached up and clasped the item around her neck letting it hang off her collar bone. The movement caught her off guard. The moment of closeness was intimate. When he was done clasping it around her neck, he let his hands fall away slowly.

"There, perfect." He smiled then cleared his throat realizing he had been swept up in the moment.

Dani looked down, and lightly touched the small oval casing with the single small stone encased within it. Her locket. A single tear rolled down her face.

"I thought it had been lost in the forest. Thank you." She spoke softly, moved by his actions.

She opened it to see the picture of her parents and the one of her siblings next to it. She once again closed it as she smiled. She held the locket in her hand feeling it between her fingers as they continued there walk.

"I saw the running shoes are being put to good use." Zachary spoke up attempting to make conversation.

Dani looked up at him. Had he been watching her that morning? "Yes, they are a perfect fit. Thank you. It felt good to be able to run once more. I must admit, the run was challenging, to say the least. The lack of movement had taken its toll." She responded with a smile and received one in return. They walked in silence the rest of the way, still too awkward to carry on.

When they reached the city hall building, he opened the door for her and let her pass by him inside, out of the cold air. They were welcomed to warmth and brightness. The ballroom was festively decorated with lights and green garland. The tables were adorned with crisp white cloths with golden banded napkins. On top sat jars with candles along with more greenery. Each table had eight chairs, each with their own dining set with plates and bowls stacked in front of the chairs, crystal glasses, and silverware neatly placed on either side of the white dishes. Dani could smell sweet and savory mixing, overloading her senses. The room was filled with people laughing, conversing, and dancing, enjoying the nights' festivities.

Zachary guided her to a table towards the front where towering windows overlooked the floor and on the opposite side, the lawn outside. Dani noticed a band softly playing in the background. The sweet melodies from a violin caught her attention. When they arrived at the table, she noticed a small card in front of one of the dining sets. Her name had been swept on it with a loose hand. The golden ink glistening in the light. She gently touched the card feeling the slight raise of her name.

"See I told you. I would have looked foolish if you hadn't joined me." He pulled out the chair for her to take a seat. As soon as she sat, he pushed her in and took the seat next to her, where a card with his name was displayed. There were two other people at the table, but they were talking amongst themselves, unaware, or lack of concern for, Dani and Zachary's presence.

"Not to be forward, but why invite me? I'm still an enemy after all." Dani held Zachary's attention, as she continued to finger the name on the card.

Without warning, he changed the subject. "Would you like to dance?" He abruptly asked as he stood. "There's still some time before dinner will be served. We can work up an appetite." Without giving Dani a chance to answer, he took her hand from the table into his and pulled her to her feet. He led her to the sleek wooden floor and placed a hand around her waist and took her hand in his. Dani started to feel warm from his touch. Together they started to move in step, matching the melody of the soft classical music being played by the quartet.

"We need to talk." Zachary looked around as he spoke, his head held high. He seemed so posed, with his back straight. But he decided this was the moment.

"We are talking." Dani commented back knowing she was being smart.

He looked down at her with a look of indication that he had caught on to her smart attitude. He then twirled her and brought her back in close and continued to talk. His look was light, but his tone conveyed a sense of urgency.

"It was always the plan for you to end up here. Your life was in danger." He spoke softly.

"Well yeah, that's because Gabe shot me." She snarled at him, feeling she needed to point out the obvious.

"How did you find out?" He asked. She didn't answer him, but instead continued to look at him, her expression was enough. He sighed. "Of course, he bragged to you about it."

"Grayson Mitchells." She stated suddenly.

"Where did you hear that name." The conversation he had planned on having with her was starting to get off track, taking turns in unexpected directions.

"Nadia. Now, who is he." She was starting to get angry.

"He's a major for the rebel forces." He gave her a straight answer, but he knew that wasn't the answer she was looking for.

"It's odd, because that's my older brother's name. But my brother died in a fire when I was seven. So, explain it to me." This time she was clear, giving him no other option but to speak the truth to her.

He didn't want to lie to her, not anymore. He knew Grayson wanted to be the one to tell her, but Zachary knew she would press.

"Your brother survived, but you've already put that together. You want to know why you were lied too. By your father, by your brother, by everyone. Am I wrong?" As expected, the look on her face indicated she was unsurprised by his answer, but still in shock at hearing it was, in fact, true.

"He wanted to be the one to tell you after I brought you to him once your wounds healed and you were ready to travel."

"Let's say I believe you. Why would my brother fake his death?" Dani asked curiously, fishing for answers.

"He didn't, your father did. And you do believe me." She said nothing but indicated she wanted him to continue. They continued to sway to the music. Ryder continued to look around for possible trouble while still glancing back at Dani.

"Your parents knew something they shouldn't. Because of it, your family was attacked. Your father was able to fake your sibling's death but because of your hospitalization...." He trailed off realizing he was overloading her with information.

"What information?" It wasn't what he expected her to ask.

"I have no idea. Neither does your brother, unfortunately. He actually thinks you might know what the information is. After all, you've spent more time with your father than anyone." Zachary twirled Dani once more and then dipped her. Dani for a moment saw the room upside down before returning to see Zachary's face.

"You said siblings. Does that mean my younger siblings are alive too?" Dani was feeling overwhelmed, but now she needed to know more. She started to cling onto the hope of her family being safe. Years of feeling a hole in her heart might be full once more.

Zachary's face turned grief-stricken. How could he fill her with the hope of her family being alive, and then destroy it? "I'm so sorry Dani, but it's just your brothers. Your sister..." He couldn't bear to speak the words to her.

"Oh, I see, I understand." The music had paused, and Zachary led her off the dance floor knowing it would be suspicious if they continued to awkwardly sway without any music to sway too.

As they sat back at their table, waiters were making their rounds for dinner, bringing the first course out. In front of Dani sat a butternut squash soup with a garnish of a brown sugar marshmallow cube.

The soup was warm going down her throat. She hadn't realized how dry her mouth had become until she started to eat. It was a lot of information to process and she had a feeling Zachary wasn't done and now she felt the loss of part of her family all over again.

She couldn't think about her sister without wanting to break down, so she pushed for something different. "You said my life had been in danger."

She whispered understanding the delicate situation. It was clear Zachary didn't want listening ears of others to overhear them speaking.

"Your father just went to Mars, yes?" Zachary slurped his soup and patted his mouth with the white napkin that had been previously laying across his lap.

"Yeah, but what does that have to do with me?" She allowed her arm to rest on the back of the fabric chair facing him.

"Simple, he's not there to protect you."

"The mission, it was all a decoy." She said slowly putting all the pieces together. It was as if someone had handed her the picture to a puzzle that she had been struggling with and now the pieces were just falling together seamlessly.

"I'm guessing Colonel Harper knows then." She suggested.

"Yes, he and your brother have been in contact about your movement since your father was assigned on this diplomatic meeting. Harpers the middleman as it were." He confirmed.

Dani sat back thinking about the information. While she thought and processed, the second course was brought out. The roasted meat and crisp potatoes looked mouthwatering, but Dani couldn't bring herself to eat. Her mind was racing, confused, and conflicted. Zachary could be lying, but for what reason. Dani knew that wasn't the case though, he seemed as if a weight had been lifted off of him by finally telling her the truth. Not only was she understanding the situation, but she was starting to understand him and the disposition he had been in.

She was still held captive by her seminally undying loyalty to her nation and her government. To believe they wanted her killed seemed impossible to process. What would she do now? She didn't want to keep fighting and defending a nation that wanted her dead. She could stay with the rebels, join their cause, but what about her friends. She needed to speak to Colonel Harper and her brother.

"Where is he?" She finally spoke, asking Zachary. "My brother, I want to see him. I want to hear this from him."

"And you will. He's waiting for us at the compound."

"Then let's go." She started to get up from her chair. Her hand was on the table, pushing up.

He grabbed her wrist and gently coaxed her back into her seat. "Hold on. Not so fast. Be patient. We will go when you're ready."

"I'm ready now." They stared at one another unblinking.

Zachary wanted to protect her, to shield her from the pain she must be feeling, the betrayal. Finally, he caved. He lowered his eyes, bowed his head and exhaled. He knew once she had made up her mind there would be no convincing her otherwise.

"Fine. I'll make arrangements to take you there." He had already done so earlier that day but didn't feel the need to load her with any more unnecessary information. He noticed that there was something else. Something itching in the back of her mind. "Was there something else?" he asked.

Dani was surprised by his question. Was she truly that readable? She shared her thoughts with him. "Jaxon Black. What do you know about him?"

He was thrown by her question. "Not much. He's a defector from the military. He found himself here and we accepted him into the town, as we do with most all defectors. Why?"

Dani felt she could trust him and decided to open her concern up to him. "I think he knew my parents. He confused me with my mother today in the library. He might know something, more. Maybe even why my family was killed. It might help us to figure out what my father was hiding."

Zachary seemed concerned, but his knowledge of the situation was lacking. He sat back in his chair, his hand resting on his chin, undoubtedly thinking. "Maybe your brother will know more." It was the only thing he could think to reply with. He truly didn't know, and he understood that must be frustrating to Dani.

*****

General Mitchells stood in the office of his comrade and loyal friend General Alpine. It was midday and the sun was shining brightly through the open windows. Alpine loved this time of year. The days were usually crisp and clear, but the breeze cooled down the grounds as the sun warmed the air. Even though the season was an indication of nature retreating into a hibernation state as the trees let go of their leaves and the plant life started to die away, losing its bright green luster from the summer months, there was still an abundance of life. Before the leaves made their descent down to the forest floor, they brighten with one last show reveling a variety of colors that set in the feeling that they had truly fallen into the season of autumn. Oranges, reds, yellows, and even pinks danced about mixing with the wind. Yes, Brigadier General Alpine adored this time of year.

"So, you're going to Mars, old friend?" Alpine spoke as he was enjoying sitting on the edge of the white window seal admiring the glistening water of a lake from afar.

"Not by choice. Unfortunately. I much rather sit idly by in my cozy chair in Eastern Command enjoying the views of my desk filled with paperwork." General Robert Mitchells commented. "You understand what this means, don't you Warren?"

He moved off the window seal and shut the windows tight behind him. He knew where this conversation was going, and it would be unwise to speak so openly about such matters. He was well aware of the prying ears that lurked in the shadows.

"I think I will take a few days and visit the academy. I hear there are a few cadets in their last years of training that have truly excelled our standard expectations by leagues. If so, then they seem like perfect candidates for a scouting mission in the northeast towards Oakden. There are some suspicious activities happening that way and I would like an accurate account of what's going on. You should come with me, say goodbye to your daughter before you head out to Mars."

Robert understood. "Might I make a suggestion for the leadership of this scouting assignment."

Alpine made a gesture indicating Robert to proceed. "My colonel, Colonel Harper. He has been under my command for more than fifteen years. I guarantee he will serve you well and ensure the safety of these young cadets along with the successfulness of the mission."

"Yes, I have heard of him. He and his first lieutenant make an excellent team. They would be fitting for this excursion." Alpine noted the look of concern on his old friend's face. "Don't worry Robert, I will ensure her safety."

*****

Zachary walked Dani back to her room and said goodnight, but not before sporadically grabbing her hand and laying a gentle kiss on to it. It took Dani by surprise. "Good night Dani Mitchells." He acted as a gentleman would. He dropped her hand from his, where it stayed frozen in midair. Dani's other hand rested on her lips where a look of daze was fixed upon her face. He grinned a sweet but mischievous smile at her reaction and then turned to leave, allowing her to her thoughts. Dani was now more curious about who Zachary Ryder was.

Her thoughts were spread ubiquitously, strained from all the new information she received. First, she needed to see her brother. She needed to talk to him and get answers. What information could her parents have had that would order their deaths. Second, she needed to reach Colonel Harper. Zachary had said Grayson was in contact with him.

It should be easy to get a message to him and hopefully back to her friends. Finally, things were starting to look up, she felt in her heart that her friends were alive and well and she would be seeing them soon. She felt she might be able to sleep through the night for the first time in weeks.

Chapter 17

Holding onto Fire

The week passed slowly. Dani would wake early in the morning and test her progress on running around the town. Every day she could run further and faster with less and less pain. Her wound was now just a pink, scarred piece of flesh. She would spend her mornings at the library, but by lunchtime Zachary would fetch her and escort her to lunch where she would end up spending the rest of the day helping to complete his daily activities and various duties the military had on the agenda for him. She was learning about the ends and outs of the rebel force along with understanding their views and hardships. Most of all though, she was enjoying spending time with Zachary and getting to know the soft, humorous man that had been shielded by the brute she had met weeks ago.

One morning, Dani awoke to a soft thump on her door. She quickly threw on a pair of sweatpants and opened the door expecting to see Zachary. Behind the door, though, was someone she didn't recognize. A young boy with blond hair and blue eyes. He couldn't have been more than fourteen. Her thoughts went to her younger brother, he would have been about the same age.

"Yes, may I help you?" Dani asked unsurely.

The boy handed her an envelope without a word spoken. She took it and turned it over, looking for Zachary's usual R but failed to see it. She looked back up at the boy confused.

"You are Dani Mitchells, correct?" The boy asked looking around.

Dani responded to his question as she looked around as well, unsure of what, or who they were supposed to be looking for. Was he not supposed to be talking to her, she wondered? The boy told her his neighbor asked him to deliver the letter to her but had no idea what it was about, and he mentioned no name. The boy said his farewells and left Dani standing in her doorway. She looked back down the hallway after the boy and then walked back into her room shutting the door behind her, as she proceeded in opening the letter.

The letter was quickly scribbled writing, requesting her presence in the library in an hour. At the bottom, it was signed by a surprising individual, Jaxon Black. She hurriedly threw on clothes and left for the library, excited by the idea of finding out this man's relationship to her parents. Maybe she'll finally get answers to questions she had been pondering since she had crossed paths with Jaxon last week. She had looked for him while she was working in the library, but he never showed after that day.

The library was empty in the still of the early morning. Miss Mackenzie wasn't even at her desk yet, though her small desk light was on. Dani wandered around the dusty library; the lights were dim. When she heard the wooded door in the front open and shut, she jumped, startled by the sudden loud bang. In the distance, she could see an elderly man walking towards her, looking around.

"Good, you got my message." He whispered to her with a raspy voice when he was a few feet away. "Please, let's find somewhere to sit down and talk." He walked away from her, heading towards a table in the middle of the room. She took a seat, her hopes high, why else would he decide to meet with her.

"Why did you ask me to meet you?" She asked him.

His knuckles were starting to turn white as his grip tighten on the back of the seat. His nerves raising as he worked up the courage to speak. "I felt that maybe you deserved some answers. Especially about your mother. See, your mother. Well, I'm... I'm the reason she died." His head was down.

He was trying to avoid Dani's eyes. What he was asked to do during the civil war with the Marsian descendants still haunted him and now he was faced with the girl whose parents he betrayed.

Dani's heart felt like it had stopped. Her stomach sinking to the ground at his word of confirmation. Her legs felt weak and she thought she might faint. "What did you just say?" She hissed. "What do you mean you're the reason?"

Jaxon took a deep breath and sat down across from her. His hands were folded neatly in his lap hiding them from Dani as if he were trying to hide the years of pain he had caused, the blood that had soaked into them from the many souls he helped destroy. They were shaking from the flashback of memories, the screams on the innocents. The faces of the dead that he'll never forget and the faces of the enemy that will never forget him. He knew by talking to Dani, she would be another enemy that would not forget him today.

"First you need to know about the civil war." He finally looked up at her only to be met with hatred in her eyes. He expected nothing less and he deserved so much more. Her parents had saved his life during the war and he repaid them with betrayal. He could still recall the events as if they were still recent as if they had happened yesterday. For him they will always be in the front of his mind, never fading.

He had been a doctor for the military, but a doctor was just his title. He was skilled in many other areas and the military utilized those other talents to their benefit. His position was to search out and experiment with new ideas that would guarantee the military a victory against any Marsian force whether it was foreign or domestic. With the possible prospect that Marsian decedents could harness the power of energy manipulation and the ability to steer it, Doctor Jaxon experimented on those from Marina, the region where those with Marsian blood lived.

He hoped within their blood would lie the secrets to gaining their abilities. What he first discovered was that the mutation that allowed them their abilities was caused by a biological reaction to a mineral native to

Mars known as Crimson Ore. If he could replicate the mutation within the earthlings, they could possibly have an advantage against Mars's special forces soldiers. Those who had been trained in controlling the energies and transforming the energies into weapons.

Years of experimenting proved futile and the citizens of Marina grew suspicious of the disappearances of their people. Rumors were starting to spread of deaths caused by the experiments and because of it, outbreaks of violence and riots had started in backlash of the military presences. Soon a full-scale attack occurred, and the military was forced to declare war against the people of Marina.

There had virtually been no military forces of any kind in the region. However, after the riots started, the eastern forces, stationed at Eastern command with military personnel, such as Dani's parents, were sent in as a control method. But through the chaos, forces from the South and even from the West were sent in to dismantle the uprising.

Within the first few years of war, thousands of lives were lost on both sides. By the end of the second uprising, tens of thousands of lives were lost. The war ended with the surrender of the remaining Marian people fleeing the nation to the other side of the wall. Those with less Marsian blood were more easily able to conceal their Marsian traits through uses such as colored contacts and other methods to conceal their red-ringed eyes. They integrated into other regions of the nation, virtually disappearing from the eyes of the government.

Jaxon recalled the events leading up to the civil war to Dani. She sat there patiently across from him taking in every violent word. While she listened, she remembered Zachary telling her of the events from his perspective. How his father was killed defending his family and fellow Marins. She still wasn't sure how her parents tied into this though.

"Your mother was a medic at the time. She would help anyone in need of attention. It didn't matter whose side they were on. One day she came to me asking questions about a marking located at the base of their neck she kept seeing on those with Marsian blood. It wasn't long until she started putting the pieces together and unraveled the true nature of the experiments. Naturally, she told your father. At the time, I supported the cause. I believed in our military. So, I....". He couldn't bring himself to finish.

"You turned them in." She responded.

Doctor Jaxon hung his head low when he heard her speak the words, he couldn't bring himself to utter. They were like fire on his tongue but hearing them out loud caused ice in his soul to emerge, freezing him where he sat. Dani no longer wanted to hear him speak, she could hear pity in his voice, and it angered her further. She stood up, the chair scooting loudly back in the quiet library. Without another word she turned and walked away leaving him in the dark corner. She felt he deserved her cold reaction and felt no guilt about leaving him in the dark. She felt no remorse for the war that fought within him to let go of the past or let it keep eating him alive, and she hoped it would do the latter.

As she stormed out of the library she bumped into Zachary. Before she recoiled backward, he grabbed her arm and righted her sturdily back onto her feet. He was elated to see her but was also surprised to see her, especially walking out of the library when he knew she had the day off and so early in the morning at that. He would have thought she would have been on her run.

"I'm so sorry. I wasn't paying..." She started to apologize before truly seeing who it was that she had smacked into. She looked up and was staring into Zachary's red and silver eyes.

"Dani, what's wrong?" He noticed a tear streaming down her face. Without a second thought, he gently wiped the tear away.

His eyes were adverted up towards the library when he heard the library door slam closed. In front of them, he watched as Jaxon was walking down the steps. 'He must have told her about her parents and the war; he thought to himself, not realizing he was still holding Dani's arm. "Come on, let's go get something warm to drink. You look cold." He wrapped his arm around her shoulder. She leaned into him and allowed him to guide her away from the library and the vicious truth she had just learned.

Even though she would have rather escaped to her room, she felt herself not wanting to refuse. She was feeling a bit cold and empty from listening to Doctor Jaxon's story. She nodded and let him guide her to a nearby coffee shop, in hopes that Zachary's company would warm her.

Dani sat at a small round table in the corner overlooked by a window. There was a thin layer of frost outlining the outside of the window. The coffee house was cozy with the dark colored walls and creamed art frames of pressed flowers lining the walls. The smell of coffee and baked goods overwhelmed Dani's senses.

Zachary sat down with a clatter in the seat opposite of her. He placed a cup of dark steaming beverage in front of her. When she took a sip, she looked confusingly up at him. What she tasted certainly wasn't coffee as she expected. It was rich with a chocolate flavor and a hint of caramel. She licked her lips and noticed the lightness of whipped topping.

"Personally, I don't like coffee and I wasn't sure how you would like yours, so I got you a hot chocolate." He took a sip of his. When he removed the cup from his bright pink lips, he sported a white mustache from the whipped topping. He licked his lips trying to get Dani to laugh but failed.

Zachary grew serious once more. "So, what did he tell you?" He sat his beverage down carefully in hopes he would not spill a single delicious drop. A waitress brought over two pastries. The steam wafted out of the crevices of the flakes. They smelled richly of spices, fruits, and nuts. Zachary took a bite and motioned for Dani to do the same. "I went to your room. Figured you'd be hungry, but obviously...." He gestured around as if his hand movement said it all. That she wasn't there.

"He told me about the conflict with Marina. About my parents and why my mother was killed. Why my family was killed." She stared into the dark cup of chocolate and explained.

"I knew your mother was killed because of information, but your father never went into it. And I never pressed, it was obviously too painful for him." He took another bite of his pastry. The two sat in silence for a long moment while Dani was lost, looking out the window. The streets were starting to become busy with people bustling to their occupations and daily routines.

"You know my father as well?" She looked at him suddenly.

Dani was unsure of how much more information could be loaded into her mind. Zachary explained how her father had saved his life and helped him into the academy. How Zachary had been assigned to look after Dani since her entrance into the academy. About selecting Hiromi to take over when he was found out as a Marina citizen.

"You have the red ring though. How did you cover that up?" She asked more out of curiosity.

"Contacts. You'd be surprised how many people live among you that are Marians." Zachary took another sip of his drink followed by a bite of his breakfast. Moments of silence passed between the two. Dani thinking about and sorting all the information.

She looked back at Zachary, bits of crumbs lining his shirt, and grabbed the handle to her cup. "Black, by the way," she lifted her cup up towards Zachary. "for next time." She released a small smile then sipped her hot chocolate, letting it warm her through. That smile was all he needed. He felt he could let her in. He was letting his guard down and he could tell her anything. The last few days had proven there was trust growing between them.

He smiled back at her. "Do you want to take a walk with me? We have some time before the trucks to take us to the main compound will arrive."

Chapter 18

OAKDEN'S DEAL

Liam walked through the threshold and was fronted with an enormous open space buzzing with activity. The black sea of uniforms working towards a single cause. The open floor was lined with rebels typing away on computers, monitoring the outside activity. Above their head's rebel leaders were pointing and shouting orders. The buzz in the room was thriving and fast.

"Welcome to Fort Ridge Crest, home of the rebel's central command." Grayson lead Colonel Harper, Lieutenant Reeves, and the cadets remaining from his squad into the large open room.

Sarah was not that impressed, all she cared about was answers, and the question she wanted an answer to more than anything was where Dani was.

"Don't worry she will be here." Grayson hadn't even needed to look back at Sarah or Liam to know what they were thinking. Their cold eyes bore into the back of his skull stinging his senses. He had felt the wave of hatred washing over him as if he was in the line of an enemy's gun barrel.

"Captain Ryder has been watching over her. He is my most trusted man. I would trust him with my life, so I feel confident trusting him with my sister's. Now," he paused turning around to look at the group of soldiers.

Sarah stood with arms crossed and dirt on her face. A man joined the major at his side and saluted. He spoke quietly, addressing the general. He nodded accepting the man's comments. "This is Sergeant Aceron. He will escort you to your quarters. Feel free to roam around and make this place feel like home, while your here. When Dani arrives, trust me, you'll know. Colonel." He nodded at the colonel and then left them to address other business.

Sergeant Aceron was a lengthy man with sunken eyes and a pointed nose. He looked as if the days were long and the nights' longer with no sleep to help ease the insomnia that had taken grip. He motioned for them to follow and led the squad out of the large room and down a hallway. At the end of the hallway, the room opened-up. To the right, the sergeant indicated a dining hall. He led them to the left where several hallways split. At the beginning of a hallway was where the sergeant had assigned the cadets sleeping quarters.

He left them to their own and trusted that their colonel would command his squad in the correct manner without having to be babysat.

Colonel Harper spoke to the dirty, tired cadets of his squad. "Each quarter has three rooms. Pearce, Evens, and Carson. You three can take the room to the left. Hunt and Katsuki. Take the right. Mitchells will be joining us in a few weeks. Go ahead and get settled, wash up, and rest. The lieutenant will fetch you when dinner is being served." The colonel left the squad to their own and rejoined Lieutenant Reeves in the command center.

The days of traveling had grown weary on him. Gravity had started to pull his shoulders down and his uniform was untamed and wrinkled. The other squad members had felt the effects of traveling as well. They were grungy with dirt staining their faces. At least they could settle in and not worry about anything for the rest of the night. He, on the other hand, still had work. He was a correspondent between the rebel leaders and the generals of Helenia who knew of the corruption and were trying to change it.

Sarah was the first to speak amongst their small group. "Well, I'm going to go take an hour-long shower. See everyone at dinner or maybe sooner, guess it depends on how I feel." Sarah didn't want to stick around and listen to Liam's conspiracies about the rebels, so before he could open his mouth to start, she left them standing there. She was spent, burned out from the trek it took to get to the rebel's camps. Twenty-five miles of trudging in mud up and down the mountains with no rest, before the rebels had finally sent a vehicle to pick them up and escort them the rest of the way to the fort. The long days had caused everyone's tempers to rise, including her own.

In his room, Liam started to unpack. His mind was telling him they weren't going anywhere anytime soon, so he might as well get comfortable. Colonel Harper had explained that there was corruption in the government. That a civil war occurred almost thirty years ago. That war chased out thousands of innocents. Those who fled formed the rebel's coalition to fight back against the government and regain their lost land. Dani's father, along with a few other generals had been working with the rebels from within. Because of it, Dani was in danger. This mission had been for her. To get her away and to safety.

Liam now sat in a room within the rebel's headquarters waiting for a guy he was supposed to trust, bring his best friend back to him. He stopped unpacking and took an unpredicted and overdue swing at the wall, denting the outer plaster. The anger boiled beneath his skin. He gripped the edge of the dresser, taking deep breaths, attempting to calm down. He hated waiting around. It made him feel useless and helpless.

He heard a knock at his bedroom door, his head snapping at the sound. Aiden walked in; he had a fresh pair of clothes on and no longer smelled like a campfire.

"Hey, the showers free." He announced to Liam softly.

"Yeah, okay thanks." Liam leaned up against the dresser, standing in front of the dent. His arms were crossed, and the days of weariness and lack of sleep aged him by years.

"You want to talk about it?" Aiden peeked around Liam but acted as if he hadn't noticed the dent. From outside the room, he had heard a loud thump but thought nothing of it. It all made sense now.

"What's there to talk about. Everything I've worked for, everything I've dedicated my life too, everything we've dedicated our lives too, is a lie. The nation I believed in has betrayed us and worse my best friend is out there and not here." He slumped to the floor and leaned his head back against the dresser, closing his eyes and softly thumped it on the wood of the drawer for a moment.

"She'll be here. And she's okay. That's what matters. Let's just get her back and we'll go from there. Okay? Now, why don't you go take a shower. Trust me, it'll wash away some of your worries. The government is tomorrow's problem. So, to speak." Aiden walked over to his friend and held out a hand. Liam reluctantly took it and allowed himself to be pulled up.

"I guess I am covered in filth." He looked down at his uniform and attempted to brush some of the dried, caked-on mud.

"Yeah, you stink too." Aiden jokingly poked at Liam as a best friend or older brother would before he left Liam to think.

Liam was locked away in the shower when a knock was heard from the front door. Finn opened the door to see a shiny new Sarah standing in the doorway. Her hair was once again blond and her face bright. The smell of dirt was now replaced with the recognizable and distinctive sweet flowers that were associated with her.

"Aiden!" Finn shouted. He moved aside for Sarah to enter. "Your girlfriends here!" Sarah softly punched him in the arm as she walked past him. He winced as if the punch had hurt him, but Sarah just smiled. Over the past week, Sarah and Finn had become good friends. Building a relationship resembling a brother and sister; love, hate relationship.

Aiden walked out of his room rubbing the excess water from his face with a towel. Sarah smiled inwardly, blushing slightly. Aiden was no longer sporting facial hair but instead was clean shaven, revealing his boyish look. He grinned a sidewards grin after noticing Sarah's shyness. He took advantage of her inability to move and laid a peck on her lips. It seemed to wake her from her trance.

"You shaved." It was all she could muster.

"Well, you kept complaining about how itchy it was getting." Aiden rubbed his chin, feeling the freshly smooth skin. Sarah looked him over and then returned Aiden's affection by placing a gentle kiss on his cheek.

"Where's Liam?" She asked Aiden and Finn as she took a seat on the couch.

"Showering." Finn replied taking a seat across from her in a lounge chair, setting his elbows on the tops of his knees.

"Does this all seem off to you guys?" She addressed them.

"What do you mean?" Liam asked emerging from the bathroom.

His hair was still dripping water, leaving little water droplet stains on his white t-shirt. He, too, was cleanly shaven, looking even younger than Aiden, the difference was his eyes. They looked haunted. She knew he hadn't been sleeping well since Dani was taken. She knew this because there were several nights when she couldn't sleep either and they would stay up by the campfire talking. One night he even caught her sneaking out of Aiden's tent. He commented that he wouldn't say anything if she didn't mention that she had noticed the tears streaming down his face.

This mission and Dani missing had indeed brought the squad together. They were more than just comrades now, they were family. They had seen every side of each other and experienced the same emotions, supporting each other through and through.

"I mean, we're just supposed to believe that our government is corrupt and tried to commit mass genocide. Now we're in the rebel's main compound and we're supposed to just join them, betraying our nation. Even if our government is screwed up, shouldn't we be there trying to change it, to fix it, or to protect the people, our people? It's our nation, it should be our responsibility. That's our job after all." She was outraged.

First, they lied to her, to everyone, about the mission, and now their hands were tied. Go along with the rebels or what? She doubted they were going to let them go and run back to their nation having obtained the knowledge they now possessed.

"I get what you're saying Sarah, but maybe this is how we help our people and nation. Maybe being on the outside, gaining the resources and the help of the rebel coalition is what we need to do. Can you honestly go back to the academy, graduate, and go about your job knowing what you know?" Finn responded.

Finn hated that they had been kept in the dark too, especially because he had been scouting with Hiromi. She had several opportunities to inform him of their plans. He would have listened, instead she didn't trust him to tell him the truth.

"What resources and help can the rebels be? They've been fighting the government for how long? Ten years? And they haven't even gained a foothold in making a breakthrough." Sarah argued in return to Finn's statement.

"Not true,". Liam had been quietly sitting back and listening, working out the pieces to the puzzle they had been dealt. He and Aiden knew things the others didn't from when Colonel Harper had come to talk to them in their room. Now everyone was looking at Liam, surprised by his sudden quiet voice.

"Think about it. When did we actually start hearing reports of a rebel force?" He asked rhetorically. "Maybe within the last four or five years. So why now? The first conflict happened over twenty years ago. Why did they not start fighting back then? What do they have now, that they didn't before?"

Aiden contributed. "Well, they've had that time to gain support from within the military. They also have had that time to gather refugees and defectors, along with weapons and gear."

"They've also had time to stage attacks that would gain them knowledge on the military's defense weaknesses. Every attack I've heard about was directed at different regional points on the wall. Also, there were very few casualties on both sides. We always knew there were groups hidden in the tree line, but they would only send a few out, and then just as fast as the attack started it would be over. Along with that, the soldiers at the wall rarely killed any rebels, only wounded. They were all taken prisoner, so now they have rebels within the nation." Finn added.

"It's as if they were planting something. No one ever checked the areas of attack afterwards. They could have been covering something else up. Taking the focus and eyes away from one spot by drawing attention to another." Aiden and Finn were going back and forth.

"It's more than that though," Liam stated. "They've been waiting."

"For what?" Sarah had a worried look on her face, as if she knew, but couldn't bring herself to say it.

"For an opportunity." Liam looked around at the three others. A knock came from the door, ending their conversation. When Liam answered the door, Hiromi was standing there.

"It's dinner time, if you guys are hungry." She commented.

The group headed back down the hall to where the dining hall was. The dining room was flooded with rebel soldiers enjoying the end of a long and daunting day. They headed for the line when Hiromi heard her name being screamed from across the room. The squad looked up to see a woman with a slender face and long black hair running towards them. She looked exactly like Hiromi, but older.

The woman embraced Hiromi, laughing all the while. "I heard you had returned, but I wasn't sure. I'm so happy you're here. Let me look at you." She pulled away and grabbed Hiromi's face, moving it about. Examining her face for anything out of the norm. "Where's Willow and Luka?"

271

"They're in the room. I don't think people would want hounds where they eat." She replied to the excited woman.

"Pish-posh don't worry about them. If they have something to say, then I dare them to say it to me." The woman held the rank of a colonel but acted as if her rank was nonexistent. She fluttered about, much as Harper did. "Hiromi, who are your friends?" She stopped to notice the rest of the squad.

"Oh yes, Schisko, this is my squad." Hiromi pointed to and named each of her squad members. "This is my older sister, Schisko."

They found themselves a table to converse and eat at. Schisko explained that Hiromi and their parents immigrated to this country. Their parents had been killed during the second conflict and it was then that Schisko understood the true evil of the government and defected to the rebel's camp. But before she could get out of the city and over the wall they were captured. Schisko had been imprisoned and tortured. Robert however, had caught wind of this and sought out Hiromi. She placed her in the military schools where she gained the position she had today. He, also, helped Schisko escape from jail and Colonel Harper snuck her past the wall.

"So, Dani's father. He's pretty much bringing everyone together then." Sarah asked.

"Well I don't know if that was his intent, but he definitely is doing his best to rescue as many as he can. After his wife and youngest daughter were murdered, it would make sense for him to go down the path he has." Schisko responded.

"But Dani doesn't know any of this." Again, Sarah felt the rage building up once more. The betrayal of it all.

"No, she doesn't, and it was for her own good. They would have killed her too." Liam stated. He knew that part all too well, remembering the night of the fire once more. How Dani was in a coma and the heartbreak he endured as he watched his best friend fall apart when she was told her whole family, besides her father died.

"And now? She's out of danger. If they haven't told her then she might try to escape. She's going to think they're still the enemy." Finn inquired, not expecting an answer.

"Are we so sure they're not?" Sarah breathed out picking at her food. Since Dani was captured, she seemed to have lost her appetite, replaced with fear, and the drive to find her best friend.

Aiden spoke attempting to comfort her. "Dani will see the mission through. Whether she knows or not she will look at this as an opportunity to gather intel on the rebels. She'll trust that we would be on our way to rescuing her. She was hurt she knows she can't do much injured and will be biding her time until she can fight without seriously injuring herself or reopening her wounds, but most likely this Captain Ryder guy has already informed her, if she believes it or not is a whole different story."

Aiden had convinced himself that Dani would stay put for the time being until things became clear to her. He just hoped his words reassured the tensions of the others and helped in easing their minds. But he was starting to worry about Sarah. She was starting to become sick, often feeling nauseous. She wasn't eating properly and was stressed about Dani and the radical changes they were all facing. He hoped when Dani arrived Sarah's mood would ease, and she would bounce back.

Sarah headed back to her room while Hiromi and her sister took the hounds for a walk. The only ones left sitting around the table were Liam, Aiden, and Finn. The dining hall had all but emptied except for a few soldiers enjoying their night. Some reminiscing and conversing with one another at other tables, while others peacefully reading or playing on a computer. The three were enjoying a card game, not ready to call it a night but needing a distraction to pass the time.

"Good evening cadets." The colonel slid into the table beside Liam.

"Colonel!" Liam spoke loudly, excitable, as if he were happy to see his commanding officer. What do you want?" His next sentence was spoken with a completely opposite tone. Liam pushed him away.

"Now is that any way to speak to your commanding officer?" The colonel stated with a light tone to his serious inquiry.

"You mean how to speak to a liar?" Liam folded a card down and picked up a new one from the pile.

"I may have deserved that. Anyways, I have a mission for Carson and Evens. I'd say all three of you but Pearce, I need you to stay here and watch over Hunt. Her, well, demeanor," Harper played with the words. "hasn't been stable since Mitchells' capture. I need someone she trusts to stay behind and watch over her. Who better to do so than, well you?" The colonel gave him a long accusing look. The intent was unmistakably marked.

"What's the mission, sir?" Finn Carson was happy to do something besides sitting around for the next few days waiting for Ryder to bring Dani to the compound.

"Wait, wait. Aren't we already on a mission?" Liam stated. A few of his cards flew out of his hands and landed face up.

"You snake! You're the liar! You had the aces!" Aiden shouted. Liam stuck his tongue out while grabbing up his cards. The colonel rolled his eyes. Through the last few weeks, he had witnessed how these cadets had grown from kids into adults, facing the challenges of a mission beyond the safety perimeters of their nation. But at this moment, all that disappeared and was replaced by the immaturity that the young cadets still harnessed.

Kyle Harper slammed a hand on the table, the table shook from the strike gathering the attention of his cadets. Who, at the moment, were reminded they were still young. "Anyways, this mission, Carson, Evens. You're going to be joining squad eight and twelve on an Arms run to Oakden."

"An Arms run sir?" Liam was slightly intrigued.

"Yes. They will be traveling northward to meet with one of the neighboring nations to gain access to additional weapons and ammunition."

"Why do they need to go, what's two extra soldiers, especially ones that are not rebels, going to do? " Aiden interrogated.

"Nothing Pearce, but I do believe it will help ease your minds. I've spent years back and forth between our nation's military and that of the rebels. I know these people. Hell, I have family here and back in Helenia. Perhaps if you spent some time with these people you will understand them and come to appreciate their cause. Their intent is not to destroy, they want to help make a change that will bring lasting peace. I'm sure you can get behind that."

Colonel Harper stood up; his hands placed on the table to help push him up as if he was struggling from weak knees. He straightened up and brushed his shirt attempting to brush away the nonexistent wrinkles.

"I'll have a list of things you should pack in your ruck. I'll have the items that you don't have sent to the room within the hour, so head back to your rooms and start packing. You need to be ready by zero eight hundred tomorrow." He started to walk away his hands cupped behind his back. "Oh, and don't worry Evens. By the time you get back, Mitchells will already be here and waiting on you." His head cocked back to look at Liam and then continued on his way.

*****

A group of soldiers stood in the open space of the round room laid in the front of the living quarters. Beyond the doors, the mountains towered over them, dividing them from their nation, Helenia. Liam looked to the towering mountains. Would they be considered defectors too? Their mission was taking longer than it should have, after all. They were a long way from home, and he was losing hope of returning anytime soon.

Suddenly Liam was accidentally shoved. A group of soldiers had been horse playing and a young man had fallen into Liam because of it. He fell to his knees in front of Liam. Liam leaned down offering a hand, embarrassed for the young man. When the young man was standing firmly in front of Liam, he noticed striking features such as dark hair and fierce eyes. The same ones he had stared into a thousand times when he looked at his best friend.

"My apologies." The young man brushed his pants off, never really looking at Liam. But Liam looked at him. He paid attention to every detail. He couldn't believe who it was. The boy's name was covered by the collar of his uniform top, but Liam already knew the name. Liam grabbed the collar and moved it aside to read the name as confirmation. The boy was confused by the sudden movement and haste of the man.

"Mitchells." Liam whispered under his breath as he slowly released the boy.

"I'm sorry, do I know you?" The boy asked skeptically.

"Conner. Your name is Conner, correct." Liam looked at the boy in the face. He attempted to try and not scare him off by knowing his first name, but his attempts seemed to fail. The boy was already on edge.

"Yes. Do you know me?" The boy took a few steps back, unsure of the stranger. This was his first mission. His older brother, Grayson, finally letting him complete some fieldwork after months of begging. He knew the other soldiers well enough, but this guy was starting to scare him a bit.

"I'm sorry. My name is Liam Evens. You probably don't remember me. You were only four the last time I saw you but," Liam was abruptly cut off by the boys sudden overreaction of glee.

"Liam!" Conner came in for a hug. He remembered Liam well. He was in his earliest memories. He and Dani had always been inseparable as if they were the twins. If Liam was here, did that mean Dani was here as well? He knew she was headed towards the compound; his brother had told him so only a few days prior. He started to look around through the crowd for her dark hair, the same as his.

"Is Dani here too! We've been waiting so long for her." His face expressing eagerness and impatience.

Liam's smile from being recognized had started to fade. "I'm afraid not." Liam stated slowly. "On our way here, she was hurt. They took her back to the town." He didn't want to give away too much detail afraid of worrying him.

"Oh, in Amire? She must be with Captain Ryder then." He rubbed his still smooth hairless face. Not even the littlest bit of stubble growing yet.

"Yeah, that sounds right." Liam attempted a smile. "Grayson said he was going to be bringing her here in a few days."

"Oh good. Well, then we have something to look forward to after the mission." Before either of them could continue conversing a deep voice called for the cadets to fall into formation and get a headcount.

Liam recognized the voice as Sergeant Aceron. Next to him, a stern looking man with the rank of captain stood straight and tall. The sergeant briefed the soldiers on the goal of the mission, how they planned on meeting with the neighboring nation towards the northeast, Oakden, to retrieve weapons and supplies that would better help the rebels with a full-frontal attack if it came to that.

Liam understood the cause for alarm. If the military decided to attack, they would be able to eliminate the rebel forces. There were children here, families, people who had been chased out of their homes and killed by the government once already. They had lived the struggle of refugees and made new homes and lives in the years following the civil war. They would stand and fight to protect what they had left, and Liam understood that more than most.

The sergeant introduced the man next to him as Captain Wyatt, who would take the lead when they made their way out of the compound in set of their mission. He explained it would take two days of travel with off-road vehicles. Each vehicle had the capacity to carry four soldiers along with their gear. An additional vehicle, three times the size of the other vehicles, would follow behind them carrying two soldiers. They would load the supplies and weapons gathered from the rebel's ally into the empty truck.

Liam and Finn stopped at the second vehicle following behind the captain and sergeant who headed to the front vehicle. They were loading their gear into the back when Liam heard a voice that was becoming recognizable. He turned to see Dani's younger brother, Conner, running up to meet them.

"Mind if I join you guys?" He asked eagerly, excited at the idea of being able to catch up with someone from his past.

Liam and Finn looked to each other, exchanging a conversation and understanding. They waved him on as they took his gear and threw it in the back with the rest of the supplies and packs. Conner climbed into the back eagerly awaiting a chance to shine in his acquired and learned knowledge to be in the field. In the last six months he had trained and studied with the military hoping to follow in his father and older brother's footsteps.

Liam stepped into the back while Finn sat up front in the passenger seat. A fourth person took to the task of driving. A woman with dark brown hair that shone red in the light. It was in a long braid that trailed down her back. Her uniform hugged her hips and curved her back. Finn couldn't help but stare at her. He caught the sight of her deep green eyes that hinted at a tinge of brown. He felt like he was being drawn into the dots that lightly specked her olive face.

Liam noticed his partner staring and quickly reached up and slapped the back of his head before the woman noticed. But his attempts were futile. The woman hoisted herself up into the large vehicle using the sidestep to assist her in pulling herself up into the seat.

"You got a staring problem cadet." She slammed closed the door and looked at Finn, her sunglasses sitting lower on the bridge of her nose. The name tape on her uniformed read Maeve and her rank indicated she was a corporal. Only one rank above himself and Liam.

"Oh, um, no." He coughed as he stalled in trying to change the subject. "Hey, Liam, how do you and Conner know each other?" He was trying to think of something to distract himself with and hopefully take the attention off himself. It seemed to work because the woman only watched Finn for a moment longer before she started the vehicle up and pulled away, following the vehicle in front of them.

Liam was enjoying a good laugh at his comrade's expense. Even when they were back home at the academy, every time the two had gone out to the bars at night, it never failed that Finn would make a fool of himself. He was awkward around anyone with a set of legs and long hair. Finn turned around and attempted to smack Liam with his hat, hopefully stopping Liam from laughing at him.

The afternoon was growing long riding in the bumpy vehicle. The road was somewhat paved but not enough to make for a smooth transition in the old vehicles. Even so, Conner and Liam seemed to have no issues falling asleep in the back. Their heads bobbing back and forth. Finn was sure at some point the two would bonk heads and secretly he was hoping for it, making for a good laugh.

The vehicle was silent, Finn was staring out the window at the surrounding woods. The trees were starting to look bare from the dead leaves falling to the ground, crowding the forest floor. What little leaves did remain had already dulled in color. The cold zapping the luster and brightness from them to help preserve the life of the tree through the harsh and frigid winter that was fast approaching. He was so intoxicated by the thoughts of running into those mountains, away from the complexity his life was becoming he didn't realize someone was continuously eyeing him.

A simple mission that he volunteered for had turned into a diplomatic nightmare.

He was unaware that Maeve was taking an interest in him. She was a Venus descent, but the traditional silver hair and eyes had eluded her. Instead, she had specks on silver embedded within her green and brown eyes. She was a corporal for the rebel military following in her father's footsteps, proud to be part of a force that would bring about the change for the nation of Helenia.

"So, you're from Helenia." She broke the silence and startled Finn from his daze.

Maeve was curious about the young man. She'd never spoken to someone who still supported the military or the corrupt nation. She had never been to Helenia. Her parents had lived in Socaster, a small town near the wall that was shadowed by Marina. They decided to evacuate a few years before the conflict with Marina, when aggression between the people and the military had started to escalate. She was not yet born, still growing in her mother's womb.

"Yeah, I am, born and raised." He looked towards her and caught her eye, but only for a moment.

She quickly looked back towards the road, focusing on driving. "It's not that bad of a place. The townspeople are nice. Everyone works hard, trying to support their families. It's not the nation, it's a few assholes who sit on self-made thrones thinking there better than everyone else." Finn felt he needed to justify his loyalty and support, his wiliness to fight for Helenia.

"And your king, don't forget him. Someone has to lead those assholes, as you put it, after all."

She hadn't even bothered to look at him, but he was staring at her now. What did she know? She only did what her rebel leaders told her to do. It was expected to have some type of power struggle with such a large and still growing nation.

"And what do you have? Some faceless leader that's telling you Helenia is completely un-savable and should be what, overtaken? Destroyed?" Finn felt himself succumbing to anger.

The tip of his ears started turning red in response to his elevated emotions. He understood his reaction to Maeve was uncalled for, yet he couldn't help himself. As soon as the colonel had told them what their so-called recon mission really involved, he was furious, feeling betrayed by not only people from the military, but from his leaders and fellow squad members.

"Whoa, soldier don't get mad at me, it certainly isn't my fault." Maeve didn't react to his outburst, assuming he was conflicted with the information thrusted upon him.

"Yeah, you're right." He felt ashamed for letting his emotions get the better of him. It wasn't this person's fault that he'd been lied too, that he had devoted his life to a military that would cover up genocide. His father and grandfather, and every other male figure of his family were military as well, serving since the conception of their nation. He wondered now what they would think of this. 'Did they know, were they a part of it? Did they blindly follow the orders of their king as he was supposed too?'

"I believed in my government and my nation. I believed I was doing good. That I'm still doing good. That I have a purpose. But now. What do I do? Where do I go from here?" Finn looked back at Liam. He was still sleeping his forehead smushed against the window and a drool path running down his face from his mouth gaping open.

"Sounds like you need a new purpose, soldier. I'm guessing that's why you're here, in this truck, to maybe find that purpose." Maeve kept driving her eyes focused and her foot never wavering from the pedal, but she understood what Finn had meant and, on some level, she understood him.

"And what's your purpose?" He caught her attention, surprised by the question. Perhaps understanding the rebels is what he needed. He had a purpose. He had had a purpose since he was selected to train in the academy. It was to protect the people of Helenia. To protect those who could not stand up and fight. He would stand up for them, shielding them, and fight against those that threaten the innocent, it didn't matter if it was foreign or domestic, and that meant his own government if that's what was necessary.

"My purpose? Well, my purpose is to help bring about the change that will better everyone." It was as simple as that. Even though she had no real connection to Helenia or her people, she knew she didn't want to be at war with them for the rest of her life, always fearing when the military was going to come in and destroy the outsiders. Wondering when that bullet would catch up with her, so she was going to help do something about it.

The sun had crept across the sky slowly. The vehicles made a stop and one by one the doors opened to allow the flood of soldiers to fall out. Each person stretching their limbs, moaning as they reached for the sky. It seemed a harmonious crack of joints could be heard throughout the clearing of long wisping grass where camp would be made.

Liam was enjoying the warmth from the fire. He sat watching as Conner and a few of the younger soldiers danced around making fools of themselves. He laughed to himself observing the shenanigans. He wondered if he looked that naive when he was drunk. As he looked on, he felt the wet, coolness of glass on the nape of his neck. As the person behind him let go of the bottle letting it slide down towards Liam's center. Liam brought his hand up just in time to catch the refreshment. Finn joined him on the grass where they had set up their tents.

"It must have been one hell of a talk while I was sleeping for her to be out there flirting with you now. Who knew our little Finny was such a charmer?" Liam took a long drink from the cracked open beer. As he took the gulp, he acknowledged the success the mission would most likely have if the person running the show was smart enough to bring beer. This apparently wasn't someone's first time.

Finn shoved his friend as they laughed enjoying the moment of simplicity. Finn looked down at his already half gone beverage wishing he had another, wishing he was back home where he could have been freely drinking without limit.

"Do you ever think we'll get back." Finn tapped on the glass bottle with the metal ring sitting on his middle finger. It was an insignia with a red crescent stone set within the metal representing his family's name. It had been passed down to him by his father and his father before him. It was something he kept with him and never took off. "Back home, to Helenia, I mean."

Liam scrunched down into his jacket allowing it to cover his neck and the ends of his hands. The sun had started to set, and the nights cool air was starting to encase the camp with the promise of a cold night and frosty air. In the morning there was sure to be frozen droplets of dew on the plants and trees along with a layer of frost stuck to the ground.

"Would it matter if we did. Can you honestly go back there, continue on with our lives as if nothing has happened? Knowing what we know? Having done what we've done, what we're doing now. I don't think it matters if they're in the wrong, or if we're in the wrong, or hell, the rebels are in the wrong, we can't go back to the academy, to our friends or our family and not feel a burning desire to do something, to help change the nation for the better. You know? Think about your sister, do you want her to grow up in a government that is ruled by paranoia and corruption?"

Liam's passion was surprising to Finn. He knew Liam over exaggerated about almost anything, but this time Finn felt his friends' words deeper within his soul. He could feel the emotion washing over him and felt Liam was right. There was no turning back now. This was something they needed to see through. They would be a part of the cause that brought about the change.

"We need more support." Finn stated. "Not from the rebels but from within our own walls. From within our nation. The people, the other cadets, they should know. They should have a say. This is our nation and it's our nation's problem; we should be the ones to fix it."

"From the sounds of it, the colonel said this has been going on for over twenty years. Since the first conflict with Marian. When people found out about the experiments, supporters against the military started to rise. The years of peace between Helenia and Marian was only because the military was needed to intervene in uprisings and riots in surrounding towns. Even today the uprisings are not just along the walls but within our own borders. People haven't forgotten, they've just been lying in wait."

"All the more reason to get home. Maeve said this weapon supply we're on our way to pick up is a game changer. The rebels are gearing up for a fight, they're ready to make their move Liam, and we need to be ready too." Finn was equally passionate. This was his fight.

The two stared off into the distance, watching the fire and the other soldiers, the moments of freedom truly appreciated and captured as they laughed, danced, and enjoyed the evening. As for Liam, Finn, and the rest of their squad, their time was up, they needed to make a decision. Would they fight alongside the rebels branding themselves as traitors, or would they stand with their military, taking on the difficult task of convincing those they've trained with to stand up and be the change that would better their nation. Both roads were daunting and formidable.

Chapter 19

INTERROGATION

It was silent in the early evening, or at least that's what time Robert's watch said it was. He and Alice had been thrown into separate cells connected to each other by a wall. 'Smart to keep us apart like this.' Robert thought as he busied himself with feeling around the walls of the dimmed cell for weaknesses. He imagined Alice would be doing the same. He listened for any sounds that might give him clues, such as how often the guards change shift, or if he could hear other voices that would indicate if the other members of the Earth party were here. Robert heard nothing, except the occasional clank of guard's feet's shifting from standing during there long shift.

There were no windows in the cell. Three white marbled walls stood strong around Robert ensuring escape to be near impossible. The only way out was through the door. The problem was that the door, just like the fourth wall was unable to be seen with the human eye. It was an electric field and glass combo, guaranteeing anyone who attempted an escape would be met with an electrifying end. He sat against his cot laid with white pristine, crisp sheets, and a single pillow. A person could go blind or delirious with the overwhelming sight of white. Perhaps that was the point.

The only way Robert could see them escaping was when, and if, someone came to interrogate them or perhaps during a prison transfer. He knew even that would be a risk, however. The guards, he imagined, would be expecting some type of resistance and would be prepared with a counter move. Robert did the only thing he could. He yelled to his cellmate next to him.

After a few moments of waiting in silence, his breathing staggered from trying to stay quiet, he was finally met with a disgruntled response, as if Alice had been too busy focused on something and Robert was interrupting her.

"Any ideas?" He asked her hopelessly.

He expected to hear what he had already deduced. That they might be shit out of luck. Even so, he could not bring himself to give up. He had a family to get back home to, and he would do anything to get back to them. With the inspiration of his family, Robert jumped up in a spur of the moment and searched over the walls once more for cracks and anomalies, anything would be better than nothing. Before he could make a full round of the cell, he heard footsteps approaching. He stood tall showing no fear. He would not give any satisfaction of defeat to the twisted prince or his guards.

Appearing before him was a guard armed with restraints and weapons. The guard held a device in hand and used it to scan the wall next to Robert's cell. He then proceeded to punch a sequence of numbers and codes into the handheld device. When he finished two bright circles appeared on one of the inner walls of the cell.

"Place your hands within the circles." The guard demanded without a hint of emotion.

"And if I refuse?" Robert asked. He looked at the guard sideways.

"Then you will be shot with an electric bolt that will leave you temporarily, but painfully paralyzed. Either way, you will comply." Again, the guard hinted at no emotion. His eyes shielded from view by dark glasses.

Robert stood watching the guard a moment longer before he reluctantly did as he was told, but upon placing his hands within the circles he immediately went weak in the knees, his energy zapped from his body. He let out a yelp of pain before he could no longer hold the weight of his own body up and fell to the ground. The hum from the electrified field stopped and the guard proceeded inside the cell to place the restraints upon Robert's wrist.

After a quick moment, Robert had gained some mobility in his legs. The loss of energy passed as quickly as it occurred. The guard helped him to his feet by placing his large hand around the underside of Robert's upper arm and led him out of the cell.

"Where are you taking me?" Robert asked, but received no response, not even a glance in his direction. As they walked down the hall, he passed the cell containing Alice. She was standing at the edge of the field, watching as Robert passed. The looks exchanged were those of encouragement and determination. A look that said if you have a chance, take that bastard out. The look was fleeting as Robert was directed down and out of the hallway.

As they walked a mental picture of the palace was being edged into Robert's mind. If they were going to escape, he wanted to know where he should run to stay safe. The guard stopped him short of a large door that slid to the side allowing them to enter. Inside was a single chair and the prince standing before that chair. The guard pushed him into the room, Robert stumbling over his own feet. He glanced back at the guard before continuing. Robert may have not been able to do much in the way of fighting at that moment, but he would keep his poise and allow the fire within him to not be extinguished.

As they approached the prince, Robert could see he was dressed in a bright pink suit. Stripes of lavender inlaid the coat and pants. His coat hung below his knees behind him and his shirt was the same color as the purple stripe. He presented himself with the same cane as before but topped his head with a different hat then the one he had been seen in earlier. One that would match his ensemble of pink and light purple. The prince was anything but subdued in his outerwear.

"General Mitchells, please take a seat." Prince Remilia addressed him, as he motioned towards the chair, his voice pitched with polite mannerism.

'As if I have a choice.' Robert thought as he was forced down into the seat by the guard's rough hand on his still weak shoulder.

"We have matters to discuss, you and I." Prince Remilia snapped his fingers over his head for a chair to sit upon. Another guard brought an exquisite chair with legs that ended in wooded curves and a seat set with a plush cushion covered in a dark purple velvet over to his prince. He pointed down in front of Robert indicating his desire for the cozy-looking chair to be placed in that location. Before he sat down, he flipped the tail of his coat as if he were taking a seat on a bench in front of a piano. He turned in the chair, his back sliding off to the side allowing him to rest his arm over the back of the chair while still holding onto his cane, playing with the top of it where a figurine of a bear's head had been carved into a piece of deep red garnet. He looked almost childish in the chair.

He brought the cane to his eye level and spun it while admiring the stone. "So, my dear Robert, tell me, what do you think your government will pay to get their generals back." He pointed the cane at Robert, the stone cane within inches of his nose.

"Nothing. You're wasting your time. They won't trade valuable information that would bring about the destruction of humanity for a couple of human lives. You might as well kill me now." Robert sat straighter attempting to display an appearance of strength and stability. He refused to let this insane prince know that he was truly terrified, terrified of never leaving Mars, of never seeing his family again, or worse, betraying Earth, letting down all of humanity.

He gulped as Prince Remilia stared at him. He could feel the young prince boring into him. "We shall see." His mouth turned into a wicked smile as he hailed for a guard to take Robert back to his cell. The guard forcefully grabbed Robert by the arm and lifted him out of the chair, his prisoner still restrained. Robert jerked attempting to at least loosen the grip knowing he wouldn't let go. Instead, the guard held on tighter and pushed Robert by the arm towards the door they came through.

As Robert was escorted back to his cell, they passed Alice with a guard of her own. Her face was red, and her lip was split. Robert's brows frowned, the heart in his chest thumping faster with the fire of rage growing within him. He was ready to fight, to protect. He could do it; the guard wouldn't be expecting him to be bold enough to try any stunts. All it would take is an unexpected and well-placed head butt to the guard's nose or thrust of his bonded hands into his chest causing a lag in his breathing. A moment, that's all he needed, a moment and he and Alice could be free once more.

As Alice grew closer, Robert saw the slight shake of her head, her mouth forming a single word. It was all Robert needed, he wasn't sure what her plan was, but he trusted her, and he would follow her lead. She was a fierce leader, stubborn to the core. Her wits were equally matched by her determination and those were unwavering. Whatever she had concocted she was going to see it through, he might as well sit back and wait for instructions from her or for her to let him in on her plan.

They passed each other and as the distance between them grew, Robert looked back and watched as the guard lead her into the room he had just departed from. The same room where Prince Remilia was, now, waiting for her. He must have slowed his pace because the guard pushed him in the small of his back, urging him to move along.

Robert sat in his cell waiting and listening for Alice to be returned to her cell. His legs were shaking, from bouncing on the balls of his feet as he sat on the edge of his bed. What had felt like hours passed before he finally heard the multiple sets of footsteps approaching. He heard the commotion of the guard releasing Alice into her cell followed by a single set of footsteps leading away, growing quieter as the distance grew.

"Hawkins?" Robert asked slightly unsure. He had no idea what they might have done to her, what kind of state she was in, or if that was even Alice in the adjoining cell. He patiently waited for a response, beads of sweat starting to form at his hairline. Seconds stretched on as if time was slowing down or stopping completely.

"He doesn't want Earth. He wants something from Earth, something that will give him an edge. His fight is with Venus." Robert could hear Alice shuffling around for an unknown reason. When he heard her stop moving, she continued. "I'm guessing you know what that something is, too."

"What does he want with Venus?" Robert didn't answer her assumption. He was trying to fit the pieces together.

"To annihilate them. Remilia knew Earth wouldn't fight with Mars because of our loyalties to Venus and our history with Mars itself. But he knew he also wouldn't have been able to bypass Earth and declare war on Venus without Earth trying to intervene. The best way to go about it was to play nice until he got what he wanted and then it wouldn't matter if Earth tried to step in." Alice slowed down. Robert could hear her gasp as if she were in pain. Her breathing was laborious, and he was sure they must have fractured a few ribs.

"Why go after Venus in the first place? It doesn't make sense." Robert urged.

"I'm not sure. It could be a power play or Venus could have a large amount of something that Remilia wants. Either way he feels his best option is to go through us first. Maybe if we play along it'll be our best chance to get home. We would have a better fighting chance if we were on our own grounds. So, what is it that he wants Mitchells?"

"A serum."

Chapter 20

WEAPONS OF MASS DESTRUCTION

Liam watched out the window as the towering mountains turned into rolling hills. The soaring, sturdy trees that had stood tall for decades were no longer visible but were replaced by scrawny, feebly trees. He was no longer looking at thickets of forest by instead brush that had started to thin as the vehicle he was in continued to drive. Soon, even the lanky trees had started to disappear and were replaced by backwoods of stocky shrubbery. The plants looked angry, armed with fierce, barbed ends that looked like they could tear a person to shreds if they attempted to saunter past them.

The looming rocky faces and dark rust colored clay soil he was accustomed too made way to blanched ivory sand. He and Finn were informed that the neighboring nation of Oakden sat near a sea causing the terrain to be soft and full of marshes. They approached the outskirts of the nation, passing through small towns. No fence, no wall of any sort. The land was open and free allowing anyone to pass through.

The brigade of vehicles started to slow as they approached a fence line. Soon Liam could see the gate with armed guards standing by and checking each vehicle that stopped in front. One guard guided a hound around the vehicles, stopping at each tire to sniff for unusual smells. Finally, it was the vehicle that Liam resided in's turn. Maeve rolled down the window and handed the guard papers and an Id with her picture on it. He glanced at the papers not even taking them from her hand. He waved them on as the gate moved up allowing them to pass through.

"We're passing into their military compound. Just like Helenia, Oakden is a military run government, but their population is one fourth the size of Helenia. For those reasons, they build bigger and better weapons. Quality over quantity as it were. Such a small nation needs a way to defeat larger opponents if war were to break out." Maeve explained to Liam and Finn as they looked slightly confused by the military's set up.

"That makes sense I suppose, but if they're so small why give away any of their weapons in the first place? You'd think they would want to keep them." Finn acquired, carrying on the conversation.

"Well, when you have more weapons then hands to shoot then I suppose you might as well sell or trade and get something out of it." Maeve answered.

She slowed the vehicle as those in front of her pulled to a stop. Captain Wyatt and Sergeant Aceron pushed closed the doors after stepping out. They shook hands with a few men dressed in what looked like a dress uniform. The green tunic with green slacks holding a line of blue running down the side of them. Their heads adorned with a green cap brimmed with a black bill. The air around them indicated higher-ranking officers.

Minutes passed before the captain waved for the rest of the squad to exit the vehicles. As Liam and Finn pushed out of their truck, they saw crates being moved and set down in front of the line of vehicles. Soldiers with crowbars wedged them between the layers of wood in an attempt to pry the tops off. Inside, rows of ammunition and firearms sat nestled in a hay-like substance. The captain and sergeant each picked up a weapon, studying it as they moved their hands over different parts of the guns. Seeming satisfied they placed the weapons back in their crates and moved on.

There was a total of twelve crates. Ten of them contained various weapons anywhere from flash bombs to firearms. The last two crates doubled the size in comparison to the other ten. What was held in those crates were supposed to be what would help the rebels to gain a victory in a fight against Helenia's military force.

The Oakden soldiers didn't take long to load the crates into the large truck while the captain and a woman of shorter status were speaking with one another. The woman would break from speaking to point and command those around her. Her voice boomed over the sandy road, echoing through the open air. In return, they would start to rush about. She was clearly in charge as she shouted commands. The look on her face was driven and full of resolve. The soldiers attempted to avoid her path as they scurried around her and on the other side of the walkway.

Liam and Finn were leaned up against the side of their vehicle waiting, as they took in the bustle and commotion. Their presences were not truly needed, in fact, it seemed none of the cadets from the rebel squads' presences was truly needed. The two other vehicles sat emptied, the cadets roaming around the area attempting to look busy, but hopelessly failing. Some were sitting on patches of grass, picking weeds, and throwing the stems on the gravel road while others walked around the vehicles, examining them for damage.

Liam and Finn laughed and conversed amongst themselves, watching the scene play out in front of them when Maeve walked towards them carrying platters of food. The smells wafted in their direction, bringing their attention to the curved woman approaching them. They straightened up as a sign of respect when she was closer.

"She's a general." She pointed with one finger towards the angry looking woman while holding the food. "One of the highest ranked generals of this nation, in fact." Maeve handed Liam and Finn the plates of food.

The shredded meats were sweating with flavorful juices. The chunked potatoes looked creamy and mixed with other items such as onions and celery. "The meat is wild boar found on the outskirts of town. The forests around here thrive with them so hunting them is encouraged." Maeve took a bite off her fork of the pulled meat, a bit of the juice running down her chin before she wiped it away with the palm of her hand.

"That general wants to see the turnover with Helenia happen as soon as possible." Maeve started to explain as she took another bite off her plate. "With the strong alliance she has helped forge with the rebel leaders, the turnover would mean a better national alliance between Helenia and

Oakden. In the last few years tensions have been on the rise between the two nations. Oakden would rather see the corruption in Helenia be eliminated before they see war with them."

"Why not take advantage of the fighting between Helenia and the rebels and seize the nation for themselves. Clearly, with the weapon power, they're strong enough to at least put up a good fight." Finn wondered. If Oakden's military force was strong then it was possible Helenia could be overthrown. Wasn't that the point of war, to gain resources and land?

"Oakden is a small nation and they're content to keep it that way. They have what they need and have no use for expansion." It was as if Maeve was inside Finn's mind.

"Then why are Helenia and Oakden not getting along?" Liam spoke up, his mouth full of food.

"Because Helenia knows Oakden is supplying the rebels with supplies. Or at least they think they do. Luckily, we're pretty sure they don't know about the weapons, or it would be war, and all the work the rebels have been building would be pointless." Maeve finished her food. Once Liam and Finn were done as well, she took up the plates and threw them in a nearby garbage bin.

The crates had finished being loaded into the truck. The captain gathered the cadets and informed them of their plans to stay the night in Oakden as honored guests, heading out in the early morning. A hotel had sported the bill for their stay and the general insisted on a feast to be thrown in honor of the promises the weapon exchange would bring to both of their causes.

Liam and Finn had established themselves in a room for the night, sharing the comfy room adorned with two beds. They each had a bed double the size of what they had been sleeping on since they joined the academy. Liam was sure he had truly never slept in a bed this size in his life. With three older brothers, he wasn't lucky enough to have his own room let alone a bed that could easily sleep four adults. He jumped off the ground with the intent of falling onto the bed and a moment later he did just that. His body was encased with fluffy white bedding and sheets. The pillows flew up into the air and landed on his face from the motion and energy of the jump.

Finn grabbed up one of the pillows before it found itself on the floor and brought it up over his head only to bring it back down, hitting Liam square in the stomach. Liam shoved aside the pillow on his face as he grabbed up the other pillow that had hit him, holding it close. He smiled a boyish smile with his eyes closed, wishing he could stay in the bed forever.

"Okay, while you sleep the night away, I'm going to go get washed up and head downstairs for the party." Finn grabbed clean clothes from his pack and headed towards the bathroom.

"You're just going to see your girlfriend." Liam taunted Finn when he was out of sight, his voice raised to ensure Finn could hear him over the running water from the shower.

"Real mature Liam." Finn hollard back knowing Liam was just trying to get a rise out him, like always.

"That wasn't a no." Liam shouted, but he received no response. Finn was either tuning him out or just didn't hear him. Liam assumed he was just being ignored. Without Dani, Sarah, or Aiden with him here, he didn't much feel like celebrating. Besides he was a Helenian, he didn't support this, he didn't want to see the people he had grown up with, his family, his neighbors, or anyone else get hurt, and with weapons of mass destruction, that's exactly what was going to happen.

Liam turned over suddenly feeling sick. How were they supposed to start a full uprising? It wasn't just the rebels, it wasn't just Oakden. There were forces within the nation who planned on attacking as well. This wasn't going to be an uprising or war; this could turn into an extermination.

*****

Liam was awoken in the night by a sudden jerk of his shoulder. He hadn't even realized he had fallen asleep. His shoes were still on and he was cuddled with the pillow Finn had thrown at him hours prior. He felt the shake again and this time it was followed by his name being called out. He sat up and then sleepily rubbed his eyes as he stretched and yawned.

"Yeah, what is it?" He asked unsure of who was even waking him.

Soon he saw the eyes he had grown so used too over the years. "Dani?" He was confused. He thought he must have still been sleeping, dreaming of his best friend like he had every night since her capture. She haunted him causing him to have unrestful nights followed by harsh mornings and longer days. He turned on the lamp sitting on the bedside in hopes of waking up. When the light flashed on, it was Conner, Dani's younger brother who was staring at him.

"Conner?" Liam grabbed the clock off the nightstand and tried to look at it through slanted eyes. It was early in the morning. He had missed the feast and the celebration as well. He glanced over at the still perfectly neat bed, untouched by hands. Finn was still away. Liam instantly became more alert, gaining a feeling that something wasn't right. "Conner it's four in the morning. Is something wrong."

"Yeah, a report just came in. It's from Helenia. My father and the rest of the Earth party that went to Mars, they haven't returned, and nobody can get a hold of them. Their signals have gone offline." There was fright in Conner's voice. It would be unmistakably disastrous for the mission to Mars to have gone wrong. It had the potential to throw the other leaders of Helenia into a fit and the proposed action of war would be closing in behind them.

Liam placed his feet on the floor, letting the ground stabilize him. He rubbed his eyes with the tips of his fingers. The understanding of what this could mean not only to their nation but to Dani, was starting to set in as he was forcing his mind and body to wake up.

"How long?" Liam asked Conner who was still standing by his bedside.

"What?" Conner was still so young. His understanding of military opposition and tactic still lacking. 'Why would Grayson allow his brother to be out here?' Liam wondered.

"How long has contact with them been dead?" Liam asked a bit harsher than intended.

"Dead?" The looks of fear growing in Conner's eyes. Liam realized he needed to be soft spoken and calm as well as not use words such as dead when the life of this boy's father was at stake.

"Lost, I mean lost. When did they lose contact with them?" Liam restated the question with a smoother tone.

"I'm...I'm not sure. They haven't said." The boy stammered. He sat down on the unused bed across from Liam. "Do you think my father is okay?" His head was down and in the low light, Liam could see tears streaming down his face. His voice was shaky and unsure.

Liam stood up and leaned over in front of Conner. He placed a hand on his shoulder in reassurance. "Conner," he brought up the boy's attention. "He's a Mitchells, there's no way in hell a prince in a fancy suit is going to keep him down. Now, let's get downstairs, grab some breakfast to take our mind off of this until we can get back to Grayson, okay." Liam attempted a smile, hoping his words would help ease Conner's stressful demeanor. It seemed it did because he nodded in agreement and led the way towards the downstairs area.

As they exited the room their noses filled with the aroma of freshly baked sweet breads, hearty meats, eggs, and vegetables. The dining area was empty, Liam suspecting many were laid up in bed nursing headaches or still working off drunken stupors. The captain, however, was up in the early morning. His head was down, staring into a cup of coffee. Liam could see the steam as he approached, leaving Conner to make a plate of food for himself on his own.

"Sir?" Liam caught the man's attention. He looked up, but not before clearly being startled by the sudden presence of another person. "The Earth parties." His tone was enough of an indication of the information he now required.

The captain kicked out the chair across from him and motioned for Liam to sit. The captain's large green boot sliding back down the edge of the chair. Liam looked back towards Conner and waved him on, an indication to take a seat, and that he would be there soon. Liam looked back at the captain and pulled the seat out, allowing himself to sit.

"What do you know?" He asked Liam as he took a sip of his coffee.

"Lost communication." Liam paused for a moment, before speaking once more. "They've been captured, haven't they?" Liam wanted confirmation.

"Your friend, the one still in town. How much does she know about her father?" He turned towards Liam. Liam was watching him like a bird about to swoop down and capture its prey. Focused. It was as if the captain knew more than he was letting on. Liam understood what he was indicating though, or what he wanted. Confirmation.

"I can't tell you that." Liam responded. It was the truth, but he could see how his statement could be interpreted.

"Can't or won't?" The captain stayed calm, revealing no emotion in his facial expressions as he took a sip of the hot coffee.

"Can't, sir, because I don't know. Apparently, she knows something, but nobody knows what and I'm pretty sure she doesn't either. Why?" Liam was not as subtle with his emotions, unfortunately.

The captain spun the spoon in his cup and then spoke. "What I think, is that that information is also wanted by the Prince. Did you know Prince Remilia asked for general Mitchells personally? He requested his presence on Mars. Odd. The Prince wants this information. He thinks it will give him more power. Let's hope that General Mitchells can hold out." He stood up, pushing in his chair and picking up his cup. "I would suggest you not let the young cadet know any of this. He might not handle it very well." He started to walk away but turned back when he was a few feet away. "Don't forget we roll out at seven."

He left Liam sitting at the table, the rage starting to boil within him. His hands on the top of the table turned to fist. He looked back at Conner who was enjoying his breakfast. Liam turned back around and took a deep breath, he had to stay in control, or he might upset Dani's younger brother. He wished she was here now more than ever. Since they had been apart, he just couldn't seem to stay in control and always felt lost and incomplete. He never realized how much he depended on her, on her presence, and on her guidance as his equal. A few more days he thought to himself. Just a few more.

The vehicles were running attempting to warm up in the cold morning air. Liam waited on a bench nearby, sitting on the top of the back of it, his pack sitting at his feet. He was lost in thought thinking about what he would say to Dani and the rest of their friends when he got back. Liam had no plans to stay with the rebels. He was going home. It was his nation, his family lived there, he needed to be there. He believed that the government needed to change, that there was corruption that needed to be sought out and destroyed but he would do it the right way, not the rebel's way.

Liam heard his name being called out as Finn ran towards him, his arm raised over his head, waving it about. Liam stepped off the bench and grabbed his pack as he met his friend. Liam was unsurprised by his appearance. Finn looked disarranged, his shirt was untucked underneath his tunic, his hair had not been combed, and his shoelaces were tangling into one another as he ran, a consequence of the laces not being tied properly.

"Man, if the colonel saw you, he'd have a fit." Liam grabbed the front of the tunic and pulled at it bringing attention to Finn's mess. "Where did you sleep last night because it certainly wasn't our room."

Finn slapped his friend's hand away. "Who said I did any sleeping?" Finn joked with Liam.

"Oh, I think you slept, I'm sure it just wasn't restful." Liam teased his friend. Finn's ears and face started to turn red and he could feel the heat from being bashful. Maeve walked up behind them as if nothing could faze her.

"What are we standing around for cadets, let's get a move on. I personally don't want to stand around in Oakden any longer then I have too. The foods good, but after last night, I'm declaring the people here to suck." She threw her pack into the back of the open trunk space. She then went to the driver's door threw it open and jumped in slamming it shut as her left foot hit the floor. A moment later the window was being rolled down and she was yelling at Liam and Finn to hurry up.

Liam pointed to Maeve with his left hand and then to Finn with his right. He then proceeded to cross his two-pointed fingers attempting to convey a message to Finn. Finn watched as Liam made a mockery of himself.

"What?" Finn finally asked. "Oh....oh! No, no, no." Finn flared his arms and hands about in front of him. "No, nothing happened between us."

"Then who?" Liam exclaimed loudly.

"With no one dumbass. I was joking. Maeve and me, we just talked." Finn said quietly.

"Then what's her problem? She got tired of listening to you ramble?" Liam pointed in Maeve's direction now confused by the harshness laced through her voice. Something was visibly bothering her.

"I do not ramble. Some drunk asshole dumped his beer on her and then proceeded to vomit on her. She turned around and punched the guy because after he threw up on her, the guy had the nerve to grope her." Finn started to explain.

"Well, hell, I did miss all the fun." Liam cut in.

"That's not even all of it. The dumb shit came back at her swinging, so I kicked his ass. She's pissed because after the whole ordeal we went back to her room to get cleaned up when we were summoned down. The captain gave us an hour-long lecture on why we don't go around punching people, especially when that person happens to be a general's son. Maeve is getting written up and has to pull extra duty for a week."

"And you?" Liam acquired.

"Well that's the great thing about it, I can't be touched. Apparently, I can go around kicking whoever's ass I want and not get in trouble. Who are they going to tell? My leadership back at the academy? In Helenia? The people they're fighting against. Yeah okay. So, there's that. It's still unfair to Maeve. The guy sexually assaulted her; he had that punch coming. Can't be helped that his nose happed to break from that punch."

"She broke the guy's nose! Oh shit! That's awesome." Liam squealed with excitement. He really had missed a lot.

"Hey, not so loud. She's still pretty pissed. Anyways let's just get out of here. After that event, I really don't want to be in this city any longer than I have to myself."

The two threw their packs in the trunk and shut it uptight. Finn took the front seat while Liam jumped in the back with Conner, who was already fast asleep. Within minutes the conga of vehicles started pulling away. The city grew smaller and smaller with every mile they drove. By tomorrow night they would be back at the compound and Dani would be there, waiting for them.

Chapter 21

MEET AND GREET

Dani waited impatiently in her room. She had paced the floors back and forth in front of the window so much that she recognized where each creak would be before her foot would land on it. Every time she passed the window, she would hover for a moment, looking for the vehicle that would take her and Zachary to the main compound. Her bag was packed, now it was just a waiting game.

It had been hours since Zachary dropped her off at her room. He told her he had unfinished business to attend to before they could depart, and he would be back before the vehicle even arrived. The time ticked by slowly. It was only eleven in the morning, but it felt much later.

Dani startled when she heard a knock at the door. She stopped pacing and looked up as the door swung open. Zachary stood in the doorway, a bag in one hand and a case in the other. Dani's eyes expanded with giddiness and warmth.

"Figured if we were leaving you might need these things back." He moved towards the bed and laid the items on top. Dani immediately rushed to the bedside and started rummaging through her military gear. Everything was all there. "I don't think they messed with anything. When they brought you in, I confiscated it and it's been sitting in my room. I promise I didn't touch anything or go through it."

"Also," he handed her the case. She took it and opened it, unsure. Inside was her knives and gun still loaded and ready to be wielded. "I'm sorry I had to keep them from you but..." before he could finish Dani was hugging him around the neck. It was an unexpected gesture and he wasn't sure if he should hug her in return or allow her to let go of her leisure.

Dani let her arms fall, suddenly feeling embarrassed. She pulled away from Zachary and proceeded to tuck her loose strands of dark hair behind her ear. "I'm sorry, I shouldn't have, I mean I didn't..." She stammered over her words unsure what to say or how to act. She was suddenly aware of his silver eyes focused on her face and it caused the tips of her ears to redden more.

Before another word could be spoken, or pass between the two, Zachary received a call over the radio he had been sporting on his hip. "Go for Ryder." He responded after unclipping it from his belt.

"Yeah, the car you requested is here." The unknown voice static over the radio.

"On my way." Ryder held the radio to his lips and responded once more before replacing the radio on his hip. "Ready to go?" He stood up from the bed and held out a hand for Dani to take hold of. She hesitantly did so, allowing herself to be pulled up. As soon as she was on her feet, she hastily let go of Zachary's warm hand. Not because she didn't want too, but because she was still unsure of how he felt towards her. They were growing close, but in which way?

"More than ready." She smiled shyly and turned to gather her things.

She slipped her knives into her pack and holstered the gun to her side. Next, she pulled over her jacket that covered up the weapon. Unless someone was looking for it, no one would know it was there. She threw on the military pack, but before she could grab up the duffel bag that had been given to her with the clothes in it, Zachary picked it.

"You're still healing. I don't want you to strain yourself too much." He smiled down at her. It was a soft smile, a genuine smile. "I just need to stop by my room and pick up my bags before we head down." Dani followed him out of the room, but before she shut the door, she took one last look, ensuring she didn't forget anything, but also it was her way of saying goodbye.

"And here we are." Zachary stopped at a door that was only a couple feet from Dani's. Literally, the next room over from hers.

"Are you serious! What the hell." Dani recoiled.

Zachary only laughed, as if he was expecting this reaction from her. Dani shook her head as she stood in the doorway. His room was dull. There was a stack of books on the table, but no other personal effects. No pictures, no nothing. His bed had been made up nice and neat, the curtains pulled back to let the light in, but the room felt and looked as empty as hers. She could feel that this was how the room had always been. That just like her, he had never truly belonged to this place.

He hustled up a pack like hers, but larger, onto his back and grabbed a large duffle bag. "Okay that's everything, let's head downstairs." Dani moved out of the doorway and made for the elevators, Zachary trailing behind her. She was almost too excited to contain herself. In a few hours she would see her family, and hopefully, get answers.

The car was waiting for them, the trunk was already open and ready for her and Zachary to place their bags in it. Before they stepped in, Dani heard a familiar voice. She turned to see Miss Mackenzie hollering after them with something in her arms. She stopped short of them and hugged Dani unexpectedly.

"Can't send you off without a proper goodbye. I made these for the road. I make the trip to the compound monthly and I know how tiresome it can be." She handed Dani a box that contained perishable items to eat. They smelled heavenly and looked mouthwatering. There were sandwiches and desserts that were still warm. "You have been a great help at the library, I'll miss it. But I'm sure we will see each other soon. Safe travels you two."

Zachary and Dani said their thanks and goodbyes before Miss Mackenzie walked away towards the library. As she did Dani caught a glimpse of something or someone. Gabe was across the street, hiding in the shadows. She could feel him staring at them, his sight boring into them. She stared back, unafraid, before Zachary caught her by the elbow, gently guiding her into the vehicle. When he noticed her looking off into the distance, he turned to see what she was looking at, but it was too late. Gabe had already disappeared into the darkness of the overcasting building.

"You okay?" He asked her concerned.

"Yeah." She responded before turning and jumping into the back seat, Zachary following in close behind her. The door was shut, and they were off.

They had left the town and were headed towards the dark forest beyond the fields where the bonfires had taken place. The sky was a rich blue with bright, fluffy white clouds hanging high above the mountains. The ride was surprisingly smooth for them traveling in a military vehicle on a poorly maintained road. The road never touched the forest but stayed close, dormant of the tree line casting shadows over the vehicle as they drove. Dani was watching outside the window, letting the world pass before her, her thoughts still thinking about Gabe, Nadia, and Penelope.

"Zachary, you said you didn't know much about Gabe, correct?" He had been leaning forward, talking to the driver, when she suddenly spoke to him. He patted the driver on the shoulder and sat back, his long legs stretching out in front of him, and his hands resting in his lap. He seemed so at peace in that moment.

"Yes." He turned towards her suddenly allowing himself to bring his full attention to her. He rested his arm on the edge of the back seat and his head. "They showed up out of nowhere without a believable explanation. Why?"

"Nadia came to my room the night of the dance. She said something that's just now hitting me."

Zachary straightened up, his attention caught, grasped by Dani's words. "And what did she say?"

"She spoke of Mars, about the military training and how she hated it. How it was especially demanding if you had abilities." Dani explained.

"Yeah, but that's known information. What does that have to do with anything?" Zachary was starting to develop a sick feeling as to where Dani was leading.

"She said she got nightmares, about Mars. They're from Mars! I bet you anything, the three of them are not defectors." Dani continued.

"You think their spies." Zachary thought about his own comment and what Dani was saying.

"Well don't you? Think about it. Especially Gabe. How he looks down on Earth and the people. The way he carries himself and brings attention to himself. What if that's all a show. To drive away from the attention to his real purpose. How often do you find him somewhere he shouldn't be? How often do you find any of them somewhere they shouldn't be, because I can think of a few times and I've only been here for a few weeks." Dani finished and waited for him to speak.

"If you think of it that way, it does make sense, too much sense actually. Shit. How did I miss that?" Zachary smacked his face with an open hand. He couldn't believe how naive he had been. "But why infiltrate the rebels, why not Helenia or any of the other nations?"

"Maybe they thought the rebels had information that would be easier to obtain. You'd have to work your way through the ranks in a nation to obtain any damaging information, and it's a lot harder to blend into a society that takes a special interest in outsiders especially ones that have red eyes as they do. Too many questions would have been asked." Dani carried on.

"But not with the rebels. They could easily pass as defectors with no extra questing required." Zachary felt like such a fool. He knew in his gut something wasn't right about Gabe from the moment the two met. He should have stuck with his instinct and acted.

The two were silent for a moment obviously thinking about the problems and uproar this travel would make, when finally, Dani spoke. "Maybe you guys should tighten your security."

Zachary turned his head to look at her, her attention had been caught by him. They were silent a moment more and then suddenly Zachary let out a hardy laugh, a genuine laugh. Dani was taken by surprise by his sudden upheaval. Then she joined him on laughing, in a moment of gloom caused by negative influences the best way to handle it was to laugh at how naive they had been.

"Well, I guess I'll be making some calls when we get to the compound. Your brother isn't going to like this at all." He moved to where his back was up against the seat and he allowed himself to stretch out once more. His legs would cramp if he kept them propped up for too long.

"I'm sorry about the extra work." Dani assured him.

"No, No." He spoke slowly. I should have seen it sooner. He just wasn't my top priority. Still isn't actually." Dani had a feeling she knew what, or who was his priority. She could feel her ears warming once more and she was confused about why she kept feeling this way around him. How could he make her feel so unsure and unsteady? "Should have clogged him harder when I had the chance." Zachary said it more to himself than to Dani.

"Wait, you punched him? No fair. I wanted to take a swing at him myself." They both shared a laugh once more. "When did that happen?" She asked him curiously.

Ryder grew serious. "When he shot you." The two of them went silent. The look they shared was of compassion and gratitude. A new relationship between the two of them had started to blossom. One of trust and understanding. The feeling of stinging dislike Dani had felt for Zachary when she had first arrived had melted away replaced with a certain fondness. She no longer felt she was a bothersome nuisance to him, but instead felt as if he wanted his time to be occupied by her.

She smiled up at him. The red in his eyes looked like fire in the sunlight, flowing as they absorbed the brightness of the day. Dani never realized how brilliant the red eyes could be until now. How alluring they could be.

"Well, thank you." She smiled a delicate smile back at him.

The drive out to the main compound was long. At one point both Zachary and Dani had fallen asleep. In the early evening, Dani was still fast asleep, cuddled up, leaning on the window, using her jacket as a pillow. Zackary surrendered his jacket over to her, draping it over her body in hopes that it would warm her. Under the jacket, he could hear her light snores and wondered if she knew she snored.

Zachary was deep in thought when they arrived at the main compound. The compound was an old-world fort. The stonework had stood the test of time and with a bit of renovation and rebuilding, the inside of the building had been updated to contain the high tech and living quarters required to maintain, operate, and house the bulk of the rebel military forces.

Upon entering through the front wall, the fort opened into a large courtyard, surrounded by eight walls that stood five stories tall. Each wall served a purpose. Some held arms rooms while others held various supplies. The operations room led underground, while the dining hall, living quarters, offices, and various other rooms that helped with the day to day living were on the furthest back wall that attached to a building that made up the bulk of the fort. The building itself was easily ten stories tall, allowing great vantage points to see any opposing force that might make their way to the rebel's front door.

The car drove through the wall as it approached and was guided around the inner wall and down through an opening leading underground to a parking deck, where all the vehicles were stored and maintained. Zachary lightly roused Dani from her sleep. She startled awake, jumping from the motion of the car stopping. She looked around startled by the lack of sunlight beaming through the car window. The yellowish-orange artificial light was dull in comparison and was unexpected.

"We're in an underground storage for the vehicles." Zachary explained.

Dani just nodded, still trying to wake up. She could tell she slept hard. Her body ached all over and her neck was stiff from lying against the window with poor support. She looked down to see an unfamiliar article of clothing laid across her. She recognized it as Zachary's jacket. The strong smell of soap and cologne from the jacket enticed her, it smelled like him, and once more she realized she was thinking about Zachary on a deeper level, her feelings for him growing. She quickly handed the jacket back to him.

"Um, thank you, for, um, covering me. It was a bit cold." Dani said shyly.

"Of course." Zachary replied awkwardly. He smiled as he took back his jacket and laced his arms through the sleeves. He could smell a hint of her scent woven through the fibers. The smell of sweet honey and lavender. He opened his door and hurried around to the other side of the car to open Dani's door, holding out a hand for her to take. She accepted it, allowing the warmth from his hand to warm hers. "We can leave the bags here. Someone will be down to get them and will take them to your room."

The two walked to the nearby elevator, stepping inside. The door closed and Zachary pushed the button with the number one on it. "So, I can take you to your room first or we can go get food, or I can take you straight to your brother. Which would you like to do first?" Zachary asked Dani.

"I guess we'll go see Grayson. I'm sure he doesn't want to be kept waiting. He never was a patient one." Dani rolled her eyes at the memories of her older brother. He would always throw some type of fit when their parents refused to do something he wanted right away. She remembered how her father would always turn it around on him and was able to trick him into waiting by making it a game or a puzzle. Her father was always about puzzles and riddles.

Zachary laughed at Dani's comment. "Oh my gosh, he really is so impatient. As soon as he says something, he wants it done right then and there."

"Yeah, you didn't have to grow up with him. If he didn't get his way, hell on earth broke loose." Dani never spoke of her siblings and she felt it was odd to do so now.

The stories and memories were foreign to her. For so many years she tried to bury her past, to forget the memories, as they were too painful to recall. Still, they slipped back in while she slept. Often, she dreamed of her mother, brothers, and her sister. She could never see their faces in her dreams, those were starting to fade, but that unmistakable dark hair that they all inherited from their mother was always recognizable.

The doors of the elevator swooshed open to a wide space. A soldier holding documents was there waiting to ride the elevator to another floor. The floor was laid with marble in the shape of a compass. Dani could smell food being cooked somewhere close, but her attention was held by something, or by someone. Someone with long blond hair and large blue eyes.

"Sarah." Dani whispered. "Sarah!" She said a bit louder, and then she was off, running towards her best friend and roommate, shouting her name. Sarah looked up at the person calling her name. Before she could start running herself, Dani was knocking into her, embracing her in the tightest hug Sarah could ever remember being given by Dani.

"Dani. I can't believe it, you're here, you're finally here." She refused to let go of Dani. Tears started to stream down her face. She had been so angry with everyone because of Dani's absence and now that she was here and that she could wrap her arms around her best friend again, all that anger started to melt away, replaced with a string of emotions.

Sarah and Dani pulled apart, allowing them to look at each other. "They said you were okay, but fuck them, I couldn't believe it until I saw you again." Sarah told her.

"I had no idea you would be here." Dani commented. She went quiet, afraid to ask the next question. Before she had to though, Sarah was answering what she was thinking.

"Everyone's okay. They're here, well, all but Finn and Liam. Oh, but don't worry," Sarah added quickly not wanting to worry Dani. "Harper sent them on a mission with a rebel's platoon. They should be back by tomorrow sometime."

Zachary walked up behind them, finally joining Dani. He had stood back, not wanting to disturb the emotional reunion, letting the two settle, but now he walked up behind Dani and placed his hand on the small of her back, alerting her to his presence. The look on Sarah's face indicated dislike and mistrust.

"You must be Ryder." Sarah spat.

"Um, yes, yes I am." Zachary said slowly.

"Sarah, this is Zachary, he took care of me while I was injured." Dani tried to smooth the tension.

"Still injured." Zachary commented.

"And who's fault was it that you were injured in the first place, Dans?" The venom in Sarah's voice had not disappeared.

"Well, it was this guy named Gabe." Dani spoke slowly, still holding her friends' hands.

"Yeah, well, who oversaw this Gabe guy? I'll tell you who, Ryder. It was his man, and it was his man that shot you."

"Sarah, I don't blame Zachary for that, and neither should you, I'll explain everything later, okay, but trust me, we can trust Zachary." Dani assured Sarah.

"No, Dani, she's right. I should have had better control over Gabe. It is my fault you were injured. You should blame me; I know I do." Zachary lowered his head, his eyes turned away from her.

"See." Sarah added. Her stance was one of rightful pride. Dani released Sarah's hand and turned to Zachary. Sarah's brows lowered as she watched her best friend interact with this stranger. She noticed Dani's body language and was sure she noticed one thing she had never seen from Dani.

"I don't blame you." She held his gaze and spoke softly to him. It was simple words, but it seemed to be all he needed to hear from her. The words rendered deeply within him. They shared a smile.

"We should be going." Zachary started, not wanting to take Dani from her friend, but he understood Grayson's inpatients at their late arrival better than most.

"Going? Going where?" Sarah asked. Dani explained that they needed to meet with her older brother, but Dani assured her that she would be back down soon, and they would have dinner and talk about the past few weeks' events.

Dani and Zachary headed upstairs to the eighth floor where offices were housed. Down a long hallway and in front of a door on the left, Dani stood, shaking with anticipation, unsure of what she would be met with. Zachary knocked on the heavy door and waited for a response. Then he opened the door and allowed Dani to pass in front of him.

"I'll be waiting right here for you. Okay." Dani nodded at him and passed through the threshold of the door.

Inside a man stood over his desk, looking down at a folder, studying it with the same look she had seen a thousand times. The frowned brows, the pinched bridge of his nose, the look of concentration, it was exactly like her father, except the dark hair. The man looked up from his paper to see a young woman standing in the doorway, her hand resting on the brass door handle. Her dark hair and high cheekbones had developed into a younger version of his late mother. "Danielle." He breathed the name in.

"No one calls me that anymore, not even Liam." She spoke to him. She couldn't bring herself to move from the shock of seeing her older brother, but Grayson, he moved, and crossed the room in four strides and took his sister in his arms, hugging her.

"I can't tell you how long I've been waiting for you to return to us. Now our family can be whole again." He pulled away from her.

"Well, almost whole." Dani said, saddened by the thought of their late mother and younger sister. Grayson was saddened by the thought as well but knew it to be true.

Grayson led her out to the balcony attached to his office. They stood outside in the cool night air talking and reminiscing of when they were children. How they would sneak fresh baked cookies, but would always get caught, well she would get caught, and to gain her brother's loyalty she would never tell on him, but their parents knew he had put her up to it and he would get in trouble anyway.

They talked about how he and Liam's older brothers would leave Liam and her in the woods to find their way back before dark, only to be forced back to fetch them. She and Liam would still be standing exactly where the four of them had left them or Liam and Dani would climb the trees and the four older brothers would have to run back to their mom's crying, having to confess how they lost their younger siblings.

Dani spoke. "I miss mom. Her smile, her smell. I used to catch dad staring at me sometimes, but I could tell he wasn't seeing me, but remembering mom. It was always heartbreaking, and I never knew how to help him." She explained to Grayson.

Grayson was watching the stars that were starting to appear in the dark sky but was listening closely to his sister speak knowing the inevitable was coming.

"Why? Why was I not allowed to know you and Conner were alive? Why keep it a secret from me? Why keep me in the dark? Do you know how alone I've been? After mom's death, dad was never the same. A piece of him died the day we buried her along with Abby. I thought it was just us. No, it was just us, and dad was too busy with work. You guys, though, you guys had each other. I was alone." Dani was feeling the sting of betrayal and hurt.

"They were watching you Dans, you don't understand how much it killed our father to put you through that. To deal with the pain of losing the four of us, to lose your whole family. And no, I will never have to feel that, and I certainly don't envy you for having to deal with that, but you do understand it was for your safety, right?" He tried to explain to her, knowing it couldn't possibly make up for the years she spent by herself, thinking what she was made to believe.

"Why watch me though? It's not like I was a threat?"

"But you are, or at least they think you are. Did our father ever talk to you about the conflict between Marian and the military?" The question threw Dani for a loop.

"No, I didn't know anything about it until a few weeks ago. Why?"

"We think our father may have told you something, or you may have seen something that was not supposed to be seen or known, that something was the cause of our family being attacked and killed. Can you think of anything, or remember anything? It could have been the smallest thing."

"No, I'm sorry. But I don't know anything." She let out a deep breath, sighing.

Grayson sighed heavily and the spoke once more. "There's something else you should know?" Dani looked up at Grayson, afraid of what he was about to tell her. "There's been a report. The earth party sent to Mars has not reported back and they lost communications with them. We think they're being held captive."

"What! But, father..." Dani started to get excited, afraid of losing another parent.

"I know, I know he's there. We think this is a play from Mars. They either want something we have, or this is a means to enact war. We have sources that say their fight is not with us though, but with Venus. So that leads us to believe they want something from us, something that would guarantee them a victory over Venus."

"Like what?" Dani asked confused.

"I don't know. It could be just a coincidence that our father is there, but he told me before he flew out that he was requested to go, by Mars. His attendance was wanted. My thought is, he knows whatever Prince Remilia thinks Earth has that will assist in his war. Which means you might know what that is too." Grayson looked at his sister. Strands of her hair blew in front of her face as she looked over the balcony towards the ground. The air was growing colder as the night started to grow longer. He could tell she was thinking that she wanted to be able to give him an answer, but she just didn't know.

"I'm sorry. I just don't know." Her fingers were laced together, hanging over the balcony. It seemed as one weight was lightened off her another was placed.

"That's okay, you're here, and you're safe, that's all that matters." Grayson spoke, but Dani could tell he was still disappointed.

"Well I may be safe, but our father's not." Dani mentioned, looking at her older brother.

"Yes, I know, and I've been in conference with the other rebel leaders. It's still too soon to make a move on our part. This information was only released today. For all we know, Helenia is already putting together a rescue party, or even making a deal with Prince Remilia. At this point, it's a waiting game. We need to see what Helenia is going to do before we act. I'll keep you posted, but don't worry, if Helenia doesn't act or doesn't act in our favor, we will. We're not going to leave Earth prisoners on Mars."

"Well if there's a rescue on our part, I want to go." Dani's face said she would not back down from this.

"Let's see how your wounds are first. Speaking of which, it's getting late and you're probably hungry and need rest. We'll talk more tomorrow." With his final words, he wished her a goodnight and dismissed her.

Chapter 22

SHORT REUNION

Sarah paced the room growing impatient waiting for Dani to return. The few moments spent with her was not nearly enough. The anticipation of seeing her again was growing, ready to burst from her chest. Every foreign footstep outside put her on alert. Every strange noise prickled at her ears. Aiden sat on the couch watching as she paced. He knew there would be no convincing her to sit down and rest, but he attempted anyways, with the slim hope that he could settle her.

"You pacing isn't going to make time go by faster or her get here sooner. She'll come when she comes. Now please, Sarah, come sit down. It's not good to stress yourself out like this."

Sarah stopped pacing to look at Aiden and then walked over to the couch to lay a kiss on his forehead. A sign of affection confirming she appreciated his concern for her well-being. Before she turned to walk away, he grabbed her hand and pulled her into his lap. But before he could return her affections, they heard a knock at the door. Sarah jumped up with haste at the potential arrival of her best friend.

She threw open the door, and there in the doorway stood Lieutenant Reeves. Sarah sighed with disappointment. Lieutenant Reeves stood, back straight, her hair in a perfect bun, her uniform neat and tidy without a single out of place crease or wrinkle. She looked clean like always.

"Sorry to disappoint Hunt. The colonel wants a word with you." Aiden stood up from his seat on the couch. "Not you Pearce." Aiden's face hardened. "Don't worry, it won't take long. Hunt will meet you in the dining hall in ten minutes. If you will Hunt, follow me please."

Lieutenant Reeves turned expecting Sarah to follow behind her. They walked down the hall towards the elevators to be delivered to the fifth floor where some of the higher-ranking commanders occupied during work hours. The elevator was slow-moving, a representative of time. They arrived at the designated floor. The floor was tiled in white polished stone with a running of royal blue carpet down the middle. The silver of the handles on each of the dark stained wooded doors glistened in the dimmed lights hanging overhead.

"No need to worry Hunt. You're not in trouble. Just relax." Reeves said without looking back at Sarah. Sarah's head was down, shadowed by fear.

This mission was supposed to reassure her she was doing the right thing by staying with a scouting unit instead of office administration, but now, everything was falling apart. Liam and Finn were on a mission with the once supposed enemy. Dani had been injured and captured, and she and Aiden were stuck in the military headquarters of the rebels. A month ago, the four friends were enjoying the weekends in town after a long week of drills and hard work bettering themselves to become the next great leaders of their nations. How did everything fall apart so quickly?

Lieutenant Reeves knocked on a door before she entered, not even bothering to wait for a response. She swung open the door, her hand stayed resting on the doorknob. The colonel sat in a dim lit room, all the lights off except for the one that sat on the desk. His head was down focused on the paperwork in front of him. It looked as if he had been lax and let his work go, letting it pile up.

"Sir." Reeves brought the attention of the colonel from his work.

"Oh, yes. Hunt, please come in." Sarah passed in front of the first lieutenant. She followed behind Sarah, guiding her to a chair in front of the desk while she continued to move on towards the desk taking her rightful side as the colonel's right-hand person.

"Hunt. I want you to go home." The colonel spoke when the two women had settled. Hunt never expected him to make that command.

"Excuse me. What do you mean you want me to go home?" Sarah started to rise from her chair as her emotions started to rise. Excitement and adrenaline taking over. The colonel waved her back down before she could completely lift from her seat.

"I want you to go back to Helenia. There is no need for you to stay here in the rebel's headquarters, sulking around. I think you would be in a better position to help if you were back in Helenia. You do want to help bring down the corruption, don't you?"

"Well, yeah, of course, sir, but I don't understand why I can't stay here. With Dani. With my squad." She was understandably upset at the idea of leaving her friends.

"Hunt, please." The colonel tried to keep her calm. He knew how much of a hothead she could be.

"What would I even be doing back in Helenia." Sarah seemed to accept rather quickly that she would be going back, without Dani, without her squad. She knew as stubborn as she was, Colonel Harper was even more so, and he was the one in command.

"Well, you won't be going back to the academy for starters. I will be signing off on yours, Pearce, and Carson's completion of academic training. Therefore, you will be entering into a unit, my unit to be precise. I want you to work as my second lieutenant under Lieutenant Reeves at Eastern Command. You'll be my eyes and ears, gathering information that might be vital and valuable to us. You'll have open access to schedules and movements, plans, everything. But it will also keep you out of suspicions. In yours and Pearce's situation, I think that might be best." The colonel leaned back in his chair, his hands resting in his lap.

Sarah accepted his answer, realizing what he was implying. "I understand, sir. Will it just be me going back home or..." Sarah trailed off. Her voice serious and filled with defeat.

"No." The colonel said with glee. "You will be having a few people accompany you. Cadet Katsuki will be joining you along with the lieutenant here and myself." He motioned towards Reeves and then back at himself. "Oh, and Cadet Pearce as well. I honestly don't think he would allow himself to stay here while you return to Helenia, anyways."

Sarah stifled her excitement. "And what about Carson and Evens, sir?"

"Well I'm not sure about Carson yet, I'll discuss it with him when they get back from Oakden. As far as Evens goes, I very much doubt that he will leave Mitchells, therefore he will be staying." There was silence, allowing Sarah to absorb his command. She seemed satisfied with what he had to say. "If you don't have any more questions, you are dismissed Cadet Hunt, or shall I say Second Lieutenant Hunt."

Sarah stood up and saluted. "Yes sir." Sarah turned and left the office hoping to not let a single tear roll down her face. The thought of this squad she had grown to love and appreciate, depending on their support and friendship, splitting up was upsetting.

Behind closed doors, Colonel Harper and Lieutenant Reeves remained. Reeves moved in front of the desk and took a seat, while Harper continued on his paperwork.

"What is it, lieutenant?" Harper asked without batting an eye at her, without taking his eyes off his work.

"Sir, permission to speak freely." She stated.

"You think I'm making the wrong decision by sending her home." He commented back to her. He felt he could read her thoughts and emotions by the level of silence and judgment she emitted.

"I think you are giving her too much credit. Sir."

"How so." He stopped working and let his hands and arms settle on his desk. His sight focused on his lieutenant. The person's opinion he trusted beyond anyone else's.

"Though her performance has been steady and her scores back at the academy for human intelligence is outstanding, I fear this last month has been detrimental to her mental health. I think seeing Cadet Mitchells getting shot may have been too much, too soon for her and now leaving after Cadet Mitchells just returned, she might not handle it well."

"This is the price of war; you know that better than most. She chose to be a soldier; she knew the risk and what came along with being a dog of the military. This is the price she pays, the price we all pay. She'll have to learn that sooner than later if she wants to survive."

Reeves didn't agree with Harper's tactics but trusted in his ability to judge people for their heart along with their strengths and weaknesses. Her faith in his leadership was always unwavering. "Yes sir."

Aiden waited by the elevator for Sarah to return. As soon as she and Lieutenant Reeves departed from the quarters, he had quickly thrown on shoes, a belt, and a sweater and rushed to the elevator. Before he could make it, though, Hiromi spotted him and stopped him by calling out his name. She had heard Dani had arrived back and wondered if they had caught wind of the news themselves. He informed her that Sarah had already spoken to her, but she was whisked away to meet with Major Grayson before the two could completely reunite. Hiromi walked to the elevator with Aiden continuing their conversation.

"Speaking of Sarah, where is she?" Hiromi asked curiously as she looked around expecting Sarah to pop up out of nowhere.

"Oh, she's, uh, she's with the colonel and lieutenant." She could tell he was anxious and on edge. He kept eyeing the elevator waiting for it to ding and the doors to swish open revealing a tall blond.

"I wouldn't worry, I'm sure they're just discussing their next plan of action with her." She tried to lessen his worry, but only seem to make things worse. His eyes went large with alarm.

"What do you mean? Do you know something we don't?" He bombarded her with questions, desperate for answers.

"Well I imagine you're going to find out soon enough, but Colonel Harper plans to start the mission back to Helenia. We need to keep up appearances and get back. If we're out much longer it will seem suspicious." She explained to him.

"When does he plan on doing this." Aiden was upset, angry even, but he guessed it was to be expected. After all, how long did they expect to stay hidden away in the mountains?

"As soon as Finn and Liam get back. I'm sorry if I've upset you. But what did you expect? We can't stay here."

"No, you're right. I guess I never expected to stay here either. I'm just not sure what we're going to be doing when we get back. After all we've learned, what do we do now." He scratched the back of his head as thoughts flooded his minds.

"It's really quite simple. We fight." She smiled up at him reassuring him that they would all be okay and then departed, heading towards her sister who was standing nearby with Hiromi's hounds.

Aiden took a deep breath and let it out slowly. He thought about what she had said. Sure, it was easy to say fight, but what was one small squad going to do? Takedown the entire Helenia military force? They weren't ready to fight, so what were they supposed to do until then? Go on with their lives as if nothing happened? Graduate from the academy and transfer to units in their trained field until then? They would be fighting alright, fighting every day to keep up this façade of being loyal to the corrupt leaders, always looking over their shoulder wondering if someone was going to figure out what really happened on this mission.

Aiden was so wrapped up in his own thoughts he not only missed the elevators' distinctive ding, but he also missed the doors opening. It wasn't until he noticed the flash of blond hair walking past him that his mind became aware of his surroundings. He called out Sarah's name as he pushed off the wall parallel with the elevator. After a few times of Aiden calling out for her. She finally stopped and turned to look at him surprised that he had been waiting for her. Her hands were wrapped in her hair that was hanging down from her ponytail.

Aiden could tell she was troubled and was lost to her own thoughts. He was sure she just received the same news he had but most likely with more detail. He asked her if she was okay knowing what the answer would be. But before they could start discussing the conversation that transpired, they were interrupted by an all too familiar voice.

*****

Zachary waited patiently on a small bench next to Major Grayson's door. Still, he couldn't seem to keep his foot and leg from jumping from his growing anxiousness. Half an hour passed, and no voices could be heard nor any movement. The hall containing the offices was empty, as to be expected since the duty day was over.

Zachary had started to grow tired listening to the white noises in his head when he heard feet scuffling followed by the distinctive turn of the door handle. The door swung opened and after a moment Dani emerged. She shut the door behind her and looked at Zachary who had hailed to his feet before she could see that he had slumped down into the bench, his legs sprawled in front of him, kicking them about from boredom.

"Were you standing the entire time?" Dani asked him jokingly.

"No, of course not. That would have been silly of me." The look on her face indicated she didn't believe him. He looked down at the bench and then moved aside for her to see. Both arms were straightened in front of him as if presenting the bench. "See, there's a bench, I was enjoying a nice sit."

Dani laughed at him. It was a short laugh, but it was enough to make him smile. "Shall we head back downstairs? I do believe we are still in our window of dining and I'm sure you must be hungry." He asked her.

"Actually, I need to find Sarah. If she caught me eating without her, well let's just say it wouldn't be Helenia you need to worry about." Dani rolled her eyes at the thought of Sarah having a fit.

She knew she would make a statement along the lines of 'she couldn't believe Dani could so peacefully eat food while she was worried sick about her,' and then follow it up with 'she couldn't believe Dani was eating while she wasn't.'

"Well then allow me to escort you to her room." They had started to walk towards the stairs, Dani leading the way. She was in no hurry to get back, knowing she was about to have to explain everything to her friends, and she rather not, plus she was enjoying her time with Zachary.

"You could just join me, you know, in general. We could go grab Sarah and most likely she'll already be with Aiden, and then we all go eat... together. It's extra company, but its good company." Dani assured him as she started her descent down the five flights of stairs.

"I don't know. I don't think your friend, Sarah, much cares for me." Zachary followed close behind her. His hand accidentally brushing against hers on the stairway railing. He paused, but only for a moment to give her space. In that time, she had stopped and looked back at him, her cheeks slightly pink from the soft and quick touch, but she waited for him to join her side.

"She's a bit protective over me, but she means well. Promise." Dani continued her descent.

They had reached the last step when the stairwell opened into the large open area connecting the front entrance, dining hall, and other hallways that contained the living quarters. Close to the elevators stood Sarah and Aiden talking amongst themselves. Sarah looked noticeably upset. It was concerning to Dani.

Dani looked up at Zachary. "At least we don't have to go looking for them." She shrugged and headed over towards her friends as she called out their names. They both looked up at the sound.

"Dani!" Aiden went in for a hug. His tall body scrunching over hers. "We're so glad you're finally back." He released her and Dani was abruptly thrown against another body when Sarah grabbed her and hugged her as well.

"Have you guys eaten yet?" Dani said between breaths as she was squeezed tightly, relieving her of all oxygen contained within her body.

"No, we decided it would be best to wait for you." Aiden replied as Sarah released Dani from her grip. Dani felt Sarah's head for a temperature in a humorous fashion.

Sarah swiped away her hand. "What was that for?"

"Just making sure you're alright. I've never known you to wait for food." Dani giggled.

"Oh, haha, very funny. I'm certainly not waiting on you now. Let's go." She led the way into the dining hall as Zachary and Aiden introduced themselves to one another.

They were close to their time limit of when food would stop being served and what was left didn't have the broadest of selections, but it was warm, and it was a substance that would fill their empty stomach. Sarah complained that it was Dani's fault, because they had to wait, while Dani just rolled her eyes. It wasn't hard to select an area to occupy, the dining hall had been emptied of all but a few people, and the group of four had their pick of seating. They chose a seat by the window in the far corner.

"So, what's wrong?" Dani asked when everyone was sitting.

"Who said anything was wrong?" Sarah asked innocently.

"Don't give me that bullshit. Spill it." Dani abruptly said.

Sarah and Aiden explain to Dani how they would be headed back to Helena as soon as Finn and Liam returned from their mission with the rebels. Dani stayed silent for a moment trying to process it. She knew she wouldn't be returning herself, that this is where she would be staying. She didn't know when she would return to Helenia, if ever. Her leaders wanted her dead, and until a revolution occurred, Helenia would remain unsafe for her. That meant she had no idea when she would get to see her friends, the family that she had made, the squad that she depended on, and had trained, and bonded with over the last four years.

Dani held back tears. She would not cry, not now. She knew she needed to be strong. To move forward and bring about an end to this corruption, not just for her, but for people like Zachary, and the others who had to flee from their homes, for all the rebels who didn't know what it meant to have a home, and for all those who were still trapped under the ideals that their leaders were in support of their happiness and good health; that they were there to build Helenia into a better nation instead of reaping the benefits brought on the backs of the people, her people.

Dani would help lead the change. She would return to Helenia, but when she did, she would be the force that the leaders would fear, the force that would drive out those who hid behind false impressions and empty promises. Those who hid behind blank faces, living atop their mountain unafraid that their world would come collapsing down around them. Dani would break down the wall that separated them from the rest of the world and those who were corrupt would have to face her and those they had wronged. The rein of their destructive and careless ruling was coming to an end and it would be by Dani's hands that they would see their demise.